EVE

ALSO BY K'WAN

Street Dreams

Hoodlum

Hood Rat

Still Hood

Gutter

Section 8

Flirt

Welfare Wifeys

Eviction Notice

Diamonds and Pearl

The Diamond Empire

EVE

K'WAN

St. Martin's Griffin
New York

Published in the United States by St. Martin's Griffin, an imprint of St. Martin's Publishing Group

EVE. Copyright © 2006 by K'wan Foye. All rights reserved. Printed in the United States of America. For information, address St. Martin's Publishing Group, 120 Broadway, New York, NY 10271.

www.stmartins.com

The Library of Congress has cataloged the first St. Martin's Griffin edition as follows:

Foye, K'wan
    Eve / K'wan Foye.— 1st ed.
      p. cm.
    ISBN 0-312-33310-2
    EAN 978-0-312-33310-2
    1. Women ex-convicts—Fiction. 2. Harlem (New York, N.Y.)—Fiction. 3. Street life—Fiction. 4. Gangs—Fiction. 5. Drug traffic—Fiction. I. Title.
    PS3606.O96E94 2006
    813'.6—dc22

                                                        2005045646

ISBN 978-1-250-62383-6 (trade paperback)
ISBN 978-1-4299-0628-9 (ebook)

Our books may be purchased in bulk for promotional, educational, or business use. Please contact your local bookseller or the Macmillan Corporate and Premium Sales Department at 1-800-221-7945, extension 5442, or by email at MacmillanSpecial Markets@macmillan.com.

Second St. Martin's Griffin Edition: May 2020

10   9   8   7   6   5   4   3   2   1

"4 MY SISTAZ"

This one is for my sistaz in the game. I know y'all didn't think I would forget about you.

My love of black women runs too deep for me not to have spun a story in honor of your strength and determination.

For my Daughters, Ni' Jaa' & Alexandria,
who keep me in the fight

PART ONE

THE VERDICT

"I'll ask you one more time, Ms. Panelli," barked the red-faced judge. "Do you wish to tell the court whose gun it was?"

"No, sir," Eve answered, nervously twirling her fingers around a lock of her hair. The county-issued jumpsuit sagged on her rail-thin body, but she tried to make it look presentable.

Eve was a striking mixture of Italian, Black, and Irish. She had smooth, olive-toned skin and at a glance, she looked more Black than anything. The only telltale signs of her mixed heritage were her red hair and blue-green eyes. When her hair wasn't braided up, it hung down to the middle of her back. Eve was one of those girls who was thick where she needed to be and slender everywhere else. With her pretty face she could've easily been a model, but the streets had a firm hold on her. That was part of the reason she found herself incarcerated at the age of seventeen.

"Ms. Panelli, I must remind you that this court will show leniency if you would just tell us who the other young men were that ran off. Now, do you wish to say anything?"

"Nope." Eve shrugged. "Ain't got nothing to say."

"Evelyn Panelli, it is in the judgement of this court that you are a threat to society as well as yourself. You have shown no remorse or regret for your offenses against the laws of our fair county. I don't know how they do it in New York City, but this is Livingston

County. You Negroes can't just roll through here disturbing law-abiding white folks. You must answer for what you've done."

This judge must be out of his mind? Eve thought. *I ain't no fucking rat. Do I wish to tell who I was with? Hell no. That ain't how Gs get down. Besides, the public defender already told me that I probably won't get more than ninety days and some probation. You go ahead and talk till your face gets redder than what it is, cracker. I ain't talking.*

Eve spared a glance over her shoulder and managed a weak smile. A few familiar faces from her crew—the Twenty-Gang—and even her disabled uncle had managed to make it to the sentencing. No Felon, and no Butter. She should've known better, though. Even as she stood there trying to stare at the judge defiantly, her stomach was doing flip-flops. She had been in trouble before, but never to this extent. She refused to rat on her friends, but the thought of being locked up didn't sit well with her.

"Evelyn Panelli, this court gladly sentences you to a term of no less than eighteen months, but no longer than two years in the Downstate Juvenile Detention Center. I can only hope than by the time you come out, you will have leaned the error of your ways."

Eve looked over at the public defender in his cheap suit. He didn't even have the common decency to look at the youth after fucking her. Eve felt like a five-dollar whore. This was the second time that a white man had shitted on her, but it would be the fucking last.

1.

Cassidy stood in the bathroom, looking in the mirror, trying to get her hair clip to stay in place. She could've kicked herself for not letting her sister, Sheeka, braid it the day before. After getting frustrated, Cassidy threw the clip into the bathroom sink and just tied her hair in a ponytail.

She tucked the yellow spandex T-shirt into her sky blue jeans, and strained to examine her ass in the mirror to make sure the fabric wasn't bunched up, giving her the "ass lumps." Normally Cassidy wouldn't dream of leaving the house without being dressed to kill, but comfort was more important than fashion for the drive ahead of her.

Cassidy was one of those girls who, no matter what they're wearing are still banging. She was a tall girl who had long straight hair. She was a nice shade of brown with a china-doll face. She was kind of on the thin side, but Cassidy had enough body to turn heads. When she walked into a room, men couldn't help but notice her.

Cassidy walked back into the room that she and Sheeka shared, and looked around in disgust. There were clothes strewn all over Sheeka's bed and the computer chair. This was just one more reason that she had to get out of her mother's house. Cassidy was more neat and organized, while Sheeka was a slob.

It took Cassidy nearly ten more minutes to find the car keys. By then she was burnt, because she was already late and had a long drive ahead of her. After finding her keys she took one last look in the mirror and headed toward the front door. When she opened it, a drunken Sheeka was standing there, trying to open the neighbor's door with her key. She stood wide-legged, trying to keep her balance on the tiled floor. Her shapely thighs threatened to tear through the fabric of her much-too-tight outfit.

Sheeka was Cassidy's sister, but they had two different fathers. Sheeka was short and dark-skinned like their mother. She was cute, but not nearly as pretty as Cassidy. For this she secretly resented her sister. She felt like people favored Cassidy because she was prettier.

"Sheeka," Cassidy said, scaring the hell out of the girl. "What the hell are you doing?"

"Hey, girl," Sheeka said with a slur. "What you doing coming outta Mr. Brown's house?"

Cassidy looked at her sister as if she had bumped her head. "Girl, you are as drunk as a skunk."

"Nah, I ain't, sis. I'm just a little tipsy. Will and them niggaz threw a party last night. It was off the hook!" Sheeka said, getting loud.

"Girl, you better keep your voice down," Cassidy warned. "If Mommy catches your ass out here all fucked up, she's likely to kill you."

"Please," Sheeka said, staggering into the house. "That woman won't be up for a few hours."

"And what time do you think it is, Sheeka?"

"'Bout . . . two or three," Sheeka said, trying to focus on her fingers as she counted off.

"Sheeka, it's six-thirty in the damn morning."

"Oops. Guess I was a lil off, huh?" Sheeka tried to walk to the bedroom but she had some trouble balancing on the stiletto heels that she was wearing. Sheeka fell flat on her face, causing her short black skirt to rise up. Cassidy looked at her little sister, disgusted as her entire ass became visible, due to a lack of panties.

"Girl, you're a mess," Cassidy scolded. As she reached down to help her sister up, her nose was assaulted by the smell of liquor and sweat. It didn't take a rocket scientist to figure out what Sheeka was doing at Will's party. She had tried to warn her sister time and again about the kinds of men who stalked those mean streets, but Sheeka was determined to do her. There wasn't but so much that Cassidy could do because Sheeka was almost eighteen.

"I don't believe this shit," Cassidy said, helping Sheeka to her feet. "What the hell were you drinking?"

"Wasn't nothing." Sheeka swayed. "Had a lil Henney, popped a few bottles. Nothing heavy. It sure was a bomb-ass party, though."

"I'll bet," Cassidy said sarcastically. She helped her sister into the bedroom and laid her down on the bed. She watched the drunken mess as she drifted instantly to sleep. Her little sister was going down the same road that their mother had danced on. She and her sister would definitely need to talk, but it would have to wait until she came back.

Felon found himself up with the chickens. He had gotten a good night's sleep, so he was feeling quite refreshed. After he had bagged up the remaining ounce of coke, he lay out to watch a movie. The movie ended up watching him. Nevertheless, he was ready for the day. He needed to get up with his partner and handle some pressing business.

Felon was a very handsome young man who danced on the borderline of being pretty. His body was athletic and muscular, but beneath baggy clothes he looked slim. He had skin the color of brown M&Ms and eyes that seemed to twinkle in certain light. Felon wasn't what you would call a lady's man, but he never found himself shorthanded when certain itches needed to be scratched.

After taking a quick shower, Felon hopped into his blue Sean Jean sweat suit and his blue New Balance shoes. After checking himself out in the mirror and making sure his smile was on a million, Felon headed for the front door. One his way there, his little brother Sammy passed him in the hallway.

Sammy was very dear to Felon. He was still a baby when their father was murdered so he really had no memory of him, but Felon carried the pain with him every day. Sammy was the reason Felon took it to the streets. He knew that he had to step up and fill their father's shoes as the man of the house. He had made a promise to himself to raise Sammy the right way and never subject him to having to go without. In a sense, Felon had traded his own life for his little brother's. Inwardly he hated the fact that he slung poison, but he really didn't have a whole lot of choices. Or at least that's what he constantly told himself.

Felon had been a bright student in high school and even had the chance to go to college. He often pondered continuing his education, but the need for money overrode that. He couldn't waste four more years in school while his family went without. He needed to make some quick cash, and the grind was the quickest way to get it. "Blow up or throw up" was how he looked at it. He did what was necessary to ensure the survival of his family.

"What up, lil nigga?" Felon asked.

"Chilling, yo," Sammy said, rubbing the sleep from his eyes. With the same dark skin and sparkling eyes, he looked like a ten-year-old version of Felon.

"You getting ready for school?"

"Uh huh."

"You got paper?" Felon asked, fishing around in his pocket.

"Nah uh."

"Here," Felon said, fishing a ten-dollar bill from his pocket.

"A man should never walk around without having some type of money in his pocket. That jewel is for free, kid." Felon rubbed his little brother's head and headed out the front door.

When Felon got downstairs to the lobby, his two soldiers were waiting for him as instructed. The first soldier was a lanky kid who bopped a little too hard when he walked. He called himself Street Wise or Wise for short. The other soldier was a five-foot Spanish kid called Goosey.

They were just two knucklehead cats from around the way that were looking to get down with somebody. Felon figured either one of two things would happen with the two. They would pan out and become good soldiers or they would be cannon fodder on a dummy mission.

"What's good, fam?" Wise asked, leaning in to hug Felon.

"Chilling," Felon said, keeping him at arm's length. He never got too personal with anyone who wasn't within his inner circle. "Check it, there're two packs in the building, right behind the door to the B stairwell. Y'all do the damn thang and by the time y'all finish them, somebody will be bringing you more. I'm out." Felon left without waiting for a response. He wasn't funny about dealing with the soldiers in the crew, but he just didn't fuck with the bird niggaz. They were good for whatever they were good for, but that was as far as it went.

Felon had gotten his hands dirty in the past, but now that he was getting his weight up a little something, he tended to stay away from the bullshit. The less he dealt with people, the less they would have to say about him. You couldn't snitch on a nigga that you knew nothing about. That motto had saved him from seeing any real lengthy bids. Felon had been behind the wall, but never for more than a few months to a year or so at a time, and that had always been because of somebody else's fuckup.

Felon felt his cell phone vibrating and wondered who the hell could be ringing him at that hour of the morning. Felon looked at his caller ID, but didn't recognize the number. When he answered the call, his ears were assaulted by the sounds Spice 1's "A Nigger Got No Heart." He knew it could only be one crazy-ass broad. "What up, Kiki?"

"My nigga, Felon," Kiki said on the other end. "What you doing up at this hour?"

"You know I don't waste a day, ma."

"I know it, boy. Say, you still wanted me to see about that thing, right?"

"For sure, ma. You got that?"

"Not yet," she said looking out the window of her truck at a chromed-out Benz. "Me and Rah bout to handle that right now. Have my money when I hit the hood, nigga."

"I got you, Kiki. Thanks." Felon hung up his phone and kept walking. Big Kiki was a part-time bouncer and a full-time criminal. She was an enforcer in the Twenty-Gang click. Both women and men feared Kiki on the streets. She was easily six feet tall and built to brawl. Kiki had a rep as being a knockout artist.

Felon ducked into the store on the corner of 132nd and Madison Avenue. When he was out early enough, he would go into the store to get a coffee, a sandwich, and a *Daily News*. He liked to spend money with the cats in that store, cause they treated everyone in the neighborhood with respect.

As he waited for his coffee and sandwich, Felon took a minute to go through the paper. On one page he read about a family getting burned out of their home in Queens. On another page he read about a little girl getting hit with a stray bullet. As he thumbed toward the back he saw that the Knicks had lost to the Raptors by twenty. Felon decided against purchasing a newspaper that morning. The world was too damn depressing.

Kiki hopped from the Eddie Bauer and looked around cautiously. They were in a quiet area of Brooklyn that consisted mostly of houses. She motioned for her partner Rah to follow. She and Rah looked like Laurel and Hardy trying to be discreet about sneaking up on someone's car. While Kiki was a big woman, Rah was a petite young girl with big eyes.

Kiki reached up under her sweatshirt and removed the "Slim-Jim" she had been concealing. She jacked the rod down into the space between the window and the door until the lock sprang. Kiki quickly slid under the wheel and disconnected the alarm system. After fumbling with the proper wires, the car came to life. Kiki gave Rah the nod and she hopped back into Kiki's truck. Kiki pulled off in the Benz, with Rah following in the truck.

When the owner of the car later found out that his car had been jacked, he complained to the police that it was hood shit. But to the two ladies who would reap the rewards of the heist, it was just another day at the office.

Spooky crept down 140th Street, making sure he stayed close to the buildings. At that time of morning, there weren't that many people about. Still, for the kind of bullshit Spooky was doing, he couldn't run the risk of getting caught. He knew that if Felon or Butter caught wind of what he was doing, his life wouldn't be worth shit.

Spooky continued to move up and down the block, serving the fiends as he went along. He kept two packs of bagged-up crack on him, so he had to pay attention to which pocket he dug into to serve each fiend. Both of the packs were identical. The only difference was that one package contained Felon's work and the other pack contained Spooky's.

That's why he had to make sure that he was on point. Felon had been kind to Spooky when he was down and out, and Spooky had repaid him by trying to slit his throat. He was selling his own work and packaging it to look like Felon's. He was still moving work for Felon while he was hustling his wares, but it was still some underhanded shit.

When Felon put Spooky on, he had promised to promote him once he had proven his worth. The promotion was taking a little too long for Spooky, so he went on the offensive. Spooky was only fifteen

years old and still lived at home, so his bills were minimal, but to
him he still needed shit. Spooky was a dude who had Gucci tastes,
with a Kmart budget. He needed to come up.

When Spooky had told his man Sean about what he had
planned, Sean's exact words were, "You're gonna fuck around and
get murdered." Sean would have no part in that scheme. Spooky
hadn't really given it much thought, though. He felt that Sean was
just being a pussy, while he was a nigga with heart. At least that's
what was going on in his ignorant-ass mind.

He figured that if he were to ever get caught, he might be able
to talk his way out of it. Felon was far from a sucker, but he was a
good dude. Spooky figured he'd give his boss a lame-ass excuse
about trying to show that he was on a come-up and needed the extra bread. Felon might beat the hell out of Spooky, but he would
probably let him keep his life.

Butter was another story altogether. A lot of niggaz in the hood
is gangsta, but Butter was downright mean. That boy got some
kinda strange thrill out of seeing people hurting. Spooky had once
heard a story about how some kid had called Butter's sister a bitch
last summer. When Butter caught the kid, he made him run out
onto the I-95. The kid had made it almost all the way across when
an eighteen-wheeler mangled him. It was a good bet that if Butter
was set on the case, Spooky would surely meet a very similar fate.
He just had to make sure that he stayed one step ahead of Felon and
his bulldog.

2.

Evelyn sat on the edge of her bunk, finishing off the last of the five cornrows that snaked over her head. She was trying to focus on the braid and finish reading the copy of Tracy Brown's *Black* that she had borrowed from one of the other girls. She almost found herself crying as the main character's life had taken a turn for the worse, but she was too gangsta for that shit.

"Panelli!" barked the brutish-looking guard. She looked more like a gorilla than a lady. "Pack ya shit, bitch. Time to roll out."

Evelyn looked up from her book and rolled her eyes. Normally she would've checked the dyke guard, but not today. It was one of those rare occasions when she decided to hold her tongue. She was being released that morning, so the minimum-wage slave could say whatever she wanted.

For the last five hundred and forty-seven days, she had made her home within the walls of DJF. It was one of the few female juvenile detention centers in the state of New York and one of the toughest. Evelyn had been laid up in the facility for about a year and a half. The gun that they had found in the car hadn't even been hers, but she wasn't going to tell the police that. Death before dishonor. That was how Twentys got down.

Evelyn gathered the last of her belongings and stuffed them into her duffel bag. She made her way around the dorm, giving "dap" to some of the girls that she was cool with. Some of the other women shot her jealous glares but didn't bother to say anything. Evelyn had proven to the other girls there that you don't fuck with Eve.

Old Pete came down the walkway, pushing his broom, sweeping up dirt that wasn't there. Pete was a local from a nearby town. He was also a career criminal who couldn't seem to get it right, and a degenerate dope fiend. Pete was one of the few men who worked in the facility. Some of the girls would let Pete sleep with them for small favors or extra privileges. Eve didn't get down like that. Pete had come at her once and she almost caught another charge. Since then she hadn't had a problem out of him.

Eve had been getting propositions from men since she was a young girl and just didn't want to hear it. Most of the time they were crass with their come-ons, and others were just perverse. But this was the price she paid for being beautiful. When she had first arrived at the facility there were a few incidents where some of the less attractive girls tested her. They soon found out that her pretty face came with a devastating right hook.

"What up, girl?" Pete asked, scratching his razor-bumped face.

"Ain't nothing," Eve said flatly, busying herself with her bag.

"So they're letting you outta here?" Pete asked, prying further.

"Seems that way, Pete."

"So," Pete said propping his broom against the door frame. "What you gonna do when you get back into the world?"

"Can't call it." She shrugged. "Try to live my life. That's all."

"Sure ya right, kid. So you gonna hook up with Felon and them when you get out? Maybe get into some of the rackets?"

"Who's Felon?" Eve asked, faking ignorance.

"Come on, Eve," Pete said, leaning in closer. "I ain't the police. You ain't gotta lie to me."

"I'm serious, Pete. I don't know nobody named Felon and I don't know what rackets you're talking about. When I hit the streets, I'm gonna try and get a job or something."

Pete must've thought that because Eve was young, she was born yesterday. Eve was hip to how Pete was getting down. She had gotten it through the grape vine that Pete was a "switch hitter." He was one of those cats that would pump the unsuspecting inmate for information and then trade it to the brass for dope or favors. Nope, Eve wasn't getting caught out there.

"Job my ass," Pete exclaimed. "You're one of the top chicks in Twenty-Gang. I heard about you on the streets, kid. They say that Evelyn Panelli, aka Eve, is one bad lady. She's always ready to get down, be it with fist or iron. The way I hear it, the streets respect ya gangsta. Not bad for a chick."

"Listen," she said, a little irritated. "That was a long time ago. I ain't wit all that shit no more. As a matter of fact, I'm feeling a little uncomfortable with your line of questioning. Why don't you ease the fuck back?" She looked him dead in the eye.

Pete thought about pressing the issue, but changed his mind when he saw the murderous look that she was giving him. Mr. Thompson, who was the director of the facility, had promised Pete an eighth of dope if he could get some dirt on the young Evelyn. He had a hard-on for the girl. Pete decided that the drugs he was promised wasn't worth getting his ass kicked or cut. Eve was quite the lethal beauty.

"My bad," Pete said, retrieving his broom. "Didn't know you were gonna get all sensitive about it."

"Ain't nothing," Eve said easily. "I just don't like people all up in my mix. That's all."

"Break this shit up," the lady guard said. "Panelli, you've got thirty seconds to get your shit and roll out. Unless you wanna stay?"

"Nah," she said throwing her duffel bag over her shoulder. "I'm outta here." Eve took one last look at the place that had been her home for what seemed like forever and was gone.

Eve followed the guard down the walkway through the different sections of the facility. She nodded at certain inmates but didn't bother to stop. As she passed through the section of the facility that served as solitary, she was suddenly halted by the sound of someone calling her name from behind one of the iron doors. Eve recognized the voice, but she knew she had to be mistaken.

"Scruggs?" she questioned, moving closer to the gate. Scruggs was a kid Eve used to go to school with. He ran with a local Blood click on her block. Even though the ladies of Twenty-Gang weren't actually a gang like the Bloods and the Crips, she and her home girls had love for the color-clad hardheads from the block. They didn't give a shit about a color. They were just some cool-ass neighborhood guys. A few of the girls were even in relationships with some of the bangers.

Scruggs was short, with a baby face. He was young, but his eyes were those of an old man. Most striking thing about him was the radiant smile that he used to hit all the girls with, the same smile that he was flashing at Eve from the six-by-six cell.

"What's good?" Scruggs asked from behind the little grated window.

"Gimmie a second," Eve said to the lady guard. The guard held up one finger to let Eve know that she had one minute. "What up, my nigga?" she asked, putting her fist to crisscrossing wires.

"Trying to live," he replied solemnly. "But I don't seem to be doing a very good job of it."

"I guess didn't nobody tell you that this was a lady's facility?" Eve joked.

"Very funny, girl. Nah, you know they had me housed a few miles from here and shit. A nigga got into something with a heavy hitter and they moved me up outta the jail. Talking some safety shit.

He fucked up, and I'm still walking 'round. Niggaz ain't hard like we, ma. I'll only be here till tomorrow, then I'm shipping further up. They're keeping me caged for my whole visit."

"What the fuck happened?"

"Man, this crab nigga tried to come at me sideways. Eve baby, you know the kid ain't no troublemaker, but I ain't have a whole lot of choices. Son came and I laced him. I carved into that boy over and over. I swung that blade until my arms got tired. The fucked-up part was . . . I did it more out of fear than anything else."

"Damn, kid." Eve sighed. "Homey died?"

"Dead as a fucking doornail, ma."

"So what's the word?"

"The word is, I'm fucked. When the bulls rolled in, I was still holding the shank."

"You gonna try to fight it?"

"Fight it," Scruggs said with a grim look on his face. "Baby-girl, I'm already in on a body. They're probably gonna try and fry me behind this shit."

"What about fam and them," Eve asked referring to Scruggs' gang. "Them niggaz ain't trying to put no money up for your lawyer?"

"Fuck them niggaz," Scruggs said. "I blame all of that dumb shit for getting me into this."

"You're talking crazy now," she said in disbelief. "That's ya click. How you gonna kick shit on em?"

"Let me put you up on something, ma. We ain't that far apart in age, but I've been at this a lot longer than you have. All that shit they kick in the hood is garbage. Don't get me wrong, there's quite a few dawgz that keep it funky, but the majority of them niggaz ain't keeping it gangsta."

"It can't be that bad, man."

"Eve, them niggaz shitted on me when I got bagged. I ain't get no visits, no packages, no letters. Not a goddamn thing. And the punch line is, I caught my case for the set. Me and that boy didn't even know each other well enough to dislike one another. Our only crimes were being from opposite sides of the color lines. This shit all chalks up to belonging. I did it all to belong."

"Don't give up, Scruggs," she pleaded. "You can get up outta this. I mean, even if you do get a lil more time on top of that you're still young. You could—"

"Fuck that," he said cutting her off. "Eve, I ain't built for the kinda time they're gonna try to give me. I'd go crazy. They got my back against the wall, ma. Just because they got me on some holdover shit in a woman's facility, don't mean I'm going out like a bitch."

"Don't start talking, Scruggs. What're you thinking about doing?"

"The only thing I can do," he said getting misty-eyed. "One of the home girls managed to slip me a lil something in here. It ain't much, but it's got a point on it. When they open this cage in the morning . . . I'm coming from the chest!" he declared.

Eve had to compose herself before she continued speaking. "That's a lot to swallow. You sure you wanna do this?"

"As sure as I can be. I was born in the system and this is where I'm gonna close my eyes. Straight like that. When they pop open this door in the morning, I'm gonna poke the first nigga that steps in here. Tell the whole hood, Eve. Tell them that I went out like a soldier."

"Let's go, Panelli," the lady guard said, getting impatient.

Eve spared a last glance at Scruggs and continued on her walk. She felt a tear roll down her cheek as she heard Scruggs bellowing in the background, *"Tell em I went out like a muthafucking soldier!"*

Eve continued to follow the female officer down the hall to freedom. It seemed as though the closer she got to the gates, the heavier her legs got. She had itched for this day every night in her dorm; now it seemed to be at hand. Just as she exited the solitary area her face took on a sudden change. She sucked her teeth and rolled her eyes as she stood face-to-face with Mr. Thompson, a short white man whose hairline seemed to be running away from his forehead. He stood there with a smug grin on his face, wearing the same brown suit that he wore every Thursday.

"Ms. Panelli," Thompson said, smiling. "Today is the big day, huh?"

"Yeah," Eve said. "I'm finally getting out."

"So you are. And what are your plans now that you're a *free woman?*"

"Don't know right off," Eve said with a shrug. "Got a few ideas that I've been kicking around."

"Umm umm," Thomson said, examining Eve over the rim of his round spectacles. "A wise man once said that too much free time is a dangerous thing."

"Yeah, well, I ain't never heard that one and frankly, it don't apply to me. All I'm trying to do is keep from landing myself back in a shit hole like this. Or worse."

"Indeed, Ms. Panelli. But what I've learned in my years as an overseer is that people like you have a hard time staying out of trouble."

"What do you mean by people like me?" Eve asked with an attitude.

"Ms. Panelli," Thomson said, matching her attitude. "I think you know just what I mean. You and those like you are animals. You murder and commit other acts of violence all in the name of corners and streets that none of you own, just to turn around and tear them down. How ridiculous. I guess that's what you folks call *keeping it real?*"

"Is this conversation going anywhere, yo?"

"Yes," Thompson said, in a matter-of-fact tone. "I don't like you, Evelyn. I don't like people like you or what you stand for. You're a blight on society. I know about your background and what happened to your family, but that's still no excuse. You're dangerous. Young, Black, and no respect for human life. But luckily for me, you're an ignorant bitch. If you had an education you'd be downright threatening."

"Fuck you," Eve hissed. "I did my muthafucking time, straight gangsta. Ain't shit you can tell me, cracker. I ain't even got to listen to this shit."

"Oh, I'm afraid you do. See, technically you're not a free woman yet. If I wanted to fuck you all I have to do is shuffle your paperwork. Yeah, I could keep your ass here for at least another week. A rather unpleasant week at that, shit-bird. Think about how you wanna play it."

Eve could feel sweat break out on her forehead. Thompson was counting on her ill temper to be her undoing. All she could think of was crushing Thompson's skull with her bare hands. Not today, though. Freedom was more important than old grudges. Scores could be settled later.

"Just as I thought," Thompson said smugly. "Take a walk, convict." As Eve walked toward the last gate Thompson stopped her short. "Eve . . . see ya soon."

Eve flexed her hands as she approached the iron gate to freedom. It was as if her legs were going to give out as she moved through the intake area. She looked at the guards scattered about the lobby and office areas. They all seemed to be staring at her mockingly. Eve couldn't help but think someone was going to block her exit and inform her of a new pending charge. Through the grace of a higher power she was permitted to make it to the exit. As she stood on the threshold, one of the male guards blew her a kiss. She smiled, flipped him the finger, and stepped through the last barrier to freedom.

3.

Eve covered her eyes against the sun's glare. They had become so attuned to the artificial lights of the prison that the fresh rays threw her off. Sure, she was allowed to venture into the prison yard a few times a week, but it wasn't the same. This was the light of freedom. The grass even seemed greener on that side of the fence. When Eve felt the drop of moisture on her, she wasn't sure if her eyes were watering from the light or they were tears of joy.

Eve spun around at the sound of a car horn. She squinted against the glare of the automobile and was able to make out a Lexus of some sort. She couldn't tell the make or model. Eve shifted her bag and looked back at the guards who were closing the gate, smiling. If it was an ambush by her rivals, she wouldn't find any sympathy with the law. She was forever the lone soldier.

Without taking her eyes off the car, Eve started walking in the direction of the nearest bus stop. The car turned with her and started to follow. Eve kept the car in her line of vision and kept strolling. Eve was able to see the car a little more clearly now. It was a GS 300. It was a few years out of date, but still very plush. It was candy Eve with chrome spinners. As Eve continued down the road she could feel the sweat rolling down her neck and pooling in the small of her back. She thought about how ironic it would be if she were to be gunned down right outside the jail. She had done harm to others in her life, so would it be wrong if she were to come to it?

"Hey," someone said out of the driver's side window. "Ain't you Eve from Twenties?"

It was on now.

"Who that?" Eve asked, dropping her bag.

"What, you don't know ya click no more?" The driver's side door opened and a familiar figure stepped out. She was a tall woman with a very pretty face.

"Get the fuck outta here," a relieved Eve said. "Cassidy?"

"Yeah, girl. What's good?"

Cassidy and Eve threw their arms around another. It had been quite a while since Eve had seen her best friend. Too long in fact. Eve and Cassidy were the closest amongst the other girls that rocked with the Twenties. They were crime partners in the world as well as respected members of their click.

"What you doing in these parts?" Eve asked.

"You know I couldn't have my sis riding home on no damn bus," Cassidy said. "Girl, it's a good thing I did come and pick you up. You look a mess," she joked.

Eve looked at the tired grey sweat suit they had given her to dress out in. The sweat suit looked as if it had seen better days. It wasn't much, but she couldn't very well come home naked. She just shrugged. "Yeah, this is some bullshit, ain't it?"

"Don't even worry about it, girl," Cassidy said retrieving a shopping bag from the backseat. "I brought some things for you. I hope they fit, though," she said pinching Eve's breast. "When did you sprout these?"

"Shut up, bitch," Eve joked. "They didn't get that much bigger."

"Eve, girl, you're holding. When they locked you up you wasn't built like this."

"Shit, I ain't running the streets acting all crazy with y'all hoes. All I really did while I was inside was read and work out."

"Just like a nigga," Cassidy teased. "Let me find out them bitches got at you in there."

"Please, it ain't even that type of party. I might look thuggish right now, but that don't mean I've lost my mind. I'm strictly dickly. Don't get it fucked up, Cassidy."

"Whatever, *Evelyn*," Cassidy said, passing her the bag. "Let's just get up outta here."

Eve gladly hopped into the plush Lexus. The interior was as lavish as the exterior. The seats were white leather and the console was trimmed in wood. It was also equipped with a TV and a PS2. Eve couldn't help but wonder where Cassidy had gotten such a nice whip.

"Damn," said Eve, rubbing her palm against the seat. "I see you've been doing big things while I was gone."

"Oh, this?" Cassidy asked, putting the car in drive. "This is a loaner. A friend of mine let me borrow it to come and pick you up."

"You've got some nice-ass friends."

"Please, Butter ain't nobody."

"Butter who?"

"Eve, you mean to tell me that you don't remember Butter from Thirty-ninth and Seventh?"

"You talking about that nappy-headed nigga who used to work with Felon?"

"Boy done got a haircut and a few dollars, girl. Him and Felon are partners now. They're the niggaz to see."

"Cassidy, you lying."

"True story, Eve. Them niggaz was ringing bells on the streets while you were gone. Him and Felon done put in a whole lot of work for Macho."

"I heard that nigga Macho got killed a while back."

"How the fuck do you think Felon and Butter got to take over the spot?"

"Them niggaz killed Macho?" Eve asked in disbelief.

"Eve, I know you ain't a gossip, but don't never repeat what I'm about to tell you."

"On the click."

"A'ight. Me and this nigga Butter been fucking around for a little while now. He's kinda cute when he cleans up and he's generous as hell with his cheese. Anyhow, me and this nigga was laid up in the telly one night. He was bumping a lil, but you know I don't fuck with that shit. If weed and liquor can't do it, then it don't need to be done. So, the yay got this nigga feeling talkative and shit. He starts telling me about how niggaz who didn't respect him was gonna get dealt with accordingly. He starts running down the line about niggaz he killed and was gonna kill, then Macho's name came up. Seems he had a personal beef with the cat from back in the days."

"What did Macho do to him?" Eve asked.

"I really don't know," Cassidy said. "But whatever it was, it must've been real fucked up. I didn't even bother to ask. To make a long story short, Felon and Butter got on with the nigga and gained his trust. As soon as they got him to drop his defenses, they murdered his ass so they could take over his spot. Niggaz in the hood wasn't stupid enough to challenge them for Macho's turf, so they've just been rocking."

"Damn," Eve exclaimed. "Let me find out everybody wants to be a killer."

"Ain't no *want* about it with these two, Eve. Felon is more laid-back, but Butter is bout that."

"I can't believe them fools done came up like that. I know Butter is a freak, but I'll bet that pretty nigga Felon is trying to hit everything moving." Eve chuckled.

"With all that money they clocking, you'd think he would. I seen him with a few cluckers, but the queen bitch is home now. Fights over, ladies. The champ is here!" Cassidy teased.

"Cut it out, Cas." Eve blushed. "I can't win something that I ain't fighting for."

"Stop fronting, Eve. I see the way he used to look, and your hot ass used to stare right back. You better be glad Uncle Bobby never caught on."

"Well, things are different now, Cassidy. I just did almost two joints in that shit box, for a gun that belonged to them niggaz. Felon and Butter skated, and I had to take the weight."

"Don't carry it like that, Evelyn. You know they didn't mean for it to go down like that. The only reason Felon didn't step up to hold that time was because of his record. They would've slain him. He tried to give Uncle Bobby money for the lawyer, but that crazy-ass old man started shooting at him. He was fucked up about what happened to you, Eve, and if you hadn't been so damn bullheaded, he could've told you himself."

"Whatever." Eve sucked her teeth and turned to the window. She knew the things she was saying were more out of anger than a grudge. She knew that Butter and Felon hadn't been directly responsible for her getting locked up. She knew the stakes when she got in the car. You play, you pay. In the early nights of her incarceration, she would lie on her bunk and cry. Not out of fear, but frustration. She placed the blame for her situation everywhere but the right place. On herself.

She often thought about Felon and what he might've been in the world doing. Did he have a girl? Did he change his mind about going back to school? She and Felon had always had a bond like brother and sister, but it eventually it had evolved into something else. It had always been on the tip of their tongues, but neither had been willing to say it.

Eve broke her silence. "What up with the crew?"

"Twenty-Gang is still Twenty-Gang," Cassidy said with a shrug. "We ride to the end. You know how that shit goes. My bitches is still crazy as hell, chasing one dream or another." Twenty-Gang started out as a few girls from 120th Street that hung out together and held each other down. As time progressed and their reputation grew, so did their number. Twenty-Gang was recognized by cats in every borough. The members of Twenty-Gang were all getting money from various hustles. Hoeing, carjacking, robbery. There were even a few of them with bodies under their belts.

"We winning?" Eve asked.

"The smart ones are. I can't make them hoes get money; they gotta want it."

"I know that's right. How's the family?"

"Mom is still mom."

"Partying her ass off?"

"You know it. But at least she's managed to hold this job at the post office down for a while."

"That's good, C. What's up with Sheeka?"

"Don't even get me started. I wanted to kill that bitch this morning."

"What happened?"

"She had the nerve to come stumbling her drunk ass in the house at damn near seven this morning. Talking bout she went to party that 'Will and them' was throwing. Little hot in the pussy bitch didn't even have no drawers on. I don't know what the fuck is up with that girl."

"She's trying to get in where she fits in," Eve said while lighting a cigarette. "Sheeka is barely eighteen, and still impressionable. She sees you getting attention from men, so she wants it too."

"I can dig it, but it ain't the same thing."

"How is it not the same, Cassidy? You fuck with niggaz for paper."

"First of all, I don't fuck all of the niggaz I talk to," Cassidy said with a little bit of an attitude. "Second of all, if I do go out and party with somebody I don't never get drunk to the point where I'm slipping. You won't never hear about none of these niggaz getting me high and running a train on me."

"You ain't gotta get defensive about it," Eve shot back. "All I was trying to say is that she's imitating what she sees."

"Look, Eve," Cassidy said, sparing her a glance. "Don't come out of lockup getting all judgmental. You might not get yours the way I get it, but ya still get it dirty. Knocking niggaz over the head is crooked too. Purse-snatcher."

"Fuck you," Eve said, giggling. "I haven't snatched a purse since I was fourteen. Hoe."

The two friends laughed and talked a little more junk as the Lexus ate up the miles back to the city. When they reached New York City, Cassidy got off the highway near Webster Avenue in the Bronx. She was starving, so they decided to roll up to a White Castle and get something to eat. Eve could also use the opportunity to change her clothes. She didn't want to hit the hood wearing that played-out sweat suit.

When they entered the fast-food joint, there weren't that many people, so they were able to immediately place their orders. While they were ordering, Eve noticed two guys watching them from a table by the window. One was light and the other was dark. When Cassidy turned around, the light-skinned one winked at her. She just wrinkled up her nose and gave them her back. By the heavy jewels that they were wearing, Cassidy knew that they were getting money somewhere, but she wasn't trying to play herself like a chicken.

Eve shook her head and laughed. She got a kick out of how men acted over a pretty face. She decided to go into the lady's room and change while Cassidy waited for the food. As Eve was headed in the direction of the bathroom, the two kids were headed in her direction. She sighed, ready to respond to whatever line they might throw at her. To Eve's surprise, they barely spared her a second look as they walked over to Cassidy. She just picked up her face and went into the bathroom.

Eve fished around inside of the bag to see what Cassidy had brought her to wear, and smiled. Eve began to pull off her sweat suit and slip into the things that Cassidy had brought for her.

The two hustlers were still trying to get a conversation out of Cassidy when Eve came out of the bathroom. When they saw the transformation, both of their jaws dropped. Eve was wearing a pair of tight-fitting, black, Lady Enyce jeans that showed off her toned thighs and well-developed ass. The red and black Lady Enyce shirt stretched over her body, advertising her 38C breasts and flat stomach. On her feet, she had on a pair of Eve-lizard skinned Sara Jordan boots with black two-inch heels. Eve had gone into the bathroom looking like a little boy and came out looking like a dime piece.

"Damn shorty," the dark-skinned one said, looking Eve up and down. "Where'd you come from?"

Eve looked at him and rolled her eyes.

"Word," he continued. "It's like that, ma?"

"Why don't y'all stop acting like that?" the light-skinned one added on. "How about we say fuck these murder burgers and go get a real meal?"

"Listen, fellas," Cassidy said, picking up her burgers. "It's nothing personal; we just don't eat meat."

"Yeah," Eve added on, "we got a 'lick-her' license."

"Liquor license?" the dark-skinned one asked, confused.

"You didn't know?" Eve asked, putting her arm around Cassidy. While the two young men looked on, still trying to make sense of what the hell they were talking about, Eve leaned in and kissed Cassidy on the mouth. They then proceeded to walk arm in arm from the fast-food joint, laughing while the two hustlers stood there bug-eyed.

4.

Butter sat in front of his big-screen television, laughing his ass off as Maury revealed test results to young couples who were seeking the identity of their kid's father. The only time you could've caught Butter out of bed before eleven was when Maury's show covered this topic. He got a kick out of the grown-ass men and woman who played themselves on national television.

Butter got his name from his butterscotch complexion. He was a short man with broad shoulders and limbs like little tree stumps. Butter had a hard face to go with his hard-ass persona. His was a shoot-you-first, fuck-a-questions kinda guy. He was Felon's bulldog and his bite was far worse than his bark.

Tynisha, the chick that Butter had lain up with the night before, came out of the back room wearing only her panties. She flopped her horse ass on the couch next to Butter and began to watch the show. Butter looked at her and sucked his teeth. He hated when people interrupted his morning talk show.

"What are you doing?" he asked, looking down at her.

"Watching the show," she responded innocently.

"Did I ask you to watch the show with me?"

"No, but I thought—"

"See," he cut her off, "that's the problem with women these days. Y'all think too damn much. Why don't you go in the kitchen and fix a nigga something to eat?"

"Damn," she said getting up. "You ain't exactly a morning person, are you?"

"Hell nah," he said, lighting the blunt clip that he had left in the ashtray. "I ain't real big on afternoons either."

"What do you want me to fix you?"

"I could give a shit. Just as long as you don't come back out this muthafucka til my show goes off. Now go ahead," he said, slapping her on her yellow ass.

Tynisha let out a giggle and ran off into the kitchen. All Butter could do was shake his head. Tynisha was cool, but she wasn't Cassidy. He found himself thinking of the tall beauty more and more. His peoples thought he was whipped. It wasn't that. He just knew a good thing when he saw it. He was quite aware of Cassidy's extracurricular activities, but he didn't really care, as long as she kept it away from him. Cassidy was fine and had a good head on her shoulders. He figured that, with a little coaxing and few well-thought-out gifts, he could reform her. That was the main reason he had let her hold his car. Unbeknown to Cassidy, Butter had big plans for her.

Butter's show was again interrupted by someone knocking on his door. Before going to the peephole, he got his 9 from under the sofa cushion. Butter never received guests this early in the morning, especially unannounced.

"Who that?" Butter asked, easing to the door.

"Me, nigga!"

Butter relaxed a little when he heard the voice. Tucking his pistol into the small of his back, he opened the door and invited his closest road dawg into his apartment. He and Felon had been down since free lunch. They had met during an awkward situation back in junior high school. Butter, a seventh grade transfer student, had moved to the neighborhood from the Bronx. It was already halfway through the school year, so most of the other children had already paired off into clicks. Butter, being short and fat at the time, often found himself alone and on the receiving end of nasty taunts.

On this particular day, after school, a group of eighth graders had Butter cornered, trying to take his Delta Force sneakers from him. The youth was outmanned and unarmed against three eighth graders and a box cutter. Still he wouldn't back down. Breaking a Snapple bottle against the ground, he squared off against his foes. The kids who had gathered around the fight cheered and instigated as blood was about to be spilled.

Suddenly the crowd parted and five youngsters stepped through, wearing war faces. Felon stood there, decked out in a Windbreaker and untied Timberlands, moved to the middle of the circle, with Bullet guarding his flank. The five-man crew surrounded the three and let Felon act as the spokesman.

"What's up with this shit, Ricky? Why it take two of y'all to get at one nigga?" Felon asked, folding his arms.

"This ain't got nothing to do with you, B." Ricky tried to smooth it out.

"I think it does," Felon replied coldly. "See, I don't like sucka shit. You having the numbers and still needing the blade seems like sucka shit to me. If you got a beef with shorty, give him the one-on."

"I'd fuck this nigga up!" Butter shouted, trying to sound like he wasn't scared to death. He never broke eye contact with Ricky or loosed the bottle.

"Break that nigga up, Rick!" someone shouted from the crowd.

"What's up?" Felon asked.

Ricky looked from his crew to Butter, then to Felon. He really wasn't much of a fighter, but he was bigger and always had his boys with him. Butter was smaller, so Ricky figured he might be able to take him. He never considered the fact that the younger boy might have hand skills. Butter blackened one of Ricky's eyes and split his lip pretty badly. After the incident the eighth graders never bothered Butter again. He was so grateful to Felon that he took to hanging around him. On a spring day, behind Booker T. Washington, Felon and Butter became friends and crime partners.

"Nigga," Butter said playfully. "You gonna fuck around and get shot popping up at a niggaz' house unannounced."

"Put that damn thing away," Felon said, inviting himself to a seat on the couch. "I tried to call ya bitch ass three or four times. Cut ya fucking phone on, dickhead."

"Oh shit," Butter said slapping himself in the forehead. "I forgot to cut that shit back on last night."

"See, that's ya own damn fault. What if it had been an emergency?"

"Then you would've handled it, kid. You know you're the eyes in back of my head, Felon."

"I know that's right," Felon said, picking up the clip and taking a pull. "From now til we leave this here for warmer climates. Smell me?"

"To hell and back again," said Butter, taking the clip. "So what the fuck is so important that you gotta come fucking with me at the crack of dawn?"

"First of all, it's after ten," Felon corrected him. "Second of all, we got a problem, son. A problem that needs to be addressed."

Before Felon could continue, Tynisha came out of the kitchen, carrying a snack tray. On the tray there was some bacon that looked like black licorice, toast that obviously had burnt, and eggs that ran more than Luke and Laura from *General Hospital*. She tried, though.

"What the fuck is that?" Butter asked.

"Your breakfast, daddy," she responded with a confused look.

"Ain't this some bullshit? It's bad enough that I gotta worry about niggaz trying to kill me on the streets, then you wanna try to poison a muthafucka?"

"The bacon is just a little overcooked because I was talking to my mother on the phone and got caught up," she explained.

"Baby, I'm not eating that shit. You can give it to Felon."

"I'm good," Felon said, putting his hands up.

"Fuck the dumb shit," Butter said, getting off the couch. "I'm gonna throw some sweats on and go get some real food. Felon, Give me a few minutes. In the meantime," he turned to Tynisha, "give my boy some of the fire top you twirking wit."

She looked at Butter with hurt in her eyes. She loved the shit out of Butter, but he didn't seem to feel the same way. He only had eyes for her home girl, Cassidy. Tynisha knew that Cassidy wasn't checking for Butter like that. She thought that if she could just show Butter what a good bitch she was, he might come around and wife her. She knew that she would be playing herself, but if Butter wanted her to knock Felon down, then she had to do it.

Felon caught Tynisha by the shoulders as she was descending, head first, into his lap. "Hold on, baby girl. I appreciate the gesture, but I'm good."

"Stop acting like a bitch," Butter said from the doorway. "Let the bitch gum you down, nigga."

"I said I'm good, Butter."

"Come on," Tynisha pleaded in an attempt to earn Butter's favor. "Let me get that up outta you, Felon."

"I said I'm good." He pushed her away.

Tynisha was offended by Felon's rejection, so she decided to take a jab at him. "Oh, I get it," she said with a wicked smirk. "Butter, looks like ya boy is still stuck on Eve."

"Bitch, I'll split yo shit if you ever come at me like that again!" Felon snapped, grabbing a fistful of the girl's hair. "I don't care if you are my dude's flavor of the month, you better recognize and show some respect!" With his point made, Felon tossed her roughly to the couch.

Tynisha had touched on a very sore spot. Felon did indeed have a thing for Eve, but he would never admit it. He had fallen for her when she first moved to the block from Brooklyn. At the time Felon was just a lil nigga causing trouble just for the hell of it. He ran with a crew of young thugs from her block. Eve had always been like one of the boys, so they often found themselves in each other's company. Most of the other guys used to tease Eve about her tomboyish nature, but Felon never did. She was his dawg and he treated her equally. Felon had even started putting her down with some of his heist. People thought that he favored her because they were crime partners, but Felon had a secret crush. Seeing as how he was a few years older than Eve, he never spoke on it. He didn't want people to think that he was a molester or anything. There was only a four-year gap between them, but that seemed like a whole lot when he was sixteen and she was only twelve.

"Let me find out she struck a nerve?" Butter teased.

"Ain't nobody strike shit. Fuck you too, nigga."

"It's all good, boo," Tynisha said, heading for the bedroom. "Eve's touching down today. See if she'll suck your little cock for you."

"Fucking nosy bitch," Felon mumbled. "Man, why you ain't tell me Eve was coming home today?"

"You're probably the only muthafucka who didn't know. You know them Twenty hoes got big mouths. Besides, I thought you wasn't checking for shorty like that."

"I ain't. Eve is my nigga, plus she gets down. I was thinking about putting her on with us."

"Hell nah, Felon. We can't put her down."

"Why the hell not, Butter?"

"Well, she's a girl for one thing. Plus, you know all of them bitches from Twenty-Gang is scandalous."

"Man, this is Eve we're talking about. The same chick that took a charge for us and never said shit."

"Hey, don't try throwing that up in my face," Butter snapped back. "I seem to remember your ass running through the woods too, Felon. Nobody wanted Eve to take the fall, but we can't change the fact that it happened. My dude, I'm all for helping the home girl out, but not by bringing her into this."

"Man, I know Eve, fam. Me and her done pulled some hellified capers together. She's built like that."

"Dawg, just because she played look-out on a few jobs don't make her hard. Eve is my nigga too, but a bitch is a bitch. Besides, the kinda stakes we're playing for are too high for her. Eve is too inexperienced to bring in on it. We can't watch our asses and hers."

"Let me put you up on something, Butter. Eve has been doing dirt since she was a shorty. Even when we were young she was always fresh. Home girl was getting down solo before we hooked up. So ain't like this is nothing new to her."

"Whatever, Felon. The only reason you're sticking up for her is because you wanna pop that."

"You wilding, son. Eve is like my little sister."

"Then you're thinking of committing incest," Butter said, laughing at his own joke. "Let me go put something on so we can dip." Butter disappeared into the bedroom, leaving Felon to his thoughts.

Felon couldn't believe the news. Little Evelyn was coming home. It had been a while since Felon had seen his lil homey. He had visited her once, but afterward she had sent him a letter requesting that he stay away. She said that it was too painful for her to see him leave at the end of the visits, knowing that she couldn't leave as well. Since then Felon had written her one letter a week. She never responded, but he kept writing.

When Eve had been in the world, they were thick as thieves. She was one of the few people who had held him down when his father passed. He poured his heart out for hours as she listened intently, never once interrupting. He told her all that was in his heart except the feelings that he had for her. This was one of his most closely guarded secrets.

Felon knew that he was doing a poor job of hiding his feelings about Eve. It was evident after she was sentenced. Felon sat with

Butter in his living room and sobbed for her when they got the news. His heart desired to be with Eve, but his logical mind was cock-blocking. What most people didn't realize was that Felon was toxic to women.

He had had girlfriends here and there. Some were good, while others were just larcenous. He seemed to attract the latter. They all wanted to be with the cats who were winning, or had the potential. They came with sweet whispers and promises of loyalty, but there was always motive. It seemed like every time he was tempted to give his heart to a woman, she showed her true colors. They wanted to be with Felon's title, not him.

Felon's outlook on women became twisted and bitter. He turned cold and calloused toward women, treating them as nothing more than objects of pleasure, for him to torment at will. Even when he found ones who were worthy, his base nature kicked in, and they too were cast aside. He wouldn't subject Eve to that, so he closed that part of his heart to her. Love was a myth, and he was too old to believe in fairy tales.

Eve sat in the passenger seat, holding her ribs. She had been laughing so hard at the two kids from White Castle that her sides threatened to split open. When she kissed Cassidy, they looked like they were gonna drop dead. Neither she nor Cassidy were gay, but they couldn't resist an opportunity to make asses out of the two young players.

"That shit was so funny," Eve said, wiping the tears from her eyes. "Them niggaz was stuck."

"Did you see the light-skinned one trying to stunt?" Cassidy asked.

"Did I? He thought he was the shit. Fake-ass 'genuine.' He wasn't hardly cute."

"They really flipped when you changed your clothes. Eve, I'm not funny style or nothing, but you're fine as hell. Me and you have always been the prettiest bitches down wit Twentys and you know it. Now that you've got a body to go with it, you're on. Eve, baby, you and me are gonna do big things. I'm gonna school you to the game and we're—"

"Hold up." Eve cut her off. "Cassidy, I ain't wit all that shit. You know I love you, C, but youz a hoe."

"Call me what you want, but you won't ever call me broke." Cassidy laughed. "But seriously, what are you gonna do now that you're home?"

"I gave it a little thought, and I don't have a particular plan. But you know I'm a survivor. I'm always gonna eat."

"Eve, I ain't one to knock nobody's hustle, but come the fuck on. You're a young lady, not some bandit. You're running around sticking niggaz up and shit instead of utilizing your natural gifts to get ahead."

"I'm not with selling ass, Cassidy."

Cassidy burst out laughing. "Eve, sometimes I forget how naive you are. I don't hardly sell ass. I'm not gonna lie and say that I don't fuck none of the niggaz that I'm dealing with, but I ain't fucking em all. As a matter of fact, I'm not even fucking most of them. Sometimes all these niggaz wanna do is sport you so they can look like the shit. If you do it right, a little conversation goes a long way."

"I hear you, Cassidy. I just feel a little funny about it. You know that ain't my style."

"Eve, you walk around here with all these people thinking you're some hardass, but I know better. I know you, remember? Besides, I seen the way you used to look at that nigga, Felon."

"Get outta here," Eve said, blushing.

"I see the way that both of you look at each other, so I know the deal."

"Cassidy, you're reading deeper into it than it is. Like you said, Felon is out here getting money. He's probably fucking all of these little nasty bitches."

"Hardly." Cassidy chuckled. "You know that man ain't tried to holla at nothing since you were away. I'm sure he's gotten some pussy here and there, but he ain't fucking with nobody like that. Let me find out you gave that nigga some the night y'all was supposed to be in Rochester?"

Cassidy was referring to the night when Eve was arrested. She had gone with Felon and Butter to Rochester, where they were supposed to sell off some guns. They had successfully gotten rid of the guns and then had some time to kill. Eve had suggested that they head back, but ol' Butter wanted to hang. He had caught wind of some club that was supposed to be popping off up that way and wanted to check it out. This would mean that they had to stay out that way for the night. Eve wasn't really feeling the idea, but Felon was. She was outvoted, so she went along.

The club turned out to be some bullshit. The drinks were watery and the music was wack. Twenty minutes after they were there, Felon slapped some kid for whispering in Eve's ear for too long. They left the club and decided to just get faded back at the hotel, which was in a low-key village called Dansville that was about a forty-five minute drive from where they sold the guns. They had made it all the way to Mount Morris before the bullshit went down.

Butter was driving navigating their small sports car down Interstate 390, while Eve was asleep in the backseat. Felon was in the passenger seat with his eyes closed, but still aware of what was going on around him. Butter decided to light a blunt and hit the cruise control for the remainder of the ride back to the hotel. The jackass decided to steer with his knees while he used a match to light the blunt, and that would prove to be their undoing.

The spark flickered to life, illuminating the interior of the vehicle. The match, however, proved to be defective. The head of the match fell off into Butter's lap. He panicked and jerked his leg, causing the car to swerve. It was only for a second, but that second was long enough for the thirsty-ass trooper behind them to think of a reason to pull them over.

Butter tried to remain calm as he dropped the blunt in his lap and put both hands on the wheel. Felon sprang to attention to see what had caused the disturbance in the vehicle's flow. He looked from his partner's face to the rearview mirror and knew what time it was. They were fucked. Unbeknownst to Eve, Felon and Butter had brought along a little insurance in the form of a P89. Felon took the gun from the glove box and dropped it on the floor. Using his right foot, he slid it beneath his seat. Butter peeped his man's play, but Eve was still asleep.

Butter tried to remain calm as he pulled the car over to the side of the road. Felon peeked over his shoulder at Eve, who was finally starting to come around. When she saw the flashing lights, her muscles automatically tensed. She knew that they didn't have anything more than weed in the car, but for some reason she didn't like the look on the gentlemen's faces.

The deputy got out of his cruiser and strutted over to their car. He was a redneck-looking character with a Confederate flag embroidered on his holster. He took his time as he strolled up to the driver's side window. Seemingly at ease, he made sure that his hand rested on the 9 he carried.

"Problem, officer?" Butter asked stupidly.

"I was hoping you could tell me," the trooper replied in a Southern drawl. "You were all over the road back there."

"Oh, is that what this is about?" Butter bared all his teeth. "I'm sorry about that. See, I was smoking a cigarette and the flame accidentally dropped into my lap."

"Is that right?"

"Yes, sir."

"Why don't you boys step out of the car?"

Felon's heart leapt into his throat. If the trooper decided to search the car, they were fucked. The look on Butter's face told Felon that he was thinking the same thing. The only one who didn't seem to realize what was going down was Eve. Felon tried to make eye contact with her, but she still wasn't catching on.

"What's this all about?" Eve asked from the backseat. Her fitted cap was pulled down, concealing part of her face and her mane of red hair, which was wrapped underneath it.

"Just step out of the car, young man," the trooper said.

Butter got out of the car, followed by Felon, who held the seat up for Eve to climb out of the backseat. As Felon helped her out of the car, he again tried to give Eve the look. She just looked at him and sucked her teeth. She was more pissed about having to get out into the night air than anything else. She had no idea that the bull-shit was about to go down.

"You boys got anything in the car that I should know about?" the trooper asked.

"Hold up," Butter protested. "Don't you wanna see my license and registration?"

"We'll come to that in a second," the trooper said, shining his flashlight into the car. "Is that weed I smell?"

"No, sir," Felon said, making sure to keep the car between himself and the trooper.

"Bullshit," the trooper said, clicking on his radio. "Yeah, this is Calhoun out on 390 South, near Mount Morris. Could you send another cruiser out this way to assist me?"

Before the dispatcher could respond, Butter hit the trooper in the jaw and took off into the woods. Felon looked from his sprint-ing partner to Eve and followed Butter's lead. Eve was in total shock. For a brief second, she was frozen in place. That second was all it took for the trooper to draw his gun and train it on Eve.

"Go ahead," he said, steadying the gun with one hand and rub-bing his jaw with the other. "You go for it and I'll give you the worst case of lead poisoning you ever did see."

Eve looked to the dark woods that her partners had disap-peared into and cursed herself for not following. She knew that they were going to take her in, but what was the worst they could do to her for a weed clip in the ashtray? Eve figured that the rednecks would slap her with a fine and turn her loose. That thought faded when the trooper pulled the pistol from under the passenger's seat. That would be the cause of Eve doing her first bid.

"I ain't fucking with Felon like that," Eve said, coming out of her flashback.

"Yeah, right," Cassidy smirked. "I saw how you got all dreamy-eyed when I mentioned his name. You can't fool me."

"Whatever." Eve brushed her off. Cassidy was more accurate in her assessment of Eve than she knew. Eve had it bad for Felon, but she figured that Felon had always seen her as just another lil chick from Twenty-Gang. She had a suspicion that he had some type of feeling toward her, but he never came clean about it, so why should she?

Cassidy stopped for a red light on 121st and 7th. Eve stared at the pedestrians crossing the street, and one in particular caught her eye. The young man she was staring out was a hulk of a cat. He easily stood six foot five and was built like a dumpster. He lumbered across the street, clutching something to his chest. He was a little heavier than the last time she had seen him, but she would know her friend anywhere.

"Stop the car, Cassidy," Eve told her.

Cassidy jumped. "Girl, what the hell is wrong with you?"

"I wanna holla at my boy," Eve said, pointing to the young man.

"Who the fuck are you talking about?" Cassidy asked, following to where Eve was pointing. When she saw who Eve was talking about, she slapped her forehead in frustration. "Come on, Eve, you can see that nigga later."

"Just stop the car." Eve said firmly. Cassidy sucked her teeth and pulled through the light to the curb. Before the car had completely stopped, Eve was on the curb, rushing to the young man.

"Beast," she called out. "Beast!"

The young man stopped in his tracks and craned his thick neck to see who was calling him. His face was twisted into a mask of rage as he eyed everyone on the block. People tripped over themselves to avoid the big man's menacing glare. Beast was ready to throw down if it was another cruel soul trying to poke fun at him. His features softened and his eyes watered up when he saw the small female coming in his direction.

"Eve?" Beast asked, flashing a jagged-toothed smile.

"Yeah," Eve said. "It's me."

"Eve!" Beast scooped her into his massive arms. "When did you come home?"

"This morning," she said, gasping for breath. "And I'd like to live long enough to enjoy it."

"Sorry," Beast said, lowering her gently to the ground. "I'm just happy to see you, Eve."

"I'm happy to see you too, Beast," Eve said, touching her now even sorer side. "Where ya headed, big fella?"

"Gotta go to the store and get food for Tom," Beast said, showing Eve that the thing he carried under his arm was a small kitten wrapped in a pillow case. "I been feeding him tuna, but I don't think he likes it."

Eve watched as Beast tenderly stroked the kitten. He might've been hard on the eyes, but Beast was a very kind soul. At least if he liked you, he was. It was hard to believe that the man-child called Beast had once been a very promising college student.

The people who didn't know him like that thought he had always been that way, but this wasn't so. Beast was a star athlete and graduated from high school with honors. He kicked it with the homeys in the hood from time to time, but they stopped hanging with him after the accident.

It was a few years ago when it happened. Beast was home for Christmas break from the University of Maryland. It was his first semester at the school, and he had marveled the faculty with his quick wit and athleticism. It was to be the beginning of a wonderful career, but that cold night in December would change his life forever.

Ever since Eve could remember, Beast had looked out for her. He was a few years her senior, so it was like a big brother, little sister type of thing. If Eve was messing up in school, Beast was on her ass. If Eve was wilding, Beast would check her. She hated his henpecking, but she knew it was for her own good.

One night Eve was in the park hanging with some of the homeys. Beast was just passing through and stopped to chat for a few minutes. About five minutes after he got there, a group of guys and girls came rolling into the park. They weren't from the hood, so it had to mean trouble.

"Which one of y'all is Eve?" the leader of the group asked.

Eve, being the bad ass that she was, stepped up. "I'm Eve," she said defiantly. The boy outweighed her by at least twenty pounds, but Evelyn Panelli was never one to back down from a fight. Be it with a guy or a girl, she was always down to squab. Eve didn't know what the boy's problem was, but she was about to find out.

The boy looked over his shoulder and motioned for one of the girls to step forward. When the fat dark-skinned chick stepped forward out of the group, Eve started to get the picture. The girl was a chick that Eve had beat the hell out of the day before for trying to bully Cassidy. Eve had whipped her out, but she seemed to be a slow learner.

"Yeah," the boy said. "I heard you and ya bitches jumped my lil sis the other night. I wasn't feeling that shit, hoe."

"First of all," Eve said, getting loud. "Didn't nobody jump ya fat-ass sister. Me and her shot a fair one and she lost. Straight like that. And second, you better watch who the fuck you're calling a hoe or you can get the same treatment."

"We'll see, Miss Badass. I'm gonna let my sister whip ya little ass. Maybe then you'll shut that big-ass mouth of yours."

"Nigga, let's do this." Eve said, sliding out of her Snorkel coat.

The girl hesitated for a minute. It was clear to everyone except her brother that she didn't want to fight. She looked from her brother to Eve and had to struggle to keep from running. She knew that Eve had beat her ass all by herself, but she had made up the jump lie so she wouldn't look soft. Now she had to get down or lay down.

The girl tried to catch Eve off guard, but the punch was fired awkwardly. Eve weaved the punch and countered with a left. Before the girl could get her balance, Eve threw a haymaker that had the girl out on her feet. When the fat girl crashed to the ground, Eve started kicking her viciously.

The girl's brother sneaked up on Eve and clocked her. To his surprise, she kept her feet and fired right back. Eve got off two good punches before Beast stepped in. He swung his mitt so hard that you could hear it cutting the wind. When the blow connected, you could hear the boy's jaw crack. Before he could hit the ground, Beast had him by the throat and was trying to juice his neck.

By this time, both crews were going head-up. Punches and kicks were flying everywhere. Eve was busy whipping on a girl and a guy near the jungle gym, so she momentarily lost sight of Beast. Suddenly a lone gunshot rang out. Eve got low while everyone else scattered. She scanned the area to see if any of hers had been hit. It was then she noticed a lone figure sprawled on the concrete.

Eve's eyes filled with tears at the sight of her slain comrade. She ran over to Beast and knelt by his side. Blood was running from a tiny hole in his forehead and pooling beneath his head. Eve sobbed for her friend. When all seemed lost, she noticed that Beast's chest was still rising and falling. It was a long shot, but she hoped that she might be able to get help and save him.

Eve ran into the middle of the street and started screaming frantically. Luckily, the park where Beast had been shot was right behind Harlem Hospital. They rushed Beast into surgery, but things didn't look good. When it was all said and done, Beast had lived but his life would never be the same. The university discharged Beast, putting an end to his college education and his football career. He would live through the shooting only to spend the rest of his days as a grown man with the mind of a child.

The homeys flipped over what had happened. They eventually caught the kid and murdered him, but the pain would never go away. They had lost a stand-up soldier in Beast. Nobody felt worse about what had happened than Eve. She knew that the whole thing was her fault. This was the reason why Eve still dealt with Beast while everyone else made fun of him. She owed him that much. Beast would forever be her friend.

"That's a nice kitten," Eve said, pushing the memories from her mind.

"Yup," Beast said, stroking the patchwork kitten. "I found him on da ave. He was all dirty so I took him home and washed him off. Now he's pretty again. Ain't he, Eve?"

"Yes, he is, Beast."

"Come on, heifer!" Cassidy shouted from the car window.

"Hold on!" Eve shouted back with an attitude.

"I don't like your friend Cassidy," Beast said, frowning. "When I say hi to her, she acts like she doesn't hear me, or whispers to her friends."

"Pay her no mind," Eve said, touching his arm. "Cassidy just has issues."

"She's mean. You know, people think I don't know they laugh at me, Eve," Beast said sadly. "They laugh at me cause I don't think as fast as them. I'm men . . . men . . . what's the word you used?"

"Mentally challenged," she reminded him.

"Yeah, that's the one. Sometimes I forget stuff. I forget a lot of stuff lately."

"Have you been taking your pills every day?"

"Nah. Sometimes I take em, but not all the time. When you went away there was nobody to make sure that I took em. Plus they make me feel icky."

"Beast, you know you have to take your pills."

"But why?"

"Because they help you to stay calm and think clearer."

"Do not. I can get calm on my own. Watch." Beast straightened out his face and tried to look serious.

"That's not what I meant, Beast. Listen, I gotta go, but I'm gonna catch up with you later to make sure you're taking care of yourself."

"You gonna come and see me?" he asked excitedly.

"Yep, and I'm bringing your favorite snack."

"You bringing Cracker Jacks?"

"Sure am."

"Yeah!" Beast shouted and pumped his fist. "Then I can show you all my new pets. I've got a snake named Bone Crusher, some fish, puppies. I had a squirrel, but Bone Crusher hugged him too hard. I buried him in Central Park."

"That's interesting, Beast. You can tell me all about it when I come over. But if you don't take your pills, no Cracker Jacks."

"I'm gonna go take em right now," Beast said, sprinting in the other direction. He had gotten about a half block before he came back. "Forgot the cat food." Beast ran into the store.

Eve stood there and waited to make sure that Beast had gotten the correct change. After making sure he was good, she headed back toward the car. People often took advantage of the big guy. Beast had a very gentle and trusting nature, but heaven help you if you got him started. Beast could snap a man's bones with little effort. The best way to handle him was just to leave him alone to his animals. Few men had made the mistake of trying Beast, and they all ended up being treated to very lengthy stays in the hospital.

5.

"Damn," Cassidy complained. "You were taking all day with that nigga."

"You know I fuck with Beast," Eve said.

"I don't know why. That boy is a headache."

"Beast is cool. You just gotta get to know him."

"Why the fuck would I wanna know him? He's a big for nothing muthafucka that always smells like a pet store."

"Cassidy, you're acting like Beast was always like this. It ain't his fault that he got shot. Have a fucking heart."

"Have a heart my ass. I'm so fucking tired of Beast and his sob story. 'College Star Shot In the Head.' We all read the paper, Eve. Shit happens in the hood. Get over it already."

"I don't fucking believe you, Cassidy. How are you gonna be so cold? Beast is one of us."

"One of y'all," Cassidy corrected. "You know I ain't wit all that thug shit. If you chose to claim that walking sideshow, be my guest. Just don't bring that nigga around me. Retard muthafucka."

"Okay, that's enough," Eve snapped. "All that shit you're popping doesn't compute to me, Cassidy. Beast is my friend, period. I don't wanna hear no more of that slick talk about him. That goes for you or any of these muthafuckas out here. That's my fucking dawg. I don't give a fuck who doesn't like it!"

Cassidy looked over at Eve to see if she was serious. Sure enough, there was steam practically coming from Eve's cornrows. Cassidy couldn't understand why Eve wouldn't let go of the guilt she carried around in her heart. It might've been her beef that got Beast shot, but it wasn't her fault. These things happen when people put themselves in high-risk situations. Cassidy decided to let the argument die. She knew Eve was bullheaded and there was no changing her mind.

"You got that, Eve," Cassidy conceded. "I didn't know you were gonna take it like that."

"It's all good," Eve said, calming down. "I just don't like people making fun of him."

"I can dig it. But fuck the dumb shit. Where we at? The liquor store? Weed spot? What's good, ma?"

"Damn, girl. I ain't been outta lockup for twenty-four hours and you're already trying to get me to OD?"

"Fuck that shit, Eve. Let's do it up!"

"I wish. I'm on paper. I can't smoke weed until next year."

"Damn, that shit is a drag," Cassidy said defeated. "Butter is on paper too, but he still smokes. He drinks this stuff to clean his piss."

"I ain't trying to go through all that shit. As much as I miss blowing trees, I ain't willing to jump through no fucking hoops for it. For all that, I just won't smoke."

"I hear ya, but they don't test for liquor. Do they?"

"Nah, I don't think so."

"So, there you have it. You'll just have to make the transition from weed head to alcoholic."

The two girls fell over each other laughing as the Lex continued with the flow of traffic.

* * *

Felon had just dropped the bombshell about what Sean had hipped him to. Just as Felon expected, Butter's solution to the problem was to kill Spooky. Felon was no stranger to violence or bloodshed, but at this stage of the game, he was trying to rise above the bullshit.

"Fuck that shit," Butter spat. "That lil ingrate muthafucka has gotta go."

Felon hushed him. "Be cool. We gotta do this smart. You and me been under a microscope since we put that piece-of-shit Macho out of his misery. The police are tight because they couldn't make that garbage-ass charge stick. Now if we go and kill Spooky all cowboy style, how's it gonna look? You gotta start using your head, partner."

"Damn! That shit just makes me tight, yo. You put that lil nigga on and he crossed us. But that's ya man, though."

"I know. I put the kid on. I knew him since he was a shorty. If he needed some extra bread, he could've come to me."

"That just goes to show that the lil bastard did it out of larceny."

"I gotta agree, the boy's gotta answer for this. But we gotta be creative about it."

"You're right." Butter snapped his fingers. "I got the perfect plan, too."

"Let a nigga in," Felon said.

"Yeah," Butter rubbed his hands together greedily. "I think you're gonna like this, Felon. Say, does your uncle still have that nail gun in his garage?"

Eve rode around with Cassidy for the better part of an hour before convincing her to swing by her uncle's pad. Eve had enjoyed taking in the sights and sounds of Harlem. She hadn't been away for a very long time, but it was long enough. Captivity could make the hours seem like days under the right conditions.

Before going home, Eve wanted to stop by the store to get a pack of Newports. Smoking was a nasty habit that she had picked up while she was away. She promised herself that she was gonna quit, but not yet. Eve's life was damn near in shambles and she had to put the pieces back together. All she had going for her was a GED, and that wouldn't be enough to get her where she needed to be.

As Eve was coming out of the store, a pair of strong arms encircled her waist from behind. Eve turned around, ready to flip out, and found a familiar face. Butter stood there, looking goofy as hell, making a kissing gesture at her.

"Boy, get off me." She swatted him.

"Damn, girl. From the way you looking, all these hoes need to get locked up," he joked.

"Fuck you, nigga," she responded.

"Eve," sang a familiar voice, coming from the left.

She felt her body involuntarily tense up. Just hearing that voice after all of this time made Eve feel some kinda way. She tried to muster up the old animosities in her mind's eye. *This was the man who you went to prison for. He blew up while you counted days.* She tried to call up the very same shield of rage that had kept her sane while incarcerated, but the flame wouldn't light. Longing overrode whatever she thought she felt, and so went the anger. If she turned around, she would surely faint. Eve closed her eyes and tried to slow her breathing. Somehow she mustered the strength to turn and face Felon.

Eve almost melted when she saw how good the months had been to Felon. His smooth chocolate skin was without a blemish or scar. The sweat suit he was wearing looked crisp, like he had just copped it. He wore a white do-rag beneath the Yankee hat that he wore cocked slightly to the side. *Time had sure been on Felon's side,* Eve thought to herself.

When Felon made eye contact with Eve, there was an instant spark. He sized her up and could've sworn his heart skipped a beat. She had filled out quite nicely while she was away. Felon didn't mean to stare, but he found that he couldn't help himself. It was like one of those scenes in the movies when everything else fades out, leaving only the two lovers. If "Shower Me with Your Love" was playing in the background, it would've been a pretty good love scene in a movie.

"Hello," Cassidy said, breaking the connection. "Damn, earth to y'all."

"Shut up, Cassidy. What up, homey?" she asked, looking at Felon.

"Chilling," he said, half smiling. "When did you touch down?"

"This morning. I'm just now hitting the streets. What's been up with you?"

"You should know. I wrote you and told you every step of the way, shorty. You trying to say you forgot how to read?"

"Nah," she said looking at her boots. "I got em."

"So why no response, ma? Nothing heavy, just let ya big bro know you were good."

Eve caught the curveball that Felon had no idea he threw. "Wasn't bout nothing." She twisted her lips. "I had to hold myself down. I couldn't let the troubles of the world invade my space. It was hard enough for me to get accustomed to the way shit worked in there, and getting letters from my peoples about how good or bad everyone else in the world was doing wouldn't have helped my cause any. I had to do what was best for the kid."

"I hear that." Felon looked her up and down. "You look more like a young lady than a little girl."

"My girl hooked me up," she said, tugging at the too-tight shirt.

"Sometimes we gotta change with the times. It looks good on you though, ma. Keep it up."

"I'll take that into consideration."

"And the boat sunk, killing all the white people," Butter cut in. "Y'all break all this *Titanic* shit up, a'ight?"

"Why you gotta play so much?" Felon asked, irritated.

"My bad, fam. I'm saying though, we're all happy to see Eve. I wanna pop a lil shit wit her too. Y'all can do the Marvin and Tammy thang on your own time."

"Shut up, Butter." Cassidy nudged him. "The only chick you gotta worry about being happy to see is me."

"You know I missed you, ma," he said, putting Cassidy in a bear hug. "You ain't wreck my car, did you?"

"No, I ain't wreck ya hoopty."

"Hoopty? Girl, you must've lost ya last mind," Butter protested. "That there is a classic. Lexus GS 300. They don't even make the chassis like that anymore. You better get up on it, baby."

"Whatever, nigga. Why, you want ya lil ride back or something?"

"Don't act like that," Butter pleaded. "I ain't stressing that car. If you need to hold on to it for a lil while longer, then do you."

"Oh." she rolled her eyes. "I thought you was getting stink over your ride."

"Nah. I'm just happy to see Eve. What up, girl?" He turned to Eve.

"Just trying to get on the right track," she said coolly.

"Speaking of which," Cassidy cut in. "Butter, can I holla at you for a second?"

"Sure," he said, following her over to the car. Cassidy whispered a few words into Butter's ear as he nodded and listened. A few seconds later he headed over to Felon. "Say, how much money you got on you?"

"What?" Felon asked, confused.

"Look, shoot me a grand or three."

"A grand or three? Nigga, what the fuck for?"

Butter grinned. "Felon, would I steer you wrong?"

"A'ight." Felon dipped into his stash and peeled off fifteen hundred dollars. Butter took the bills and headed in Eve's direction. Felon looked on in shock as Butter added twenty-two hundred of his own to the pot and presented it to Eve.

"Baby girl," Butter began, "this ain't much, but it's a lil something to keep ya belly full for a minute."

Eve stared quizzically at the wad of bills in Butter's hand. She wondered what Cassidy had whispered into this lion's ear to turn him into a pussycat. Eve hadn't accepted Felon's or Butter's help while she was away, so the noble thing would've been to decline the money. Eve was hardly thinking about nobility as she snatched the bills and stuffed them into the pockets of her too-tight jeans.

"Just call it a contribution to the 'We Love Eve' fund," Felon added.

"Be careful, baby boy," she warned. "Love is a very powerful word. It can heal or harm, depending on how it's used."

"That's why it can never fall into the wrong hands," he shot back. "Love is for the free of spirit. The dreamer. Tell me," he said, leaning in to whisper to her, "what do you dream about?"

Eve felt herself getting moist as Felon's breath tickled her neck. She couldn't believe he was still able to get to her like this. Only this time it was different. It was no longer the fantasies of a young girl, but the desires of a woman.

"So, talk to me, people," Cassidy said. "Are we hanging or what?"

"I ain't got nothing to do," Butter started. "How about we—"

"We got that thing, remember?" Felon cut in.

Butter caught on. "Oh shit. Sorry about that, ladies. Look, we'll get up wit y'all later on. Eve, it's good to have you back, nigga."

"Good to be back." She waved.

"I'll see you later, shorty," Felon commented as he walked off.

"Count on it, big-timer. Count on it." Eve smirked as she watched her childhood fantasy bop away.

6.

Cassidy dropped Eve off in front of her building and instructed her to be ready by ten. Reluctantly, Eve agreed. She didn't really care for the party scene, but she had been down for a while. She walked up to the building she called home and shook her head in disgust. The shabby brown tenement looked as if it would collapse at any time. Nonetheless, this was where Eve was released to. Her uncle Bobby's apartment.

As Eve approached the building, she caught more than a few glances from the hustlers posted up. Some of them looked at her as fresh meat, while others tried to shoot her an intimidating glare. To their surprise, she returned each stare in kind.

"What's really hood?" asked a brown-skinned kid, taking the initiative. His hair was braided in a swirl with a long plat at the end. He wore a purple FUBU shirt with the matching purple Nikes. He came in Eve's direction with a confident swagger. "How you doing, ma?" he pressed.

"I'm good," Eve said, trying to sidestep conversation.

"Damn, baby. It's like that?"

"Straight cheese," Eve told him.

"Stuck-up bitch," capped one of the other hustlers.

Eve stopped in her tracks and turned to face the group. "What happened?" she asked. "Repeat it. You got something you wanna say, nigga? Speak up!"

"Shorty got a lot of mouth," the big-mouth hustler said. "You better watch that shit, yo."

"Man, y'all got me fucked up," Eve informed them. "I'm passing through and you're talking crazy. Is there a problem?"

"Yo, check this out, bitch—"

"Hold that down, B," someone in the group said. "Is that Eve?"

"Who that?" Eve asked.

"Who you want it to be?" the older man asked, stepping forward. "It's me, young'n. Bullet."

Eve's wheels spun for a minute trying to recognize the thirty-something cat talking to her. Bullet wasn't short, nor was he tall. He just was. His face bore scars of the many correctional facilities he had been a guest of. Bullet was an old-school gangsta. He was only in his early thirties, but he had served under some of the greatest street legends of the eighties and nineties. Bullet got his name from all the lead that he had taken over the years. He had taken a good amount, but he had issued out double. Bullet could've been one of the greats, but he chose to be among the soldiers. No one knew his logic for it, but that's just how he was. Bullet was both respected and feared in the tristate area.

"Bullet?" Eve said, with recognition finally setting in. "Get the fuck outta here!"

"What's up, baby girl?" he said, hugging her. "Been a long time, cousin."

"I be knowing," Eve said, blushing. "I'm home for good, though."

"Shit, I'd like to think so, Eve. But you know how I've been doing over the years. I'll bust a nigga brain for a lil bit of change, know what I mean?"

"I know that's right," Eve agreed. "So you still in the game, Bullet?"

"What else is there, Eve, baby? I got five kids, ma. I gotta eat and provide for them."

"You still slinging dick wit ya lead, huh Bullet?"

"If I don't somebody else will. These niggaz." Bullet grabbed the smart-mouthed hustler by the neck. "You gotta excuse ignorant-ass youngsters, Eve. These niggaz don't know no better. Say, lil nigga," Bullet addressed his captive, "you know who the fuck this is?" The hustler shook his head dumbly. "Punk, this is Eve. She's the hardest young bitch on these streets. This lady will carve yo disrespectful tongue out yo muthafuck'n head, chump. Say you fucking sorry, nigga!"

"Sorry," he squawked.

"Ignorant muthafucka." Bullet tossed him to the ground. "Good to have you home, Eve. How you living these days?"

"Like a soldier," she said. "Speaking of which, I need to ask you about something." She stepped out of earshot of the group and Bullet followed.

"What's on ya mind, shorty?"

"I need a come-up," she said seriously.

"Ain't this some shit." He folded his muscular arms. "You ain't been home for a few hours and you're plotting."

"Ya protégée is hurting right now, Bullet. The parole board is supposed to be hooking me up with a gig, but I really ain't trying to slave for thirty dollars a day."

"I feel you, sis, but ain't nothing but trouble come with this lifestyle. You just did a bid and I'd hate to see you down again. If you're uptight, I can float you a few dollars till you get on ya feet."

"I know, and I appreciate the gesture, but you know that ain't how Eve do. I gotta grind for mine, I don't believe in handouts."

"Determined as ever, just like back in the day."

"You know how it is, Bullet. I'm gonna do me whether you put me on a lick or not."

"Very true." He chuckled. "Tell you what, if I catch wind of something, I'll think about putting you down."

"Fair enough." She smiled.

"You bout to go up and see Uncle Bobby?" he motioned towards the building.

"That's where the bulls can find me," she joked. "You know how it be when you down."

"I do. You know that been my winter home since a shorty," he reminisced. "But that was a long time ago. I was running around with you and Felon like I didn't have any sense."

"I see Felon is still on a grind."

"Shit, counting money ain't no grind. That boy got his wings. Felon is still my nigga, but he don't deal with this here. Everybody knows that ya man ain't slinging iron no more. He's slinging birds now. We hold this," Bullet spread his arms, "by the law of the land. Do or die. You know what it is round here, Eve."

"I know that's right, but I'm trying to see my piece of the pie too. You better get up on it." She punched him in the arm.

"Whatever, Eve. You know where to find me, right?"

"Indeed." She nodded. Eve shot the loudmouth hustler a glance, followed by a mocking chuckle. Dap was issued to the soldiers who saluted her, and she dismissed those who hit her with the screw face. She had no idea what the odds were of her winning the conflict with the young hustler, but she knew that she had never been a sucka and she didn't intend on becoming one.

Eve climbed the last landing of the five-story walk-up, breathing heavily. Her new habit seemed to be having an effect on her body. Quitting was an option that she would definitely keep open, but it would wait til another time. Eve had issues, and in her mind the cigarettes helped.

She stood in front of her uncle's apartment and hesitated before knocking. It had been her home since she was young, but now the place felt alien to her. Her uncle had written from time to time, but he never got a response either. Eve ducked him out of shame. She was ashamed that as smart as she was, she ended up catching a charge for a stupid-ass reason. She examined the chipping brown paint in the door and saw the spot where she had carved her name. Eve traced the carving with her index finger. Memories.

Deciding that she was beginning to feel stupid, Eve knocked on the door. She tapped three times, causing paint chips to shake loose and float to the ground. At first there was nothing, then a lock clicked. A bolt could be heard sliding loose, followed by another lock. After the strange clicking orchestra came to a cease, the door sprung open. No one stood to take responsibility for opening the portal, but it was an invitation nonetheless.

Eve cautiously stepped through the doorway and closed it behind her. She found herself standing at the end of a long hallway that she remembered all too well. Eve still had the scar on her forehead from when she hit it on the closet door. Her uncle would always tell her about running back and forth but she never listened. The results were a permanent mark.

Different pictures lined the walls of the long hallways. There were pictures of family members, whom she hadn't seen in a while and probably never would again. There were also pictures of her Uncle Bobby from his days in the service. He looked young and regal standing among his fellow soldiers. They were all smiling and brandishing weapons. He still kept in contact with some of the guys from his unit. They even managed to get together every year or so. She remembered the grand old stories that he told about the war and his part in it. She also remembered the nights when he would wake up screaming from nightmares brought on by the conflict.

There was one picture in particular that gave Eve pause. She ran her fingers across the frame, wiping away the dust that had settled on the protective glass. It was of a couple and a little girl. The man in the picture had smooth tan skin and wavy auburn hair. A thin mustache lined his upper lip and curved downward at the ends. The woman had a caramel complexion, with long black hair, a round face, and attractive full lips. She smiled lovingly at the man in the picture and her hazel eyes held the sparkle of happiness. In the center of the picture was a little girl wearing two pigtails. A lone tear ran down Eve's face as she remembered the tragedy that had befallen her parents.

She couldn't have been more than nine or so at the time, but the memories were still fresh in her mind. It was New Years Eve as she huddled with her parents in front of the television, waiting for Dick Clark to count down to the new year. Her parents weren't rich, but they weren't hurting either. Eve was provided with all of the comforts and love that a little girl should have. These were happy times for her. The calm before the storm.

Her father, who was a mixture of Italian and Irish, was a soldier in a local mob family. Because of his mixed heritage, he could never be officially inducted into the secret society, but he was still a respected man on the streets. Everyone loved Joe-Joe Panelli, but there were also those who were jealous of him. Some people figured that a half-breed wop with a nigger for a wife didn't deserve the kind of respect and attention that Joe had earned.

Her mother was one of the fairest women in Harlem. Shanice Jones was a college student who moonlighted as a lounge waitress in order to finance her education. She had met Joe through her brother Bobby, and the attraction was instant. Even with the threat of being disowned by his family, he pledged his love to Shanice and asked the beautiful Black woman to be his wife. Shanice accepted his offer and they had been together ever since.

"Mommy," asked a young Evelyn. "Could I get some ice cream while we wait for the ball to drop?"

"Evelyn, you know eating ice cream at this hour is gonna give you nightmares," Shanice scolded. "Wait until tomorrow."

"Come on, baby," Joe said in his deep voice. "It's New Years. I don't think it would hurt much if we gave Eve some ice cream."

Eve tried to keep from squealing with joy as she listened to her father work his magic. She knew that whenever her mother told her something, she could always look to her father to be on her side. He was Eve's hero.

"You two kill me," Shanice joked as she got up from the couch and headed for the kitchen. "Always trying to double-team somebody."

Joe looked over at Eve and winked. She smiled back at him and flashed the "okay" sign. As usual, her father had come through for her. She was as close to him as any daughter can get to a father. Even though his skin was different, Eve never saw him as black or white. To her, he was just daddy.

Eve followed her mother to the kitchen and watched in anticipation as her mother scooped the Heath Bar ice cream into a little glass bowl. From the kitchen doorway, Eve heard a knock at the door. She thought that it might be Uncle Bobby or one of her father's friends who had come to bring in the new year with them. When Joe opened the door and she saw the expression on his face, her young mind told her that something was wrong.

Shanice, who was still unaware of the visitor, continued to prepare Eve's snack while the little girl watched the exchange. The intruder was a young white man wearing a grey suit under his black overcoat. His jet black hair was slicked down and combed back, giving him an old-school mobster look. He flashed a wicked grin, like he knew something no one else did. His eyes had to be his most defining feature. They were the coldest blue that Evelyn had ever seen, even on a white man. He stepped through the doorway without being invited and began speaking to Joe. Eve had never seen the man before, but something about him didn't sit right with her.

The man said something that caused him to turn beet red. Joe began to growl something in retort, but Eve's Italian was scratchy at best. Whatever the exchange of words was, they weren't pleasant. The two men became more animated as the argument went on. The visitor said something and nodded in Eve's direction. When Joe turned around and noticed his daughter watching, the visitor made his move.

He removed a small pistol with a silencer from the pocket of his overcoat and raised it to an unsuspecting Joe's face. When Joe noticed the fear etched across his little girl's face, he spun around to the intruder. The last thing he saw was the muzzle flashes as the intruder squeezed the trigger. Joe's forehead exploded and he collapsed. He was dead before he hit the carpet.

A split second before Joe was sent to the next life, Shanice came to see what had distracted Eve. When she saw her husband killed, she dropped the glass bowl, shattering it on the kitchen tiles. Hearing the sound of the bowl breaking brought the intruder's attention to the two females in the kitchen. He stepped over Joe's body and came in their direction.

Shanice saw his intentions written all over his face. She ushered Evelyn into the farthest corner of the kitchen and armed herself with the largest knife she could find. When the intruder came into the kitchen, he was greeted by a mother who sought to save the life of her child at any cost, even if it meant sacrificing her own life.

The knife bit deeply into the intruder's arm, causing him to bellow out in pain. She tried to come back for another slice, but he was ready. Using his slashed arm to block the blow, he came around with the other hand and clocked Shanice with the gun. She stumbled, but managed to keep her wits long enough to launch another attack. That was when Eve heard the chirp.

From where she was standing, Eve couldn't really see what was going on. All she could see was her mother's back and the intruder's face. A dot appeared on her back and quickly began to grow. The intruder wore a wicked grin as Shanice began to stagger from the impact. The pain in her chest was intense, but her paternal instincts wouldn't let her forget Evelyn. Her life had already been forfeited, but the child must survive.

Again, without fear for her own life, Shanice tried to defend her child. When the intruder raised his pistol in Evelyn's direction, Shanice threw her weight into him. Instead of pressing the attack, Shanice darted for the child. The killer let off three wild shots. One shot destroyed Grandma's clock, while the other struck a falling Shanice. The third hit Evelyn.

Shanice collapsed to her knees over the fallen child. Blood was splattered on the wall and edges of the refrigerator. Shanice covered her child as best she could while the intruder kept firing. When the smoke cleared, the intruder stood over the two prone woman and spat. As he was leaving the apartment, he paused to watch Dick Clark bring in the new year. He left the mother and child for dead, but he wasn't quite through enough.

A neighbor, who had been spying through her peephole, called the police. When they got there, the intruder was long gone, but they found a two dead people and a little girl, who was shot up and barely breathing. They rushed Eve to the hospital, where she was treated for gunshot wounds to the chest and leg.

When the police questioned young Evelyn, she told them honestly that she didn't know the man who killed her parents. She didn't know him, but she would never forget his face, his cold blue stare, or that wicked grin. They asked her a few more questions, then turned her over to the state. It was all downhill from there.

"Evelyn," called a gruff voice from the rear of the house. "You gonna stand there gawking at them pictures or you gonna come in here so I can get a look at you?"

Eve sighed and placed the picture back on the wall. She kissed her fingertips and placed one on both of her parents' faces before continuing down the hall. As she drew closer to the living room, she caught sight of a Minicam that was mounted in the ceiling. Uncle Bobby had always been a strange one, but even this was a little extreme.

Eve entered the tiny living room and looked around nostalgically. Uncle Bobby still had the same living room furniture that he had when her parents were alive. It was even still covered in plastic. The tan carpet has crisscrossed tire marks on it. No doubt the work of Uncle Bobby. A writing table sat near the window, giving them a clear view of the avenue. Off to the right was Uncle Bobby's room. Eve took a deep breath and proceeded.

Uncle Bobby looked as wild as ever. He was still sporting the same Afro that he had when he and Joe were running partners, years ago. Only now it was sprinkled with flakes of grey. He was draped in his usual green army fatigues and flack vest. A bayonet was strapped to his ankle and a tiny gun turret was mounted on the arm of his chair. The glare from the half dozen video monitors behind Bobby illuminated his face in a sick blue light as he grinned at his sister's child.

"Come here, girl," Bobby said, spreading his arms. "Give ya uncle some love."

Eve half bent and embraced her uncle. At first she wasn't sure how he was going to react. Eve had snubbed him for her whole bid. It wasn't done out of malice, but she was going through something that she needed to handle alone. Bobby greeting her with love made her feel at ease. He was probably still gonna give her the lecture of her life, but that was his way. The important thing was that the both of them were back amongst family. All they had left was each other.

"Good to see you, Uncle Bobby," she said genuinely. "Good to see you."

"It's good to see you too," he said holding her at arm's length. "You look good."

She looked down. "Thanks. Cassidy brought me this stuff to come home in."

"Cassidy came to pick you up? How's she been? I see her riding round with this one or that one from time to time, but she ain't been by since you went away."

"She's chilling."

"Umm hmm," Bobby said suspiciously. "I see her fast-ass little sister is following right in her footsteps. I hear she be up in them strip clubs doing private dances. They say a few fellas been wit her."

"Uncle Bobby, how is it that you never leave the house, but you know some of everything about what's going on in the streets?"

"Cause I was born wit my ear to the street and it's still there. You think about that when and if you thinking about cutting up. Hear?"

"Come on, Uncle Bobby, why you gotta cut right in? Ain't you happy to see me?"

"Hell yeah, and I'm trying to keep you around. Them streets ain't nothing nice, girl."

"This ain't the sixties," she said.

"Shit," he spat. "You ain't gotta tell me. We was real gangstas in the sixties. Not like these rap babies out here," he said, nodding out the window. "We had codes back then. Rules. Everybody ate, cause we respected the rules. If you got out of line, you got put down. Simple as that."

"I'll keep that in mind," she said, heading for her bedroom.

"You better learn to listen to somebody, Eve," he called after her. "There's nothing out there but trouble. If you know like I know, you'll try to get a job or go to school and get yo yellow tail up out this. You see what happened to Big Joe."

Eve froze. She felt her body tense up as once again the memories were dredged up. "My father was murdered in his home," she said with her voice dripping venom. "He was murdered by the same guinea muthafuckas that y'all worked for, remember?"

"Do I remember?" he asked, returning her cold glare. "Damn right I remember. It was them same muthafuckas who put me in this here sports coupe," he said pounding on the wheelchair. "Dealing with Franko and his people was just as good as signing a deal with the devil, but we was too young and dumb to see it. Course, it probably wouldn't have made a difference if we had. Thought we was somebody cause they said so. Red and Black was what they called us." Uncle Bobby had to compose himself before speaking again. "I'm sorry, Eve. I know you're still hurting from it. The worst part is, it'll always feel like my fault."

"Your fault," she said, softening her voice from earlier. "Wasn't nothing you could've done."

"I should've done something," he said, unsheathing his bayonet and waving it at no one in particular. "I came for em though, Eve. They took my only sister and my only friend, so I went for em. Again and again, I went for em. When they whipped my ass, I came back. When they shot me, I came back. Again and again, taking it to them crackers, baby. I killed a good amount of em. Never did get who I wanted. The last time I went back, they sent me home in this thing," he said, patting the chair. "Poked me full of holes and tossed me off a bridge." He chuckled, as if getting tossed off a bridge was funny. "Thought they'd killed, me. Cocksuckers. Broke my back, but I'm still here. I'll get em one day."

"Don't worry about it," she said, stroking his face. "We'll get them one day."

Eve left her uncle sitting there, holding his bayonet, looking at his monitors, waiting for a war that never seemed to come. Eve felt kind of bad about the way she had spoken to her uncle Bobby. Out of everybody, he probably took her parents' murders the hardest. He was overseas on his last tour when they were killed. He never even got a chance to say good-bye. Eve would have to go back and apologize to her uncle, but that would wait. She had to reacquaint herself with the streets.

7.

Spooky stood inside of Jimmy Jazz on 125th Street, looking over their selection of jeans. He had a pocket full of money and decided to buy himself a new fit. He had already brought a new chain and matching bracelet the week before and now he was ready to bust out with it. But one couldn't wear new jewels without a new fit. Which is what brought him to the store.

"Spooky," called a voice to his rear. "What up, nigga?"

Spooky turned around to see Sean standing behind him. "What's good?" he said, giving Sean a pound. "Fuck you doing over here?"

"Same as you, dawg. Trying to get something to wear for the weekend. I hear they had the sale going on today. I see you heard about it, though."

"Nah, I ain't come to bargain shop," he said arrogantly flashing a knot of money. "I came to get right."

"Whooo weee," Sean said. "You holding, kid. I guess ya lil scheme came off?"

"What it look like? I told you Felon and them was some salad-ass niggaz. They ain't bout shit."

"Scared of you, kid." Sean smirked. "Where you headed after this?"

"I'm going to the liquor store and hit the block."

"I was bout to do the same thing," Sean lied. "You wanna ride with me?"

"Oh, you pushing?"

"Nah, my man drove me up. We got room for you, dick."

"Say no more."

Sean led Spooky from the store and out to the street. Sean felt kind of bad about what was about to go down, but he figured Spooky had brought it on himself. Maybe an ass-whipping was what he needed. Either way, it didn't matter to him. Butter had promised him a few dollars plus Spooky's corner for his services. Spooky would get over it.

"Right over here," Sean said, opening the door to a tented Taurus. "Let's get up outta here."

Spooky tossed his bags into the backseat and climbed in. He relaxed himself on the plush leather seats and admired the car. It was a simple but well-kept automobile. When Spooky looked up to see Butter behind the wheel, he almost soiled the very seats that he had been admiring. Butter looked over his shoulder and smiled at Spooky. Spooky thought about making a run for it, but when Felon slid onto the seat beside him, he knew he was cornered.

"What up, Spook?" Felon asked calmly.

Spooky measured Felon's approach and noted that he kept his hand in the pocket of his jacket. Things were beginning to look worse and worse. He reasoned that if he played it cool, he might get out of this one. For all he knew, they probably didn't even know that he had been stealing. When he noticed Butter kept cutting his eyes at him from the rearview, his chances slimmed a bit.

"Damn, Sean. You ain't tell me you was rolling with the homeys," Spooky said sarcastically. Sean just turned around in the front seat and looked out the window. Spooky vowed that if he made it out of this shit he was going to kill Sean's ass.

"What's really good with you?" Felon asked, rephrasing his initial question.

"Chilling, y'all," Spooky said, trying to sound cool when he was really shook. "Which liquor store we going to?"

"Gotta make a lil stop first," Butter said from the front seat. "Won't take long. Right over the bridge, in the Bronx."

"The Bronx? Why we going all the way up there, Butter?"

"Cause I said so. Now shut the fuck up and stop being a back-seat driver."

No sympathy there.

"What's been up with you, Felon?" Spooky asked, trying another angle.

"I'm good," Felon responded, still with his hand in his pocket.

"Ain't seen y'all in a minute. Don't come through the block too much no more."

"That's because y'all doing such a good job out there," Felon said.

Felon spoke in an even tone. Spooky tried to read his face, but it was useless. The fact that Felon had no anger in his tone gave Spooky hope. Then things got worse.

"How's ya mom, yo?" Butter asked from the front seat.

The threat had been made. There was no edge to Butter's words, but Spooky knew it was a threat. Had Felon asked about his mother, it would've been nothing. But Butter never got personal like that with him. Spooky wanted to break down and cry, but he held his composure. He decided to use Butter's question to strengthen his sympathy plea.

"She ain't been doing so good," Spooky lied. "She's been back and forth to the hospital about her heart."

"Sorry to hear that," Felon said sincerely.

"Yeah, that shit is fucked up," Butter cut in. "I know how expensive hospital bills can be. Shit, I done put quite a few muthafuckas in St. Luke's, myself. You need to hold something to help out with the bills?'"

"Nah, I'm good." Spooky said, beginning to sweat.

"You sure?" Butter pressed. "It wouldn't be nothing to throw you a few dollars. Matter of fact, you can even take it out of the pack money."

Spooky didn't miss the curveball that Butter threw, nor did he miss the look that Felon shot him. It was a pretty good bet that they were on to him. Spooky felt the weight of the .25 in his waist and thought about going for it. When he saw Felon's jaw clenching and unclenching he decided it against it. There were no illusions in Spooky's mind as to what Felon was holding in his pocket.

For the remainder of the ride, there was an uncomfortable silence. Spooky tried to strike up small talk, but the occupants of the car were nonreceptive. Felon just looked silently out the window, while Butter smirked behind the wheel. Spooky wondered if he could choke Sean before either Felon or Butter put a slug in him.

Butter exited on Webster Avenue. After getting off the highway they pulled in behind an auto-repair shop. It was after hours so the little spot was closed. Spooky looked around his final resting place and wished for the umpteenth time that he hadn't been so damn greedy.

"Come on," Butter said, stepping out of the car.

Spooky looked at Felon for a sign, but found none. Reluctantly he got out of the car, with Felon following closely behind him. Sean timidly brought up the rear. Spooky looked at his former friend and again thoughts of murder ran through his head.

"Come on," Butter said, leading the quartet farther into the recesses of the garage. "My uncle left something for me back here. I'm gonna snatch it up and we out."

Spooky walked behind Butter, and Sean followed hesitantly. To his surprise, Felon hung back. When he looked back at his other boss, Felon stared right back at him, his eyes cold. Spooky's feet suddenly began to feel like lead. He thought about running, but he was in the middle of nowhere and sure to be cut down before he could reach any kind of cover. His only hope was to catch Butter slipping when they got behind the garage. He knew Sean's punk ass would be light work.

"It's right in here," Butter said, nodding toward a leaning shed in the rear of the garage. "Spooky, get the door while I try to find a light or something."

Spooky looked at Sean, who had his eyes glued to the ground, and proceeded in the direction of the shed. As he passed Butter, he saw the shorter man reaching into his waistband. It was now or never. Spooky swung with all of his might and clocked Butter on the chin. Butter staggered from the blow but kept his feet. He spat blood on the floor and smiled at a terrified Spooky.

"You got more heart than I gave you credit for," Butter hissed, drawing his nine. "Never let it be said I was a stingy nigga. Take these shits wit you, faggot!"

Spooky tried to reach, but the first bullet had already shattered his collar bone. The young man hit the ground and howled in pain. When he tried to get up, Butter stepped over him and put one in his gut. As Spooky lay on the ground, bleeding out, he could see Butter trying to hand the gun off to Sean. The young man looked at the pistol but didn't reach for it. Murder wasn't part of the plan.

"Put one in this nigga!" Butter ordered. Sean began to tremble but still didn't reach for the gun. "Won't be no weak links on this team," Butter growled, "or muthafucking witnesses to this murder."

Sean knew what time it was with Butter. If he didn't pop Spooky, he would probably wind up dead too. Survival was the code of the streets, so he took the pistol. He took one look at his pleading friend and popped him in the head. At least he didn't have to suffer.

"I was beginning to worry about you," Butter joked as he took the gun from Sean's shaking hand. "Help me with this shit," Butter said, clearing out a pile of old car parts in the corner. When they had moved the rubble, there were two six-foot holes dug in the dirt.

"Why two holes?" Sean asked, not knowing if he really wanted the answer.

"In case you didn't pull the trigger," Butter said seriously.

Sean just watched quietly Butter tossed Spooky into the hole. His greed had gotten him in way deeper than he ever meant to be. He belonged to Butter and Felon now and there was nothing he could do about it.

Felon stood in the front of the garage, smoking a cigarette and thinking about Eve. His lovely Evelyn. Seeing her that afternoon had been shocking enough, but seeing the transformation she had undergone was an unexpected pleasure indeed. She was the same hard-ass Eve, but she had grown up quite a bit.

The sounds of a scuffle, then gunfire, told Felon that the job had been done. He tried to tell himself that he felt bad about having Spooky clipped, but it wasn't a very convincing lie. He had known the boy and his family for years, but this was business. Spooky was wrong and had to be dealt with. Had they let him slide, everyone would've tried to put their hand in the cookie jar. It was better to nip it in the bud early.

After about fifteen minutes of waiting, Butter came from behind the garage, followed by Sean. Everything seemed fine at first, but then Felon noticed the look on Sean's face. The boy looked as if he had just seen a ghost. It didn't take a rocket scientist to know what his problem was. Felon had asked Butter not to mark Sean. He was only there to help lure Spooky in, then assist with getting rid of the body. Butter must've missed that part. He thought that making a man kill made him stronger. In some cases it did, but in other cases it had a reverse effect. The murderer could wind up traumatized by the experience. Felon would have to keep a close eye on Sean for the next few weeks and he would definitely have to check Butter.

8.

Eve sat on the edge of her bed, looking around her bedroom. It had been her home more often than it hadn't, but it felt like a new place. Her uncle Bobby had kept the room exactly as she left it. In fact, he never even bothered to clean it. Dust hung on everything, from her furniture to the stack of books in the corner.

Eve's room wasn't typical of what one would expect of her. She had a full-sized bed, a writing table, and one of those portable closets. On the walls hung pictures of famous Black women, from Evelyn Baker to Queen Latifah. Eve always respected powerful sisters throughout history. Even though she was half white, she knew nothing about their culture, as she had never spent any time around her father's family.

Eve walked over to her portable closet and began to thumb through it for something to wear. She really didn't feel like going out, but the home girls were throwing a party and she had to attend. She thought about making up an excuse but brushed off the idea.

She had been locked down for a while, so having some fun would do her good.

She frowned in disappointment when she came up with nothing. All of her gear was either played out, dirty, or didn't fit anymore. As luck would have it, she came across an outfit that she had never worn and tried it on. It was a Pepe denim skirt with a matching jacket that was cut short in the back. When she tried it on in the full-length mirror, it rose up in the back, a little another testament to how she had filled out. She then took out a pair of smoke-gray loafers, for comfort.

Eve's bedroom line rang, drawing her attention away from the mess that was her wardrobe. She had to dig through a pile of clothes to find the phone, but at least her uncle had kept the line active while she was away.

"Yo," Eve said into the line.

"What up, bitch?" the caller asked.

"Bitch? Muthafucka, I think you got the wrong number."

"It's Keisha, silly ass."

"Oh shit." Eve chuckled. "What up?"

Keisha was a girl who ran with Twenty-Gang. She wasn't really anybody in the crew, but she kept it kinda funky. Before Eve had gone away, she and Keisha had partnered up on a couple of jobs. Keisha would get with the nigga, tap his pockets, and when she was done, set him up to get robbed by Eve. They weren't the tightest members of the click, but they did square business.

"I heard you just touched down?" Keisha asked excitedly.

"Yeah," Eve responded, lighting a Newport. "Cassidy picked me up this morning. But, to what do I owe the pleasure of this call? I know it ain't a social ring."

"Business, never personal," Keisha said. "When I heard you was back in the world, I had to give you a shout to see what was up. You still down for yours?"

"Always," Eve said confidently. "Just tell me whose throat it is."

"Knucklehead-ass nigga from the Stuy." Keisha sucked her

teeth. "Think his floss game is up. Bout time for the boy to learn how Twenty get down. Feel me?"

"All day." Eve smiled. "We'll get up and go over the details."

"That's what's up, Eve. I'll talk to you later. Oh, and it's good to have you home. One."

"One."

Eve needed some income coming in and her girl Keisha came through. This was part of the reason that she loved her click. After being home for less than twenty-four hours, she had a lead. One hand washed the other and two hands picked a nigga bone clean.

During the ride back to Harlem, there was an uncomfortable silence. Sean sat in the backseat, clearly terrified, and Butter stared out the passenger window chain-smoking. Every now and again, he would turn around to look at Sean and chuckle softly. He seemed to be getting a kick out of the young man's rattled nerves. Felon just watched it all from the driver's seat. He wasn't thrilled about how Butter had carried out the hit and, as soon as they deposited Sean in front of his building, he confronted Butter about it.

"Was that shit really necessary?" Felon asked, looking over at his partner.

"What you talking bout, fam?" Butter asked naively.

"Cut the shit, B. You know just what I'm talking about. I asked you not to involve that boy in the hit."

"Fuck that shit." Butter waved him off. "It's good for the boy's character."

"Butter, how is traumatizing the lil nigga good for his character? Him and Spooky was peoples and you had him take part in your little execution. All you did was complicate the situation more than it had to be."

"All I'm trying to do is look out for our team, yo," Butter said seriously. "There can be no weak links in this chain. The stronger we are, the longer we can play this game. You know how the shit goes, Felon. You can't be too careful with these lil niggaz out here. You gotta test em to see what they're really made of. I was just making sure we wouldn't have a problem with the kid later on down the line. Now, he's gotta be loyal to us."

"Just because you made that kid kill his man, doesn't mean he has to be anymore loyal to us," Felon informed him. "What if he snaps and goes to the police or starts running his mouth?"

"Then we kill him, his momma, and any fucking body else that he might love." Butter chuckled.

"That's your fucking problem," Felon snapped, "Iron ain't always the answer, son. You so goddamn quick to prove ya gangsta. We done popped mad niggaz on the street when we was playing them corners. Now is the time when we supposed to be stacking chips and keeping a low profile. Ain't you learned discretion yet?"

"Fuck that discretion shit, yo! Discretion didn't get us to where we are. The hammer did. Niggaz gotta know we ain't playing. Having a bunch of weak-ass niggaz around us ain't gonna solidify our spot in the game. You gotta be heartless. Besides, I'm tired of being the only nigga putting in work."

"What you trying to say?" Felon asked, cutting his eyes at his partner. "You acting like your hammer is the only one spitting?"

"I ain't mean it like that, kid," Butter assured him. "What I'm saying is, you don't spend time in the trenches like that. This is our thing, but I'm out there with the soldiers every night. I know what it is, Felon."

"Nigga, I ain't got time to play grunt. I'm the one making sure the money is right and things are running smoothly."

"And I love you for it." Butter smiled. "I'm cool with what I do. I'm a field general and I ain't got no problem with it, but allow me to do my job, fam. I gotta keep these muthafuckas in line the best way I know how. Two of my favorites are fear and manipulation. When these niggaz fear you, they can be manipulated to do just about anything. Like ya man Sean. I know the kid ain't no killer, but he knew too much. I had to set him out like that. Now, you're right about him possibly snapping and going to the police, but if he does, he's guaranteed a healthy bid too. It was a judgment call."

"Some fucking judgment," Felon mumbled. "We did what we had to do to take over Macho's shit and that was cool, but there ain't no need for us to be putting unnecessary heat on ourselves. Just be cool."

"Fuck cool, Felon. I'm bout my paper and the operation. All that cool shit will get you tried. This ain't no *Fortune* five hundred corporation, we're street hustler. These niggaz ain't people, they're fucking animals. The law of the jungle is: only the strong. I ain't never been weak and I ain't never gonna be weak!"

"Your head is like fucking rock." Felon exhaled.

"And my gun is like a storm. Niggaz run for shelter or get wet the fuck up! Straight like that. Now fuck all this faggot shit you talking. Take me back to the hood so I can change my clothes. I'm bout to get fresh and go party with my boo. You need to stop playing and come get you some pussy."

Felon just shrugged his shoulders and kept driving. He could sit there and try to get through to Butter for the rest of the night, but he still wouldn't make the man understand where he was coming from. Butter was just one of those niggaz. Continuing the argument would get Felon nowhere, so he decided to leave the conversation alone and focus on the party. His boo was home and he had to make sure he was correct when he saw her again.

The sound of her phone ringing, again, brought Eve out of her nod. She hadn't even realized that she had gone to sleep. Her digital clock read eleven twenty-five, so she knew just who it was on the other end. If it had been anything else, Cassidy would've been late, but for a party she always seemed to be on time.

"Yo." Eve yawned.

"Bitch, I know you ain't sleep." Cassidy sucked her teeth.

"No," she lied. "I'm up."

"You need to come on, Eve. We're gonna be late."

"Okay, okay. Gimmie like a half and I'll be ready."

"Eve, we're parked in front of your building. You've got twenty minutes before we start blowing this horn up," Cassidy threatened.

"Yeah? Well don't come crying to me when Uncle Bobby starts tossing grenades out the window," she cracked. "See you in twenty." Eve hung up before Cassidy could say anything.

Felon stood in the full-length mirror, admiring himself. He wasn't really the dress-up type, but you couldn't deny the fact that he cleaned up well. For the evening's festivities he selected a pair of black slacks that weren't tight, but fitted him. His forest green shirt was buttoned almost to the top. Beneath it, you could see his chiseled collarbone and the neckline of his tank top. His green Stacy Adams clicked on the hardwood floor as he strutted toward his bedroom door. He took one last look at the mirror to make sure his waves were spinning out of control and smiled. He was ready to ball.

When Felon got outside, Butter was already waiting. The was a first, because the man was notoriously tardy. Much like his partner, Butter was dressed to impress. He was decked out in a tailored gray suit that had a three-quarter jacket. The black mock neck hugged his broad chest, but wasn't tight. In the center was a red and yellow gold medallion. The two sized each other up and smiled.

"Whooo-weee," Butter squealed. "Look at my nigga! Man, Ron O'Neal ain't got nothing on you. Pimp hard!"

"I do what I can, when I can," Felon said, popping his shoulders.

"Well, let's see if you can manage to get yourself some pussy tonight," Butter said, adjusting his friend's platinum cross.

"All you think about is pussy." Felon swatted him away.

"Don't forget money." Butter smiled. "Fuck the dumb shit. It's gonna be a lot of hoes at the spot tonight. I'm trying to slide wit at least two of them. You just make sure you don't cramp my style wit you celibate ass."

"Don't worry about me. I'll be okay."

"Probably gonna be up in Eve's ass all night."

"Why you always sweating me?" Felon asked defensively.

"Cause you open and you won't admit it. My nigga, I know you better than you know yourself. Now, you can stunt for everybody else, but I'm not convinced. You're stuck on her."

"How you figure that?"

"Felon." Butter folded his arms, "How many girls you been wit since Eve went away?"

"Nigga, I done fucked plenty of bitches," Felon said proudly.

"Don't avoid the question. I didn't ask how many girls you fucked. I asked how many you been wit."

Felon was silent.

"That's just what I'm talking about," Butter continued. "I've seen women come and go. Some of them been hoes, but some of them been nice too. But for some reason, you ain't tried to seriously hook up with none of them. When Eve left, she took your heart with her, didn't she?"

"Butter, that's bullshit," Felon said, trying to sound convincing. "I could say the same for you. You hook up wit a chick for a while, then you get bored. So somebody holding onto your heart too?"

"I'm a different case, baby. I don't love these hoes." Butter winked.

"Whatever. Let's just go." Felon had an attitude, but he couldn't be mad. Butter had seen right through him. His insides burned whenever he was in Eve's presence. He craved her, but time and again, heart battled against logic. *They're all scandalous. No, Eve is different. You'll only hurt her. How many broken hearts?* He shook his head, trying to get a grip. The tingling in his stomach told him that he would have to get the Eve situation under control, sooner or later.

Eighteen minutes after she had hung up with Cassidy, Eve was out the door. She had almost gotten delayed in the shower. It had been quite some time since she was able to take a shower without someone standing next to her. She wanted to stay under the water a while longer, but she knew Cassidy would probably make good on her threat. She really didn't need to hear her uncle's mouth anymore that night.

Eve trotted down the stairs. She had to stop a few times to adjust her skirt, cause it kept riding up on her. When she bought it, the skirt was a little loose on her. Now that she had gained a bit of thigh and ass, it was snug. Eve really didn't do short skirts, because she was self-conscious about the bullet scar on her leg.

"Bout time," Cassidy said, with her hands on her hips. "You know how long we've been out here waiting?"

"I said, my bad," Eve brushed past her.

Cassidy looked her over. "Baby girl, you working that lil denim piece." She turned and switched toward the car. A group of guys passed by and threw catcalls at the girls. Cassidy was looking good enough to eat. She was wearing a black dress that hung low in the back and showed off way too much cleavage. The stiletto heels she was standing on made her look more statuesque that she already was. Eve watched her friend strut her stuff and smiled.

Eve got into the passenger seat and greeted Rhonda, who was rolling a blunt in the back. Rhonda was one of those girls who had a very pretty face but couldn't keep her weight down. Most of the time she wore big clothes to try and draw attention from her size, but it was apparent that Cassidy had a hand in her outfit that night. She wore a halterlike dress that squeezed her around the midsection and pushed up her double-D breasts. Her hair was cut into layers and rinsed in a plum hue.

"What up, Eve?" Rhonda asked in her squeaky voice.

"Nothing much." Eve smiled, "just glad to be home."

"I know that's right. I did time before and it wasn't nothing nice."

"Bitch, please," Cassidy said, putting the car in gear, "spending the weekend in jail does not count as doing time."

"Two days or two years, it's all time," Rhonda said, trying to add merit to her imprisonment.

"Anyway," Cassidy said, rolling her eyes.

"You ready to get your swerve on, Eve?" Rhonda asked.

"I don't know about no swerving," Eve said, looking out the window at the passing sights, "but I could use a good time."

"You could use a good dick." Cassidy snickered.

"Fuck you," Eve said, sticking her middle finger up playfully. "I ain't no hoe, like you."

"There you go, getting me confused. See," Cassidy said, stopping for a red light, "I ain't no hoe. I'm a woman who enjoys life's simple pleasures. I gets mine, that's without a doubt, but its only because I believe in keeping my pussy from rusting. A bitch like you probably got cobwebs on ya shit."

"You wish." Eve chuckled.

"I know you, baby girl. Your pussy ain't never had a good workout. Then again, I might be wrong. I heard them bitches in jail get real freaky. One of them turn you out, boo?"

"I don't think so. I might be rough, but I ain't a vegetarian. Every girl needs a lil meat in her diet," Eve said, giving Rhonda a high five.

"I should hope so," Cassidy said, moving through the green light, "cause ya man is gonna be there tonight. You need to stop playing and give him some."

"Here we go again." Eve sighed. "First of all, Felon ain't my man. Second of all, I'll hold on to *my* virginity until *I'm* ready to let it go."

"Eve, you're still a virgin?" Rhonda asked, covering her mouth in shock.

"You say it like it's a bad thing," Eve said, turning to face Rhonda.

"I'm not saying that. It's just . . . strange," Rhonda said, trying to clean it up.

"Eve is saving herself," Cassidy added. "She's waiting for some square-ass nigga to come riding in on a white horse and sweep her off her feet. Yeah, right!"

"Cassidy, you always gotta amp some shit." Eve rolled her eyes. "I didn't say all that. I'm just waiting."

"For what?"

Eve didn't have an answer for the question. People would often tease her about not liking guys. Some would even go as far as speculating about her sexual orientation. Eve was totally heterosexual, but she wasn't as open about men as her friends were. For as hard as she was on the outside, she was totally sheepish when it came to the opposite sex. She was almost eighteen and could count on one hand how many times she had even kissed a guy. She just wasn't as caught up in them as most girls her age. Eve wasn't saving herself for marriage or anything like that, she was just waiting for the right guy to come along.

9.

Felon sat in the booth, sipping a glass of Moet nectar. The club was slowly but surely filling up. Felon detested crowds. If you had more than five or six people in a room at one time, he was on edge. That's why he chose to stay in the booth. From where he was sitting, he could see the whole dance floor and the bar. He made it a point to never be in a position where someone could get the drop on him.

There were plenty of players from all over New York in the house. Some he was cool with, some he wasn't. He greeted his associates, and kept a watchful eye on his rivals. They noticed Felon sitting there, alone, but no one dared try anything. Even if they did, he wasn't worried about it. The .38 strapped to his ankle would've squashed any confrontation before it got out of hand.

A shadow loomed over Felon. "Buy a taste for an old project nigga?"

Felon had his pistol halfway drawn when he noticed who the voice belonged to. Bullet stood over him dressed in a black turtleneck and black jeans. His leather peacoat was totally buttoned, with the exception of the bottom three. This made it easier for him to draw whatever he was carrying, a trick that he had passed onto Felon early in the game.

Just seeing his elder brought back memories of days long gone. They had been cool for years. Felon was robbing cats before hooking up with Bullet, but he was the one who taught him how to do it the right way. Sitting in a staircase or a car, scoping out a vic. The stale smell of tobacco on Bullet's breath as he whispered for the youngster not to blow the element of surprise. They had pulled quite a few capers together.

"What's good, nigga? You almost got popped creeping on me like that," Felon joked.

"Yeah, but all you would've done was knock the wind outta me wit that punk-ass thirty-eight," Bullet tapped his knuckles against his Teflon breastplate.

"Sit your know-it-all ass down." Felon used his foot and slid a chair out for Bullet. The robber baron oozed into the chair and angled it so he could see all around him. "I know you ain't in here plotting," Felon continued.

"Nah, I just stepped out for a drink." Bullet smiled.

"Bullshit. Bullet, Eve is out on parole. Don't start that shit with her up in here."

"Come on, nigga. You know I love Eve same as you do. Well, maybe not the same." Bullet raised an eyebrow. "Point is, I'm not in here casing the joint. On another note, how's the new gig treating you?"

"I can't complain."

"I hear that. I see you shining and all," Bullet motioned toward Felon's chain.

"I like to throw it on every now and again." Felon adjusted the piece.

The conversation was momentarily paused when the waitress approached their table. From the wooden tray she was carrying she produced two shots of Henny. She placed one in front of Bullet and the other in front of Felon. She smiled briefly and sauntered back into the crowd. Felon looked at Bullet quizzically, but Bullet just winked.

"Can you still hold yak, or has that fancy living killed your taste for anything except champagne?" Bullet teased.

"A'int nothing changed but the decimal point." Felon slid the glass closer to himself.

"Road to the riches and all that. I can dig it. I still get mine the old fashion way, knocking niggaz over the head. You ain't too far gone from the game to remember what that feels like, right?"

"Yeah, I remember. Hiding in corners, laying on a vic. Those was the days man, but they're giving out too much job for that snatch-and-grab shit. I'm good with that old thug-ass shit."

"You need to hear yaself, kid," Bullet chuckled. "You getting paper, and I ain't mad at you, but you've become the same kinda nigga we used to scheme on."

Felon had never really thought about it like that. When he and Bullet were getting down, they made it a point never to rob civilians. Stores and gas stations didn't count, but when they were plotting on individuals, they were usually drug dealers and underworld players. They figured that they were doing the community a service by relieving the parasites of their goods. Not only that, they were more lucrative heists.

"So, what you trying to tell me? Because I'm holding a lil weight, I'm fair game?" asked Felon, keeping his eyes on Bullet. They had been friends once, but time and envy could be a corrupter.

"Easy, chief." Bullet placed his hands on the table. "Anybody lift your goods, it won't be me. And if I catch em, I'll make em sorry they ever fucked with a friend of mine."

"Glad to know I'm still considered a friend and not a turncoat."

"Felon, I don't care what you do for your bread, we always gonna be cool. I can't say that I don't miss you at my side."

"I wish I could say that I'm tempted by the offer, but you could always see through my lies." Felon shrugged.

"Yeah, I guess everybody ain't meant to go down in history."

"Fuck history, my dude. I'm trying to secure my future." Felon laughed. "Man, fuck the dumb shit. Why don't you hang out for a minute? Eve and the girls should be here soon."

"Nah, I got some people to see. I just wanted to have a drink wit my nigga and see how you been."

"That's love, fam. Let's toast." Felon raised his shot. "To friendship!"

"And long paper," Bullet added.

The two men touched glasses and downed the liquid fire. Felon reiterated his invitation for Bullet to hang, but he declined a second time. After shaking hands and promising to stay in touch, Felon watched Bullet get up and blend into the crowd. He wondered who had been unlucky enough to garner the burglar's attention for the evening.

"What up, Felon?" a voice called out from his left. Felon glanced over casually as a Puerto Rican girl came into view. "Long time, huh?"

Felon gave her a half smile and nodded. He ran her face through his mental Rolodex and tried to pull up her file. Shorty "had that." She was tall and shapely, with a rose tattooed over her left breast. He knew her face but couldn't remember her name. Her brown eyes drank him in as she invited herself to seat.

"You don't remember me, do you?" she asked seductively. Felon didn't respond; he just continued to stare. "Well, let me refresh your memory." She slid her tongue out of her mouth and wagged it at him. When she fully extended it, it easily touched her chin.

"Oh, shit. What up, Carmen?" Felon said, remembering the wild night he had with her. Felon had met Carmen at an after-hours spot. Knowing who he was, she immediately jumped on his dick. Later that night, he took her to a hotel and gave her a shot. Her sex was all that, and her head game almost made him lose his cool. As she deep-throated him, she stretched her tongue under his balls and nearly to his ass. Shorty was a major freak.

"I should punch you," she said playfully. "How you gonna forget my name?"

"I could never forget your name, ma," he lied. "I'm just a lil high."

"Umm hmm," she said, suspiciously. "So, what you doing up in here? I thought you didn't do the club thing."

"I don't. I just felt like stepping out tonight. Ain't about nothing."

"You're looking good, baby," she said, looking him up and down.

"You ain't looking too bad either," he said, returning her stare.

"You in here by yourself?"

"Nah, me and Butter rolled together."

"That's what's up," she said, anticipating Felon inside her again. "I'm here with my girl, Cee-Cee. Maybe we can all get something to eat later."

"Anything is possible."

"What up, my nigga?" a feminine voice called. Felon knew who it was without even looking. Cassidy appeared from the crowd, with Rhonda and Eve in tow. When he looked up at Eve, he could've sworn he saw anger in her eyes. When she peeped him looking, she straightened her face. Interesting.

"What's up, ladies?" Felon said with an innocent smile.

"Chilling. Who's your friend?" Cassidy looked Carmen up and down.

"Oh," Felon said, as if he had forgotten about his uninvited guest, "this is Carmen. Carmen, this is Cassidy, Rhonda, and Eve."

"What's up?" Carmen said in a very uninterested tone. "Felon." she turned her attention back to him. "I'm about to go find Cee-Cee. I'll see you later?"

"We'll see," he said, cutting his eyes at Eve.

Carmen didn't miss the look. It pissed her off, but she didn't comment on it. She looked at Eve and walked off. Had it been anyone else, Carmen might've popped a little shit, but she knew better. Though she wasn't from Harlem, she knew what was up with Twenty-Gang.

"Felon," Cassidy said, sliding into the booth on his right side, "I don't know why you fuck with these lil nasty bitches."

"Cassidy, you don't even know her. How do you know she's nasty?" he protested.

"She just looks nasty." Eve tried to slide into the booth next to Cassidy, but she stopped her short. "Hold up, Eve. Rhonda, come sit by me, so we can smoke this blunt. Eve, you sit on the other side of Felon."

Eve shot Cassidy a look and reluctantly went to sit on the other side. She slid into the booth, but didn't acknowledge him. She thought about him with the freaked-out Puerto Rican and gritted her teeth. Eve didn't know if she was tight because Felon had been all up in the girl's face, or the fact that she was even letting it bother her. She had to shake it off and stay focused. There was too much to be done for her to be stunting who Felon was fucking.

"What y'all drinking?" Felon asked, in a lazy tone.

"You know I'm a classy chick, so don't order me nothing hard," Cassidy warned. "I'll take a glass of white zinf, for the moment."

"I'll take a whiskey sour," Rhonda added.

"You can get me—," Eve began.

"Nah." He cut her off. "Just come with me. I can't carry everything by myself."

Eve slid out of the booth and stepped to the side to wait for Felon. He eased out behind her, still holding his glass of Mo. Eve took in the measure of his mode for the evening. She nodded her head in silent approval of his outfit. She had never really seen Felon dressed up. Back when they used to hit local spots, his idea of dressed was a sweater and some jeans. Things had changed some since she went away.

Felon didn't catch Eve's appraisal, but Cassidy did. She peeped her girl giving the new money man the once-over. She winked at Eve when they made eye contact. Eve stuck her tongue out and mouthed *nosy bitch*. Felon turned up his flute and drained the last corner of champagne. His placed the glass down and licked the remainder from his lips. Eve peeped that too.

Butter shook the dice in his right fist while his money flailed in his left. There were about four or five other men huddled around him. Weed smoke engulfed the bathroom, largely in part to the blunt of Sour Diesel that hung from the side of his lips. The bracelet that dangled from his wrist looked like a string of tears when the dim light bounced off it. Butter had come in the bathroom to take a leak when he discovered the dice game. Being that he was a nigga constantly chasing paper, he saw it as a come-up.

"Five to you, fam and I got ya man covered for his light-ass two," Butter said, eyes sweeping every player. "Hold that!" Butter shot the dice across the dingy tile, skipping once before they hit the wall. The dice did their wicked dance while everyone looked on in awe. Duce was the point. "Shit!" Butter cursed. A seven-thousand-dollar two. Butter had only come into the club with about eight or nine thousand. It was still early and he hadn't even begun to do it up.

"Oh, shit!" someone shouted.

"Five hundred he duce or less," Teddy added in. He was one of the young boys Felon had recruited. He was sixteen years old, and didn't give a fuck about too much of anything. Teddy had no home or family to speak of. All he knew was the street. Felon put him on, and he had proven a valuable asset. He was wild as hell, but Felon felt like he could help mold the youngster.

"I'll take that bet," Spanish Carlos said, lighting a Newport.

The roller picked up the dice and went into his spiel. "You about to loose ya money, lil nigga," Dre said, adjusting his crotch with his free hand. Dre was an old head who still fashioned himself to be hip. He was easily forty-five but tried to carry himself like he was twenty-five. He had on a pair of olive slacks and some knockoff Gucci loafers. Some of his teeth were missing, while others were rotting. Most he just covered up with gold. When he moved, his three gold chains clanged together, sounding like a ghost's rattling.

"Shoot the dice," someone said.

Dre went into his two-step and tossed the dice with a funny twist. They danced around, like nobles at some regal event, before they finally stopped and announced the winner.

"One-hundred and twenty-third Street!"

"Fuck!" Dre shouted.

"Ante up, fellas," Butter said, holding out his palms. Dre's partner put two thousand in his left palm and walked away, broke and sucking his teeth. Dre dropped some bills in Butter's right palm, but it felt off. After a quick scan through the bills, it only counted out to be thirty-five hundred. Butter looked at Dre as if he had asked him a strange question.

"Hey, Butter, baby. You know, I'm good for it." Dre smiled. "I'll come through the hood tomorrow and drop the difference."

"You didn't ace tomorrow. You aced just now," Butter said in an easy tone. Some of the spectators had backed up a step or two, knowing Butter's reputation for violence.

"Hold on, Butter." Dre lowered his voice a bit. "I know you ain't stunting that short change."

"Dre." Butter shrugged. "You lost. If I would've lost, I'd have paid you. Can I get mine?"

"Butter . . . man, I got my lady here wit me and . . ."

"I ain't tell yo to blow ya cash, fam," Butter said, hooking his thumbs into the loop of his pants. With his jacket pushed back, the butt of a pistol was visible. "Now, I ain't got nothing to do with what got on between you and ya shorty. You play, you pay. Why we gotta do it like this?"

"Butter, all I got is five hundred left on me," Dre said, emptying his pockets. "Allow me that, man."

Butter knew how this was gonna play out. Dre was gonna give him a hard time about the money, plus he didn't have it all anyway. He was having a good night and didn't want to waste it by arguing with Dre. He was a short-change motherfucker and Butter should've known better than to bet such stakes with him.

"A'ight." Butter nodded. "Keep ya lil five hundred. Make sure you got my paper tomorrow, Dre."

"I got you, my nigga." Dre made to pass Butter, but a firm hand held him up.

"Chill for a minute." Butter backed him up. "I'm gonna need some collateral. Take ya shine off."

"What?"

"Ya shine, Dre. I need something solid to hold on to, until I get my paper. I got you, my nigga." Butter smiled.

Dre's partner went to step over, but Teddy stopped him short. "Shhh," he warned, placing a gloved finger over his lips. "This is grown folks' business." Dre's partner looked down and saw that Teddy was holding a shotgun, sawed down to nearly the size of a handgun. He quickly retraced his steps and went to lean against the sink. Teddy kept one eye on Dre's partner and the other on anyone else who might have felt some type of way about what was going on.

"Why you gotta be on ya bullshit?" Dre said, seeing the armed youngster.

"I ain't tripping," Butter said. "Dre, you still my nigga, but I gotta make sure I get mine. This ain't personal."

Dre shot daggers at Teddy and Butter as he began to take off his rings and chains. He could imagine the look on his girl's face when they got back to the party. He was supposed to be a tough guy, but he came back from the bathroom stripped? He could already feel it ringing off in his head. Butter was playing him, and it was something that he wouldn't forget anytime soon.

Butter took the jewelry into his jacket pocket and flashed Dre a smile. "Don't take it like that, yo. This is just business. Come see me later on and I'll buy you a drink." Butter strolled out of the bathroom, with Teddy bringing up the rear.

A brand new Neptune's joint was blaring from the speakers, so everyone rushed the dance floor. Felon and Eve bumped their way through the crowded club, trying to reach the bar area. Every so often, Felon would brush up against Eve's butt. At first she thought it was an accident, but after the third time, she recognized it as flirting. When he got close enough to do it again, she backed into him and started swaying to the beat.

Felon was almost knocked off balance by the unexpected move. He wasn't much of a dancer, but he couldn't let his little homey show him up. Felon moved behind Eve and started lightly grinding against her. When she felt him becoming erect, she moved away. He tried to ease back behind her but she pushed him away, offering a naughty smile.

When they finally made it across the room, she stepped aside and let him take the lead. Eve stood a few paces from the bar while she waited for Felon to order their drinks. She busied herself looking around at some of the people in the club. As usual, some of the girls had next to nothing on, their asses and chests hanging out. Eve saw nothing wrong with showing a little skin every so often, but the way they did it was tasteless.

"Let me find out," Felon whispered in her ear.

She almost shivered. "Let you find out what?" she asked.

"That you checking these niggaz out?" He winked.

"Please. Can't no nigga in here do shit for me. These cornball muthafuckas ain't even my style."

"Yeah, right. I could see you digging one of these thirty-something-ass niggaz," he teased. "Probably get yaself a sugar daddy and shit."

"Felon, you got jokes." Eve chuckled. "At least it wouldn't be a hood rat. I ain't know you had a thang for them fake video hoes."

"You wish. You need to stop being so hard on men and let a nigga in."

"For what? So they can play with my feelings, then fuck me over? No thanks, Felon."

"Eve, every nigga ain't evil. There are some good brothers out there, ma."

"Show me a guy that professes to be good, and I'll show you a nigga that's gonna bounce at the first sign of trouble. A nigga is always gonna be around when shit is good, but eventually they all go. It's in your nature."

"Come on with that, Eve."

"Felon, it's the truth. Every nigga I've ever known had an ulterior motive. They get what they want and abandon you. Present company included." The last statement had slipped out in the heat of the moment. She saw the brief look of hurt flash across Felon's eyes and wished she hadn't gone there. "Sorry," she whispered. "Me and men haven't really seen eye to eye since my father was killed. Felon, I didn't mean—"

"Stop it," he said, fake mushing her. A change of topic was in order. "So what you got lined up, now that you're home?"

"You know the routine. 'Gainful employment,' 'stay out of trouble.'" She held her fingers up, mimicking quotation marks.

"Where you trying to work?" he asked.

"I don't really know." She shrugged. "You know me, I jack for my bread, but being on paper complicates that a little."

"Eve, don't you think you're getting too old for that? You're about to turn eighteen, ma. Don't you think it's time for you to start acting like a lady?"

Eve placed her hands on her hips. "Felon, I know you're not preaching to me. You sell drugs and you're lecturing me about growing up? What, you gonna be the one to grow old and retire?"

"It ain't like that wit me."

"Then what's it like, Felon?"

"We're not gonna make this about me." He flipped it. "I could've sworn we're talking about you. Look, Eve. I ain't gonna argue with you about it. All I'm saying is; you got a lotta potential, ma. Don't waste that shit on the streets. You can be or do anything you want in life."

"Anything?" she asked very seriously.

"Anything," he said, equally serious.

"Your drinks, sir," the barmaid called, breaking the moment.

Eve took a step back and turned her eyes away. Felon paused, looking at Eve. He turned and retrieved the drinks from the smiling waitress. He handed her two and he took two. During the walk back to their table, neither said a word. No words needed be said. There was a sort of electricity between Eve and Felon. They both knew it, and they both knew it would have to be addressed sooner than later.

"What're you so cheesy about?" Cassidy asked, noticing the grin on Butter's face.

"Cause I'm so happy to see you," he said, sliding into the booth next to her.

"I'll bet," she said, not hiding the fact that she didn't believe him. "Where you been all night?"

"Mingling and shit," he capped. "You know the hood loves me. Now come here and give me a kiss." Butter pulled Cassidy to him in anticipation of throwing his tongue in her mouth. Cassidy smiled and kissed him on the cheek. "It's like that?" he asked, clearly disappointed.

"Butter, you know I ain't wit sucking all on no nigga's face in public. I got you though, boo."

Butter sucked his teeth and sulked like a child, denied the privilege of going outside. He fancied himself as someone who knew all there was to know about women, but when it came to Cassidy, he was stumped. Even before he got his weight up, he had been courting the beauty. He showered her with affection and catered to her every want and need. Cassidy had it better than any chick he had ever dealt with, but she still fed him with a long-handled spoon. She knew he saw other women, just like she saw other guys, but she was his number one. Butter was trying to wife Cassidy, but she wasn't having it. He would continue to bide his time, though. Butter was a man who was used to getting what he wanted.

"What up, little sis?" Butter asked, turning his attention to Eve.

"Taking it light," she said, sipping her Hennessey Sour.

"I know that's right. Yo, shorty," Butter said, stopping a waitress, "bring us a bottle of Crys." The waitress went off to get Butter's champagne. "So," he continued, "how's life in the free world?"

"Can't complain. I'm just glad to be home, ya know?" she said, downing the last of her drink.

"Fortunately, I don't." Butter smiled. "I ain't never been caught for none of my bullshit, and I'm trying to keep it that way. But seriously, how was it in there?"

"Man," she shook her head, "it wasn't nothing nice. I mean, the spot they had me in wasn't the worst, but it wasn't fun. I didn't get into too much drama, but just being up in that piece was horrible. The food tasted like shit, and there were roaches everywhere. I'm gonna cherish my freedom."

"And we're gonna make sure of it," Cassidy added.

Everyone at the table nodded in agreement. Eve was still the baby of the crew. They all tried to look out for her like a little sister, even if she rebelled against them every chance she got. That was just her way.

The waitress eventually made it back to the table. In one hand she held the bucket, which had a bottle of Crystal tucked securely into a mountain of ice. In the other hand, she held several plastic champagne flutes. She sat the glasses down and filled them all halfway. She hesitated for a moment and cast a glance at Butter. Apparently she was waiting for a tip. Butter took the opportunity to stunt for the crowd.

"Here you go, ma," he said, peeling off five hundred of Dre's money. "Keep the change." The waitress gave him a seductive smile and melted back into the crowd.

"I hear that, big time," Cassidy said.

"It's only money." Butter winked. "I'd like to propose a toast." He raised his glass. "To Eve. Baby, we're glad to have you back amongst us, and we're all gonna do our part to keep your crazy ass out of trouble."

"To Eve." Felon added to it.

"To Eve!" they all said in unison.

Eve crossed her legs, raised her glass, and toasted with her friends.

For the next few minutes, everyone drank and made small talk. Every so often Eve would notice Felon staring at her. Whenever she tried to meet his gaze, he turned away. Between the heat and the alcohol, Eve was feeling good. She decided to take the opportunity to fuck with Felon. Sliding one foot from her loafer, she began rubbing it up and down Felon's shin. She could see the look of surprise in his face and smiled at him. He sat there dumbfounded for a few seconds, then took it a step beyond, placing the foot on his lap.

Out of view of everyone else, he began to massage it. Felon's strong hands sent goose bumps up her leg. His hands worked her instep and heel, expertly tempting her to close her eyes. She looked over at Felon, who was now wearing a triumphant look on his face. Quite unexpectedly she began to feel moisture building between her legs. It had been quite some time since she had been touched by a guy, and it was never like that.

The goose bumps up Eve's thigh caused butterflies in her stomach. She eyed Felon hungrily and he returned the stare. Visions of him taking those same muscular hands and gripping her about the waist caused her to blush. At that moment Felon looked like an object of pleasure that had been placed on the earth solely for her. Carmen passed behind their booth and touched Felon's shoulder. He paused momentarily, turning to see who it was. By the time he returned his attention to Eve, her facial expression had changed.

Eve glared at the girl and removed her foot from Felon's lap. When he tried to reach for it again, she moved it farther out of his reach and slipped it back into the shoe. Felon looked defeated and she was just pissed that a wayward lay had broken such a magical spell.

Eve managed to put the situation with Carmen behind her and

get back into the flow. The childhood friends drank and talked shit until the joint closed. Eve was having so much fun that she found herself getting teary-eyed several times over the course of the night. Felon had disappeared sometime during the night. Eve didn't miss the fact that Carmen had seemed to vanish also. Butter and Cassidy had plans to spend the evening together, so they dropped Eve and Rhonda off on the way.

During the elevator ride in Butter's apartment building, Cassidy fondled him. She stroked his penis through the thin slacks and whispered into his ear. He pressed the back of his head against the wall and moaned softly as she licked his exposed throat. By the time they made it into the apartment, Butter was hopping out of his clothes.

He lay back on the couch while Cassidy did a little dance for him. She slowly peeled out of her dress while Butter eyed her hungrily. When she was stripped down to just her white thong she moved to the couch and leaned over him, supporting her weight with her arms. Her chocolate nipples dangled above him while he touched each one with his tongue. The sensation sent chills down Cassidy's spine, but she had other plans for his mouth.

Standing on the couch with a leg on either side, she held her vagina near his face. The sweet scent of her mingled with the light tinge of sweat made Butter begin to salivate. Cassidy knew just how to bring the beast out of a man. She dipped her hips in his direction, but kept her love box out of his reach. When Butter felt as if he could take it no more, he grabbed her roughly by the hips and pulled her to him.

With his hands still fastened around her waist, Butter ripped her thong off with his teeth. He kissed her first on her belly button, then down near her vagina. Cassidy squealed and giggled as his tongue found the object of its desire. He thrust his tongue deep inside her, then alternated between tongue-fucking her and sucking her clit. Cassidy's body tensed and she began to climax. Waves of tremors overcame her as she came in sprays. Butter was careful not to let one drop of Cassidy's essence escape his parched throat.

Cassidy sighed, enjoying the oral pleasure he was giving her. After letting go one more burst, she decided to show him who was really the boss. She planned to hit Butter up for enough cheddar a new summer wardrobe. So she went to work

Cassidy abruptly pulled herself away from his skillful mouth, causing a wet sucking noise. Butter rose to pull her back down, but she put her hand against his chest and shook her head. She leaned in and began kissing her juice from his mouth, then worked her way south. Pulling his nine-inch penis from his boxers, Cassidy one-hand massaged him. Then she dipped her head beneath his balls and started licking in a circular motion. Butter panted and stroked the back of her neck in anticipation.

Once he was good and swollen, Cassidy put the head in her mouth. Butter's eyes began to flutter as the heat radiated from below his waist to the rest of his body. She licked around the rim of his dick with the tip of her tongue while massaging his balls with her free hand. Then she got into it and started to bob up and down on his dick, each time taking a little more into her throat. Butter could've sworn he was going to black out when she took the whole thing.

From the way his body trembled and his dick was getting even harder, she knew he was about to pop. But she wasn't ready yet. She pulled back and gripped the head of his penis roughly. Reaching beneath the couch cushion, Cassidy produced a Magnum. Butter always kept a stash nearby. After using her teeth to rip open the wrapper, she used her mouth to roll it on him. When she deemed it moist enough, she mounted him. The heat from Cassidy's mouth was nothing compared to the inferno that was her pussy. She ground on him slowly at first, then began to buck wildly.

Butter's eyes rolled back in his head as she took him to the moon and back. He grabbed her about the waist so tight that she knew his hands would leave a bruise. It would be well worth it when he set that paper out. Opening her eyes to admire her handywork, she noticed Butter's face had twisted into a hideous mask. *Oh, no, the fuck he ain't,* she thought to herself. Becoming stiff as a board, Butter exploded into the condom. He bucked a few more times, then his body went limp. But his dick was still hard and Cassidy had every intention on getting hers. She continued to ride his dick until she had pleased herself twice more. Once satisfied, she lay against his heaving chest and joined him in peaceful slumber.

10.

Eve was up and out early the next morning. She was never one to sleep late, but today she had added motivation. It would be her first meeting with her parole officer. Eve removed the necessary documents from her duffel bag and placed them into a black Coach purse. Normally she didn't bother with them, but she had to present certain documents to her PO and didn't want to risk losing them. She dressed in a pair of tight-fitting blue jeans and a form-fitting black T-shirt that made her red hair and blue-green eyes stand out. It was a nice day, but there was a slight chill in the air. This suited her fine, because she had slight hangover from the night before. Before she went away, Eve had been able to hold her liquor just as well as any guy from the crew, but after being sober for so long, she had the tolerance of a novice. She welcomed the cool breeze against her face.

The block was relatively empty, considering it was nine in the morning. The only people on the streets were the working class and the hustlers serving the fiends their morning wake-up. Eve ignored the youngsters making their transactions and kept stepping. The faces might have changed, but the routine was still the same.

She still had some time before she had to be downtown, so Eve stopped in the corner bodega on 124th and 7th to get something in her system. Her stomach told her that she was starving, but her common sense told her to eat light. The last thing she needed was to be on the train and catch a bad case of the shits. She decided to get a bagel and some orange juice to hold her until she came back up top. When she got to the counter, she was greeted by the store owner.

"Is that little Eve?" he asked, giving her a yellowing smile.

"What up, ahck?" she said, giving him dap.

"Haven't seen you in a while."

"I've been away. Had to take a little vacation." She shrugged, placing her wrists together to mimic being cuffed.

"You were locked down?" he said, genuinely concerned. Mohammad was one of the coolest store owners in Harlem. The whole hood might not have had love for him, but they respected him. He was good to the people he serviced. If you were tight with him, he had no problem giving out store credit or stashing your package, but if you crossed him, he had no problem touching you. On more than one occasion, Eve had witnessed Mohammad and his brothers locking some unsuspecting loudmouth in the store and putting the smack down.

"Yeah," she nodded, "but I'm home now."

"Praise Allah," he said, giving her a warm smile. "How's your friend, Cassidy?"

"She's cool."

"Tell her to come by and see me." Mohammad had a thing for Cassidy longer than Butter did. He was always giving her free goods and trying to holla, but Cassidy wasn't interested. It's not that she had anything against him, but he wasn't the most attractive cat. Mohammad was short, with funny-shaped ears, and was going bald on the top.

"A'ight, ahck." Eve reached into her pocket to pay for her breakfast, but he stopped her short.

"Don't insult me, Eve. You're just coming home, so it's on me. You just make sure you stay out of trouble. Okay?"

"Sure thing. Later, Mo." Eve gave him dap and left the store. She strolled farther north and cut across 125th. The business owners were just opening their shops or standing around, swapping the latest gossip. Opposite the stores were the book vendors. These had to be some of the hardest working cats on two-fifth. Rain, sleet, or snow, they were out there with their tables. Eve stopped at one of the tables to purchase a book. She enjoyed reading on the train as opposed to sleeping or sitting around looking stupid.

A book called *Hoodlum* caught her eye, so she picked it up to read the synopsis. When she saw that it was written by K'wan, she purchased it. He was one of her favorite authors and you couldn't go wrong with one of his novels. With the novel tucked in her purse, she continued her trek to the A train.

As Eve rounded the corner of St. Nicholas, a familiar face caught her eye. The girl was about five-four with a curvaceous body. Her leather miniskirt bareley covered her shapely ass. She stood, wide legged in her thigh-high boots, talking to one of the cab drivers. Her hair was cut a little shorter, but Eve recognized the face.

"Jasmine?" Eve called out.

Jasmine turned around, eyes wide with shock. She thought it might've been her mother, or someone who knew her family, so she was prepared to take off running. When she recognized Eve, the fear gave way to a warm smile. "Eve!" she squealed. "What's up, girl?"

"Chilling." Eve leaned in and hugged her. "What you doing out here?"

"Trying to live," Jasmine responded, trying to look like she wasn't embarrassed that Eve had caught her. Jasmine was one of the junior members of Twenty-Gang. She couldn't have been more than fifteen or sixteen, but she had the body of a full-grown woman. When Eve left, Jasmine was just another little girl, trying to find out where she belonged in the world. Apparently she had. Her search for acceptance landed her on the hoe stroll.

"Trying to live, huh?" Eve twisted her lips. "What are you really doing out here? I know you ain't doing what I think you're doing."

"Come on, Eve. Don't start. I'm just trying to get my weight up," Jasmine whined.

"Looks like you're doing a little more than trying to get your weight up. What're you doing out here with these hard-luck mutha-fuckas?"

"If they spending, I'm winning," Jasmine said, trying to make a joke out of the situation.

"Jasmine, don't play with me," Eve said in a deadly tone. "You ain't nothing but a baby, and you're out here selling your ass?"

"Come on, baby," the cab driver yelled out the window, "you getting in or what?"

"Hell no, she ain't getting in," Eve said, walking over to the cab.

"You're pretty," the cab driver said, licking his lips. "No need to hate, baby. I got enough money to take the both of you on."

"What you working with?" Eve asked, formulating a plan in her head. She cocked her hip, leaned down into the passenger side window, and gave him a cold smile. He was mesmerized by her ocean-like eyes and toasted skin. The cab driver pulled out a wad of bills, which Eve leaned in and snatched. "Let me let you in on a secret. That girl you're trying to pick up is a baby. As in: not legal. I just saved your stupid ass from a charge."

He looked stunned, then angry. "You stupid bitch! You're trying to get me locked up. Get away!" the driver shouted angrily at Jasmine.

"Eve!" Jasmine barked.

"What? You feeling bold?" Eve asked, folding her arms over her chest.

Jasmine, realizing who she was talking to, toned her voice down. "You're taking money out of my pocket."

"I'm trying to save your life. Your lil ass ain't got no business out here. You're gonna fuck around and make the headlines. Does your mother know you're out here?"

"No," Jasmine said, looking at her boots. "I ran away."

"Why did you do a fool thing like that?"

"Her boyfriend. About six months ago, Mom started dating this guy from a Hundred and Thirty-first. The old dude that hangs out by the supermarket. Wears a patch over his eye."

"I know who you mean," Eve said, searching through her mind. "What about him?"

"Well, about two weeks into the relationship, he starts staying with us. He throws moms a few dollars from his SSI check once a month, so she's loving this nigga. Well, he started coming on to me. It was real subtle at first, but after subtlety doesn't work, he gets on his gorilla shit. I woke up one day and found him standing over my bed touching himself."

"That's some sick shit," Eve said, heated. "Did you tell your mom about it?"

"I told her," she sniffled, "but he said that it was the other way around and I tried to come on to him. Naturally, she believed him. She starts calling me all kinds of whores and cursing me out over this nigga. That night I packed my shit and got in the wind. I've been staying from place to place and trying to turn tricks, just so I wouldn't starve out here. I didn't know what else to do, Eve."

Eve could feel the rage mounting inside her. Jasmine was barely more than a child. The thought of a grown-ass man trying her like that caused Eve's blood to boil. "Check it," Eve said, handing Jasmine the cab driver's bankroll. "Go get yourself a room somewhere. Take a shower and put on some respectable clothes. I'm gonna handle this for you."

"Eve, I don't want you going back to jail over this," Jasmine pleaded.

"Quit talking crazy." Eve stroked her cheek. "Twenty-Gang takes care of their own."

"But Eve—"

"Just do like I told you, Jasmine. Meet me on the block at about eight-thirty and this shit is gonna get handled." Eve hugged Jasmine and escorted her to another cab.

"Hey," the first cab driver said, hopping out of his ride, "what about my money?"

"You mean *my* money, chump." Eve glared at him. "You're out here trying to have sex with minors. That's illegal in this country, and a capital crime when it's one of my peoples. Now, you got three choices. One, you try for this money and I end up beating the hell out of you. Two, I could report you for this and cause a big stink. Three, you get the fuck out of here and take it as a learning experience."

The cab driver sized Eve up and thought about it. He easily outweighed her, but something in Eve's eyes screamed trouble. If she did report him to the police, they would find out that he was in the country illegally, and that would be a bad thing. He decided to leave the situation alone. The driver flipped Eve the finger and sped off in his cab.

Eve stood there and waited until Jasmine was safely away before she descended into the train station. She was prepared to do battle with the cab driver, but she was glad that she didn't have to. It seemed that the hood was full of surprises since last she came through. Felon and Butter were top dawgz and little Jasmine was selling ass. Eve had her work cut out for her. No matter what, though, Evelyn Panelli was home and everyone was going to know it.

11.

Cassidy leaned against Butter's Lexus, cleaning her nails. She had been waiting for him for a whole five minutes and was beginning to get impatient. He could be insensitive at times. Cassidy had things she needed to do. Her hair appointment was at twelve, then she had to go all the way down to Ninety-sixth Street to get her feet done up. After all this was done, she had to check on her girls to see what was going on that night.

Butter came bopping out of the building, wearing sky blue jeans and a pair of blue and white Jordans. His wife beater was slightly visible beneath his crispy white T. He smiled broadly at Cassidy, but she turned her head.

"Why you acting like that, ma?" Butter asked, hopping down the last two steps of the stoop.

"You had me out here all morning." She snaked her neck.

"You need to stop lying." He sucked his teeth. "You only been out here a few minutes. I'm doing you a favor, so you need to cool out wit yo stank ass!"

"Nigga, don't come out here acting like I need them lil ones you setting out. If you feel like that, I can get the money from somewhere else," Cassidy challenged.

"Cassidy, you need to get off that shit. I keep telling you, I'm all you need, baby. Why you keep fucking wit them sucka-ass niggaz like that?"

"Butter." She looked him up and down, "I ain't ya girl."

"That's my point. Cassidy, I'm trying to make an honest woman out of you."

"Honest?" She folded her arms. "Nigga, please. You wouldn't know honest if it slapped you in the face. Butter, you always talking about wife'n somebody. Let me ask you this; how you gonna wife me, wit all the little chicken-head bitches you deal with?"

"Cassidy, them girls don't mean nothing to me. I mean, they're fun, but it doesn't really get deeper than that. I want somebody I can grow with. I want you, ma."

Cassidy tried her hardest to hide her smile from Butter. He was so cute when he was pleading. She didn't put him through the motions because she was mean. She was just showing him what it felt like to walk in a woman's shoes. She couldn't even count how many of her girls swooned and acted crazy over some dick. This wasn't just limited to her click, but women all over the world. Cassidy wanted to show Butter just how powerful the pussy was.

"Butter." She smiled warmly, "you're a sweetheart, really. But you know how I feel about my freedom. I ain't ready for no man just yet. But when I am, you'll be the first to know."

Butter just looked at her. He was good enough to keep her pockets stuffed and let her ride around in his whip, but he couldn't get Cassidy to commit. He had dozens of women throwing themselves at him, but his nose was open for Cassidy. It was times like those when he wondered why he even bothered.

"Come on, boo," she said, running her hand from his chest to his crotch, "don't feel funny about it. I'm just trying to focus on me right now."

As Cassidy massaged his crotch, he remembered just why he bothered with her. Butter's heart melted under Cassidy's touch. He reached into his pocket and broke her off, just like he knew he would. No sooner had he laid the money in her palm than Felon came walking out of the building.

"Trick-ass nigga," Felon remarked, passing the couple.

"Don't hate," Cassidy said, kissing Butter on the cheek.

"Whatever," Felon said, scanning the block. His gaze stopped on a white Benz coasting up the block. Felon's hand immediately went to the Glock that he had tucked in his belt. He looked to see if Butter was on point, but his partner was already moving to his side with his gun drawn. As the car got closer, they both breathed a sigh of relief.

The Benz pulled up to the curb where the duo was standing. A Black man, appearing to be in his late twenties to early thirties, climbed out of the driver's side. He nodded to Felon, then to Butter. They knew the man as Big Steve. Steve was about six-five, with a massive chest and a stone jaw. He was loyal to his employer and merciless to his enemies. Steve walked to the rear of the car and held the door open for Carlo.

Carlo stepped out of the car, wearing a powder-blue linen suit. The shirt was unbuttoned at the top, exposing a platinum choker. He ran a bony hand over his smooth jaw and sized the two men up. Butter hated when Carlo glared at them. Carlo's pale blue eyes always gave him the chills. The man stepped to the curb and nodded to Felon.

Felon nodded. "Carlo, what da deal?"

"Chilling," Carlo responded. "Just came through to see how you boys were doing. Been a while since I've seen you."

"Everything is everything. Just holding down the block, kid."

"I'll never understand you guys." Carlo smirked. "All the money you pull in and you can't seem to steer clear of these corners."

"This is where the action is," Butter said. "Gotta be in the streets to know what's going on."

Carlo glanced at Butter, then turned his attention back to Felon. "This guy." Carlo chuckled. "You need to help your boy broaden his horizons."

"Butter is fine the way he is," Felon said, keeping his tone even but his glare cold.

"If you say so. And who is this?" Carlo asked, looking at Cassidy.

"She was just leaving," Butter said, blocking Carlo's view.

Carlo eyed the shapely girl and licked his lips. Even though he was Italian, he had a serious thing for Black girls. He undressed Cassidy with his eyes and she did the same to him. She allowed Butter to escort her back to the car, but not before giving Carlo one last look. She knew money when she smelled it.

"Walk with me," Carlo said, walking down the block. Felon looked over at Butter, then took up a pace next to Carlo. "What's new in the streets?"

"Shit is shit." Felon shrugged. "Money is rolling in, same as always."

"Heard through the grapevine that you guys had a little problem up here? Somebody's sticking their hand in the cookie jar?"

"Where'd you hear that, Carlo?"

"Hey, people talk and I listen."

"Well, you've been misinformed," Felon lied. "No problems here."

"See that it stays that way," Carlo said in a commanding tone.

Felon looked at the thin man standing next to him and all he could do was chuckle. Carlo was a smug little bastard. He thought because his grandfather had a seat on the commission he had a right to talk to people like shit. He usually didn't mean anything by it. He was just an asshole by nature. Felon hardly took Carlo seriously, but Butter couldn't stand him. He often fantasized about killing Carlo, but Felon wouldn't let him. For one thing, it would bring mob heat down on them. For another, they were getting major paper through Carlo's people. Felon liked things the way they were. Profitable.

"Got some new shit coming in," Carlo said, lighting his Marlboro. "High-grade shit. You guys think you can handle it?"

Felon chuckled. "Carlo, that's a dumb-ass question. We can sell anything you put in the hood. When and where?"

"First shipment comes in tomorrow night. They'll be some people there waiting for you. You go in, switch cars, and leave. I'm gonna have Steve and one of my people ride with you."

"Why the extra security?" Felon asked. "Me and Butter usually do the pickups on our own."

"This ain't a regular pickup, pal. This is the *real* deal. We just got a hookup with these guys in Colombia. This shit has never been sold in the states."

"That sounds like some serious shit," Felon said, calculating the money they would make. "Is it that good?"

"Is it good?" Carlo asked, as if he couldn't believe Felon was questioning him on it. "Let me tell you a story. About a week ago, we get a key of this shit to sample. The guy we used gets a free high and a few dollars in his pocket, but he got greedy. Decides he wants to skim a little for himself. The thing is, this guy doesn't know what he's lifting is a hundred percent pure. To make a long story short, we found him three days later. We had one of our doctors check him out. Seems his brain had swollen up and started bleeding."

"Damn," Felon sighed.

"Now you see why we don't want anything to go wrong. Felon, once we put this on the streets, we're gonna lock shit down. We can all get rich off this!"

Felon nodded his approval. The shit they had out was good, but it was only a few steps above what the competition was doing. They were holding the block down, but they needed to step their game up if they wanted to really get it popping. Felon looked at Carlo, who was smiling devilishly. It was as if those cold-ass eyes could read his mind.

"Fuck that nigga talking about?" Butter asked, watching the tail-lights of the Benz fade away.

"My nigga," Felon said, smiling at Butter, "that cracker is about to make us rich."

"Fuck is you talking about, fam?"

"Let him tell it, we've got some shit coming in that's gonna shut the rest of the muthafuckas down."

Butter sucked his teeth. "You believe that shit?"

"He hasn't steered us wrong so far."

"Felon, I don't know why you be acting like that honkey is so fucking cool. You know he don't give a fuck about us."

"Yeah, but we're making good money together," Felon pointed out.

"Fuck him," Butter spat. "We don't need that muthafucka. Acting all high and mighty cause his peoples is in the mob. Fuck all them dago muthafuckas. Let that white boy fuck around and old granddad might get an anonymous phone call. Shit, if they knew he was slinging drugs they'd probably kill him for me."

"What are you, fucking stupid?" Felon glared at him. "Butter, if them Sicilians get wind that we're helping him move this shit, they're gonna clip us all. You need to watch what you say outta your mouth."

"What you acting all paranoid for? It's just me and you talking."

"Butter, I don't even want you thinking that shit. You'll fuck around and get drunk and say it in front of the wrong niggaz. Shit, let me see a few million first before someone puts a bullet in my head. You hear what I'm saying to you, partner?"

"Yeah," Butter grunted, "I hear you. Look, all I'm saying is that nigga ain't got as much say-so as he thinks. He ain't really doing shit that we can't do ourselves."

"True, but he serves his purpose. Just like he uses us, we use him. Fair exchange isn't robbery. Shit, did you forget who helped us take over in the first place?"

Felon had a point. Before them, Carlo had been doing business with Macho. Macho had made quite a bit of money for Carlo, but the Dominican became lax. Carlo caught wind of Butter and Felon's little scheme before they could pull the caper off, but instead of turning them in, he decided it would be more profitable to aid them.

The night Macho was murdered, Macho had been sitting in Mc-Donald's parking lot waiting for Carlo. Carlo never showed up, but Butter and Felon did. They killed Macho, his bodyguard, and the young women who were with them. Leave no stone unturned.

"That's old shit," Butter said. "We them niggaz now. Fuck Carlo!"

"Easy," Felon said, placing a hand on Butter's shoulder. "It's in our best interest to keep him with us. When and if that changes, you can do what you want."

Butter nodded, but he still didn't agree with Felon. To him, Carlo was a spoiled rich kid, living in his father's shadow. He didn't answer to anyone, and that included Carlo. Whether Felon agreed or not, Butter planned to kill Carlo as soon as he gave him a reason to.

"I don't like that nigga." Steve said, peering at the shrinking forms of Butter and Felon in the rearview. "He's always poking his chest out."

"I ain't got a lot of love for the psychotic prick either. Butter is a headache." Carlo lit his cigarette.

"Carlo, why don't you let me get rid of that chump? Felon is the real brains behind the shit anyway. We don't need both of them."

"I had thought about that too. The thing is, Felon won't cut him off. He's stuck on this loyalty shit. As long as Felon keeps him under control, I'll tolerate him."

"Carlo, he's gonna be a problem. I can tell by those funny-ass looks he keeps giving us. One of these days he's gonna feel lucky and cause a real problem."

"Get the fuck outta here." Carlo waved him off. "He's crazy, but hardly stupid. Besides, I got more pressing issues."

"What's up?" Steve asked, looking at Carlo through the rearview.

"I got it on good authority that a cube truck filled with some prime shit is scheduled to disappear off the George Washington

Bridge," Carlo leaned in to whisper to Steve. "Give you one guess
where it's supposed to end up."

"Staten Island?"

"You got it. That half a fag, Jimmy V, is gonna make a killing
off that shit!"

"Yeah, he's a lucky shit. Those guys in SI get all the perks,
while we take what we can. But that falls under Jimmy and his
crew's jurisdiction. We can't hit it."

"Six weeks ago, a couple of goons knock over a UPS truck. From
this truck they stole a shitload of blank credit cards. Cards that were
supposed to be distributed by me. I lost out on some big money
when I couldn't make good on those orders." Carlo cringed, thinking about the hit to his bankroll. "I know it was Jimmy's people, but
I couldn't prove it, so Dad said I had to let it ride. I say fuck that."

"Carlo, I already know what you're thinking." Steve shook his
massive head. "If we hit Jimmy's shipment and someone fingers us,
it's gonna raise a hell of a stink."

"I know. That's why we gotta get somebody else to pull it off.
Somebody who can't be traced back to us."

Steve's wheels began to spin as he went through his roster of
underworld associates to find someone capable of pulling the job
off. "I got it!" He snapped his fingers. "I know a guy, real hard cat.
Use to run a crew in Manhattan. These jokers would steal the collar
off a priest if they thought it could bring in a few dollars."

"Do you think you can get him for this?" Carlo asked excitedly.

"I should be able to track him down."

"Make it happen, Steve. Tell him it's paying top dollar. If his
crew can pull it off, maybe we got some more work for them."

"I'll get right on it, chief." Steve pulled out his cell and began to
make some phone calls. Carlo sat back and chuckled as he imagined
the look on Jimmy V's face when he got word that his hijack had
been hijacked.

As Steve was disappearing out the door, Carlo had a thought.
"Steve. As long as we're at it, might as well kill two birds with one
stone."

"What else you need?" asked Steve.

"Contact that spade. Josey Whales or whatever he calls himself."

"The Outlaw? What do you want with Johnny Black?"

Carlo's eyes flickered. "What do you think? I want somebody clipped."

12.

The meeting with her parole officer came and went smoothly. The fifty-something woman alternated between staring at Eve over her wire-rimmed glasses and scribbling on her note tablet. Since Eve didn't have any immediate employment plans, her parole officer said she'd get her into a job-development program. Eve liked to call them plantations. They worked you like a dog, and barely paid you enough to buy a Metrocard.

Everything else the PO said sounded like gibberish. She asked some routine questions, took her urine, and let her go. Now she had the rest of the day to kill. A wise man once said, "Too much time is a dangerous thing." So she decided to do something with hers. She had taken care of her legal issues; now it was time to get down to survival.

She needed a hammer, and knew the easiest person to get one from was Bullet. She could've gone to Felon or Butter, but she didn't feel like answering the questions that would come with it.

Besides, she wanted to establish her independence outside her big brother's shadow.

Bullet's movements were so routine that they could've been detrimental to his health if he wasn't so notoriously vicious. He was posted up near the Metro North station, the same place you could always find him around that time. Bullet preyed on the passengers who rode the line. He appeared to be moving in on a middle-aged white man in search of a taxi when Eve approached.

"Taxi, mister?" Bullet smiled at the man.

"Ah, I'll just catch a yellow," the man said suspiciously as he looked Bullet up and down.

"You don't wanna do that, mister. Those guys are always trying to rip tourists off. They rig the meters so you're charged an arm and a leg."

"And I suppose you Gypsy cab drivers are much more reasonable?" The man arched an eyebrow.

"Oh, I ain't no taxi, sir. I'm just down on my luck for gas money right now, and I could use the extra bread. Tell you what, if you're going to a destination in Manhattan, I'll only charge you ten bucks."

At the mention of the discounted rate, the man began to weigh his options. The ride to West Forty-first Street was sure to run him between twenty and twenty-five dollars, depending on traffic. It was unlike him to accept rides from strangers, but the thought of saving fifteen dollars made him ponder it. Besides, if the young man tried anything he'd be shocked to find himself staring down the barrel of the nickel-plated .22 that he always carried when taking the train. Just as he was about to accept the offer, Eve intervened.

"Sorry, mister," she said, taking Bullet by the arm, "this taxi's taken."

"See here, young lady. I was here first," he protested.

"Yeah, he was here first." Bullet nudged her.

"I know, but my sister's water just broke and I gotta get to the hospital right away. There's another cab right over there that can take you wherever you're going."

"Well, seeing how it's a medical emergency, I guess you should take it. Tell your sister congratulations on the new addition." The man picked up his bags and waved farewell as he went off to catch another cab.

Bullet faced her. "What the hell was that about?"

"I need a favor from you."

"A favor? Baby girl, you just blew my phone bill. Why should I do you a favor?"

"Because you love me, and I'm your favorite student." She batted her eyes.

"What do you want, Eve?"

"I need a hammer."

He eyed her. "A hammer, for what?"

"I just need one. Come on, Bullet."

"Jesus, you love trouble, don't you?"

"Bullet, would you rather I came to you for it, or approach one of these larcenous niggaz in the hood?"

Bullet looked at her beautiful face and saw the same little girl he had taught how to pick locks four years prior. He never could deny her when she asked for something. "Come on." He started off down a side street. They came to a stop next to Bullet's beat-up Chevy. He got behind the wheel and motioned for her to get in the other side.

"You still pushing this piece of shit?" she teased.

"You better watch it, Eve. This is my Thursday car." Bullet fished around under the driver's seat until he found what he was looking for. He handed her a black Beretta that had electrical tape around the handle.

"Does this thing even work?"

"Course it works. Just a little beat up." He smiled. "That little number has gotten me out of quite a few jams. If you get knocked with it . . ."

"I didn't get it from you," she finished his sentence. "Thanks, Bullet." She tucked the gun in her purse and moved to step out of the cat. She was halfway out when she leaned back in. She kissed Bullet on his rough cheek and made her exit.

Now that she was armed, Eve felt a bit better. The Beretta was a little on the old side, and it wasn't the most powerful gun she'd had, but it would do. If she was lucky, she'd never have to use it. Before going to her final destination, she made a pit stop by her crib to change. When she was done, the reflection that stared back at her in the full-length mirror was totally different. She reemerged from her building wearing black army fatigues and a fitted cap.

Beast lived in a beat-up building on 132nd and Eighth. The few people who were conversing in front parted and fell silent when Eve came through. She made sure to make eye contact with each of the men as she passed. When she began her climb up the stairs, she could smell the urine and other foul stenches. People lived in the building, but it was mostly used as a hideaway for undesirables. Dogs were kept on some of the higher floors, while addicts got high on the lower ones.

Beast lived on the top floor, which was one of the worst. The floors were cracked up and had holes in certain areas. Eve made sure not to touch the walls, unsure of what would come away on her hands. So many trash bags and other discarded items littered the floor that the walk to Beast's apartment was like navigating an obstacle course. She knocked on the faded burgundy slab and waited.

She looked around at the wartorn hallway. It was amazing how some people were forced to live. The government was so busy funding staged wars that they had forgotten about the people they had been created to service in the first place. Sad was the state of the world.

After a moment, Eve heard stirring beyond the door. First she heard clawed feet scampering back and forth. Knowing Beast, it was some stray that he picked up. Her ears finally registered his lumbering footsteps approaching. Beast opened the door, wearing a mask of pure irritation. He was naked from the waist up, wearing a pair of faded black sweat pants. He glared at the young man dressed in all black and sneered viciously. Only when Eve removed her hat did his face soften.

"Hi, Eve!" he squealed. "What're you doing here?"

"I told you I would come and visit." She smiled. "You gonna leave me out here, or can I come in?"

"Sure," he said, ushering her into the apartment.

Beast's apartment stunk to high hell, but Eve ignored it. She stepped over a puddle of urine that was beginning to dry in the hallway. He had three bedrooms. One he kept for himself; the other two were for his pets. Eve could hear the animals becoming restless as a stranger's scent entered the house. Dogs barked and birds squawked in some of the back rooms. Eve paid no attention to the noise as she followed her friend into the living room.

Unlike the rest of the house, the living room was relatively clean. There was a coffee table, sofa, and a love seat. The furniture wasn't top of the line, but it wasn't stained with animal excrement. Beast sat on the sofa, taking up a good portion of it, and motioned for Eve to sit in the love seat.

"I'm so happy to see you, Eve. No one comes to visit me since you left," he said, sounding more like a child than she remembered.

"Well, I'm home now, and you know I'll make sure you're okay," she assured him. "Did you take your medication today?"

"I was just gonna do it." Beast retrieved the pill bottle from his pocket and shook a few into his hand. He tossed the pills into his mouth and swallowed them dry. "See," he said, opening his mouth for Eve to inspect, "all gone."

"That's my boy." She smiled. "Now, I got something for you." Eve dug into her pocket and pulled out a box of Cracker Jacks. Beast snatched the box from her so fast that he almost took a finger with him. With the glee of a small child, he tore the top from the box and began to devour the caramel treats. Eve found herself feel a mix of joy and sorrow. She was very happy to see her friend, but it was heartbreaking to see what he had become.

"Cracker Jacks are the best," he said, licking his sticky fingers. "Thanks, Eve."

"You know I'd do anything for you," she told him. "So what you been up to?"

"Nothing much. My friends keep me real busy." By friends, he meant the array of animals that he cared for. Besides Eve, they were all he had. As if on cue, the kitten he showed her the day before came hopping onto his lap. Beast stroked the kitten's head affectionately.

"So you gonna sit in the house playing Doctor Doolittle, or we hitting the streets?" she asked.

"Okay," he said standing, but still cradling the kitten. "Let me put my shirt on first."

While Beast disappeared, Eve decided to have a look into the kennel. It had been a while since she had been to her friend's house. Beast was always known for keeping strange animals, and she was curious to see what he was housing these days. When Eve opened the door, her curiosity almost made her wretch.

The smell of urine and animal waste rushed her senses. The stink was so bad, she was afraid it would get caught in her clothes. She peered into the room and observed Beast's circus. Apparently this was the room he reserved for the larger animals. Chained to opposite corners of the room were three dogs. Two were pits and the third looked like some mixed breed. All of the animals bore scars and tooth marks in their hides. Obviously someone had been fighting them before they came under Beast's care.

After seeing the first room, she decided that she didn't want to see the other one. She closed the door continued down the hall. Several dust-covered pictures hung crookedly along the left wall. She took one down and felt her eyes water. Beast was crouched, in his football uniform, holding Eve on his shoulder. If he'd never taken such a liking to her, he might've been more in life. The more she thought about that fateful night, the more fitting her nickname became. Before she could embarrass herself by crying, Beast came out of the bedroom.

"What's wrong?" he asked, with a child's innocence.

"Nothing," she responded. Eve kissed her fingers and ran them across his image before following him out the door.

Bullet watched from the shadows as the man he was supposed to meet entered the school yard. The big man was alone, but Bullet could see the glint of metal from the pistol he had dangling at his side. Big Steve was still as paranoid as ever. Bullet couldn't blame him, though. When you lived as they did, being too relaxed could get you an early retirement plan in potter's field.

He and Steve had something of a history. They both came up in the crack era and had occasionally been allies on Riker's Island. When the big man had called him, he was a bit suspicious at first. Since going to work for the Italians, Steve had distanced himself from his hood ties. He and Bullet would still speak when they passed in the streets, but it didn't go beyond that. When Steve called to request a meeting, Bullet found it odd, but his curiosity wouldn't allow him to decline.

Steve strode right past Bullet's hiding place but didn't notice the seasoned criminal lurking. He had gotten about three feet when he heard the faint sounds of shuffling gravel to his rear. He started to turn around, but the feeling of cold steel at the base of his skull froze him. He had been caught slipping.

"Sup, Steve," Bullet whispered.

"B-Bullet? What's with the gun?" Steve asked in an unsteady voice.

"I was gonna ask you the same thing," Bullet replied, removing Steve's pistol and placing it into his jacket pocket. "Old friends don't talk business over pistols."

"Chill, man. That shit ain't bout nothing. You expected me to come down to this shit hole and not be strapped? Come the fuck on."

"Yeah, I can understand that." Bullet lowered his weapon, but neglected to return Steve's. "Anyhow, you said you had a proposition for me, nigga?"

"Yeah, man. How would you like to make yourself a whole lot of cake?" Steve asked slyly.

"Shit, who wouldn't? What's your angle?"

"Ain't no angle, Bullet. My people just need some work done, and I think you're the best man for the job."

"Or the best patsy for the fall." Bullet shot back. "What you need from me?"

"What else? I need you to steal something."

13.

Carlo bucked like a wild bull while the prostitute he had picked up grabbed the sheets and moaned. Her bronze ass was whelped and bruised from his vicious blows. She cried out in pain, but he ignored her.

"Yeah, bitch," he snarled, "you love this cock, don't you?" Carlo grabbed her viciously by the waist and flipped her over. Her silky hair was stuck to her face by sweat, but still allowed glimpses of her brown eyes. He stroked her gently and let his imagination go. He imagined that the girl was someone else. She was a tall Black woman with a curvaceous body. Cassidy smiled at him wickedly, beckoning for more. In his delusion, she called for him to stroke her harder.

The more intense the image, the harder Carlo stroked. He began to plow into the girl with animalistic fury. She began to whine and try to slow him down, but Carlo was caught up in the moment. He pumped harder and harder while the girl screamed out. Just as he was about to cum, he opened his eyes so he could kiss

Cassidy. To his dismay, the Puerto Rican girl lay there beneath him.

Something in Carlo clicked. He bared his teeth and started to pump the girl as hard as he could. She tried to put her arms up and he slapped them away. When it became irritating, he began slapping her in the face. The girl screamed, but no one would come to help her. The apartment was empty, save for Carlo's bodyguards.

He threw his head back and howled as he released in the girl. When he was spent, he rolled off her and slouched over the side of the bed. The girl leapt from the bed with fear twinkling in her eyes. She scrambled around, frantically trying to gather her clothes. Carlo eyed her for a few moments before he bothered to speak.

"Sometimes I get a little crazy." He shrugged. The girl looked at him as if she wanted to stick a knife in his back while Carlo dug into his pants pocket. "We won't have a problem," he said, holding out several hundreds, "will we?"

The girl looked from the money to Carlo as if he had lost his mind. She felt violated and dirty, but what could she do? Carlo was the son of a mob boss. There was no one she could go to with it. She wiped her face and took the money. She spared one more glance at the motionless man and fled.

"Sorry I'm late, Dad. Had to stop and take care of something on the way here," Carlo said, flopping down on the sofa.

"So you say. Probably laid up wit one of them nigger whores." Franko De Nardi was as vicious at the age of fifty as he was at twenty-one. His face sagged a bit more and the edges of his hair were going gray, but his eyes still flashed blue menace. Franko had been laying bodies for the mob for over twenty years. After enough blood had been shed, they allowed him to retire to a nice-sized house in Long Island. He might've been retired from the execution game, but he still had his hands waist deep in dirt.

"So what's so important that I had to come down here and couldn't hear it over the phone?" Carlo asked, not bothering to hide his impatience.

"What do I always tell you about those fucking phones, Carlo? Guess you won't be happy until you're doing time with some ballooned-up spade in Attica."

"Sorry, Pop."

"Anyhow, I called you in to check on things with those guys you got to move this shit."

"Like I told you, Pop, it's in the bag. Felon is a stand-up dude."

"You put too much faith in these people, Carlo." Franko sat next to Carlo and patted his leg. "Trust is a fool's suicide. But I'm sure you know that."

"Sure. I learned from the best." Carlo smiled, trying to avoid a lecture.

"You damn well better, Carlo. This ain't your everyday shit. A lot of people got clipped trying to get it in. Shit, it damn near cost me my soul for the piece were getting. There can't be any fuck-ups."

"It's like I said," Carlo spoke, trying to control the natural fear he had of his father, "Felon can handle it."

"You make sure that he can. If we play our cards right, we stand to make a fortune. This stuff is way more potent than what everybody else has got. Out in the bush, they call it 'Body Bag.' You know how many people OD'd while the chemists were trying to get the mix right? You can cut this shit to hell and still knock a horse out."

"Geez, you act like I'm stupid or something, Dad. All we gotta do is pick the van up and drive off with the shit. Simple."

"Watch your mouth!" Franko said, pointing a chubby finger at his only son. "I'm your father, not one of those fucking punks you're used to dealing with."

"Sorry," Carlo whispered.

"Don't be sorry, be careful. Now, make sure these guys don't fuck it up. They handle this right and they'll be *'moving on up,'*" Frank sang, mimicking the theme song from the Jeffersons.

"I got you, Pop. Can I go now?"

"Yeah, kid. Get outta here."

Carlo could tell that his father was pissed but didn't say anything. He knew how important the deal was without his father constantly pointing it out. Besides that, his mind was elsewhere. Ever since he had seen her, he couldn't keep his mind off Cassidy. He knew she was one of Butter's bitches, but the look in her eyes said she would play the game. That was all the invitation Carlo needed.

Jack Hayes stood against the liquor store, puffing his Newport and shooting shit with his crew. He was a lanky man, with a bald head and a dusty black patch over his eye. His lips were pink and discolored from all the years of drinking, but that still didn't stop him from smearing lip balm on them, trying to win back the natural luster.

Eve strolled up 131st Street with her hands tucked into her pockets. She had spotted Jack from down the block, but he wasn't paying her any mind. With her hair tucked up into her fitted cap and the oversized army jacket she wore, Eve could've easily been mistaken for a boy. Jack didn't even spare her a second look as she brushed past him and went into the liquor store.

Eve had her back to Jack, but she was using the faint reflection in the partition to clock his movements. When she brushed past him on the way in, she didn't feel a bulge, so it was a safe bet that he wasn't armed. But just in case, she had her pistol firmly tucked into her hand. Jack's movements were sluggish and somewhat clumsy, suggesting that he had been drinking already. The whole thing should go over smoothly, but if it didn't, she had a B plan. After purchasing her liquor, Eve headed back outside. This time, when she bumped Jack it was almost hard enough to knock him over.

"Say, man. Why don't you watch where you're going?" Jack said, angrily.

"Shouldn't have yo drunk ass in the doorway," she said, staring him directly in the eye.

"Lil nigga, you must not know who you're talking to."

"I know just who I'm talking to," Eve said, taking a step closer. "A drunk-ass old man who likes to touch little girls."

Before Jack could say anything else, Eve was in motion. She caught him with a two-piece to the chin, but it didn't drop him. When Jack tried to right himself, Eve cracked him with the bottle. His two companions would've come to his rescue, but Beast had them both secured about the throat.

"Sit yo punk ass up," Eve said, grabbing Jack by the collar and partially lifting him. "Let me tell you something," she said, sticking the pistol to his temple, "Jasmine is my peoples. She down wit Twenty-Gang, muthafucka. If I ever hear talk of you putting your hands on her again, I'm gonna put two in you. Understand?"

Jack nodded.

"Good," she said. "Now this is what you gonna do. You're gonna go by the house, pick up whatever you got there, and get the fuck gone. If you I hear you took longer than ten minutes to make the shit happen, you gonna have to answer to my homey." Eve motioned toward Beast.

Jack looked at the monstrosity holding his two friends and nearly wet his pants. He had it good at Cora's. She catered to him and had a fine-ass daughter who, until that moment, he planned on fucking. The young man who had hit him and his huge friend had changed that plan significantly.

Cassidy came out of the bodega, chewing a Snicker's bar and clutching a Dutch Master. A Jamaican kid she dealt with had given her some high-grade weed and she couldn't wait to try it. She stepped into the street at the intersection and immediately jumped back on the curb as a white Benz screeched to a halt in front of her. She started to flip, but held it when she saw the face in the backseat.

"How you doing?" Carlo asked, smiling at her.

"I'm a'ight," she responded, trying to sound uninterested.

"You're Butter's girl, right?"

"I ain't nobody's girl."

"Then I guess I'm not stepping on anybody's toes by talking to you?"

"No harm in talking." She smiled.

Carlo openly looked Cassidy up and down. The pink sweat suit she wore hugged her body, accentuating her breasts and hips. Carlo had to fight off the erection that was trying to punch its way through his pants. He was totally smitten with Cassidy.

"Why don't you get in?" he asked, opening the door.

"Nah, I don't get into cars with strangers, but you can get out and talk to me," she told him.

Carlo smiled and stepped out of the vehicle. Cassidy couldn't help but admire his style. His clothes looked as crisp as the day they came from the store and his jewels were polished to a finish. Cassidy wasn't really into white boys, but he was very easy on the eyes.

"What's your name?" he asked, leaning on the Benz.

"Cassidy," she responded, licking a smudge of chocolate from her upper lip.

"Cassidy, beautiful Cassidy. Anybody ever tell you that you look like a model?"

"Yeah, every lame-ass nigga trying to holla."

"Then I won't tell you," he countered.

"Very funny," she said, preparing to cross the street.

"Hold on," he said, touching her gently on the arm. "I didn't mean any disrespect, I'm just trying to strike up conversation. Why are you acting like you're in such a rush?"

"Cause time is money," she said flatly.

"Oh, I see." He smiled. "You're bout your paper, huh?"

"Please believe it. No offense, sweetie, but if I'm gonna put in time with somebody, he has to at least have something going for himself."

"Baby, I got the whole world in my hands. My name is Carlo; everybody knows me."

"I don't know you," she lied. Cassidy knew full well who Carlo was. He was the man behind Butter and Felon's rise to power. As far as street players went, he was the man to see.

"That's a shame." He shook his head. "Maybe you could get to know me?"

Even as Cassidy and Carlo exchanged game, a plan started unfolding in her head. She knew she was wrong, because Carlo did business with Butter, but she couldn't let the opportunity pass her by. The hustlers she dealt with had cake, but not on the level of Carlo De Nardi. Where they had a few thousands, he had millions.

When Eve hit the block, some of the home girls were gathered on the stoop. Big Kiki was engaged in a conversation with Rah. When Kiki saw the youngster approaching her, wearing a fitted cap and army jacket, she took a defensive stance.

Eve nodded. "Sup, Twenties?"

"Eve?" Kiki asked, straining her eyes. "Girl, you need to stop rolling up on people like that. You trying to get blasted?"

"You wasn't gonna do shit." Eve smiled.

"You got that right," Kiki said, pulling a nine from under her sweatshirt. "This lil bitch do all my squabbling for me."

"What's good?" Eve asked, giving them both dap.

"Waiting on Cassidy's slow ass to come back with the Dutch so we can blaze," Rah said.

"Pothead bitches," Eve joked.

"What up, big boy? Fuck you doing out here away from your zoo?" Kiki asked, acknowledging Beast.

"Nothing, just hanging with Eve," Beast replied sheepishly.

"We got some E&J popping off." Kiki exposed the bottle. "Your PO don't test for liquor, right?"

"Hell nah," Eve replied. "Pour me a cup."

The girls stood around, talking shit and sipping brandy. Big Kiki was one of the few members of Twenty-Gang who moved like Eve did. While most of the other girls were plotting on dudes or worried about primping, Kiki's mind was always on her scratch. She and Eve didn't always see eye to eye, but there was a mutual respect. About a quarter of the way into the bottle, Cassidy came walking up the block.

"Look at y'all." She sucked her teeth, "Drinking on the stoop like some corner boys. Ain't y'all bitches got no class?"

"Fuck you, sack chaser," Kiki shot back. "You need to come get some of this liquor fo we drink it all."

"Sup, C." Eve nodded.

"Chilling like I do, baby girl."

"Hi, Cassidy." Beast smiled. Cassidy just looked at him and rolled her eyes.

"What took you so long to come back with the Dutch?" Kiki asked.

"Girl, you know I got a fan club. I just bagged me a piece of prime real estate," Cassidy bragged.

"Who's baby daddy you trying to fuck now?" Eve teased her.

"Baby, you got it fucked up. This nigga ain't got no baby mama. And if he did, the bitch shouldn't have been slipping. More to the point, I think I just hit the muthafucking lotto!"

"That's the same shit you said about Butter," Kiki reminded her.

"Nah, Kiki. This nigga ain't no street lieutenant. He's the man behind the man."

"Well, don't keep us guessing. Who is it?" Rah wanted to know.

"Carlo!" Cassidy smirked.

"Scandalous bitch." Kiki covered her mouth.

"Butter is going to kill you." Rah shook her head.

"Who the fuck is Carlo?" Eve asked, totally lost.

"Eve, you've been away that long that you don't know who Carlo De Nardi is? That's the nigga supplying Felon and them niggaz," Kiki told her.

Eve looked at Cassidy in total disbelief. Even though Butter wasn't her man, to fuck with someone he did business with was a bad move. If what her friend was doing ever got out, and it probably would, it could land her in a world of shit. Eve didn't know Carlo personally, but she knew his name. His father and grandfather were tied into one of New York's five families. She had never seen either of them, but remembered reading about them in the paper.

"That's some snake shit," Eve said coldly.

"Call it what you want, but I'm trying to get mine," Cassidy said in a matter-of-fact tone. "Besides, Butter ain't my man."

"Yeah, but you're fucking him," Eve pointed out.

"Sweetie, don't be so dense. Me and Butter are cool, but it's more of a business arrangement than anything. He pays to play. Same as everybody else."

"Cassidy, you know that boy is gonna flip if he finds out. You're dead wrong!" Eve said.

"Let me hip you to something, before you start that preaching shit." Cassidy snaked her neck. "I'm my own woman. Ain't no nigga out here got a claim on this pussy. That means I'm free to fuck whoever I want. Butter does him and I do me. Ain't nobody tell him to catch feelings. He knew what it was from the gate."

"Cassidy, this shit is gonna blow up in your face. You're playing a dangerous game," Eve protested.

"No more dangerous than you running around strapped while you're on parole," Cassidy shot back. "Don't start with me tonight, Evelyn."

Eve wanted to wring Cassidy's neck. True, she was single and free to do whatever she wanted, but this situation was different. Butter wasn't just some nigga, he was fam. They all grew up together and she should've had more respect for him than that. Luckily for Cassidy, Jasmine came walking up the block before Eve could dwell on it further.

"I'll be back," Eve said over her shoulder to Beast. She strolled down the block and met Jasmine halfway. Jasmine had abandoned her whore outfit for a simple pair of jeans and sneakers. Gone was the paint around her lips and eyes, giving way to her clear skin. She looked more like a little girl now than the streetwalker she had been that morning.

"Hey," Jasmine said sheepishly.

"You look much better now," Eve said, touching her face.

"Amazing what a nap and a shower can do." She smiled.

Jasmine paused for a moment before continuing. "Eve, I spoke to my mom a little while ago. She told me that Jack is moving out. I just wanted to say—"

"Save it," Eve said. "I told you, Twenties take care of there own. Go on home, Jazzy. I think you and your mom need to talk."

Jasmine didn't want the older home girl to see her cry, but she couldn't help it. It was the first time someone had ever done anything for her and didn't ask for something in return. She didn't know why Eve did it, but she was glad that she did. Jasmine hugged Eve as tight as she could, then turned and left.

14.

Eve was awakened by the sound of her phone ringing. She looked at the clock and saw that it was barely ten o'clock. She wondered who, other than her PO, would have the gall to be ringing her phone at that hour. She picked up the receiver with the intention of flipping, but calmed down when she heard the voice on the other end.

"What up, Eve?" Keisha said.

"What's popping, Twenty?" Eve replied.

"Listen," Keisha said, "I know you was probably still sleep, but this was the only time I could get away to call you. Remember the cat we discussed?"

"Yeah. The nigga from Brooklyn who you want jacked. What about him?"

"Well, I've been with him for the last day or so. Poor fool is trying to make a hoe a house-wife, but that's his bad. Tonight is the night, ma. You ready?"

"All day," Eve assured her. "What's the plan?"

Eve stayed on the phone with Keisha for about ten minutes while they went over the details of the setup. It would be tricky, but Eve knew she could pull it off. Robbery was her craft. After hanging up the phone with Keisha, she decided that it would be a waste of time to go back to sleep.

In her mind she went over the things that would need to be done before her meeting that evening. She rolled out of bed and took out an outfit for the day. The first thing she had to do was find something to wear. She still had some paper left from what the homeys had given her, but she needed something to go on top of that. When her hand brushed against the pistol under her pillow she knew just how to get it.

Sean sat on the dingy bed in his motel room, smoking a cigarette. His nerves had been shot ever since Butter had forced him to participate in Spooky's murder. He hadn't slept in days. Every time he closed his eyes he saw himself helping Butter put Spooky in the ditch. Spooky was wrong for stealing, but Butter had no right to kill him. The sick bastard got a thrill out of watching him die. Sean's hands were just as dirty. He could've refused, or maybe even gone to the police, but he hadn't done either. Even if he had tried to alter Spooky's fate, it would've sealed his own. The walls were beginning to close in on Sean, and he couldn't take it.

After swallowing down another mouthful of vodka, he stubbed what was left of the Newport into the ashtray. Overhead, a light flickered in its socket. Dragging a chair to the middle of the room, he climbed up and inspected the bulb. It blinked once more, then held its illumination.

Connected to a thin beam next to the light fixture was a leather belt. Sean checked the double knot to make sure it would hold, then looped the other end around his neck. Adjusting the noose, he pulled the buckle against his Adam's apple. He knew he deserved to be punished for his role in the murder, but wondered if he could do it to himself. The cheap folding chair gave under his weight, not letting the question linger in his mind for very long.

Maria Chin moved casually through the aisles of the tiny grocery store, checking the stock on the shelves. She turned cans of peas and moved on to the creamed corn. Her husband had already done the stock as he did every morning, but she still moved from aisle to aisle as if it hadn't been done yet. She kept one eye on the shelves and the other on the group of school kids who had come into the store.

The children from the local junior high school always came to the store to buy their lunches and supply of junk food for the day. Every so often kids would shoplift, so the Chins were cautious of young people. Especially Blacks.

"Yo, they got the new Mystic, son," proclaimed a young man sporting an Afro. The two boys rummaged through the drink cooler, clowning and examining the different flavored beverages. One boy almost dropped a bottle as his friend shoved him.

"You break, you buy," Maria said nastily.

"Damn, ain't nobody gonna break nothing." Afro sucked his teeth.

"Hurry up and buy," she insisted.

No matter how much money they spent in the store, it was always the same thing with the Chins. They catered to the white kids, but treated all the Blacks and Hispanics as if they were going to steal. The two boys laughed at the lady's accent and continued what they were doing. After a bit more deliberation, they took their items to the counter and waited for her husband, Artie Chin, to ring them up.

"One fifty," Artie said, placing the Mystic into a paper bag.

"One fifty? These joints is only a dollar uptown," Afro protested.

"Then you go uptown and buy," Artie said, not bothering to hide his dislike for the colored children.

"Y'all always on that bullshit," the second boy said, "Ching chong muthafuckas."

"You watch you mouth." Artie pointed a crooked finger. "You no like, you no buy. Get out!"

"Fuck you!" Afro shouted, knocking over a candy rack. The two boys laughed at the damage they had caused and ran from the store.

At the moment they were making their exit, the Chins noticed a young man coming into the store. He was wearing a fitted cap and a bright red bandanna tied around his neck. Before Maria could position herself to spy on the young man, he pulled the bandanna around the lower half of his face and produced a large pistol from his hoodie.

"Y'all know what it is," he said, aiming the gun at Artie. "Empty the muthafucking register!"

"We don't want trouble," Maria pleaded.

"Fuck that! Bitch, get yo ass over here by this old muthafucka!" he demanded, waving her over to the register. Maria cautiously did as she was told.

"You Blacks always give trouble. We all oppressed," Artie said, trying to be diplomatic.

"You trying to be funny?" the young man asked, pressing the gun against Maria's temple. "Fuck that oppressed shit. You better get that muthafucking drawer open before I pop this bitch!"

Artie nervously fumbled around with the register keys until the bell sounded and the drawer popped open. He stuffed the bills into a paper bag and handed it to the young man. After taking a brief glance into the bag, the young man looked at Artie like he was stupid.

"You trying to be funny? Fuck this chump change. Set the real shit out," the young man said, hopping over the counter. His braids flapped back and forth as he looked from Maria to Artie. After frisking Artie, he found a large roll of money tucked in the older man's sock. "See," he said, holding up the roll for Artie to inspect, "you almost made me pop yo dumb ass for this shit."

"Please, just go!" Artie tried to keep from shouting.

"Yeah, so you can hit the panic button on me? Y'all slant-eyed muthafuckas must think I'm stupid." the young man ran his hand along under the counter until he found what he was looking for. Using a pocket knife, he pried the panic button from its mount and cut the wires. The Chins looked on in shock as they realized they weren't dealing with a run-of-the-mill stickup kid.

"This how we gonna do this," the young man said, making his way back over the counter. "Me and this bitch are gonna take a little walk. Now you keep your cool and I'll let her go, but if I hear the police on my heels, this hoe is gonna get one in the brain."

"Don't hurt my wife!" Artie shouted.

"Fuck is wrong with you?" the young man said, slapping Artie with his free hand. "You trying to bring the heat, son? I don't want this bitch. She's just gonna make sure I get off the block without a problem. Now, let's go, bitch."

Artie and Maria Chin had been robbed before, but never like this. The young man with the braids knew just what he was doing. Never before had Artie felt so helpless as when he watched Eve walk out of his store, clutching his wife about the arm.

"Cassidy! Cassidy! Girl, you gotta see this shit."

Cassidy reluctantly pulled her head from under the pillow to see what her sister was shouting about. It was twelve o'clock in the afternoon and she usually didn't get up until one, when the stories came on. Sheeka knew she was dead wrong for breaking her rest.

After another few minutes of coaxing, she got out of bed and slipped on her Baby Phat bathrobe. With all the enthusiasm of a man walking the green mile, Cassidy made her way down the hall to the living room. When she entered, her eyes widened in surprise. Sheeka stood in the midst of three dozen long-stemmed roses, holding a Teddy bear dressed like a bellhop.

"Girl, you must've laid it on this nigga," Sheeka teased, holding a white card.

"Shut up, stupid," Cassidy snapped, snatching the card from Sheeka. The card only contained four words and a signature.

Meet me for dinner tonight.
Carlo

Cassidy couldn't fight back the smile that creased her lips. She hadn't spent more than five minutes with Carlo and he was already tricking bread on her. Definitely a plus. Upon closer examination of the bear, she noticed the tennis bracelet tied around his neck. Carlo knew how to do it up. She was so busy swooning over the gifts that she never bothered to realize that she had never given him her address.

Eve got off the train on 125th Street, grinning and whistling a tune. After she left the Chin's grocery store, she had pushed Maria down into a pile of garbage and made her escape. The robbery had gone off without a hitch, and she was nine hundred dollars richer for it. Not bad for a few minutes of work. Now she was ready to shop.

She moved in and out of the various stores on 125th, picking out things she needed and things she just wanted. Eve loved shopping, and she got a kick out of the weird looks she was drawing, picking out thongs and bras from a lingerie store. She was still dressed like a boy so she could only imagine how it must've looked.

After she finished shopping, Eve decided to head back to the block. Before going upstairs she wanted to pick up some Cracker Jacks for Beast and a few cans of food for his kitty. Inside the store, Eve bumped into a familiar face. He was tall and muscular, with a scar that ran from his ear to his cheek. His boxed braids hung down to his shoulders and were tied off by red rubber bands. If a person couldn't guess his affiliation by the numerous tattoos on his neck and arms, the red bandanna hanging from his right back pocket was a dead giveaway.

"Brother Bone," she said, easing up behind him.

Bone reflexively went for his hammer, but stayed his hand when he saw who was addressing him. "Eve? Baby girl, that you?"

"Who did you think it was?" she asked, punching him in the arm.

"Never can tell these days, ma," he said, ruffling the newspaper in his hand. "Gutter and them fool-ass niggaz from Harlem done turn this muthafucka out. It's open season on anything in red. Most of these niggaz be tucking they flags, but I'm true to my shit. Word to mine."

"Fuck had you so caught up that I could've snuck up on you?" she asked.

"You ain't heard?" He handed her the *Daily News*. When Eve read the headline, her heart almost dropped.

INMATE MURDERS PRISON GUARD AT JUVENILE DETENTION CENTER

She already knew what the article would say, but she read it anyhow.

Michael Scruggs, 18, was awaiting transfer to stand trial for the murder of a rival gang member in another facility. When correction officers opened his cell to transport him, Scruggs attacked them with a homemade knife. Scruggs was killed in the battle, but not before he wounded one officer and killed another. Officer Kevin Murphy, 31, was pronounced dead at later that evening from injuries to the chest and neck. He leaves behind a wife and three daughters. Authorities are still investigating how Scruggs got the knife into his cell.

"Damn, he went and did it," Eve said to no one in particular.

"You knew about this shit, Eve?" Bone asked.

"Yeah," she said, wiping a stray tear from her cheek, "I talked to him on the morning I got out. He was going through a thang, so

I figured he was just talking. I didn't think he would really do it."

"Yeah, ma. That nigga went out G style. Pigs took my little man outta here. Me and the crew gonna party it up for the homey. The set had much love for him, ma."

Eve's mind went back to the conversation she had with Scruggs on her way out. Bone was part of the very same crew that had abandoned Scruggs when he got locked up. Now he was talking about how they were all broken up and how much love the crew had for him. It all sounded like bullshit to her. Eve was so twisted by the news that she didn't even bother to get her items from the store. She gave Bone dap and went her way.

The news of Scruggs' death had her shaken, to say the least. The world around her was changing and it wasn't for the better. Black kids were losing their lives left and right, all in the name of nonsense. It was times like those that Eve had thought about hanging up her pistol and going straight, but what would she do? She had gotten her GED, but other than that, she really didn't have any skills. She could always try to make the best out of it and go into one of the job-placement programs that they offered parolees, but she couldn't see herself slaving for pennies. No. She would just have to get it how she got it until a better idea came to her.

She trekked up the stairs to her apartment so she could put her bags away. After what had happened, she needed to get low and get her thoughts together. She had hoped that Uncle Bobby would either be sleeping or too busy to notice her, but no such luck. When she entered the apartment, he was parked in the living room watching a documentary on the World War II. He shot her a suspicious look as she passed with the bags.

"Been shopping?" he asked, chewing on the filter of his cigarette.

"Yeah, I had to go pick up a few things," she said, trying to keep it moving.

"Don't look like no few things to me. Looks like a whole lot of something."

"You know how us women are, Uncle Bobby."

"Sit down for a minute, Evelyn." She thought about protesting, but the look on his face said that he wasn't trying to hear that. With a sigh she flopped on the couch. "So, what's going on with you?" he asked.

"Nothing much. Just taking it light."

"Joe-Joe, I ain't flew here, I grew here. I ain't never been no fool," he told her. "You ain't been home forty-eight hours and you hardly been here."

"Come on, Uncle Bobby. I'm just trying to readjust to society," she whined.

"That's bullshit and you know it, girl. Evelyn, I might not have no legs, but my eyes and ears work just fine. When you got out of lockup, you didn't have a pot to piss in, now you're shopping and carrying on to all hours of the night. Don't let one of them slick-talking niggers get you into some shit you can't get out of."

"You know me better than that," she responded.

"Indeed I do. That's how I know you ain't up to no good out there."

"Listen, a few of the home boys scraped some money up and gave it to me as a welcome-home present," she half lied.

"I'll just bet," he said, examining her. "And what did you have to do for that money?"

"Not a damn thing. I ain't no hoe," she said defensively.

"You watch your mouth and I never said you was no hoe. I just know that something don't come for nothing. Whatever you're up to, don't be no fool."

"Never that. I got too much up here," she said, pointing at her head, "to go out like a sucker."

"I sure hope so. Freedom is a precious thing, Evelyn. If your time away ain't taught you nothing else, it should've taught you that."

Bobby and Eve talked for a while longer before he excused her to her room. Uncle Bobby might've been getting on in years, but he was still sharp as ever. She respected his concern for her, but really didn't have time for the sermons. It was a cold world, this she could testify to firsthand. People who waited around for it to come to them were destined to starve. Eve knew that if you wanted something in life, you had to go out and take it.

15.

Carlo was a man who liked the finer things in life. Fine clothes, fine women, and fine furnishings. The luxurious apartment he owned on Central Park West was among the finest the city had to offer. The walls of the sunk-in living room were painted an eggshell white. The plush green carpet was so thick that you could pitch a quarter into it and have a hard time finding it. The four-piece sectional, imported straight from Palermo, was decorated in swirling green and gold patterns. Along shelves and on mantles were pictures of prestigious-looking Italians, and in the center, Carlo held court.

"Gentlemen, it's about to snow in Harlem." Carlo smiled, letting the weed smoke seep out through his mouth and nose. With his blue eyes shining through the mist, Carlo looked almost demonic. He knew that the strange color of his eyes made men uncomfortable, and he played on that for effect. It was a tactic his father had taught him early in the game. Present with him were his two capos.

Tony was a short man who was shaped something like a soccer ball. He had wavy brown hair that he always wore slicked to his head like an old-world gangster. Franko and Tony's father had done business together back in the days, so the boys spent a lot of time together growing up. Carlo trusted him as if he was his own blood.

Salvatore actually was his blood. He was his first cousin, on his mother's side. Unlike Carlo, Sal had been born in Sicily. He had just finished high school and was allowed to finish his studies in America. Uncle Franko had promised to look after the boy, so he allowed Carlo to give him a job. He was eighteen and dangerous.

"You think them niggers are gonna pull it off, C?" Tony asked.

"That kid Felon has got a head for numbers. Then when you add that fucking pit bull he runs with, *minga!* They'll pull it off."

"I don't get it," Sal said in a heavy accent, "why you do business with these guys? In Sicily, they're servants, mistresses. Here, you do business with them?"

"This is the land of opportunity, cousin," Carlo said with a casual smile. "You gotta see past the color lines to make the big bucks. These kids are from the streets, so this shit is already in em. We're just giving them something to work with. This thing goes off like we expect it to, we'll all be able to get a nice taste. Fuck these few blocks we're holding, we could take over the whole borough."

"Why not the city?" Tony added.

"That's what I'm talking about." Carlo patted him on the shoulder. "Wishful thinking. Trust me on this one, guys." Carlo's phone ringing interrupted their conversation. He listened for a second, then covered the receiver. "Listen guys, I gotta take this. I'll get with you later on."

"Thank you for the flowers," Cassidy said, cradling her phone. "And the tennis bracelet was beautiful."

"You don't have to thank me, Cassidy. Someone like you should always be surrounded by beautiful things." Carlo was always slick with his words. "You really wanna thank me, then accept my dinner invitation."

"I don't really know you to be alone with you," she said, toying. "I mean, for all I know you could be some kind of sicko."

"Cut it out, Cassidy. You know I ain't no kind of monster. I'll tell you what, we can do it at a restaurant of your choosing. That way they'll be plenty of people around."

"Sounds fair, I guess."

"So, I'll come through your block at about . . . seven-thirty. How's that?"

"No, don't come through here," she blurted out a little too quickly. "I'll meet you somewhere."

"What, your man gonna spot us?" Carlo asked suspiciously.

"Nah, I told you I ain't got no man," Cassidy insisted, going back to her "in control" tone, "I just don't want these niggaz around here all in my business. I'll meet you in front of White Castle on a Hundred and Twenty-fifth. You know where that is?"

"Of course I do."

"Good. How's Amy Ruth's sound to you?"

"I've never been there," he admitted.

"All right, then that's where we'll go. I'll see you later, Cassidy."

"Later, Carlo." Cassidy disconnected the call and immediately headed for her closet. She had chosen Amy Ruth's because it was reasonably priced. Not that she gave a damn about what he had to come out of his pocket with; it was all just a part of her G. She would have Carlo believing that she was a humble girl just out to find a good man to take care of her. He'd fall for it and she'd be getting hit with paper from time to time. This was all just a preliminary to the big show.

Keisha lay flat on her stomach, propped up on her elbows. The full length gray fur was hiked up just a little bit in the back, exposing a small amount of cheek. She rolled over to her side and began to suck on her fingers. She took her free hand and slid it down across her round breast and began to massage her clit. Paul watched the show and tried not to slobber all over himself.

Slowly she beckoned for him to join her, which he did all too happily. Starting with his head and ending with his penis, Keisha kissed him softly. When she took him into her mouth, Paul almost came. He had never felt something that warm and tender. A few times, he had to look down to make sure she hadn't slipped him into her raw.

When she felt his penis swelling like he wanted to cum, she stopped. Paul tried to push her head down, but she pushed him away. Instead of continuing with her head job, she just brushed her nail against the shaft. Precum began to leak from the head and run down the sides. She figured he was about ready.

Keisha reached under the pillow and pulled out a ribbed condom. She popped it in her mouth and applied it to Paul's penis. When the condom was in place, Keisha climbed on his wood and went for what she knew. She leaned over to one side so she could get a better grip on the edge of the bed and began to buck wildly. Both of them made animal-like grunts as they explored each other. Paul made a series of ugly faces, then sighed as if someone had let all the air out of him.

Keisha looked at Paul in disgust. He always came before she got into her groove. Even though he spent paper, she expected to at least get a nut once in a while. Paul had most definitely outlived his usefulness.

"Daddy," she sang, "you're the best."

"You know I do what I can, when I can," Paul said, breathing hard.

"I'm in a good mood now. Baby, we still going out tonight?" When Paul looked like he was going to flake, she added. "I feel like shaking my ass tonight." She saw the light go on in his eyes immediately. He seemed to like watching her dance almost as much as fucking her.

"I guess we can still go," he said. "I don't really fuck with The Lab like that, but there's supposed to be a big party in there tonight."

She clapped excitedly. "Yeah, let's get pretty and stunt tonight."

Paul felt nothing but joy in his life when he looked at Keisha. From the moment he met her, he was smitten. She was fine as hell and her head game was choice. Paul had started neglecting the shorties he already had and had cut others loose. Since he had been with her, it had been about Keisha and only Keisha.

"Listen, baby," he said, pulling her down to the bed, "these last couple of days have been the best. I never met nobody like you, ma. We need to stop bullshitting and see where we can go with this. Word."

"You mean that?" she asked with glassy eyes.

"For real. I mean, I ain't say I wanna get married or nothing, but I'm trying to fuck with you like that. Be my girl, Keisha?"

"Of course," she said, letting a tear run down her cheek. "I'll be your girl!"

They both hugged and let tears flow freely. Paul was crying because he was happy, she was crying because she hadn't expected him to be such an easy mark. Paul was cool, but there was no way she could be his girl. After Eve plucked him clean, there was no way he'd be able to afford her.

Dre sat behind the wheel of his '88 Regal, watching the comings and goings of the hood. He inhaled deeply on his Newport in silent contemplation of his task. A member of Felon's crew, named Vinny, passed right by his car and never spared Dre a second look. He watched the young man meet up with two of his friends and pile into a late-model truck. He thought about following him to see what he might learn, but decided against it. He would wait on bigger prey.

About forty-five minutes after the boys departed, Dre peeped Butter come out of the building. He could hear his heart pounding in his chest as he relived the night the youngster had punked him. Butter had showed his ass and made Dre look like a fool, but he would pay for it.

"That him?" asked a voice from the backseat.

"Yeah," Dre croaked, "that's him."

Johnny Black leaned forward so he could get a better look at his intended target. In the dimly lit car, all you could see of Johnny was his teeth and the whites of his eyes. His pupils were pitch black and devoid of any kind of shine. He wasn't even old enough to drink, but he knew how to make a man lie down. The Outlaw, as he was called, would take nearly any job.

"A'ight." Johnny nodded. "I'll take care of it. Like I told your man, half up front."

"Damn, y'all young niggaz is so impatient. Always in a rush for some shit. I got paper, nigga, so don't play me like a fraud. I ain't gonna jerk you," Dre said, directing his anger for Butter at Johnny.

"Oh, I know that, Dre," Johnny said coldly, but never taking his eyes off Butter, "cause we both know how much I enjoy my work." Dre looked at Johnny, but the youngster never turned to meet his gaze.

16.

Eve and Bullet walked up to the address Keisha had given them and looked around. It was a quiet block in Flatbush that was lined with small houses and trees. It was a good thing that they had parked the van a block away, because it would've probably looked suspicious sitting in the driveway.

"Pretty nice joint," Bullet said, sizing up the residence, "but I ain't impressed."

"It's not what's on the outside, it's what the vic could be hiding on the inside. You taught me that," she reminded him, slipping on a pair of rubber gloves.

The duo made their way around to the back door and set to work on the lock. Eve was skeptical about bringing someone else in on the job, but she knew she would need help. Bullet was the perfect man for the job. He picked the lock with the skill of someone who had over a decade of breaking and entering under his belt. Within minutes they were stalking through Paul's house.

The place was decorated in simple blacks and whites. The living room boasted a fifty-five-inch color television, equipped with a surround-sound system. The TV could stay, but the system was definitely getting lifted. Kiesha had told Eve exactly where the good shit was and said anything else she carted out was hers.

"Damn, I thought you said this cat had some paper" Bullet whispered.

"Be easy. The good shit is upstairs." Eve led Bullet upstairs to a tastefully decorated bedroom. A twenty-inch plasma TV was mounted to the wall, but a wooden canopy bed dominated most of the bedroom. With some help from Bullet, Eve moved the bed and examined the floorboards. The floor was polished to a shine except in one spot where the colors didn't quite match. To the untrained eye it wouldn't have seemed unusual, but Eve knew just what she was looking for.

She gave the spot a good stomp and the floor caved in. The stacks of money that were once piled neatly in the floor were yanked out and thrown into a pillowcase. Inside the dresser drawer, Paul had watches and other accessories lying out in plain sight. This was definitely a kid who wasn't used to money. Within an hour, Eve and Bullet had taken nearly everything that wasn't nailed down and stacked it neatly next to the front door. There were CD players, the TVs that were small enough to carry, and some more odds and ends. A very nice haul, but the real kicker was when Eve went into the deep freezer. There were at least four and a half kilos stacked next to some ice cream.

"Whoo-weee!" Bullet squealed and rubbed his hands together greedily.

"This is what I'm talking about," she said, hefting one of the birds. "See, Bullet, I told you this would be a sweet run!"

"You sure did," he said, picking her up and spinning around. "Eve, I could kiss you."

"You do and I'm gonna knock your ass out," she warned. "Quit playing and put me down. We got stealing to do. Go get the van, while I get the stuff ready."

Bullet went for the van, while Eve prepared their haul for transport. In less than a minute Bullet was pulling the Rent-A-Center
van they borrowed in the driveway. As they were loading their
items, some of the neighbors watched as Paul had a good amount
of his furnishings repossessed.

Eve beamed like a girl after her prom night as she thumbed through
the bills again. "This was a big score."

"It's a'ight," Bullet said casually, steering with one hand and
lighting a dangling cigarette with the other.

"A'ight?" She raised her eyebrow. "Nigga, we caked off!"

"We caught a good lick, Eve, but once this shit gets split up the
take'll be mediocre."

"I don't believe you." She sat up. "This shit was like taking
candy from a baby, but you're throwing jabs at it. Oh, I suppose
you would've cleared more preying on tourists by the Metro North
station?" she asked, her tone challenging.

"That's small change, Eve. I'm talking about hitting a big score.
Bigger than the few thousand we're gonna pull in for this stuff." He
nodded toward the cargo compartment.

"If you got something on your mind, I'm listening."

"Eve, what I'm about to run down to you is for your ears only.
Understand?"

She nodded.

"I know a guy who's tied in with some guineas downtown.
They need a caper done, and they commissioned me for the job.
It's paying big bucks, baby. Bucks that I'd split down the middle
with you. Now, I got a bunch of lil niggaz that I could call on and
they would help me pull the job off for next to nothing . . ."

"So why are *we* having this conversation?" she asked suspiciously.

"I was getting to that, speed racer. Like I was saying, I got
a bunch of youngsters that'd come along for the ride, but they ain't
dependable. They lil niggaz smoke too much damn weed. The last

thing I need is for some high-ass joker to fuck the situation up. You don't smoke weed and you hardly drink. You're one of the sharpest people I know, and more importantly, *I* trained you."

"Okay." She nodded. "What's the score?"

"A truck is supposed to be coming into the city carrying portable CD players," he began. "Not them cheap shits. I'm talking about high quality. I don't know how much these mobsters are pulling off em and I really don't care. What I do know is that the job pays close to six figures."

"For some damn CD players?" she asked.

"Like I said, not my concern. All I'm worried about is what we'll be walking away with. Look, I didn't even want to bring you into this at first. We won't be the only people trying to swipe this truck. There might even be some gunplay involved. I know you ain't got no plans on being a career criminal, but this might be my shot at the big time. I need someone that I can trust with my life to pull this off."

"And that would be little old me?"

"Baby girl, I'd bet on you to win any day."

Eve thought about it momentarily. She had robbed people and establishments, but never a moving object. She knew that the Italians were relentless about things like hijacking. Whereas the Blacks and browns made most of their illegal cream by hustling or other such vices, the mobsters were thieves. Most of them would rather steal till the end of their days rather than taint themselves or their families with drug affiliation. Then she recalled what he said about possible gunplay. Who else wanted the truck badly enough to shed blood for it? Rival crews? Another mob family? There were too many variables for her to decide right away.

"Give me some time to think on it," she finally said. "I got something else I gotta take care of tonight, but you'll have my answer soon."

"Sure, Eve. But don't think too long. I gotta take this, with or without you, baby."

* * *

A few hours after the robbery, Eve found herself making yet another quick change. Seemed as if she was doing that a lot as of late. The constant switch between Evelyn and Eve could be dizzying at times, but it was necessary. The way she had chosen to live her life made it so.

She touched a delicate finger to one of the bags forming under her eyes and frowned when she noticed her nails. They were chipped. She doubted that anyone else had noticed, except maybe Cassidy. Her friend was always concerned about appearance and material possessions, but they weren't as high on her priority list.

People never really knew what to make of Eve. Even as a little girl, she'd rather play cops and robbers with the boys than jump rope with the girls. She felt that men were simpler and easier to figure out than their complicated opposites. Women were always so fickle and conflictive. That was the reason why she was referred to as hard. She always figured it was easier to embrace the rough nature of her larcenous comrades than try to adapt to the femininity of her sisters. It was hard for a little girl to really understand what it was to become a young lady without anyone to teach her. From the time her mother died, there was never an elder woman for Eve to confide in or learn from. All Eve had around her were men.

As Eve got older, she noticed something within her began to change. With the development of her body and mind came the development of certain feelings. She felt somehow different since her return home. She had tried to explain it to Cassidy, in hopes of getting some type of insight, but her best friend simply laughed it off and told her, "You're finally discovering the bitch, trapped under all that nigga." Eve had mixed emotions about the half joke, but she let it go.

She pushed the trivial thought from her mind and focused on business. She pulled a stocking cap over her braids, which were beginning to fuzz up, and put a fitted one over that. Checking her scowl once more in the mirror to see if it was passable, she dubbed herself ready. It was time for phase two of the plan.

* * *

Cassidy sat and watched Carlo gobble down his second piece of cobbler. He had attacked his entrée as if ribs and collard greens were something totally alien to him. For the better part of the night they had been feeling each other out. Cassidy told him about her mother and fast-ass sister, and Carlo talked about life growing up in a Sicilian household. He didn't talk too much about his family, and whenever it came to his father, he changed the subject.

"So, Cassidy, how come you hang around with Butter if he isn't your man?" Carlo asked out of the clear blue.

"I don't hang around," Cassidy corrected him. "Butter and I are see each other sometimes."

"What's the difference?"

"The difference is, he and I aren't exclusive. Why, does the fact that I was seeing someone bother you?"

"Nah." He wiped his mouth. "You're grown. See who you want. I just got a problem with you seeing someone that I'm doing business with."

"Well, I don't see either of your names on this pussy," she whispered to him.

"Really? And how would I go about getting my name on it?" he asked.

"Play your cards right and time might tell," she teased. "It takes a certain kind of man to handle me."

"Baby, cut the game. I got money and power."

"So?"

"So, that makes me the best man for the job."

"Let you tell it," she shot back.

"Cassidy, cut it out. I'm working with some long dough and you know it. Anything that Butter's ever given you, I can buy four of em. Money talks and bullshit runs a marathon."

"Let's get something straight," Cassidy said, sitting up straight, "I ain't no hoe. True, I like nice shit and I like to be papered, but that doesn't mean I'm gonna let any nigga waving some cash taste this. It ain't that kind of party, boo."

"Whoa, don't take it like that. I didn't mean no disrespect," he said, trying to recover. "All I'm saying is, you're a dime, Cassidy. A girl like you needs a guy that can take care of her. I'm not talking about letting you hold a car or spending a little dough on you. I'm talking about letting you see how the other half lives."

"You talk a good one," she said, relaxing again.

"Yeah, but I can back it up. Come on, baby, don't act like you don't know what I'm about."

Cassidy and Carlo talked for a little while longer, then called for the check. After they ate, he took her to a nice lounge in the village for drinks. She was turned on by the kind of attention they got. Everywhere they went people treated Carlo like he was a VIP. Nothing was too much for Franko De Nardi's kid. Cassidy had decided that maybe she had finally hooked the big fish with Carlo. If he kept moving the way he did, his name would be etched on her pussy sooner than she thought.

The line of people waiting to get into The Lab was ridiculous. People were staked out from the entrance all the way to Throop. A rapper from the neighborhood, who had managed to make it big, was taking the stage. The jam was going to be the place to be for the evening.

The line being so long was something Eve hadn't counted on. If she waited, her vic would be gone by the time she got inside. Not bothering to try her luck, Eve made her way over to the VIP line. The bouncers were checking credentials, waving in the somebodys and sending the nobodys to the regular line. The hundred-dollar bill she palmed and handed to the bouncer made her somebody that night.

This part of the plan had almost been scrapped. They had pillaged the vic's house for all its valuables and were sure to get a good chunk of change from the fence. Robbing the young hustler himself really wasn't necessary at that point, but Eve figured all or nothing.

Now she found herself slithering through the Bed Stuy under-world.

She was surprised to see that the inside of the club wasn't that crowded. The bouncers were probably making people wait so they could claim they were overcrowded and charge more money. This was something that worked in Eve's favor. She would be able to re-trieve her package without drawing much attention. She parked herself and waited for the bartender to notice her uplifted hand.

The girl pouring the drinks was a shapely young lady with a round face. Her spandex top advertised her large breasts to every-one who had eyes. She swaggered over to Eve and leaned in so that her cleavage would be exposed.

The bartender, asked "What you drinking?"

"Gimmie a shot of Henny," Eve said, trying to sound as manly as possible.

The bartender winked at Eve and strutted over to fix her drink. Before she could get to pouring, one of the staff caught her atten-tion and whispered something in her ear. Eve figured she could get what she had to get and come back for her drink. With her order al-ready placed, she ambled over to the bathroom.

When she opened the bathroom door, a cloud of smoke hit her in the face. A few guys were standing around, smoking or using the urinals, but no one spared Eve a second look. She walked over to the mirror to give herself the onceover. She was wearing a black leather blazer over a red button-up. She had quite the time tying her breasts down so they didn't bulge through the material. The match-ing leather pants were two sizes too big, so as not to show too much of her ass. As usual, her braids hung down her back from beneath her black fitted cap. She looked like one of the boys.

Using the mirror, as opposed to turning around, she scanned the stall doors. On the third stall from the door, she found what she was looking for. A "Live on Lenox" sticker was plastered to the closed stall door. Without attracting too much attention, Eve made her way to the stall.

To her disappointment, it was occupied. She went back over to the mirror, started fixing her braids, and tried to wait out the occupant. Fifteen minutes had passed and still nothing. People had started to look at her funny, so she knew she had to make a move. Getting fed up, she knocked on the stall door.

"Occupied!" someone shouted from inside the stall. Eve waited another minute or two and knocked again. "I said, occupied!" the same voice shouted.

"I need to get in there," Eve said, trying to sound masculine.

"Use another stall," the occupant responded.

"Look, I'll give you fifty dollars to let me use this stall," Eve offered. After another minute, the door sprung open. A Black dude in a pink button-up and matching cap came out of the stall, followed by a skinny white dude. From the inflammation around the white dude's nose, Eve guessed what they were up to. Eve handed the Black dude the fifty and closed herself inside the stall.

She slammed the seat down and dropped her pants to her ankles, giving anyone who might be looking the impression that she was using the bathroom. She reached behind the toilet and found just what she was looking for. She ripped the wad of tape loose and came up with a .25, just where Keisha said it would be.

Keisha had come down to the club earlier that day to plant the gun. She was fucking one of the bouncers, so it wasn't hard for her to get into the club before it opened. She gave him a shot of head as payment and went about her business. She was going through all this just to set a nigga up. Eve made a note of how dangerous an enemy Keisha could be if it came down to it.

Butter and Felon arrived to pick up Steve right on time. To their surprise, he wasn't alone. There was an Italian cat with him, sporting a black ponytail. Steve informed him that Sal was one of Carlo's men and had to go along. Butter didn't like it, but Felon just shrugged. They parked Butter's car and climbed into the truck, with Steve behind the wheel.

On the way to the pier the only sound was the radio playing low. Each man was locked in his own thoughts. Steve watched the road, while Sal sat in the back next to Butter, playing with a switch-blade. Felon was going over the plan again, while Butter tried to keep his eyes on everyone at once. After a few miles of driving, the pier came into view.

"When we get in there, let me do all the talking," Felon said to the occupants of the car.

"Who made you boss?" Sal asked.

"Carlo, that's who," Steve spoke up. "Sal, be cool and let Felon handle this. We're just the muscle."

Sal didn't like the idea of taking orders from Blacks, but if this is what Carlo wanted, this is what it would be. The truck pulled up to a wire fence and flashed its high beams twice. There was a brief pause and the gate began to slide open. Steve navigated the truck to the back of a storage area and parked next to an identical one. Five Spanish cats got out of the twin and awaited their guest. Felon got out and motioned for the other three to stay in the car.

"You Felon?" asked a Spanish kid with a curly Afro.

"You Tito?" Felon shot back.

"Who your friends?" Tito asked, without bothering to answer Felon's question.

"Those my peoples," Felon responded shortly.

"Why they no get out?"

"Same reason you probably got niggaz stashed all throughout this bitch." Felon looked around cautiously. "Come on, papi, you ain't here to do business with them. I'm the man to see."

One of the men mumbled something in Spanish and Tito waved him off. "You tell them to get out of the car, or we no deal," Tito demanded.

"What kind of shit is this?" Felon asked. "You trying to pull something?"

"We no pull nothing. We just wanna see who we're dealing with. Tell them get out and we deal. No trouble."

Felon stared Tito down for a long minute without moving. He didn't like the way it was going down, but he held his face. Tito and his boys could just be downright paranoid, or it could be a setup. Felon shrugged it off, telling himself that the Spanish crew wouldn't be stupid enough to cross Carlo. Even if they did try something, he knew he and his partner were strapped. And even if he didn't show it, Felon had a good idea that Sal was holding too. He looked over his shoulder and motioned for the others to join him.

One by one they filed out of the truck. Steve posted against the truck while Sal flanked Tito's crew. Butter came and stood by Felon's side, with the shotgun tucked in the arm of his full-length leather jacket.

"So we gonna do this or what?" Felon shrugged.

"Okay," Tito nodded, seemingly satisfied. "Sorry about that. Can't be too careful. We do business now."

Felon motioned to Steve, who popped the rear of the truck. One of Tito's boys, followed by Sal, went to inspect the cases carrying the money. After a long moment he gave Tito the nod.

Felon held the keys out to Tito, but snatched them back when he reached. "I believe you have something for me?"

Tito made a face and handed Felon the keys. He tossed them to Butter, who went to inspect the cargo. At first Butter couldn't find anything, but one of Tito's men showed him how to work the false floor. Butter quickly sifted through the packages and nodded in approval to Felon. Without another word, the two crews switched trucks. Felon and his people waited a full fifteen minutes after Tito had gone to pull out of the lot and hit the southbound traffic. Each man wore a broad smile all the way to the Bronx. The deal had gone off without a hitch, but Felon was just barely forcing down the lump that had crawled into his throat.

The crowd was noticeably thicker when Eve came out of the bathroom. The music was blaring and bodies were rubbing against each other, making the temperature in the club thirty degrees higher.

After a bit of shoving, Eve was finally able to make her way back to the bar.

The bartender noticed Eve and abandoned her conversation. "Hey, you're back." She smiled. "I thought you left."

"Sorry about that. Some things take a little longer than others," Eve responded with a wink. Eve wasn't into girls, but paying the role of a man, it would've been strange if she hadn't. The bartender placed the drink down with a piece of paper attached to the bottom of the glass.

"It's on the house." She smiled. "Listen, I get off around three-thirty. Holla at me." The bartender gave Eve another seductive look and waggled her shapely ass back down to the other end of the bar.

The night dragged on, and Eve still hadn't spotted her mark. She was beginning to wonder if she should abandon the mission when she spotted Keisha on the dance floor. They made eye contact, but neither made a move toward the other. She locked eyes with Eve and motioned toward the area near the stage. A slim kid, wearing a thick chain, was talking to a point guard from the New York Knicks. Eve nodded at Keisha, confirming he had been tagged.

Eve would've liked to watch from the bar, but the bartender kept coming on to her, so she decided to change her position. When the entertainment went to take the stage, Eve moved to a dark corner. Everyone else watched the show, but Eve kept her eye on Paul. He and Keisha sat at a private table, where she grinded on his lap and made sure he got roaring drunk.

About halfway through the show, Paul made his way toward the bathroom. Eve decided now would be as good a time as any to make her move. Just about everyone in the club had their eyes glued to the stage, so the bathroom should be relatively empty. Even if it wasn't, this would probably be her best chance. She just hoped he had enough valuables on him to make it worth-while. Before Eve went in the bathroom, she stopped at the bar and got a bottle of water.

The bathroom was empty except for Paul and one other man. Eve held the water at her side and took the urinal next to Paul. She stuck her hand inside her pants and put the tip of the bottle through her zipper. Slowly she began to pour the water out, giving off the appearance that she was peeing. She spared a sideways glance at Paul and saw that he was having trouble focusing. When the other man finally left the bathroom, Eve made her move.

"Don't fucking move," she said, placing the pistol to his head.

"Fuck is this shit?" Paul slurred. "You know who I am?"

"Yeah, a nigga about to get robbed. Come up off all that shit!"

"Muthafucka!" Paul cursed. He tried to examine Eve's face, but she forced his head down with the pistol. He reluctantly handed her his chain. She watched him very carefully as he took off his watch and rings. The door came open, drawing Eve's attention for a split second. That was all Paul needed.

He caught Eve with a left, causing her to stagger back. He tried to advance the attack, but she was ready for him. She blocked with her left arm and clocked him in the temple with the gun. Blood trickled down his face, but he held his footing. As tough as he came, she came tougher. A solid left put him on his back.

"Punk-ass nigga," Eve said, wiping a speck of blood from her lip. She knelt down next to Paul and began digging through his pockets. All in all, she lifted four thousand in cash and several pieces of jewelry. With a triumphant grin Eve stuffed her take into her pants pockets. She gave him one last kick for good measure and slipped from the bathroom.

When Eve rejoined the party, the show was wrapping up. The whole crowd was going crazy, but Eve hardly noticed. She was too busy trying to get to the door. Getting through the crowd was like trying to navigate through pea soup. People were bumping and shouting as the rapper went into his last set. She had just about made it to the door when she heard the shots.

Paul was standing on shaky legs in the middle of the crowd. One of his boys rushed over to see what was going on and he pointed in

Eve's direction. The man drew a gun and pointed it at her back. For all of the planning she had done with Keisha, neither of them had factored in another gun. As soon as she ducked, the first shot whistled over her head.

Everyone ducked and tried to rush the door. It was all she could do to keep from getting trampled. Using the chaos as cover, she made a dash for the exit. She looked up just in time to see the same guy who had come into the bathroom pointing the bouncers in her direction. If she had the time she would've put one in the snitch, but time wasn't on her side. With the rush of people there was no way she could make it out before either Paul's people or the bouncers got to her. She needed an exit, quick.

Eve held her pistol in the air and fired off two shots. Everyone within ten feet of her scattered like roaches. When a hole opened up she broke for the fire door. One of the bouncers tried to grab her, but she avoided him by ducking around a guy who was trying to shield his girl from the crowd. She lucked out with the first bouncer, but the second one got a grip on her jacket.

She tried to break loose, but the mammoth guard had a grip of steel. The whole security force was coming at Eve from one direction while Paul and his people approached from the other. She fought against the bouncer, but he easily outweighed her by over a hundred pounds. As he drew her in closer, she saw her impending capture. With no other options, she abandoned her jacket, leaving him clutching leather.

Eve scrambled on her hands and knees to the door. A good Samaritan blocked Eve's path to freedom. Apparently he had never heard the old saying about a caged rat. Using all her strength, and the barrel of the gun, she knocked him clean out and burst through the doors to freedom.

Legs pumping and muscles aching, she darted up back streets and across avenues. Her chest heaved as she kept a steady pace through the bowels of Bedford Stuyvesant, heading toward East New York. Had things gone according to plan, she would've been able to speed-walk the few blocks to where she had a rental car parked. But things hadn't gone according to plan, had they? Around Atlantic Avenue and an irrelevant side street she wouldn't remember the day after, Eve was able to catch a cab.

Only when she was sure the police weren't purusing her and they were safely away from the scene, did she breathe easy. Some calls were just too close. For her greed she found herself nearly captured or executed. Neither were acceptable options. She almost caught an asshole full of time and a bullet in the back for a few thousand dollars. The stakes were being raised, but the score was still the same. If she intended not to starve, Eve needed to step her game up.

17.

Young Sammy darted in and out of the small stores in the Green
Acres Mall while his older double brought up the rear. For their
successful pickup and distribution of the new drug to the rightful
people, Carlo had thrown them all a little something extra, Felon
more so than the rest. He decided to use some of his money and
take his little brother shopping.

"Come on, Keith. I wanna see if they got the new NBA game!"
Sammy shouted excitedly, running into video-game store. Felon
shrugged and followed.

They stayed in the store for about twenty minutes as Sammy
mulled over the different games and tried to explain the differences
to his big brother. Felon nodded as if he understood, but he really
didn't. As far as video games went, he got off the bandwagon after
Super Nintendo. Still, it brought him joy just to see Sammy happy.
Had Felon himself been a little more guided on the road of life, he
might not have veered from the path. He wasn't complaining, just

thinking. There was really nothing he could do about it at that point. He was knee-deep in it and had no intentions on turning back. "All or nothing," he whispered.

"What'd you say, Keith?" Sammy asked, looking up from the game cover he was reading.

"Nothing," Felon told him.

Donnie lounged near Foot Locker with his partner Rich, trying to rap to a young lady and her two friends. The girls had brushed them off and kept it moving. It had been the same story for them all day. They weren't the most attractive young men in the borough. Donnie was rail thin with dusty brown hair and splotched brown skin. Rich was light skinned with a chipped tooth and a funny-shaped head.

"Fuck you, bitches!" Donnie yelled in true hater fashion.

"Ya ass wasn't that fat anyway!" Rich added.

"Can't stand these Queens bitches." Donnie spat on the floor. "They're all stuck-up."

"Fuck it, let's go get outta here and head back to Harlem."

"Come on." Donnie began walking toward the exit, but caught a glimpse of a familiar face. He searched his mental Rolodex, trying to place the face. Suddenly it hit him like a fist. "Yo, check that shit, son." He tapped Rich and nodded toward the game store.

"What, you wanna buy a video game?" Rich asked, confused.

"No, dumb ass. I'm talking about homey that just came outta there."

"Duke wit his seed? What about him?"

"I know that kid. That's the nigga that robbed me last winter, son," Donnie said angrily.

"Donnie, you high or something? How the fuck do you know that's the same kid?"

"His walk," Donnie said seriously. "He had that same cocky-ass swagger when he walked away with my chain."

"So, what you wanna do?"

"We gonna roll on that nigga," Donnie declared, patting the gun in his waistband.

"He wit his seed, yo."

"Fuck that. That nigga gotta answer for that shit. Let's go." Donnie moved for the food court, and Rich reluctantly followed.

Glancing at his watch, Felon noticed it was getting late. The sun would soon be setting and he would be needed in the hood. He and Sammy left the game store and made their way to the food court. Felon absently rubbed the back of his neck as a chill went up his back. He stopped short and looked around, but could find nothing out of the ordinary. Shaking off his uneasiness, Felon carried his and Sammy's tray to a free table.

Sammy stuffed the ketchup-soaked fry into his mouth and rambled on about something that had happened to his science teacher. Felon nodded from time to time, but his attention was elsewhere. The sensation he was feeling was the equivalent of being watched when you're the only one in the room.

His eyes vigilantly swept back and forth through the food court, searching for something out of the ordinary. Just when he was about to chalk it up to paranoia, he saw something that set off warning bells in his head. Seated near the exit were two men who appeared to be in their twenties. He would've dismissed them, but the brown-skinned one kept staring at him. As he focused on the Ruff Ryder T-shirt the kid was wearing, it dawned on him that he had seen the same two jokers icing him outside the game store. It didn't take a rocket scientist to realize they were up to no good.

Felon found himself between a rock and a hard place. Had he been alone, or with his team, he would've just approached the duo, but Sammy was with him. He couldn't subject his little brother to the violence of his lifestyle. He thought about calling Butter or Teddy, but there was no telling how long it would take one or both of them to reach him. His only hope was to try and ditch them.

"Time to go, Sammy," Felon told his little brother.

"Aw, Keith. I wanted to hit another store," Sammy whined.

"You've hit enough stores for the day, kid. Besides, Mom will kill me if I don't get you back in time for dinner." Felon scooped his bags with one hand and placed the other on the butt of the nine in his pocket. Ushering Sammy in front of him, they headed for the exit furthest from the boys.

As they crossed the ground level, Felon peeped the two boys get up to follow. He cursed silently under his breath for being caught so far from home. He wanted to scoop up Sammy and break into a run, but he didn't want to risk tipping the boys off and getting shot in the back for it, so he kept a steady pace. When he stepped out into the darkening parking lot, Felon stopped Sammy short.

"Hold on, Sam. I got a special job for you." He dug into his pocket and fished out the car keys. "I think I left my phone in the food court. Why don't you go start the car and I'll be right behind you?" Sammy reached for the keys excitedly, but Felon snatched them back. "Start it, Sammy. Don't move it."

"Aw, man." Sammy huffed as he took the keys and went off to do as he was told.

When Sammy was a safe enough distance away, Felon darted back the way he came. When he checked his gun, the grip was nearly soaked from his sweating palm. He wiped his hands on his pants so his aim would be true when and if it came to it. He concealed himself in the shadows near the doorway and waited.

After about two minutes, the two young boys came bumbling out of the mall. The one with the dark skin held a small-caliber handgun at his side, while the other boy brandished a knife. They looked around, dumbfounded, trying to figure out where their prey had gone. Felon didn't keep them in suspense long.

While they stood there and argued about who was the cause of Felon's escape, he peeled away from the shadows. The boy with the knife was about to shout a warning to his friend, but the bullet was already making its exit through his chest. Before the brown-skinned boy could hit the ground, Felon dumped two more in him. With the brown-skinned boy taken care of, Felon turned his attention to the light-skinned one.

"Don't shoot! I'm just a kid," Rich pleaded.

"And you'll never become an adult," Felon hissed. He shot the kid twice in the face. Before the body hit the ground, Felon vanished.

"What's going on?" Sammy asked nervously as Felon climbed behind the wheel and put the car in gear.

"Nothing," he said in a too-calm voice, "just some kids playing with firecrackers." With that said, they merged with traffic and headed back to Manhattan.

Eve and Bullet sat in a stolen Cutlass, on a side block near the gas station on 149th. Steve had given them the route the truck would be using, and the 145th Street Bridge was how it was to enter Manhattan. The two robbers made small talk, but only so one wouldn't hear how loud the other's heart was beating. They chain-smoked cigarettes and waited on their score.

"How much longer?" Eve asked impatiently.

"Cool out, Eve. We ain't been here that long," Bullet responded, lighting another cigarette with the burning ember of the one he had just smoked.

There was a rumbling in the distance that made both of them sit bolt upright. In the rearview, they spotted a large cubed truck motoring along under the overpass. It was still several blocks away, but at that hour of the night they were able to hear it approaching. Under normal circumstances this was an unusual route for a truck to be taking, but this wasn't a normal delivery. The driver had been paid by Jimmy V to allow the truck to be stolen by two of his men, but what the driver didn't know was that the people about to spring their trap on him didn't work for Jimmy V.

"You know what to do?" Bullet asked, checking his double-barreled shotgun. She nodded. "Good." Bullet gave a cautious glance around and disappeared into the shadows, clutching a plastic canister.

Eve slid behind the wheel and gunned the engine. After checking the rounds on the tech that sat beside her on the vacated passenger seat, she made a broken U-turn. When the car was positioned to face oncoming traffic, Eve flicked on the high beams and got out to stand behind the car. When she heard the blaring horn, she raised the tech and stood ready.

Butch Carter was a working-class citizen from Southside Jamaica, Queens. He had been a part of the 1422 truckers' union for just over eighteen months before a coworker put him on to a scheme to earn some extra bread. Every so often they would arrange for a truck to get knocked off by one of several organized crime families from in and around the tristate area. This was Butch's first run.

His instructions for the mission were quite simple. He was to take the 149th Street Bridge into Manhattan and detour to get gas near the West Side Highway. During the detour, he would quietly turn the truck over to members of Jimmy V's crew. He would later file a report with the police, stating that he was robbed at gunpoint by several Puerto Rican men. He would later be paid three thousand dollars for his role in the heist.

At first he was skeptical about undertaking the mission on his own, but the same coworker who had plugged him to the hustle assured him that everything would go smoothly. So far this had held true. He had successfully driven the truck from the warehouse in Westbury, Connecticut, to the Bronx without incident. Butch smiled and thought about how sweet the job was when he was assaulted by a set of high beams directly in front of him.

"Are you fucking serious?" Butter asked in disbelief.

"Right there at the mall, son. And I had Sammy with me!" Felon fumed.

"What you wanna do?" Butter asked in anticipation.

"Ain't shit else to do. I laid both them pussies down."

"Did you know the kids?"

"One of them looked familiar," Felon said, frowning, "but I don't think I knew em. They was some bold muthafuckas though."

"That's what I be trying to tell you, son." Butter paced his living room. "If these muthafuckas don't fear you, they gonna come. Niggaz think twice before coming at me, cause they know I don't play that. I come with two guns, dumping!"

"Mo money, mo problems," Felon mumbled.

"True story. Felon, we them niggaz now, so these jokers are gonna be feeling in a way. Like maybe they're owed a piece of what we built. It's up to us to stand these faggots off and let them know where they stand on the food chain. This shit was light, but please believe it gets deeper."

"Larcenist muthafuckas." Felon lit his Newport. "Acting like I can't do me. You gotta feed these niggaz with a long-handled spoon. Yo man, I'm bout to buy moms a house and get my own lil piece of something where I can lay my head."

"Shit, I ain't going nowhere," Butter declared.

"Butter, you about to be rolling in dough. How you just gonna stay on the block where you're shitting?"

Butter stopped his pacing and stared at Felon briefly, as if pondering his question. He reached down and picked up the nickel-plated nine from the table. "These is the last days, baby boy," he said staring hypnotically at the barrel. "If I gotta go out, I'm going out in style."

The glare blinded Butch, causing him to raise his arm protectively while he slapped the horn. Disoriented by the sudden burst of light, he couldn't judge just how far out in front of him the other car was. Just as he began pumping the brakes, a second car slammed into the side of his truck. The larger auto began to slide sideways as the minivan continued to push against it. Through blurry eyes and with a shaky grip, he swung the truck off to the side, trying to gain its independence from the van and avoid the car in front of him. His vision cleared just in time for him to see the pillar speeding directly toward him.

The truck smacked the steel column, producing a deafening ring. Butch's head smacked off the headrest and collided with the wheel. The whole cabin danced white and spun in circles, but Butch managed to stay conscious. Blood gushed down his forehead and into his left eye. He tried the door but found the van had it pinned. When he turned to crawl out the passenger door, a shotgun barrel clocked him in the forehead.

While Bullet climbed the side of the truck, Eve made her way toward him. She backed down the street, holding the tech low in a two-handed grip. Her heart beat against her chest as she scanned the block for police or witnesses. Her job in the heist was key in its success. Bullet had long ago schooled Eve to the art of theft, but this was something different. Hijacking, kidnapping, grand theft auto. If something went wrong, it'd sound like a football score at the sentencing.

"Get the fuck out!" Bullet ordered.

"What the fuck are you doing?" The round-faced Irishman groaned. "You guys weren't supposed to hurt me. I thought you were supposed to wait until I got to the West Side."

"Clown, I don't know what the fuck you're talking about. Now, if I gotta tell you to get out one more time, they're gonna have to scrub you out," Bullet threatened.

Butch looked at the scarfaced Black man and realized something was wrong. These were not Jimmy V's people. His mind raced as he thought about what a fuckup he was. His first time out and he managed to get his load ripped off by the wrong crew. There would be hell to pay behind this. The fear of having the mob on his ass outweighed the fear of the man holding the pump to his face. In an act of pure stupidity, Butch palmed the .32 he kept in the truck cabin.

"Come on, fat boy," Bullet said impatiently. He had now opened the door to the cabin.

"Okay, take it easy." Butch inched toward Bullet.

"Hurry up!" Eve shouted from the driver's side.

"Be easy!" Bullet shot back. The split second his attention was drawn was enough time for Butch to make his move. The larger man swiftly trained the gat on Bullet. Seeing what was about to go down, Bullet tried to throw himself from the doorway. Butch let off two frantic shots. One hit Bullet in his upper chest, laying him out.

Eve saw the flash and was frozen in place. Her mentor flew from the doorway, landing hard on the pavement. The truck driver crawled across the front seat and made for the open door. In the blink of an eye, the whole thing had gone sour. Eve looked from her fallen mentor to the fleeing vic and decided she had to do something. She squeezed the trigger of the tech and the gun rattled off in her hand.

Having never fired one, she misjudged the kick. The bullets struck the front of the grill and busted a window, but missed the driver. When she rounded the front of the truck, the driver was climbing down from the cabin, still holding the pistol. He spotted Eve and opened fire. She managed to dodge the bullets, but fumbled her grip on the tech. By the time she got the gun back under control, the vic was jogging down the side of the truck.

Instinctively she raised the gun and fired. The bullets ricocheted off the side of the truck, sparking where they struck. She had let off almost seven shots before she hit him. One bullet pierced his lung while the other cut through his calf. Butch limped and hit the ground face first. Eve ran to Bullet's side to examine him.

"Bullet!" she shook him. "You okay?"

"Yeah." He swatted her off. "I'll be better if you stop shaking me," Bullet ripped his sweat shirt and examined the slug that was stuck to his vest. "Nigga tried to get me."

"You had me worried. Next time . . ." Her statement was cut off when Bullet's arm shot out snake quick. He snatched the tech from her before she even realized he was moving. Bullet fired the gun one-handed, cutting into Butch, who had been trying to get a bead on Eve.

"Next time you gotta put a nigga down, take him out the game. Understand?" He looked at her seriously. She nodded, still shocked at how effortlessly he killed. "Good. Now, help me into the truck so we can get the fuck outta here and get paid."

18.

Steve stood back and shook his head in disbelief as Bullet steered the truck into the garage in Flatbush. He and Tony had placed a wager on whether Bullet would be able to pull it off or not. The Italians figured Bullet to be a nigger stickup kid who wouldn't be able to pull off something of that magnitude. The slightly banged up but very full truck steaming in front of them made Tony the loser.

No one knew better than Carlo's crew how important this shipment was. Not only was it a slap in Jimmy V's face, but it would strengthen their team. Bullet didn't know it, but he had earned Steve a great deal of favor with the De Nardi organization.

"I don't believe he pulled it off," Tony chuckled.

"I told Carlo Bullet was good." Steve smiled. "Jimmy V is gonna shit his pants." He waved for the men to empty the truck and Bullet to join him.

Steve had expected a crew of hardened gunslingers to climb from the truck, wearing screw faces, but there were only two occupants. The stickup man emerged from the battered truck, favoring his left arm, followed by a young man dressed in fatigues. The passenger had his hat pulled low, so Steve couldn't really see his features. He did, however, notice that the man seemed to be overly concerned about Bullet's ailing shoulder. Steve wondered if his old associate had developed a taste for little boys.

"You pulled it off." Steve shook Bullet's hand enthusiastically.

"Was there any doubt?" Bullet replied.

"Nah," Steve cut his eyes at Tony. "I told my people you were good. I just never expected to work with just the two of you." He let his gaze linger on Eve, as if waiting for an introduction.

"Oh," Bullet caught on, "this is—"

"E." She cut him off in a deep voice.

"Yeah." He nodded in understanding. "This is E. He schooled under me a few years back."

Steve sized up Eve, but she made it a point to avoid direct eye contact. Steve could tell Bullet's protégée was young from his smooth face. His hands weren't hard or callused, so he guessed he wasn't a fighter. The grip on the tech suggested a trigger man. Outside of what he deduced on the physical, Steve couldn't deduce much about the boy named E, but if Bullet vouched for him, then he was good.

"Well, you and your teacher are some top-notch thieves." Steve smiled. One of the men unloading the truck carried a crate over to Steve and laid it at his feet. Steve pried the lid off and extracted a handgun from the straw padding. It had a squared frame and an extended barrel.

"Muthafucka," Bullet said in surprise. "Nigga, you said we was stealing CD players?"

"Some things are on the need-to-know basis." Steve handed Bullet a pistol and took another one out for Eve. "From our friends in Germany. Sorry we kept you guys in the dark about it, but the boss felt it was for the best. Don't worry about it, though. With the job you guys pulled off, I think I can convince the boss to put you on payroll."

Eve looked from the smiling giant to the pistol in her hand. So this is why they were willing to pay so much for the job. They had just lifted a small arsenal for the De Nardi family. And if they decided to retain her services, what would it mean for her life?

Johnny sat cross-legged on a stack of pillows, watching. The apartment had been padlocked by the sheriff's department, but it was nothing for The Outlaw to pick it. It was one of many talents. The windows were mostly boarded up, which suited him fine since he only needed one. Before setting up, he had loosened one of the boards just enough to see the avenue but not to run the risk of being spotted. Mounted in front of the window was a tripod, supporting a thirty-caliber assault rifle. He toggled the crosshairs on the sight to get a better look at his target.

Butter stood on the avenue with some of the locals, talking to a man who Johnny recognized from his notes as Vinny. They were carelessly joking and lounging, not even realizing that death loomed mere yards away. Johnny zoomed in on Butter, focusing on his broad chest. He could almost see the man's heart beating through the powerful monocle. He slowly moved the crosshairs from his chest to his head.

Johnny leveled the cross with Butter's eye and fingered the trigger. Sweat dripped into his eye, but he didn't allow himself to blink. He grinned menacingly as he fantasized Butter's head exploding when the shell split it. His penis began to rise against his jeans, causing a print in the denim. Butter said his good-byes and left his crew. "Another time," Johnny whispered, toggling the crosshairs, sighting another target.

Vinny gave Butter dap and watched him until he was safely in the car. After his boss departed, he went back to join his crew in front of the bodega. They were in the middle of a discussion about the latest rap group when Vinny felt something slam into his chest. He winced at the stinging and looked down to see a pool of red forming. At first he thought he was shot, but there was no pain. Vinny touched his fingers to the spot and examined them. "Paint?"

PART TWO

WINDS OF CHANGE

19.

As the weather got warmer, Eve's life took a turn for the better. Just as Steve had indicated, the De Nardis put Eve and Bullet on the payroll. They commissioned them from time to time to do jobs that they didn't want to dirty their hands with. It was mostly shake-downs and burglarizing establishments that didn't want to play ball with the family. The jobs only came every so often, but they paid handsomely.

She had stopped reporting to the job developer and found work at a temp agency. Eve would work in different office buildings a few days a week, just to tell her PO she was gainfully employed and have a reportable source of income. This also allowed her schedule to be flexible. Her main source of income was still jacking.

With the money she was making from the Italians, Eve was fi-nally able to start improving her quality of life. She had tossed out her old clothes and went shopping for a whole new wardrobe. She bought a lot of jeans, sneakers, and boots, and some designer pieces that covered outfits for stepping out as well as seduction. She tried to ignore the fact that she was thinking of Felon when she bought the sexier outfits.

One was a dress that she had ordered from Marshall Field's, via a catalog. It was a form-fitting black dress with a V-cut back. She stood in the full-length mirror admiring how the dress fit her body. It hugged her about the hips, showing off her hourglass figure. She fixed her hair into different styles, imagining what it would be like to step out in the piece with some handsome chocolate Adonis (preferably Felon), making their grand entrance at some social event. They would turn every head as they glided across the threshold. *Yeah, if Felon ever* . . . She smoothed her hands over the dress, sighed, wiggled out of it, and hung it in the closet. She shook her head.

Felon and Butter were on the come-up. Slowly but surely they were outclassing the competition. Word had it they had some new product that was causing everyone else to close up shop. Butter was still playing the block, flossing and acting a fool. Felon was a different case. Aside from an occasional cameo, he really didn't come through the block that often.

Eve missed spending time with him, but she wasn't totally against the separation. Whenever he was around him her heart raced and her thoughts became incoherent. She felt like some chickenhead swooning over an unrealistic crush. She managed to keep her cool more often than she didn't, but there was no denying the fire than burned within her.

She had feelings for Felon, and she knew that he felt something for her, but was it right? Though Felon never meant for her to go to jail, he still abandoned her. Who was to say that he wouldn't do the same with her heart? She knew that he felt something for her, but she also knew that he'd never admit it, and she probably wouldn't either. They shared a special friendship that most people would never experience in this lifetime. If they went the extra step, things would change. She tried to shake it off and focus on something else, but she couldn't. Eve had never honestly been in love, but she knew that what she felt for Felon went beyond a schoolgirl's crush.

Now that she had a little money put up, she wore her trademark cornrows a little less. When she wasn't on a job, she would go to the Dominicans and let them style her hair. When she first started going, her hairdresser thought she was Spanish and would try to converse with her in the native tongue. When Eve explained her heritage, the dresser laughed and told her she didn't look like a white girl.

Eve was always a pretty girl, but since her wardrobe upgrade, she turned plenty of heads. Catcalls and compliments followed her like a shadow. It took some getting used to, but she learned to accept the attention.

When Eve wasn't stealing or working at the temp agency, she occupied herself with movies. She was always spending large sums of money on DVDs or taking in flicks. She didn't know if it was the solitude, or living vicariously through the characters on the screen, but watching movies soothed her. She didn't always undertake the task alone. Eve had even gone on dates. Guys from various boroughs were checking for the pretty redhead. Some of the guys she met were real cool, but it never went beyond one date. Her heart was elsewhere.

Twenty-Gang was still Twenty-Gang, but they were seeing less and less of Cassidy. Since she had started seeing Carlo, she had been less active in the affairs of the streets. In a way it was a good thing. Cassidy needed someone to keep her ass off the streets and out of different men's beds. Eve had reluctantly accepted her relationship with Carlo. If her friend was happy, then she was happy for her. She still didn't agree with the move, though.

Cassidy was curled up on Carlo's king-sized bed, reading a copy of *Road Dawgz*. She wasn't really a reader, but she loved this particular author's work. He was one of the more powerful voices in the game. Things had been good since she hooked up with Carlo. He stayed true to his word and treated her like a queen.

Cassidy had gear before, but Carlo stepped up her game. She had pieces from every designer and more shoes that she knew what to do with. In addition to keeping her fly, Carlo got her mobile. Cassidy was now the owner of a Honda Civic. It was three years old, but it was hers. She didn't even care that she hadn't met his parents. Carlo told her that his parents had "old world" values. They knew he dabbled in dark meat, but they'd shit a brick if he ever brought one home. It didn't matter as long as she was taken care of.

Carlo slid into the bed behind her and started nibbling on her neck. She knew what he wanted. She reached behind her and started massaging his penis. When it was good and hard, she slipped him inside her. Carlo started off slow until he found his rhythm. Cassidy threw it back at him, letting out a soft moan. They spooned for a while, then Carlo flipped her over and started hitting it from the back.

Cassidy bit her bottom lip and hissed as Carlo slid in and out of her. He gripped her small waist and began to hammer into her harder and harder. Cassidy clawed at the sheets and begged for him to keep going. Carlo worked his hands up her back and let them come to rest on her neck. She arched her back and threw her head back in ecstasy He rubbed her delicate tendons and gradually began to apply pressure.

It felt good to Cassidy at first, but the pressure got more and more intense. She tried to motion for him to loosen up, but he didn't seem to notice. The deeper he pumped, the tighter his grip became. Cassidy could feel him cutting off her wind and began to panic. She tried to thrash and even managed to let out a muffled shriek, but he still didn't let up. Carlo was lost in the moment. Harder and tighter, Carlo went to work. Just as Cassidy was about to pass out, Carlo exploded. His hands came away from her neck and he collapsed on his side.

"Goddamn, Carlo!" she rasped and scrambled from the bed. "You almost fucking choked me to death."

"Chill, baby. It was just getting good, that's all," he managed to say between deep breaths.

"Carlo, I like to get a little kinky too, but you almost choked me out. This shit is wack." Cassidy began gathering her clothes from the floor, deciding that she had had enough of Carlo's shit. Carlo's kind of sex was beginning to get too painful for her. First, he had damn near ripped a bald spot in her head. Then there was the time he bit her until he drew blood. Now it was affixiation.

"Come on, baby," he said, sliding his arm around her waist, "I didn't mean to get so rough with you. Your stuff is just so good that I got caught up. Don't be like that."

"I don't like this rough shit, Carlo," she told him.

"Cassidy, all I can say is I'm sorry and try to make it up to you. Tell you what." He managed to get her to sit on the edge of the bed. "How bout I give you some spending money and you go out and have yourself a good time?"

"How much?" she asked, trying not to let her greed shine through.

Carlo smiled, knowing her weakness. He reached under the bed and pulled out a Nike box. He double-checked the contents and handed it to Cassidy. "Knock yaself out."

Cassidy shook the shoebox near her ear and smiled. She planted a kiss on his forehead and went into the bathroom without uttering a word of thanks. Carlo just lay back on the bed and smiled. Money couldn't buy love, but it could make a woman put up with a lot of shit. Cassidy was proof of that. Carlo lit a cigarette and let his thoughts roam to who he would bed down and fuck bloody after Cassidy left.

"Mac . . . I move rocks and pounds, taking over small blocks and towns!" Butter sang into his Mac 11 machine gun while Bennie Segal killed the truck. Teddy sat behind the steering wheel and shook his head.

"That's why I fuck wit you, son." Teddy passed the blunt off. "You about the only nigga I know that's crazier than me."

"You gotta be crazy out this bitch, Ted. The hood only respects gangstas," Butter said.

"And who's more gangsta than us?"

"Not a muthafucka walking on two legs. We puts in nuff work, kid."

"Speaking of work, what's up with Felon?" Teddy asked, turning off Morningside and onto 125th.

"Got his head stuck in the sand some damn where." Butter passed the blunt back.

"Been a while since he rolled through the block. He ain't got no love for the hood?" Teddy half joked.

"You know Felon ain't like that, lil nigga," Butter said, defending his homey. "He love the hood, but he don't like to be in it if he ain't gotta be. See, niggaz like us love to be in the mix. We get off on this kinda shit, but that ain't where Felon's head is at. He on his 'trying to plan for a rainy day' shit."

"Fuck that. A nigga could be dead tomorrow. I'm trying to do me, now!" Teddy declared. Butter nodded but didn't discuss Felon further with Teddy. "Yo, what's up with Cassidy?"

"Man, fuck her." Butter sucked his teeth. "She act like she ain't got time for a nigga no more. Probably found somebody else to scratch her fucking itch."

"Bitches is like that, yo." Teddy said.

"Watch ya mouth, lil nigga. I'm the only one that can talk about that bitch like that." Butter laughed at his own twisted humor.

Seventh Avenue was packed. The nice weather had brought out Harlem's finest, stunting with whips or standing around trying to bag girls. Butter lowered the driver's side window of the Escalade and let his arm dangle out the window. The yellow diamond on his pinky caught the attention of a quite a few ladies on the strip and two young men.

"That's that nigga right there," Johnny said to Knowledge.

"That big-head nigga?" Knowledge asked, pointing at the red truck.

"Yeah. Make it clean, son."

"I got you, Black," Knowledge said, adjusting the belt of his pants. The Beretta tucked in his waist kept pulling them down. After giving a brief look-around, Knowledge went in the direction of the truck.

Johnny leaned against the wall and watched. Big Steve, by way of Dre, had paid him to kill Butter, but he wasn't a stupid man. He had done his homework on the kid and found out that he could be quite a headache. Johnny was hardly afraid of going head to head with Butter, but he needed to know what he was up against. If Knowledge succeeded in killing Butter, that would be cool, but if he didn't, Johnny would know how to approach, based on Knowledge's sacrifice.

A girl and her friends were trying to get Butter's attention and were doing a pretty good job of it. They were all dressed in too-short shorts and Air Maxes. Butter could see the nipples of the light-skinned one poking through her wife beater. He licked his lips hungrily and decided he would have one, if not all, of the girls that evening.

"Stop the car, son," Butter said, already hopping out of the car.

Teddy shook his head and proceeded double-park on the corner. He wanted a shot of the young love box too, but he had class about his shit. He figured that he was that nigga, and a bitch should be chasing him down. He was leaning over to put his gun on the passenger seat when he caught a motion in the rearview mirror. The kid was just walking down the block, so Teddy almost brushed him off. The thing that caught his attention, though, was the fact that he was staring at Butter.

Butter had his back to Knowledge, so he never saw him coming. He was stunting for the girls, letting them touch his chain and flashing cash, when Knowledge crept on him. The only thing that made him aware of something being wrong was the look of horror on the girl's faces. Butter turned around and found himself staring down the barrel of the Beretta. Knowledge placed his finger on the trigger and all hell broke loose.

* * *

Felon sat in front of his television watching *Carlito's Way*. No matter how many times he watched that movie, the irony in it never ceased to amaze him. Carlito wanted to get out of the game and live happily ever after. Yeah, right.

Felon poured himself another glass of Henny and lit a blunt. He watched the smoke seep from his nose and dissipate into the air. "Getting out." That was something that crept into Felon's brain every so often. What would he do if he got out? Maybe get a job? Not likely. In the streets, he was a star. In the working world, who would he be other than another nigga living from check to check?

The thought was laughable. Him being anything other than what he was seemed like wishful thinking. The grind was where it was for him. He didn't relish the thought of working for twenty or thirty years, just to retire on a pension. His family needed things, and the streets provided him with the means to provide for them. The life of a hustler was a cold one, but Felon would rather be cold and rich than broke and warm.

Teddy leaned around the back of the truck and started dumping. Before Knowledge even knew what was jumping off, his shoulder exploded. As if that wasn't bad enough, Butter laid into him with a straight right. The whole world went woozy and Knowledge found himself on his back.

People were running left and right, but Teddy brushed through the crowd like he didn't even notice them. Knowledge had managed to make it to his knees when Teddy pressed the .357 against his temple. Knowledge looked into Teddy's eyes and saw only malice before his brains hit the sidewalk. Butter and Teddy forgot about the girls and headed back to the truck, never even noticing Johnny Black still leaning against the wall.

20.

The next morning, Teddy sat in the folding chair, thumbing his PS2 controller back and forth. To his right sat Spoon, toggling the other controller. Vinny and Mike stood near the door, awaiting instructions. Felon paced the floor, trying to make heads or tails of what he had just been told.

"These muthafuckas got nerve," Spoon said with a bit of venom in his voice. "How they gonna try to come at son?"

"That shit was crazy, Felon. Homey just came up and tried to pop him," Teddy added.

"Shit!" Felon cursed. He should've seen it coming. Butter was the kind of cat who couldn't get money and fall back. He had to flash. He had to have the biggest mouth in the room, and the most girls on his dick. Felon constantly warned him about his cavalier attitude, but the boy was hardheaded.

"What we gonna do, chief?" asked Teddy.

Felon paused momentarily and glanced at Teddy. It was a damn good question. The money was rolling in, so the last thing he needed was a war fucking up the flow. Yet he couldn't let a crime like this go unpunished. Butter was like a brother to him. Any man who tried to lay hands on his family had to be dealt with. But the fact still remained that no one knew who was behind it. The shooter was dead, so he wasn't telling. Felon needed time to devise a game plan, but he had to throw the wolves a bone to calm them.

"We gonna handle this shit," Felon said, slamming his palm. "Spoon, y'all niggaz hit the streets and see what you can dig up. Teddy, I want you to stay close to Butter. I'm gonna put some guys on y'all as extra muscle until we get to the bottom of this shit." The men prepared to leave and carry out their various assignments. Before Teddy left, Felon called after him. "That nigga is like my brother, Teddy."

"I got you, fam. You know how I do." He tugged at the gun in his pants. Teddy saluted Felon and left the man to his thoughts.

The store on Seventh was crowded with people buying water and ice, trying to beat the heat. It was unseasonably warm that day and everyone was feeling it. Kids darted in and out, stealing or tossing their money on the counter without bothering to wait their turn. Beast stood patiently on the line waiting to pay for his purchases.

Three brawny men came barging into the store, knocking a path through people as they went. They were dressed in jeans and T-shirts, all covered in plaster. They rummaged through one of the freezers, retrieving forty ounces and bottles of water. Two of them took their places on the line, but the cockier of the trio bullied his way to the front of the line. He cut right in front of Beast just as he had reached the counter.

"Ah, excuse me. I was here first." Beast said as politely as he could. The man, who was almost a foot taller than Beast, ignored him. "Sir?"

"Fuck outta here!" the man barked, never bothering to turn around.

"I don't want any trouble. I just wanna pay for my stuff and go," Beast pleaded.

Now the man did turn around and size Beast up. His cold brown gaze bore down on the young man, challenging him to lock eyes. When Beast turned away, the man figured him for a coward. With nothing better to do, he decided to embarrass the mentally challenged young man and try and make himself look like somebody in the process.

"Yo, can't you understand English?" The man cocked his head. "I said, get the fuck outta here, retard!" The man poked his finger into Beast's chest to punctuate his last remark. Mistake.

By the time the man saw the rage building in Beast's eyes, it was far too late. Beast grabbed his finger and snapped it like a twig. The man's shriek and the sound of his bone snapping brought his two friends to Beast's rear. One was foolish enough to smash a bottle against Beast's head, which only seemed to enrage him more. With an animalistic snarl Beast whirled around and grabbed him by the neck. With almost an effortless toss, the attacker was airborne.

The third of the trio pulled a pocketknife. In an act of desperation he tried to cut his way out of the store. Beast caught the knife-wielding hand in one of his massive paws, covering everything except the blade. Using his thumb, he snapped the metal and glared at the man. When he opened his mouth to scream, Beast smashed his fist into it. His face made a crunching sound as the man crumbled. Beast then turned his attention back to the original threat.

"I'm not retarded!" he snarled into the man's face. "Do you hear me?! I'm not! I'm not!"

"Sorry, man," the construction worker sobbed.

Beast eyed him closely, as if he was trying to decide if he wanted to eat him or not. The man was so terrified that he pissed his pants. Beast looked down at the stream of urine and scrunched up his nose. Deciding that enough damage had been done for the day, he dropped the man on his back and returned to the counter. The store owner was terrified, thinking that the violence wasn't over yet, but Beast did something that surprised everyone in the store. He apologized, paid for his goods, and left.

* * *

Eve sat on a milk crate, trying her best not to melt in the heat. She was dressed in a pair of sky blue Baby Phat sweat pants that hugged her curves and a matching baby-doll tank top. Sweat soaked the neckline, giving it an almost transparent effect. Her nipples pressed against the cotton ever so slightly. Her hair was blown out and hung from beneath the Blue Jays fitted cap she wore pulled firmly on her head. The brim did little to hide her from the sun. To her relief, Beast came walking up the block.

"Here ya go," he said, handing her a bottle of water from the bag he was carrying. "Nice and cold."

"Good looking, Beast," she said, accepting the water. Eve turned the bottle up and began to down the refreshing liquid. Beads of sweat began to run down her neck, finishing the saturation job on the tank top. When she finished the water she noticed Beast staring at her with a puzzled look on his face.

"What's wrong?" she asked.

"Nothing," he said, turning away.

"Beast, I saw the way you were looking at me. What's up?"

"You're different, Eve."

"What do you mean, I'm different? I haven't changed, Beast."

"Yes, you have. You're prettier now."

"Thanks, I think. Beast, I'm getting older, so I'm filling out in certain places. Girls do that, ya know."

"I know that," he said as if it should've been painfully obvious to her. "I don't like it."

"Why? Don't you want me to grow up?"

"That's not what I mean. I don't like the way guys look at you now. They look like they wanna do bad things to you."

"I'll bet they do," she said, patting his cheek. "That's just how guys look at girls. It's been happening since the dawn of time."

"I still don't like it," he said, folding his arms.

The conversation was broken up by a silver Acura pulling up to the curb. Eve couldn't see through the window, so she immediately inched closer to the small pistol stashed in a doughnut box. Ever since her brush, she had been paranoid. If trouble was about to pop, she would make sure her and Beast's asses were covered. She cracked a broad smile when her friend stepped out of the ride.

"What up, my nigga?" Cassidy sang, strutting up to the sidewalk. She was wearing a dress that dropped down in the front, showing off her cleavage. The alligator slip-ons she wore looked like they were fresh off the shelf. Even the scarf she had tied around her neck looked like money.

"C-style, what up, ma?" Eve gave her dap. "I ain't seen you in a minute!"

"I been handling mine," Cassidy said, spinning around to show off the fit.

"Doing big things, Cas. I can't even be mad at you. That fit is off the hook."

"Carlo bought it for me."

"Big spender," Eve said sarcastically.

"Don't hate, bitch," Cassidy smiled. "Look at your ass, looking like a lady. Who's dick you sucking that got you open?"

"Don't play with me, heifer. I don't suck dick!" Eve exclaimed.

"Not yet."

"Forget you." Eve waved her off. "These is just some sweats. You're killing em though. That dress must've cost a grip."

"Ain't my money. Who gives a fuck?"

"You ain't right, C. Say, what're you doing with that scarf on as hot as it is?" Eve yanked at the scarf, but before she could get it off, Cassidy stopped her. Eve spotted the black-and-blue marks on her friend's neck and screwed her face. "What's that?"

"A'int nothing," Cassidy said, retying the scarf.

"Looks like something, Cas. Don't bullshit me. That nigga hitting you?"

"Hell no," Cassidy said, defensively. "That nigga ain't crazy. He just gets a little rough when we're fucking. You know I got that good shit, Eve."

"Cassidy, I hope you ain't lying to me. You know how I get down when it comes to you. You're the closest thing I got to a sister and the only family I got outside of Uncle Bobby. I'd gladly kill a muthafucka for you, Cas."

"That's why you'll forever be my ace," Cassidy said, getting teary-eyed. Just as the water began to fall, a pair of hands covered Cassidy's eyes. She knew from the familiar smell of Cool Water who it was. "Boy, quit playing." Cassidy spun around.

"Whoa," Butter said, holding his hands up. "That ain't no way to treat your future baby daddy."

"Nigga, please. I ain't trying to have no kids with your crazy ass. Butter, you've got too many damn issues."

"That's the life of a superstar." He shrugged. "What's up wit you though? I ain't heard from you in a minute."

"I've been busy," she said shortly.

"I hear that hot shit. So, what's up wit me and you?"

"Nothing," she responded.

"Cassidy." He scratched his head, "I ain't the sharpest knife in the drawer, but I sense you ain't feeling me like that."

"Don't take it personal. A bitch just got a lot on her plate right now. It's still love, boo-boo."

Eve watched the exchange between the two but said nothing. For all the shit Cassidy talked about not belonging to anyone, she still hadn't managed to tell Butter about her involvement with Carlo. Eve continued to watch Cassidy half answer questions and dodge advances until she grew tired of it.

"What's with the extra muscle?" she asked, changing the flow of their conversation. There were two men whom Eve didn't recognize standing near Butter's truck. Teddy was behind the wheel.

"Just some bullshit," he said casually. "Some nigga made a move on me, so Felon suggested that I get some baby-sitters. I told him I'm good, but you know how he can be."

"How is he?" she asked, trying to sound uninterested.

"Why don't you call and ask him? The number is still the same," he said with a wink. Eve responded by giving him the finger.

"Anyhow," he continued, "Cas, we need to hook up, ma. Catch a movie or something."

"I'll call you," she said, brushing him off.

"A'ight." Butter looked at Cassidy sadly. He cared for Cassidy and thought she was starting to get feelings for him, but she was colder than ever. She acted like they had never shared any good times. Fuck her! Cassidy was acting like a typical bitch. He didn't need her; he was a ghetto star and could have any bitch he wanted. Butter said his good-byes and bounced.

"That was some cold shit," Eve said to Cassidy.

"What is it now?" Cassidy asked, as if she didn't want to hear it.

"You ain't always gotta treat him like that. You know how he feels about you."

"Come on with that shit, Eve. It ain't happening between me and Butter. Carlo is taking care of me and I care about him."

"Do you care about him, or what he's doing for you?" Eve asked.

"What's the difference?"

"Big difference, baby girl. All you'll be is a showpiece to him. That dago ain't trying to wife you."

"Look, all I know is he's getting what he wants and I'm getting what I want. Listen to you trying to explain affairs of the heart to me. What you need to do is go to Felon and tell him how you feel, before one of these skank-ass bitches slide up into your spot."

"Please, they can have him," Eve said, folding her arms.

"You can't front for me. I've known you too long. Evelyn."

One of the reasons that Cassidy irritated the hell out of Eve was that, no matter what type of front she tried to put on, Cassidy could see through it. In truth, her heart ached for Felon, but her mind made her numb to it. Felon had been a good confidant to her for a good number of years. If she took that extra step, things would change. And what if it didn't work? Felon was a man and therefore he could only be trusted to a certain extent. She wasn't sure if she was willing to give up a friend for a shot in the dark.

"Listen," Cassidy said, cutting into her thoughts, "we gonna stand out here and bullshit, or you gonna come and help me spend some of Carlo's money?"

Eve looked at Beast, then back to Cassidy.

"Okay, he can come too," Cassidy said reluctantly. The three of them climbed into Cassidy's Acura, with Beast taking up the entire backseat, and headed to the Green Acres Mall.

"Keith, how much longer are you gonna make me wear this blindfold?" Mrs. Johnson asked.

"We're almost there, Ma," Felon assured her. They had been driving for the better part if an hour and Felon's mother was getting restless. Sammy sat in the backseat snickering because he knew about the surprise. After about another twenty minutes, Felon pulled up in a quiet suburb in Westchester County.

"Come on," he said helping his mother out of the car. He lead her a few paces and removed the blindfold. Mrs. Johnson found herself speechless.

It was a small Victorian house, surrounded by neatly trimmed grass. A beautiful L-shaped porch outlined the house, giving it a regal presence. The house wasn't in top condition, but it was still very nice. Once Felon put some work into it, it would be beautiful again.

"What is this?" Mrs. Johnson asked, looking at the house.

"Surprise, Mommy!" Sammy shouted.

"It's for you, Ma," Felon said with a smile.

"How did you—"

"Don't even worry about it," he said, kissing her forehead. "It's bought and paid for, Ma. I've been saving the money for the last couple of years. I know the guy who owned it, so he gave me a good deal."

"I can't believe it," she said, still staring at the house in astonishment.

"Believe it, Ma. It's yours. You can move in as soon as the repairs are finished. You've been taking care of me all my life and I wanted to do something for you."

"Thank you," she said, hugging him. "Thank you so much."

Felon felt a warm tear run down his cheek. All the years of doing dirt were finally starting to pay off. He had been getting money before, but when Carlo had hit him with the new product, his income damn near tripled. Now that he had gotten his mother and little brother out of the way, he could get his grind on without fearing for their safety. It was time to get it popping.

"So, any ideas?" Teddy asked, putting the finishing touches on a blunt of haze.

"Nigga, if I knew who tried to have me killed, they'd be dead," Butter snapped. He didn't admit it to his young'n, but his nerves were fried. He was that nigga in the streets, yet someone had been bold enough to try to lay hands on him. If it hadn't been for Teddy, Butter would've been a statistic. The worst part it, he had crossed so many people there was no telling who had tried to touch him.

"We gotta stay on point," Teddy said, lighting the blunt. "Just because they missed the first time, doesn't mean they're gonna be sloppy with the next hit."

"Them muthafuckas come at me again." Butter picked up the sawed-off that was sitting on the table. "And they gonna go out in a blaze of glory, son."

"Butter, you know I'm always down to bust my hammer for you, but we gotta be smart about this shit. You're a made man, so whoever tried this shit has got balls the size of Canada or be connected to some real powerful muthafuckas. You get into it with anybody lately?"

"Not that I can think of. I mean, I lay my pimp hand down on these suckers on the block, but that shit is usual."

"Nah, Butter," Teddy waved him off. "This shit goes deeper than some block shit. For a muthafucka to try and have you clapped in such a public place has really got a hard on for you. This shit is personal."

"Ted, niggaz hate just for the sake of hating. I'm that nigga on the block, so muthafuckas envy me. I haven't done anything fucked up enough for a nigga to take it personal. Man, for all we know it could've been some random nigga trying to get his stripes."

"Butter, we gotta be overlooking something." Teddy stood up and began pacing the floor. With the blunt hanging out the side of his mouth and his arms folded behind his back, he looked like a black-ass Castro. Suddenly his pacing stopped and he looked at Butter. "What about that nigga from the club?"

"What nigga from the club?" Butter asked, lighting his blunt. The extra blunt doubled the size of the already lingering weed cloud.

"The old head. He was in the club the night Eve came out. You cuffed his jewelery."

"Oh, punk-ass Dre?" Butter chuckled. "That nigga ain't bout shit, fam. He damn sure ain't got the weight or heart to come at me."

"Don't underestimate that cat, B. you embarrassed him in front of his peoples. I know I would've taken that shit real personal."

Butter reclined in the folding chair and scratched his chin. Could Dre think to mount an attack against him? Not likely. He did some dirt back in the day, but he was a nobody in the age of the modern gangsta. To have a hit put on a man of Butter's caliber took paper. Dre was a broke-ass nigga trying to hold onto a legacy. Even if he had held a grudge, why would he have waited so long to move? It had to be someone else.

"I don't think it's Dre." Butter shook his head. "He ain't got the paper. Its gotta be someone else. Maybe even an upstart crew?"

"Fuck it. Either way, we're not gonna be caught slipping. You niggaz is my meal ticket. Can't let you go dying on me," Teddy joked and threw his arm playfully over Butter's shoulder.

Butter had a lot of love for Teddy. Felon had recruited him, but he and Butter seemed to share a lot of the same interest. Violence.

Eve was nearly out on her feet after the day she had had with Cassidy. They hit Green Acres Mall, then drove out to another spot in

New Jersey, with Cassidy stopping in nearly every store. Eve had brought a few items for herself, but Cassidy had gone to work. The fact that she had too many bags to carry on her own was the reason that Eve found herself walking into the den of Carlo De Nardi.

Eve was impressed by the high-rise building. It was a gray structure with a green canopy bearing its address. A balding Hispanic man held the door for them and helped carry the bags across the carpeted lobby to the elevator. The car was plated in gold and didn't have so much as a smudge on it.

They stepped off the elevator onto the eleventh floor. The hallway was carpeted in the same maroon as the lobby. Rows of soft lighting lined the walls, shining a faint glow on the wallpaper. At the end of the hall, a man sat on a stool reading a newspaper. He looked up at Cassidy and spoke into a hand radio. Only after a response came through did he look at Cassidy and wave her forward. Eve followed her friend into the apartment, never once taking her eyes off the bodyguard.

Carlo's apartment was decorated just as she would've expected it to be. The best of everything. From the plush carpet to the expensive furniture, Carlo had set it out. Cassidy left Eve in the living room while she disappeared into the bedroom. Eve took a moment to look around the place. She ran her hands along the edge of his big-screen TV and imagined how a playoff game would look on it. Carlo's stereo system sat in a glass case with two rail-thin speakers flanking them. She was taken by the décor of the place, but her eyes lingered one on side of the room in particular.

Eve moved close to the wall and began to examine the pictures. They depicted what she assumed was Carlo's family. Sicilian men of all shapes and sizes, striking regal poses. As she moved down the line, her eyes came to rest on the last two pictures. The one at the end of the row was of Carlo, and the other was of his father. Something about the man's face made Eve's body shiver. It was as if someone had run an ice cube down the small of her back. For some reason she was afraid.

The closest she had ever come to catching a glimpse of Franko De Nardi was in blurred newspaper clippings. This picture however, depicted him in great detail. His slick hair, the bushy eyebrows. You could look into his cold blue eyes and tell he was a killer. That's probably why Eve felt so creepy looking at him.

After her inspection of the portraits, Eve parked herself on the couch. She was immediately engulfed by the soft leather. She had to readjust herself so as not to look like she was stretched out. After a few minutes passed she began to feel herself getting tired. She wished Cassidy would hurry up so she could drop her off. Just as she was about to call to her friend, she heard shouting.

"What the fuck? You don't know how to knock?" Carlo shouted, still leaning over the plate of cocaine.

"Sorry, I just . . . what the fuck?" Cassidy said, seeing the plate. "Carlo, what's going on?"

"I'm trying to get fucking high. What does it look like?" he asked.

"Since when do you sniff?" she asked.

"Come on, Cas. Don't be a square. It's just a little coke. Geez, you act like you walked in on me hitting the pipe or something. What am I, some fucking junkie here?"

"No, Carlo. It just surprised me."

"Come here," he said, patting his thigh. Cassidy timidly walked over and complied. "Why you gotta act all crazy?" He nuzzled against her earlobe.

"Carlo, how do expect me to act when I come here and find you sniffing coke? Come on now."

"Don't act like I'm the first person you've dealt with that snorts. Don't gimmie that shit. Listen baby," he said, scooping a small amount of powder onto his finger, "this shit is purely recreational. It's so low-grade that you can barely get right. Try a little."

Cassidy frowned her face and turned away from the powder. She knew plenty of people who sniffed, but it wasn't her thing. If weed and drinks couldn't do it, it wouldn't get done. Cassidy refused the coke and got up from Carlo's lap, almost knocking the coke over.

"Fucking-A, Cassidy!"

"I told you, I don't want any!" she shouted.

"You know, you can be a real fucking brat sometimes," he said venomously. "I take better care of you than that fucking shmuck Butter ever did, and all you do is complain. What the fuck is this shit?"

"Hold on," she said, pointing a finger at him, "don't you be coming out ya mouth to me like that. I ain't wanna them hood rat bitches you're used to dealing with. Check ya self!"

"Who the fuck do you think you're talking to?" Before Cassidy could blink, Carlo was standing inches away from her. Seeing the maddened look in his eye caused her to back up a step. Carlo's eyes flashed pure rage as spittle flew from his mouth. "I ain't some fucking street-corner hump! You better watch your fucking mouth. Before I—"

"Before what?" she asked defiantly. Her heart was pumping damn near out of her chest, but she tried her best not to show Carlo that she was afraid.

He stared at her, clenching his fist. Just when Cassidy thought he was about to knock her out, Carlo turned and kicked over the table with the coke. "Shit!" he yelled. "Cassidy, I'm gonna fuck you up one of these days."

"Yeah, right," she said snatching her purse. "This shit is wack!" Cassidy spun and headed for the door.

"So you just gonna leave?" he called after her. "Fuck it then! I don't need you. Run back to the fucking ghetto!"

Eve was on her way down the hall when Cassidy came storming out of the master bedroom. Her face was contorted into a mask of rage, giving Eve pause. Without uttering a word, Cassidy strode past Eve to the front door. Eve looked back at the half-opened bedroom door and could see what looked like sugar spilled on the carpet. After a moment's hesitation, she followed her friend out the door.

Johnny Black sat on a bar stool within the murky recesses of Lucky's bar, listening to Dre rant. Ever since receiving news of the botched hit on Butter he had been a wreck. Johnny wasn't moved at all. It was part of his plan.

"Man, how you gonna fuck it up, Johnny?" Dre asked for the eighth time.

"I told you that I'd take care of it, didn't I?" Johnny asked, looking up from his Pepsi.

"Fuck that shit," Dre said, advancing on the youngster. "You were paid good money for that hit and you fucked it up. I want answers, goddamn it!"

Before Dre could take another step, Johnny was on him. He grabbed Dre about the collar with his right hand and gripped his pistol with the left. Dre tried to pull away, but Johnny spun him around so that Dre's back was now against the bar. Dre's boys tried to move, but Johnny raised the pistol to Dre's head. He flashed a wicked smile at the men, causing them to back up.

"Let me tell you something," Johnny hissed. "First of all, you watch how you talk to me, muthafucka. I done put enough niggaz to sleep, so laying yo bum ass out is light. Second of all, it might be your beef, but it sure as hell ain't your bread paying for this boy's nap. You're acting like you run things all of a sudden. What kind of fucking fool do you take me for? I know it's Carlo's money that's paying for this hit. You're just a fall guy in case something goes wrong. Ass-munch. I does this shit here, so be the fuck cool and let me handle my business. We understand each other?" Dre nodded. "Good," Johnny said, pushing him roughly on the bar.

Still holding his pistol at his side, Johnny backed out of the bar. Dre and his crew looked at him angrily, but no one moved to try and stop him. If Johnny hadn't proven anything else, he had proven that he was quite dangerous.

* * *

Butter coasted down Lenox Avenue at about five miles an hour. He had a blunt hanging out of his mouth and Big Tymers' "1 Stunner" blasting from his speakers. He was smiling and waving like the president as people admired his new red CLK with the red and gold rims. It was one of the two new cars he had purchased since becoming the man. He was truly playing the roll of a ghetto star.

At 116th he cut over to 7th then made his way back up toward 118th. He double-parked the CLK in front the T-shirt spot and checked the clip of the P89 that rode in the passenger seat. After tucking the gun in his waistband, he hopped out of the ride and greeted his public.

A group of young men were posted up on the corner, watching Butter with envy. He knew that they were sizing him up, but he also knew that they were aware of who he was, so they wouldn't try him. The word had gotten out about his little phantom war and he was taking no prisoners.

Butter went into the store and purchased a 5X black T-shirt. He slipped the black T-shirt over the bulletproof vest that he had taken to wearing and looped his dinner plate–sized medallion back around his neck. It was hot as hell, and the vest had him sweating like a runaway slave, but he couldn't afford to take chances. It was like Teddy said, "Just because they missed once, doesn't mean they'll miss again." If a nigga did come for him, they'd be in for the shock of their life. In addition to the P89 he carried, his trusty sawed-off was tucked in the backseat.

When Butter came out of the store, he noticed that a young lady had joined the group of dudes on the corner. She was dark skinned with an ass shaped like an apple. Just by her body language, he could tell that she was a hood bitch. Just like he liked them. The young men were trying to lay their mack game down, but they had nothing on Butter.

He stood in front of the store until he made eye contact with the girl. When he was sure he had her attention, he walked slowly to his ride. Even without looking back, he could still feel her eyes on him. Butter leaned against the car and gave her a seductive look. He paused momentarily, then motioned for the girl to come to him. Like a hypnosis patient, she did as he requested. The young men shot them angry looks and cursed under their breath, but they didn't want it with one of Harlem's new kings.

"What's up, baby?" he said, licking his lips.

"Chilling," she said, looking from him to the car. "What's up wit you?"

"Trying to figure out what you're doing over there with them lil niggaz, instead of checking for the kid."

"Oh, yeah? And who are you that I should be checking for?"

"I'm that nigga, baby. You ain't know?"

"Is that right?" she said, placing her hands on her hips.

"Indeed it is, boo. Listen, fuck the dumb shit. Why don't you hop in and go for a spin with me? We can get to know each other and shit," he said, adjusting his crotch.

"I don't be hopping in niggaz' cars I don't know."

"The name is Butter, baby, aka Butter soft, aka every woman's dream."

She chuckled. "You're a funny guy."

"You don't know the half." He smiled. "Listen, boo. I'd love to stand out here kicking the shit with you, but time is money. Either you're rolling, or you ain't." Butter didn't wait for an answer. He walked around to the driver's side and got behind the wheel. Before he could start the car, the girl had hopped in. By the time he made it to 135th, he had his dick buried in her throat. Yes, he truly was the number-one stunner.

21.

It had been several days since the incident at Carlo's, but it was still on Eve's mind. Cassidy was upset about something, but she was closemouthed during the ride back to the hood. Eve brought it up a few more times, but Cassidy would always brush it off. She didn't want to pry. When her friend wanted to speak on it, she would.

"Come on, Monster," Beast said, pulling a large pit bull behind him. Monster was a wreck of a beast. He had patchy gray fur and one eye. His head was easily as large as a ten-pound bowling ball, and the dog weighed at least eighty pounds. Beast had found Monster about a month or so after Eve got locked up. He had lost a fight and the owner had left him to die in a lot. Luckily for the dog, Beast found him and was able to save his life. They had been together ever since.

"That muthafucka's gonna bite you one day," Eve teased him. She hiked through the grass beside him wearing a pair of blue denim shorts that were tight around the ass and thigh. Leaves crunched under her three-quarter Timberlands.

"Nah, ah. Monster is a good boy," Beast assured her, patting him on the head.

They strolled through the park for a few more blocks and exited on 116th Street. When they stepped from the park, there was a group of girls sitting on the bench, smoking a blunt. Eve didn't know the girls, but she recognized Sheeka sitting with them.

"Sup, sis?" Eve said, walking over.

"What's good, Eve?" Sheeka responded between pulls.

"Chilling. What your lil ass doing, sitting on the parkside, getting high?"

"It's only weed," Sheeka said, trying to justify it.

"The shit is still a drug. Let me holla at you for a second." Eve motioned for Sheeka to follow her out of earshot. When they had gotten a few feet away, she said, "What's up wit Cas?"

"Damned if I know." Sheeka shrugged. "I don't see that chick like that."

"Don't y'all live in the same house?"

"Yeah, but Cassidy is hardly home. She pops up once and a while, but she always with that Carlo cat. What's his story, Eve?"

"Bad news," Eve said flatly. "You notice anything strange from the few times she does come around?"

"Not that I could tell. Something going on?"

"I don't know, Sheeka. That's what I'm trying to find out."

"That nigga better not be fucking with my sister!" Sheeka said, heatedly.

"Calm down, sis. I didn't say anything was going on, Sheeka. I'm just making sure Cassidy is good. Just keep your eyes and your ears open for me."

"I got you, Eve."

Eve and Sheeka returned to the girls on the bench. Sheeka resumed her session, and Eve left with Beast. She told herself that she was just being overly protective of Cassidy, but something in her gut told her that something was up with Carlo. Fuck it. Cassidy was a grown woman and totally capable of handling herself. Carlo might've been caked up, but he was hardly stupid.

* * *

Felon sat at a back table inside of One Fish Two Fish, picking over a lobster tail. Every time he came to the restaurant he ordered the same thing. Steak with a lobster tail. He savored the rich taste of the Maine lobster, smothered with butter and a twist of lemon. As he took another mouthful of the shellfish, he reflected on the days when he couldn't afford to eat lobster. That was a long time ago. Ever since they had started moving the new product, Felon could afford to eat whatever he wanted.

Carlo had stayed true to his word and they were seeing long paper. Felon and his family would be moving into their new house at the end of the month. Life was good. But for all the riches he was gaining, he still felt empty. The game was good to him, but he was still alone. He was never shy of company, cause every chick wanted to see the man who was holding the bag. But they were just jump-offs. What he lacked was someone to share his accomplishments with.

These were the times when he thought of Eve. She had grown up and filled out quite nicely. Over the last few weeks he had made it a point to avoid her. It seemed as if when he was around her, the beast in him screamed to come out. Many a night he envisioned what it might be like to be inside her. The other night at the club, every fiber of him said to go home and give her the fucking of her life. He felt almost ashamed to think about her like that, but he was a man and she was a woman. It was the natural law of things.

There was so much he needed to say to her, but he couldn't find the words. There were times that he would post up in the hood and just watch her move. The man in him said to approach her and express himself, but the coward in him made him watch from a distance.

He had considered just taking her off to the side and letting her know what time it was, but then what? What if she reciprocated the feelings and they took it a step beyond friendship? Felon already had an idea how that would end up. He'd fuck her, then when he got bored, he'd cast her to the side. He told himself that he loved her and it would be different, but the sad fact was that he didn't know how to be any other way.

Felon's meal was interrupted when he spotted Carlo's Benz pull up. This was the reason he chose to sit facing the window. He could see anyone approaching the restaurant. He sat tapping his fork as Big Steve held the door for his boss. Carlo didn't even look around when he came in. He nodded to the hostess and made his way to Felon's table. Without waiting for an invitation, Carlo sat in the chair opposite Felon.

"What's up, buddy?" Carlo smiled.

"How'd you know I was here?" Felon asked.

"Man, we're like the feds. We know everything, pissan. What you got there?" Carlo asked, looking at Felon's plate.

"Carlo," Felon began, putting his fork down, "no disrespect, but is there a reason you're here?"

"Isn't there always a reason?" Carlo smiled. "I need to talk to you about your boy."

"Butter? What about him?"

"I hear he's been pretty busy?"

"Business ain't gonna handle itself," Felon replied flatly.

"Yeah, I know, but when does handling business become excess?"

"Carlo, what are you getting at?" Felon asked, beginning to get an idea of where the conversation was going.

"I'm talking about all the attention he's drawing to himself and us."

"Really?" Felon asked, playing dumb.

"Come on, Felon," Carlo said, helping himself to a potato on Felon's plate. "You an I both know what I'm talking about. This guy acts like he's the mayor or something. He's riding up and down Eighth Avenue doing doughnuts in a seventy-five thousand dollar automobile. What the fuck, Felon? People downtown are gonna start asking questions about him sooner or later. Questions that my people might not wanna answer. You know what I'm saying?"

"Come on, Carlo. You know Butter is excessive. He just high-balls a bit."

"If he wanted to high-ball, he should've stayed on the corner," Carlo spat. "Not only is he flashing, his name got attached to a murder on a Hundred and Twenty-fifth. What kind of shit is that? We're not doing some small numbers anymore, pal. We play this right and we'll all be rich. I don't need some cowboy who ain't used to nothing fucking that up!"

"I'll talk to Butter," Felon said, sipping his water.

"If you say so," Carlo said, standing, "but this shit is still bad for business. We can't have Butter running like he doesn't have any home training. It doesn't look good on my family or yours. You better talk some sense into him before it's out of your hands."

"I said I'll talk to him."

"I know you will, Felon. Just hope he listens." Carlo nodded and headed for the door. Felon sat there wondering what Butter might've gotten himself into, and what kind of position it put him in. He dropped some money on the table and left the restaurant.

Cassidy stood at the counter in Macy's paying for her purchase. After the incident with Carlo, she had refused to see him for a few days. She wouldn't take his calls or see him. Carlo had tried sending her gifts, but she sent them back. The only reason she accepted this gift was because Carlo had finally started speaking a language she understood. Cash.

Cassidy's cell rang off, causing her to put her bags down to answer it. She hoped it wasn't Carlo checking in on her, cause she really didn't feel like talking to him just yet. She had people to see and plans to make. Without checking the caller ID, she answered the phone with an attitude.

"Yeah, who is this?"

"Hold on, ma," Butter said. "It's me."

"Oh, sorry, Butter," she said, feeling a little silly.

"Everything cool with you?" he asked, concerned.

"Yeah, just some hood shit. What made you decide to dial my number?"

"Just wanted to see what was up with you. What, that nigga so far up your ass he screening your calls?" he joked.

"Not even. I'm still me, nigga."

"I hear that. Yo, I wanted to see if you was coming through the spot tomorrow night."

"What's going down tomorrow?" she asked, switching hands between the bag and her cell.

"How you gonna forget Felon's birthday?"

"Damn, I forgot he had a birthday coming up. But it ain't til like next week, right?"

"Yeah, it's in a few days. We decided to do something a little early, though. You know Twenty-Gang gotta come out."

"All day," she agreed. "I'll holla at the girls and we'll swing through. Butter, how did you get that stiff-ass nigga to agree to a party?"

"Cause he doesn't know it's a party. He think we going out for drinks, on some niggaz, shit."

"You know he's gonna be mad."

"Fuck it. We gotta do it up for son. Make sure you bring Eve."

Cassidy laughed. "There you go."

"For real. She need to quit fronting and give my man some pussy. Why don't you holla at her?"

"Please, boy. I ain't got no control over Joe-Joe's pussy."

"Just make sure you bring her, and wear that dress that I like to see you in."

"Don't start that. But look, I gotta go. Hit me tomorrow with the details and I'll make sure the home girls show out."

"A'ight, ma. One."

Cassidy ended the call with Butter and smiled. It was nice to hear from him. She gave him grief when she was with him, but she kind of missed what they had. At least Butter showered her with attention. She decided that she would wear that dress for him. Carlo could show his ass all he wanted, cause Cassidy knew that none of the other bitches he was dealing with had anything on her.

No sooner had Butter hung up with Cassidy than someone was ringing his doorbell. He grabbed his sawed-off from the coffee table and eased to the door. Careful not to put his body in the line of fire if someone should shoot through door, Butter leaned over to the peephole. When he saw who it was, he lowered the shotgun and opened the door.

"What da deal, B?" Butter asked as Felon brushed past him.

"Maintaining," Felon said, crossing the living room and hitting the bar. "I hear you been a busy man."

"You know how I do," Butter said modestly.

"Ghetto superstar." Felon smiled and sipped his drink.

"I can't help it if the hood loves me." Butter popped his collar.

"Butter, it's okay to have love in the hood, but don't you think you might be overdoing it a bit?"

"Fuck that." Butter waved him off. "I'm enjoying my life. I'm getting money!"

"Just because you're getting money doesn't mean you have to tell the world. We gotta keep a low profile with our shit."

"Low profile? Nigga, is you crazy? Do you hear Jay-Z telling Dame Dash to keep a low profile? Hell, no. Them niggaz is balling out of control. They earned their paper, and they're flossing it."

"Butter, they also have legal holdings to account for their balling," Felon pointed out. "You ain't got shit to account for this here," his arms swept the plush apartment. "You want the Feds breathing down your neck?"

"Fuck the Feds! If they wanna come, let em come. I'll tell you this much. By the time they catch up with me, I'll have lived one hell of a life."

Felon massaged his temples in frustration. Talking to Butter was like talking to a brick wall. He understood where his man came from, so it was only right for him to wanna enjoy his money. But his behavior could potentially bring heat that neither of them needed. Felon had too much invested in their move to let Butter's wild-ass ways fuck it up.

"Fuck this shit." Butter patted him on the back. "If it'll get you to stop bitching, I'll be easy with my profiling. You done crying now?"

"Fuck you," Felon shot back. "I'm trying to keep you free long enough to enjoy this paper, kid."

"I ain't going nowhere, Felon. I'm gonna handle my end and we gonna see paper."

"A'ight," Felon sighed, giving him dap. "I'll holla at you later." Felon walked from Butter's apartment, hoping that was the last warning he'd have to issue, but knowing it wasn't.

22.

"I can't believe I let y'all talk me into this shit," Eve said, tugging at her blouse.

"Why don't you stop whining?" Cassidy sucked her teeth. "You act like one night away from the block is gonna kill you. You need to get out more often."

"Besides, you look cute, Eve." Sheeka winked.

Eve had been getting compliments all night. After quite a bit of convincing, she had agreed to let Cassidy and Sheeka gas her into a girls' night out. Cassidy claimed she felt like she wasn't spending enough time with her peoples. Eve didn't really want to go, but she agreed to anyway.

Eve had on a pair of tight-fitting, black, three-quarter knickers. From the rear her ass looked like a heart. Her black Prada sandals criss-crossed up her toned calves, giving her more of a brick-house appeal. She wore a sleeveless white top that caressed her delicate neck and was tied off in the front, showing off her tight abs. Sheeka had flat-twisted Eve's hair into spirals that snaked up the side and back of her head.

"I ain't staying long." Eve folded her arms.

"Don't be like that," Cassidy said, pulling her along. "Our click is gonna be up in there. We're gonna get drunk and have fun."

"Y'all can get drunk. Somebody's gotta stay sober so you don't end up playing yourselves."

"Whatever," Cassidy said, pulling her friend through the doors of The Sugar Shack. "Just come on." She tried to contain a smile, knowing who Eve would encounter once they got inside.

The bouncers barely spared the girls a second look as they crossed the threshold. There were a good amount of people inside the lounge, but it wasn't crowded. As Eve and her crew passed by the one of the tables, a kid sporting a wavy czar touched her hand. Eve glanced at him but kept moving. She thought that he was attractive, but she figured she'd just have a few drinks and keep it easy. All that changed when she saw Felon sitting at one of the tables in the back.

Felon and Teddy were crying-laughing as they watched Butter try to sing along with an R. Kelly song to a young lady he was dancing with. He half stumbled, half swayed, clutching a bottle of champagne, trying to hit the high note. It was an act of pure comedy.

Felon sipped on his Remy and continued to talk shit with his boys. He didn't want to come out at first, but he was glad that he did. He had been so consumed by the hustle that he rarely got to enjoy his life. He missed being able to just kick it with his peoples and talk shit. A shadow looming over him caused Felon to turn around. His breath was almost stolen from him when he saw Eve standing behind Cassidy and Sheeka.

He caught her eye and immediately felt his heart begin to pump faster. It had been a while since he had been in such close proximity to Eve and she was looking damn good. Looking at the tricks the lights were playing on the warm shades of her hair made him want to reach out and run his fingers through it. Felon almost gave deed to thought, but settled on a simple hello.

"What's up, nigga?" Cassidy sang.

"Sup, Cas. What y'all doing in here?" he asked.

"I invited them," Butter cut in, draping a drunk arm over Eve's shoulder. "Damn, you looking good, baby girl."

"Get yo drunk ass off me." Eve removed his arm.

"Oh, shit. I don't want Felon getting mad at me for touching on his boo."

"Why you play so much?" Felon said, embarrassed as hell.

"Cause he's a silly muthafucka," Eve said.

"Teddy, why don't you get up and let a lady sit down?" Cassidy suggested.

"A'ight, damn," he said, sliding off the chair.

"As a matter of fact, Sheeka wants a drink." Cassidy said.

"I do?" Sheeka asked, dumbfounded.

"Yes, you do." Finally catching the hint, Sheeka went off with Teddy to the bar. "What's good in the hood, Felon?" Cassidy picked up. "Ain't seen you in a while."

"I could say the same for you," he said, giving Cassidy a look like he knew something he wasn't supposed to.

"I've been around."

"Fuck that," Butter said, "we need some drinks." He summoned the waitress, who took their orders, then went to fetch them.

After the drinks arrived at the table the quartet sipped champagne and made small talk. Eve found herself sipping a little faster than she normally would out of nervousness. Every time she looked at Felon, she couldn't help but think how much she wanted him. His shape-up was crisp as usual and he smelled like roses. More than once she thought she felt a dampness in her panties.

Felon tried to be discreet with the lustful glances he was sending Eve's way. He had never seen her wear her hair like that, but he liked the style on her. It made her look regal. Her lids were lightly brushed with a mahogany powder and her lips painted to match. Every time she laughed or shifted her position, his eyes went to her ample breasts, which looked like they were threatening to spill from her shirt. When her scent wafted into his nose, his dick began to rise ever so slightly.

Throughout the whole evening, Felon and Eve made it a point to avoid eye contact. They conversed with the rest of the group, but there was no intimacy to it. Cassidy excused herself to go to the lady's room, leaving Eve with Butter and Felon. At least she hadn't left them alone. Things were awkward, but everyone was having a good time. That all changed when Carlo walked in.

"Fuck invited this nigga?" Butter said venomously.

"Fuck should I know? It was your little plan," Felon answered.

"Butter, don't start," Eve warned. "I gotta use the bathroom." Eve got up and went to warn her friend just before Carlo made it to their table.

"Sup, fellas?" Carlo greeted them.

"Chilling, Carlo," Felon replied.

Butter just nodded.

"I see you guys are in here having a good time," Carlo said, inviting himself to a seat.

"It was kind of a private party," Butter said, staring directly at Carlo.

"Oh, was I interrupting?" asked Carlo, but he made no move to get up.

"Nah, you're good," Felon cut in. "We're just having some drinks for my birthday."

"Your birthday? This calls for a celebration." Carlo motioned for the waitress and requested three more bottles of champagne. "It's not every day a man gets to celebrate one more year on earth."

"It's just another day to me, man," Felon said.

"What, are you kidding? It's a freak'n joyous occasion. Some guys don't get to make it to their prime."

"We wouldn't know nothing about that," Butter added to the mix. "Me and my niggaz is gonna live forever."

"Wishful thinking." Carlo smiled.

On the other side of the lounge, Eve and Cassidy moved silently along the bar. Cassidy had thrown a fit when Eve delivered the news about Carlo being there. She was having a good time, and he was sure to blow it. Eve convinced her that they should just leave and make up a story to tell Butter and Felon another time. In all truthfulness, Eve just wanted to be away from Felon.

They slipped back and forth through the crowd of people, trying to find Sheeka so they could go. They spotted her across the room, lounging with Teddy, and moved to retrieve her. Cassidy had successfully made it to where her sister was sitting without being seen. Now all they had to do was slide out and no one would be the wiser. That's around the time when Butter's drunk ass blew it up.

"Cas!" he shouted from across the room. "Where you going, ma?"

Cassidy turned slowly in his direction and smiled. Carlo was sitting on the other side of Felon, but she could see him staring at her. This was the last thing she needed. If Butter was going to find out about her and Carlo, she didn't want it to be like this. There was nothing she could do about it at that point but put on her game face.

"You leaving?" Butter asked as Cassidy approached the table followed by Teddy and Sheeka, with Eve bringing up the rear.

"Nah, I was checking on Sheeka," Cassidy lied.

"I wasn't gonna hurt her," Teddy joked.

"Hey, Cas," Carlo spoke up.

"What's up?" she said with a weak smile.

"Y'all know each other?" Butter asked, surprised. He kept looking from Cassidy to Carlo. Eve just put her head down.

"Sure we do," he said, smiling.

Butter saw the sarcastic look on Carlo's face, and Cassidy wouldn't look at him at all. Suddenly it all made sense to him. "Hold up. This is why you stopped fucking wit me?" asked Butter, pointing at Carlo.

"Hold up, Butter . . ."

"Hold up my ass," he cut her off. "Cassidy, you fucking with Carlo?" Her silence was enough of an answer for him. "Muthafucka!" Butter rose from his seat, holding the champagne bottle. Big Steve took a step in the direction of the table, but Teddy blocked his path. He didn't draw his weapon, but his eyes told Steve that he wouldn't hesitate. The situation was about to get very ugly. Just as the violence was about to pop off, Felon rose and stood between them.

"Ease up, my nigga. Don't do it like that," Felon said, placing a hand on Butter's chest.

"Don't do it like that?" Butter slurred. "What about how they did it?"

"Butter, I'm not your girl. It's not like I was creeping on you by seeing Carlo." Cassidy said defensively.

"Cassidy, don't even try to justify this shit. Yeah, you might not be my man's girl, but you were fucking him. Now you're fucking his partner? Yo, shit like that can get a nigga killed." Felon said venomously.

"It ain't that serious, Felon. It's just a piece of trim." Carlo said mockingly.

"Fuck you!" Butter snapped, trying to get at Carlo.

"Cool out," Felon said, restraining Butter.

"You watch your fucking self," Carlo warned, pointing a finger at Butter. "Felon, you better teach this guy some manners before he gets himself fucked up."

"Everybody, calm the fuck down! Carlo, hold them threats," Felon demanded. "Ain't nothing popping off in here tonight. Butter, put the fucking bottle down. Now!"

Butter's face was still twisted into a mask of rage. Cassidy had hurt him very deeply. He would've dealt with it a little better if she had gone outside his camp, but she had the nerve to fuck someone he did business with on the regular basis. The more he thought about it, the madder he got. He knew that if he didn't put some space between himself and the turncoats something was going to happen.

Eve watched the exchange, holding her breath. She knew that something would end up happening because of Cassidy's poor choices in men. At first she thought Butter was going to press the issue and crash Carlo with the bottle, but to her surprise, he just kicked the table over and headed for the door. As he passed her, she could see the hurt in his eyes. Not really caring to be around for the fallout, Eve slid out behind Butter.

"What kind of bullshit is this?" Felon asked, looking from Carlo to Cassidy.

Carlo shrugged. "Hey, your boy flipped out."

"Carlo, you knew he was seeing Cassidy, so why fuck with her? You violated, son."

"Felon, Butter is *your* boy. I do business with *you,* and *you* do business with *him.* I ain't got nothing to do with that arrangement," Carlo said. "I was attracted to Cassidy, she was attracted to me, and the rest is history. I don't hang with the kid, so how did I violate?"

Technically, Carlo had a point. He and Butter did business together, but it's not like they had a personal relationship. Cassidy was looking for a come-up and Carlo was giving her what she wanted; he was just getting some pussy in the exchange. That still didn't change the fact that what they did was fucked up. Butter had genuine love for Cassidy, and she totally disregarded it by the snake move she pulled.

"Felon, I know you're tight, but I didn't mean any disrespect. She told me that she didn't mess with him like that," Carlo told him.

"Yo, Cas. I'm real disappointed in you. You're supposed to have more class than that," Felon said coldly.

Cassidy was momentarily speechless. The words stung, but coming from Felon's mouth made them hurt more. They had grown up together and shared many a good time over the years. She thought about crying, but didn't want to give either of them the satisfaction. "Fuck this," she said, storming out the door.

Carlo called after her, but she never stopped. Felon just flared his nostrils and stared at Carlo. Sheeka looked around, wondering what had just happened, and went to join her sister.

"I had so much love for that girl, Eve," Butter sobbed into the bottle. He had held his cool when he was inside the lounge, but once he was alone, he let himself go. Eve had walked up the block and found him on a stoop, sobbing.

"It's all good," she rubbed his back.

"I ain't all good," he insisted, guzzling from the bottle. "I know Cassidy is a girl that likes to have nice shit, so I tried to give her what she wanted. I guess my paper wasn't long enough?"

Butter continued to rant while Eve tried to console him. A few minutes later, Eve saw Cassidy and Sheeka come out of the lounge. Cassidy stared in their direction, but Eve waved her off. There was no telling what the alcohol and his sorrow would cause Butter to do if he saw her. Eve motioned that she would call Cassidy, to which she nodded and left.

The next person to come out was Felon. He paced back and forth in front of the spot, trying to kill a Newport in three pulls. He glared over at Butter but didn't move in their direction. Even from a few yards up, Eve could see the hurt in Felon's eyes. He looked like he had the weight of the world on his shoulders. In a sense he did. Carlo had been a valuable asset to them and their cause, but the bad blood between him and Butter was threatening to spoil that.

"How is he?" Felon asked, finally approaching them.

"He'll be a'ight," Eve responded.

"She dissed me, fam," Butter slurred.

Felon wanted to bark on Butter, but he knew his friend was going through something. This was the reason why he didn't want to get close to anyone. The hurt a female could inflict on you was worse than a gunshot. Gunshot wounds heal, but broken hearts could only be treated.

"Get up," Felon said, helping Butter off the stoop. "Time to go home."

"Fucking played me!" Butter yelled, nearly causing Felon to fall over.

"Let me help you," Eve said, taking Butter's other arm.

"Damn, that nigga twisted," Teddy said, approaching the spectacle.

"Shut up and go get the car," Felon snapped. Teddy laughed and did as he was told. "I got it, Eve."

She sucked her teeth. "Stop trying to be so fucking hard and let me help you get him home. I care about Butter too."

Felon glared at Eve but didn't try to force her to go. Together they helped Butter into the back of the truck. Teddy drove while Felon sat in the passenger's seat. Eve rode in the back, keeping a damp paper towel pressed against Butter's forehead.

"I'm sick of niggaz!" Cassidy shouted, taking her clothes off.

"Stop yelling," Sheeka complained from her bed.

"I'm for real," Cassidy said. "I'm tired of these muthafuckas and the headaches they bring with them."

"Face it, you slipped up. You bought this headache on yourself, big sis. What made you think you could dangle both of them niggaz and not get caught?"

"I wasn't *dangling* nobody. Butter wasn't my man, and Carlo was taking care of me. I ain't do shit wrong."

Sheeka yawned. "Then why are you so damn mad?"

"I'm not mad. I'm sick. Sick with men and all their shit!"

"So you gonna switch to girls?" Sheeka joked.

"I said sick, not crazy."

"Cas, forget about that shit. It was fun while it lasted."

"Fuck both of them. I'm that bitch," Cassidy declared, climbing into her bed. Butter and Carlo could both go to hell. It would only be a matter of time before something else came along. The sisters talked for a while longer, then decided to turn it in. Before long, they were both fast asleep and men troubles were totally forgotten.

23.

Eve and Felon dragged Butter through the apartment door. He was damn near out on his feet, so it was no easy task. To make matters worse, he stank to high hell. On the way home, Butter had started throwing up out the rear window of the truck. Dried vomit stained his chin and the front of his shirt. With some effort they managed to get Butter to his bedroom. They tossed him on the bed, but he continued snoring. He was out like a light.

Felon proceeded to remove Butter's shoes so he could sleep comfortably. Eve watched, admiring Felon for being such a good friend. This was one of the reasons she was so attracted to him. Felon was a hood nigga, but he was also very compassionate. She watched his muscles rippling beneath his shirt as he performed his task. Eve found herself reaching out to touch him but pulled back. She quickly exited the room, leaving Felon to his task.

Carlo sat in the middle of his living room, snorting cocaine and drinking Dominican rum. He couldn't believe that Butter had tried to raise up on him. Butter had to know that if he laid his hands on him, it was a death sentence, but he had tried it anyway. It was amazing what the power of the pussy could do to some men. Cassidy had great pussy, so Carlo totally understood.

Speaking of Cassidy, what was he to do about his little ghetto flower? Carlo knew it would only be a matter of time before the black bitch became a headache. Cassidy was a pro in bed and after some coaxing, even participated in some of Carlo's little games. He hadn't got her to sleep with him and another woman yet, but it was on his list. He had fun with her, and thought that he might even keep her around for a while. She was angry, but it would blow over. Toss her a few dollars and she'd be right back on his dick. She might not have snorted or smoked, but she was an addict like the rest.

Eve was sitting on Butter's couch, sipping a glass of juice, when Felon came out of the bedroom. She had kicked off her sandals and was flexing her toes in the plush carpet. Felon hadn't noticed them in the club, but in soft living room lights he surveyed her airbrushed toenails. They were the same silver and black orchid print that coated her nails. Felon managed to tear his gaze away from her long enough to make his way to the bar. He poured himself a glass of Henny and joined her on the couch.

"I see you made yourself at home," he joked.

"I figured you were gonna be a while. Besides, me feet were starting to hurt," she said, wiggling her toes.

"I know how it be with the bunions." He nudged her.

"Boy, please. Ain't nobody got no bunions." They shared a brief laugh, then there was silence. This was the first time they had been alone together. She pretended to be watching the television, but she was really looking at Felon. In that light, he still looked like the teenaged boy she used to pull heists with. From his flawless black skin to his angular jaw, he was still as intriguing to her as he had been back then.

Felon could tell Eve was looking at him. If there was one thing he learned from being in the streets, it was to be able to tell when someone was clocking you. Felon could feel his palms beginning to sweat. It was funny how even at that age a girl could make him feel like that. Maybe it was being so close to her, or it could've been the liquor, but Felon could feel heat mounting in his gut. Usually they had someone to act as a buffer, but this particular evening he and Eve were alone.

"What you looking at?" he said, catching her off guard.

"I ain't looking at you," she said, sticking her tongue out. Between the heat and the alcohol, Eve found herself feeling playful.

"You know your face could freeze like that."

"Bullshit." She fanned him off.

"It's true."

"Well, you know your liver could rot, drinking that shit," she shot back.

"As if you care," Felon said, emptying his glass and getting up to get another.

"Cut it out, Felon. You know I got love for all y'all crazy asses."

"I don't doubt it," he said, returning to the couch with his glass, "but that ain't the kind of love I'm talking about." Felon shocked himself with that statement. He had been thinking it, but he hadn't intended on saying it. The liquor had loosened his tongue and he had put it out there. He couldn't take it back now.

Cassidy was awakened by the chirping of her cell phone. She sucked her teeth in frustration, because she had just dropped off to sleep not long before. Without looking at the caller ID, she answered it with a major attitude.

Sheeka too was awakened by the late-night call. She wondered who the hell it might be calling at that hour, but with Cassidy, you never could tell. She lay there, pretending to be asleep, while Cassidy exchanged heated words with whoever was on the other end. After about five minutes of going back and forth, Cassidy ended the call. Glad that her sister's late-night drama hadn't cut too deep into her rest, Sheeka dropped back off to sleep.

* * *

"Felon, what you talking about?" Eve asked, knowing full well what he meant.

"Baby girl," he said, gathering his courage, "how long we gonna play this game?" He touched her thigh gently.

"Felon, your ass is tipsy. Let's not go there right now." Eve tried to get up, but he pulled her back down. He used a little more force than he intended and she landed on his lap. He thought she was going to pull away again, but to his surprise she didn't. They sat there for a while, gazing at each other.

"Evelyn, why don't you want me?"

She opened her mouth to answer, but nothing came out. Looking into his beautiful brown eyes, Eve couldn't think of anything but the emotions that she had kept locked away for so long. Eve wanted to tell him how she felt. She wanted to tell him that she had wanted him for as long as she could remember, but the words escaped her. This is when Felon did the unexpected.

Slowly he leaned into Eve's space. She wanted to pull back, but her heart wouldn't let her. Before she could ask him to stop, their lips met. Felon kissed her deeply, tenderly. Tiny shocks shot from her toes to the top of her head. As if moving of its own accord, her tongue met his and performed a lover's dance.

Felon eased her back on the couch and undid Eve's blouse. He kissed her neck and worked his way down to her breasts. Just above her left breast there was a tattoo of the number 20 with wings on either side. Beneath the tat, she still carried the bullet wound from the night of her parent's execution. When he unclamped her bra, her breasts popped out and called to him. They sat up like two golden mounds. Her already erect nipples stiffened even more under his gentle kisses. They explored each others' bodies with fingers and hungry kisses. She gently nibbled at his neck, causing Felon to moan in ecstasy.

Eve wanted Felon as bad as she wanted her freedom when she was locked down. She popped open his shirt and began to lick his muscular chest. When he undid her pants, she didn't resist. Eve could feel her sex begin to warm and moisten. She took his hand and guided it down to her pussy. Felon gently inserted his finger into her, and Eve gasped. He felt so good that she could feel herself releasing in his hand. He slid her pants down and began to kiss her stomach. Felon worked his way down to her clit.

When his tongue entered her, it felt like liquid fire. She had heard Cassidy and the others talk about what oral sex felt like, but she never imagined that it would be like this. He licked her like an ice-cream cone on a summer day. She grabbed his head and begged him not to stop. When he felt like he was about to explode, Felon removed a condom from his pocket and moved over to enter her. Eve pressed her hands against his chest to stop him.

"What's wrong, baby?" he panted.

"What if Teddy comes up?" she asked.

"Don't worry about him. He'll call first," he said, kissing her again. "Eve, baby. I've wanted you for so long, let me make love to you." He resumed planting kisses on her and stealthily slipped the condom on.

Eve melted under his touch. Her body quaked as tiny sparks flickered and died in every one of her nerve endings. After all this time, she was about to give herself to the man she truly loved. No matter how wrong her logical brain told her it was, her heart and the moisture building in her pussy told her it was right. She would have this man, but she had to lay her cards on the table first.

"Felon, before we do this, I need to know it's real." She said.

"Oh, it's real as can be, ma. I want to be inside you, and you want me inside you." He said, playing with her moist clit. "Let me in, boo."

"Felon, I've never done this before," she told him.

Felon stared down at her with raised eyebrows. "You're a virgin?" he asked, totally surprised. Eve sucked her teeth in embarrassment. "Hold on, baby." He stroked her cheek. "It's cool. I just didn't know you were a virgin."

"Something wrong with that?" she asked defensively.

"No, no, baby. That's cool. I just didn't know. That's all. I'll be gentle."

Eve was still hesitant, but once he began kissing her belly again, she loosened up. He tried to position her on the couch so she would be as comfortable as possible, but to his surprise, she opted to get on the floor. She slid down onto the carpet and waited for him to join her. He balanced himself on his arms so she wouldn't be crushed under the weight. On his first attempt at entering her, Eve flinched and scooted back.

He crawled up to where she was lying and wrapped one arm tenderly around her waist. He gazed deeply into her eyes and she could've sworn he mouthed "I love you." They looked into each other's eyes as he slowly began entering her.

As soon as he got the head in, she tensed and dug her nails into his back. Her love tunnel was the tightest he had ever felt, slowly yielding, allowing him entry. Felon had to clench his teeth together in order to keep from crying out. Eve felt like heaven. Slowly and methodically he began to stroke her. She panted helplessly and soon they established a rhythm.

Felon pumped into her and Eve threw it back. The pain had faded and she was floating on a cloud. If she had known sex was that good, she might not have waited so long. She moaned and cursed as Felon took her to highs that the weed or the liquor never could. Tears rolled down her cheeks as she came over and over. Felon came shortly after and the two lay in each others' arms, spent.

When Teddy dropped Eve and Felon off in front of Butter's building, he figured they would be a while, so he decided to get some work done. There were still some unturned stones relating to Butter's attempted murder that needed to be looked into. After stopping to pick some extra muscle, he hit the streets in search of his prey.

Teddy sat slouched behind the wheel of the Tahoe, smoking a blunt and observing the street directly in front of him. He had been watching the tiny bar for the last hour, but nothing eventful had happened yet. The two goons in the backseat were beginning to get antsy. They were soldiers, and recon wasn't one of their strong points.

"Yo, we've been here for hours," a nobody named Rocco complained.

"And we'll be here as long as it takes," Teddy said coldly. "Nigga, you ain't getting paid to keep time, you getting paid to put in work. So until that time comes, shut the fuck up and let me think!" Rocco started to beef, but there was no doubt that Teddy would use the .357 that sat on his lap.

Teddy watched the bar for twenty more minutes; then something interesting happened. A customized motorcycle rolled to a stop in front of the bar. It was black, with extended handle-bars. The rider was low to the ground, but not as low as one would be on a traditional chopper. He could still manage to get on and off with minimal effort. The bike wasn't like anything Teddy had ever seen, or at least not in that combination. It appeared to be built entirely of different cycles. The rider revved the bike, causing the pipes to release a ghostly wail.

Dre came out of the bar, followed by two of his boys and the girl from the club. Dre approached the rider while his companions hung back. Teddy pulled out a digital camera and took a few shots of the meeting. Dre handed the man an envelope and mouthed something to the rider. When he lifted the visor of his helmet, he had his back to Teddy, so there was no way to tell who was behind the mask.

The whole thing gave him food for thought. Butter didn't think Dre had anything to do with the attempted hit, but Teddy's gut told him differently. Now he caught the suspect doing back-door deals with an unknown conspirator. All of the pieces hadn't come together yet, but Teddy got the picture. Dre would be simple to touch, but the rider was another issue. He had no idea of the man's identity, or what he was capable of. He would be the key to all of it. Teddy hadn't seen his face, but someone was sure to have a line on the owner of the bike.

After the rider departed Dre and his people walked from the bar to a Chevy that was parked a few cars down. Dre got in the back with his lady and the two men piled in the front. The engine rattled and the car rolled out into traffic. Teddy counted to twenty and rolled out in the opposite direction.

Felon was awakened from his peaceful slumber by his cell phone ringing. He popped up, almost forgetting where he was, but relaxed when he saw Eve lying next to him, sound asleep. He smiled at her, remembering the mind-blowing sex they had just engaged in. If it were up to him, he would've lain there with her forever, but seeing Teddy's number in the caller ID meant that business needed to be attended to.

"Yo," Felon said into the phone. As soon as Teddy began speaking, Felon's face became grim. He listened intently as the young gunner ran down his suspicions. Felon didn't like what he was hearing.

"A'ight," he said. "Stay on that nigga. If he's dirty, snatch his ass up. One." Felon ended the call and resumed his position next to Eve.

24.

The next afternoon Butter sat in his apartment, seething. He had been embarrassed and betrayed, all at the same time. Whenever he thought about it, he saw Cassidy's nonchalant demeanor and Carlo's smug-ass grin. At the time, he wanted nothing more than to kill them both where he stood, but what would it have solved? Carlo would still have one up on him, and Cassidy would still be a snake in the grass. She would get what was coming to her, just like everyone else.

"What's good?" Teddy asked, walking up on Butter.

"Shit," Butter answered without turning around.

"Man, you've been looking out that window for hours. Fuck is you trying to do, spot the Goodyear blimp?" Teddy's attempt at humor went totally over Butter's head. Seeing that wasn't working, he tried a different approach. "Yo, I checked that kid Dre out. The boy is looking real suspect. Seen him talking to some motorcycle nigga that I didn't recognize. I think the kid is filthy."

"You still on that shit?" Butter asked in a very uninterested tone. "Dre ain't bout shit. Ain't nobody tried nothing lately either." Butter went back to looking out the window.

"Yo, kid, whether you know it or not, it's a lot of animosity coming your way from the streets right now. You and Felon done officially made it. You think muthafuckas is happy to see that? You better look at the writing on the wall, cousin."

"Teddy, you better stop letting Felon fill your head with that bullshit. I'm a fucking accident waiting to happen. Niggaz ain't stupid enough to try me again. You only get one chance. Besides, I got other shit on my mind. Can't believe this backstabbing bitch," he groaned.

"If I was you, I'd get my head in the game, son. Fuck what happened with that bitch."

"What you mean by that?" Butter asked, turning a questioning glare at Teddy.

"Nothing." Teddy looked away. "All I'm saying is, you gotta keep a clear head about this. I know how you feel about shorty, but let's not forget what's going on out here. Somebody tried to off you, kid."

Butter snorted. "Teddy, go head with that shit. Homey wasn't the first nigga who tried me, and he won't be the last. But you know what? Everybody that comes for a piece of me, is gonna end up just like that clown on One hundred and twenty-fifth."

"Butter, man, I just think—"

"Yo, we don't keep you around to think," Butter said, cutting him off. "You acting like this bitch got me slipping or something. I'm still that nigga, and that ain't never gonna change. Every muthafucka has their day. Fuck that bitch and fuck these sucka-ass niggaz out here." Butter turned on Teddy with murder in his eyes. For a second, Teddy wasn't sure if Butter was gonna wild out or not. To his relief, Butter just grabbed his sweatshirt and stormed out of the apartment.

Officer Andy Lapelsky was a third-rate cop and a top-notch degenerate. In addition to being a lousy husband, miserable father, and a gambler who was constantly in the red, Andy was a drug addict. This is the reason why he found his rest being broken in the wee hours of the morning.

Rolling over and clicking on the light, Andy fumbled with the phone. He rubbed a freckled hand across his eye and croaked into the receiver, "Yeah?"

Hearing the voice on the other end, he immediately sat up. The speaker wasn't frantic or even shaken, considering what Andy had just heard. He banged his fist against his forehead and cursed the caller in a hushed tone so as not to wake his wife. After mumbling a few instructions into the receiver, Andy hung up.

As if his life weren't already complicated enough, he had to get himself into debt to make it worse. Andy was in debt to quite a few people, and one of them had just called in a favor. Andy would've loved to tell the caller to piss off and refuse any part of it, but he didn't have the heart. Instead he began to put a plan together.

He gently slipped from the bed and grabbed his pants and shirt. He crept from the bedroom and dressed in the hall. Normally he would've awakened his wife to tell he was leaving, but he hadn't had ample time to come up with an excuse. He would have one for her when he returned in the morning.

Eugene Benett was a landmark in the Hunts Point area of the Bronx. For the last few years, he could be found roaming the back alleys and lots, rummaging through the trash. On good nights, the pimps and would pay him to watch their cars and the hoes would tip him to play lookout while they turned their tricks. Between that and his other hustles, Eugene made enough money to keep his belly full and stay high.

He had just left the gas station, raiding their garbage for cans. It was a dry night, but he had enough to get his fix. Dragging his cart full of junk behind him, Eugene cut down the back street to see where he could score a high. At the end of an alley he spotted a sofa and several piles of old clothes someone had tossed out. Eugene moved hurriedly to the rubble to see what he could recover. If he was lucky, he'd be able to get the good stuff before any of the other homeless people could pick it over.

Apparently it had been a lover's spat. There were boxes with men's clothes spilling out of them. Bad luck for the poor slob who was running around the city half naked. Good luck for Eugene who was in need of a new wardrobe. Amongst the clothes were several garbage bags. Prying one of them open, Eugene found more clothes. When he moved to the second bag, he caught a glimpse of something beneath it. At first he couldn't make out what it was, but when he reached out to touch it, he immediately jerked his hand back. It was a nipple.

Every fiber of his being told him to bolt, but natural curiosity made him push the bag aside. Beneath the pile of trash he discovered a body. Eugene almost threw up as he looked at the battered corpse of a young woman. Her face was bruised and a deep gash ran along her temple. Eugene staggered back and ran from the alley, screaming.

Carlo came strolling out of his building reading the *Daily News*. Sal brought up his rear, his eyes sweeping the block, looking for an invisible foe. Big Steve leaned against the car, smoking a cigarette, looking at his watch.

"What's up, Steve?" Carlo asked, sniffling.

"I've been waiting for a half hour, man," Steve said, a little irritated.

"I was tying up some loose ends," Carlo smiled, climbing into the backseat.

"I'll bet," Steve said, walking around to the driver's side.

"Say, did that spook Johnny Black finish the job yet?"

"Not that I know of. Dre told me he flexed on him though."

"Dre probably shot his mouth off to the kid. That fucking Outlaw is a mean son of a bitch." Carlo laughed.

"Carlo, why didn't you just deal with Johnny yourself instead of doing it through Dre?"

"Guilt by association, pal." Carlo smiled. "It wouldn't look good on me if my partner found out that I got his boy clipped, would it? Besides, it's more fun watching niggers cut each other down in the streets." He erupted into laughter.

"Fucking asshole." Steve mumbled.

"What the hell is wrong with you?"

"Nothing," Steve grumbled, "I just got some shit on my mind."

"Whatever. Geez, smells like pine in here."

"I took the car to get washed," Steve reminded him. "Where're we going?"

"I dunno. I feel like partying." Carlo smiled. "Let's roll through that spot in Queens. I hear that got a lotta fine black broads in there. How bout it, Sal?" Carlo addressed his cousin. Sal just shrugged.

Big Steve glared at the two Italians through the rearview mirror. He hated how Carlo and people like him played gangsta in the streets. Where he came from cats grinded because they had to. In Carlo's fucked-up circle, they played gangster, emulating the old heads. The age of the real mobster was surely dying out if worms like Carlo could come to power.

And was Steve any better? There was nothing fake about his gangsta, but he worked for a sick little fuck. He had always known Carlo was a snake, but watching him move lately, he was beneath even a snake. Still he served him. When Steve had taken the job he had been promised wealth and power. He no idea that it would come at the price of his soul.

Eve's latest job assignment was at an office building. She worked at a shipping company several days a week, answering phones and running errands. The days were usually pretty light, limiting her duties to fielding a few phone calls and an occasional coffee run. Her boss didn't stress her about how she dressed, so she was allowed the luxury of showing up in jeans and Timberlands. The arrangement was perfect for her.

For the last couple of days, she had been trying to busy herself with work. She went to work and came home, limiting the time she spent on the block. Her girls would try and coax her to hang, but she would shoot them down with an excuse. Eve didn't mean to alienate her click, but she had things on her mind that she needed to sort out.

Ever since she had given herself to Felon, she had been avoiding him like the plague. When he called her cell, she sent him to voice mail. When he called her house, she wouldn't pick up. He had even gone as far as calling Uncle Bobby's line, but Eve had made him lie and say she wasn't there.

No matter how much she ducked him, she couldn't seem to get him out of her mind. She was a jumble of nerves about the whole thing. Having sex with Felon was a mistake for several reasons, none of which mattered at the time. Eve prided herself on strength and self-control. Felon had managed to break through her shell and she gave in. It wasn't like he had taken advantage of her, but she felt awkward about it. She tried to look at him in that same brotherly light, but things had changed, as she knew they would.

She wanted to be with Felon, but it would never work. It was common knowledge that he and Butter had dozens of groupies running around the five boroughs. Eve wasn't into competition, nor was she into fighting over a man. She was above that, but she knew it would only be a matter of time before she would've had to slap a bitch for getting out of pocket.

Next to a relationship ruining their friendship, Eve was her own biggest obstacle. She had some serious emotional issues that she wasn't ready to address yet. Her whole life had been one big tragedy and it left a deep scar on her soul. She had to sort her feelings out and work on overcoming these things before she could complement someone else. What she and Felon shared was great, but until she got herself together they couldn't be.

Another unresolved situation was what had happened between Cassidy and Butter. Just as Eve had predicted, it blew up in her face. She felt bad for Cassidy getting caught up, but she felt worse for Butter. To say that he was embarrassed wouldn't even do it justice. Cassidy and Carlo's relationship coming out the way it did was ugly. Butter was hurt, so there was no telling what he would do.

Eve could remember the smug look on Carlo's face when the shit hit the fan. His blue eyes shone with triumph as he watched Butter stagger from the lounge. Eve hadn't missed that. It was the first time she had seen Carlo in person, and she found herself just as uneasy as when she was looking at the pictures. Something radiated from him that made her very uncomfortable.

Eve opened the newspaper, trying to take her mind off the whirlwind her life was turning into. As soon as she opened the paper, she wished she hadn't. The newspaper never seemed to report anything good. All you ever read about were murders, homelessness, and other depressing issues.

Just under a story about the FBI hiring the mob to dig up some graveyard, a highlighted piece caught Eve's eye. The article was so small that she might have missed it. "Prostitute Found Slain," the headline read. A homeless man found the body of a young woman somewhere in the Bronx. She had been raped and beaten, then her body had been stuffed under some garbage bags on a side street. Not wanting to read anymore, Eve flipped the page.

What kind of city was New York becoming if women could be murdered at random like that? Granted, the girl was a prostitute, so it was partially her fault, but what gave someone the right to do that? It was spooky to think just how easy it was for some sick fuck to prey on you in the city. And people wondered why she carried heat.

Putting the paper down, Eve decided to give Cassidy a call. She remembered that she hadn't spoken to her since the incident. Even though she was ducking most of her phone calls, she couldn't remember Cassidy's being among them. She figured that Cassidy was still tight over what happened. She couldn't blame anyone but herself for it, though. Eve decided to reach out to her and see where her head was at.

After the fourth ring, Cassidy's voice mail clicked on. Eve tried her one more time with the same result. It wasn't unusual for Cassidy not to answer her cell if she was with a guy, but she usually picked up for her.

The next call she placed was to Cassidy's house. Sheeka picked up on the third ring. Eve made small talk, then inquired about Cassidy. Sheeka informed her that she hadn't seen her sister in a day or so. She told Eve about Cassidy getting the late-night phone call and not being there when she woke up the next morning. Sheeka suggested that Cassidy might be shacked up with some cat, and told Eve she'd have her call if she spoke to her.

Eve hung up the phone and stared out the dingy window. It wasn't unlike Cassidy to disappear for days at a time, but she would've at least left word with someone that she was all right. Sheeka hadn't seen her and Cassidy wasn't picking up her phone. Suddenly the hairs on the back of Eve's neck began to stand up.

When Eve got off work, she stopped by her house to change clothes. She was meeting Sheeka and Beast so they could roll to the movies. Cassidy was still MIA, and she still wasn't taking Felon's calls. She was worried sick, and her heart was pulling her in a million different directions at once, but other than that, life was peachy.

As she was making her way back to the train station, she spotted Felon sitting behind the wheel of his minivan. Her heart immediately began to beat faster and faster the closer she got to the van. She had rehearsed what she wanted to say to him, but her mind drew a blank. She decided to forego the dialog and just speak from her heart. She had to let Felon know what was going on inside her.

When she was almost upon the van, she noticed a second shape inside with him. She couldn't tell who it was because of the tinted windows, but she could tell it was a female. Anger and hurt feelings almost caused her to charge the van and beat the hell out of both of them, but she checked herself. Technically, she and Felon weren't an item, so she had no cause to flip. That still didn't stop her from feeling like a fool for giving herself to him.

"Guess that's the game for you," she whispered to herself. Eve felt like crying, but no man was worth her tears. Instead, she held her head up and walked down the street like she was the queen of Harlem.

"I really appreciate this, Marcy," Felon said to the dark-skinned girl sitting next to him.

"Felon, don't even trip. That's my little brother, so I don't mind." She smiled. "He better not get used to this shit, though. This is my first and last time. Nobody told his dumb ass to get locked up."

"We all catch a bad break sometimes, Marcy. Tell him I'll send somebody up with some bread later on in the week, a'ight?"

"I'll tell him. While I'm thinking about it, what's good with me and you?"

Felon chuckled. "Come on, Marcy. Don't put a nigga on the spot like that. I'm damn near married."

"She must be a special lady, to have convinced you to settle down."

"She is." He reflected on Eve.

"Can't knock a girl for trying." she winked. "Later, Felon."

Felon watched Marcy saunter away through the rearview mirror and admired her healthy ass. He would've loved to crack that, but it would've only made things more complicated for him. His heart and his brain were having a heated argument, and for once his heart was winning. Felon looked at the shit-eating grin that he was wearing in the rearview and could've sworn he saw Eve disappear around the corner.

25.

Glo was the brainchild of a woman named Gloria Guzmand. The whole place consisted of five chairs, two sinks, and three hair dryers. The work stations were black marble and the mirrors were lined in silver. It was a relatively small salon, but they had consistent clientele. On the weekends it was always packed, and they had discounts on wash-and-set's during certain days of the week.

It was almost closing time, so most of the patrons had gone already. Eve lounged in one of the swivel chairs while Beast occupied three of the waiting room chairs, looking through a *National Geographic* magazine. She and Beast were waiting for Sheeka to boil this woman's hair after she had finished braiding it. Sheeka was the only Black girl working in a salon full of Dominican women. She was their braider.

"I hope this movie is as good as they saying," Sheeka said, dipping the woman's ends into the scalding water, "I don't wanna pay my ten dollars and end up mad."

"Rah said it was tight," Eve said.

"Since when that dizzy bitch start thinking for herself?" Sheeka twisted her lips. "If Kiki told her that shit tasted like sugar, she'd be the first one on line with a spoon." The whole salon fell out laughing.

"Yo, you got in touch with your sister yet?" Eve asked, trying to occupy herself with thoughts that didn't include Felon.

"Nah. That heifer still ain't called nobody. She's probably still mad about getting busted," Sheeka said.

"You think so?"

"Hell, yes. Let me tell you something about my sister. I might be the youngest, but Cassidy has always been the brat. Even when we were little, if things didn't go her way, Cassidy threw a fit. One time, she ran away for three days. Moms bust that ass when she got hungry and came home."

"Yeah, Cas can be like that," Eve said, "but that doesn't explain why she isn't picking up her cell. Aren't you worried?"

"Eve, if I had a dollar for every time Cassidy pulled a disappearing act, I'd be a rich bitch. Cassidy is grown. When she decides to start acting like it, she'll come home."

"I'd still feel better if I'd spoken to her."

"Oh-oh," Beast said from the doorway. Eve looked over just in time to see two uniformed officers coming through the salon door. At first she panicked, but she regained her cool when she remembered she wasn't strapped.

"RaSheeka Brown." one of the officers stepped forward.

"Ah . . . I'm she," Sheeka said, stepping forward.

"Can you come with us, please?"

"Is there a problem?" Eve asked.

"And whom might you be?" the second officer asked.

"Her sister," Eve lied.

"This isn't really the place to discuss it," the first officer said, stepping toward Sheeka. "If you'll just come with us, we'll explain everything."

Sheeka looked back and found the whole salon staring at her. She asked one of the girls to finish the woman's hair while she got her purse. Her heart raced at a million miles a minute trying to think what the police could want with her. She hadn't done anything, but maybe it had something to do with one of the dudes she dealt with? Reluctantly she allowed them to usher her out the door, with Eve on their heels.

"I wanna go too." Beast loomed over the second officer. Beast glared at the officers, making their hands inch towards their guns. Eve told him to go home and she would come by later.

Of all the places Eve imagined herself ending up, the morgue was not one of them. Sheeka thought the police had come to arrest her, but that wasn't it. They had picked her up in connection with the slain prostitute from the Bronx. When they first found the woman, there was nothing in her purse but eighty-two dollars and half of a pack of cigarettes. During a second examination of the Gucci purse they found a rip in the lining. Inside the rip was one of Glo's cards with Sheeka's name on it.

They asked Sheeka a bunch of questions about her relationship to the girl, but she couldn't help them. Finally they said that if Sheeka had seen the girl, she might remember her. Sheeka, of course, refused to identify the body. After some coaxing she agreed to look at some pictures of her, but only if Eve could be present with her. Since Eve was Sheeka's "sister," they didn't raise too much of a stink. Now they found themselves sitting in a cold office, waiting for the coroner and one of the officers to come back with the pictures.

After what seemed like forever, the officer who had come to the salon came into the office, followed by a man wearing a lab coat. After a brief introduction, the coroner laid a white folder on the table in front of Sheeka. She swallowed hard and allowed herself to look at the picture. As soon as Sheeka laid eyes on the picture, she mumbled something incoherent and passed out. If it wasn't for the officer, she'd have hit the floor.

Eve leaned over to look at the picture and see how bad the girl was. The girl's face was swollen and bruised, so it took a second for the light to go off. Eve could feel her head begin to swim and her mouth water. She tried to blink, but her eyes wouldn't comply. The girl they found was Cassidy.

When Sheeka woke up, the realization of what she saw had set in. She immediately began screaming and wailing. It took three officers and a sedative to calm her down. The shock of seeing her sister like that made something in her snap. As she was in no condition to answer any more questions, when the detective came in, he directed them toward Eve.

"So, she was your sister?" the detective asked. He sat across from Eve wearing a black mock neck and chinos.

"Yes," Eve said numbly. "Cassidy. Her name was Cassidy."

"I see," he said, scribbling in his notepad. "How long was your sister a . . . working girl?"

"A what?" Eve asked, staring up at him. She searched his artificially tanned face to see if she had heard him wrong.

"Ms. . . . ah . . ."

"Panelli."

"Yes. Ms. Panelli, we have reason to believe that the young lady in question was indeed a prostitute."

"Why, because you found her on Hunts Point?" Eve asked, heated.

"Ma'am, not only did we find her on Hunts Point, but we have several other clues as to her activities. There were signs of penetration in her anus as well as her vagina. In addition to that, forensics detected several different semen samples. Look, I know this is hard, but—"

"Hard my ass!" she roared. "Cassidy wasn't no prostitute. I don't care what your labs say, I know her better than I know myself!"

"Ms. Panelli, may I remind you where you are?" he said, raising his voice.

"Fuck where I'm at. My best friend was murdered and you're trying to convince me that she was selling ass, instead of trying to find out who did it."

"Ms. Panelli, I didn't know the young lady, but I do know the facts. Now, either your sister was a prostitute or someone went through a hell of a lot of trouble to make her look like one. Either way, she was murdered and we will catch who did it. You sitting in here shouting isn't gonna help the situation."

"Man, fuck this shit," Eve said, standing up and heading for the door.

"Ms. Panelli, we're not finished talking."

"Nah, we're finished. Until you find out who killed Cassidy, I ain't got shit else to say to you." Eve slammed the door, rattling the pen holder on the desk.

When Eve got back upstairs, the desk sergeant informed her that Sheeka had been taken to the hospital and would most likely be kept overnight for observation. Eve left the precinct in a world of hurt. Her best friend had been beaten like a dog and tossed in an alley. What kind of monster could do such a thing? Cassidy might have done some foul things, but she didn't deserve to go out like that.

She walked down the darkened streets with no direction. She crossed over block after block, absorbed in her pain. She had managed to hold it together in front of the detective, but now that she was alone, she cried openly. A few people spared her a glance, but no one bothered her.

How could this have happened? At first Eve thought that it might've been an angry lover, but she pushed the thought from her mind. Cassidy dealt with men for their money, not their cunning. She dealt with a few dudes who had bodies under their belts, but they were more the type to use guns or knives. Something like this didn't fit any of their profiles. This was the work of someone with a deep sickness.

Eve went over the events of the last few days and tried to find a clue as to what had happened. To her knowledge, Cassidy hadn't really been in the streets since she started seeing Carlo. She came through the block to check her crew every now and again, but other than that, she had been keeping a low profile. She couldn't think of anyone Cassidy might've come into contact with who would've wanted to murder her.

The fact that she was murdered was terrible by itself, but the way it was done was the unnerving part. She didn't doubt the evidence the police found, but she knew they were wrong about her. Cassidy was a little loose, but she wasn't a prostitute. Someone wanted the police to believe Cassidy was a hoe.

Not even remembering her cell phone, Eve sought out a pay phone. She had to call the one person who could help her world stop spinning and try and make sense of all the madness. Felon. It didn't even matter that she had seen him with the mystery women. All she could think was that he would know what to do. He would know how to make the hurting stop. She had to dial the number twice before she finally got him. Just hearing his voice made her want to break down, but she had to be the rock of the crew. She had to pull herself together and find out what went down with Cassidy. Not only was Cassidy a part of her click, she was family. Whoever was responsible for it, Eve would make sure they suffered before she let them die.

Butter had been wailing nonstop since Felon had relayed Eve's message. He had slammed his fist through the minibar, cutting it up, but that didn't stop his raging. Seeing that the bar wasn't putting up a fight, Butter snatched a bottle of scotch from the wreckage and began to guzzle it.

Felon didn't even want to imagine what Butter was going through. He had lost friends in the struggle, but never someone whom he held dear. Seeing the pain in his friend's eyes, he wanted to collapse on his knees beside him. He wanted to reach out and comfort Butter, but he knew there was nothing he could say or do to ease the pain. Instead, Felon stood by and watched as his friend mourned for his lover.

* * *

When Felon came downstairs, Eve was sitting on the steps of Butter's apartment building. Beast ran one of his huge hands down her back, attempting to comfort his friend. He tensed up when he saw Felon's shadow looming, but returned to caring for Eve when he saw who it was. Felon sat on the steps next to them.

"How is he?" Eve asked, wiping her eyes.

"My nigga took it hard," Felon whispered. He looked at Eve's face in the pale moonlight and could see that her eyes were puffy from crying. He reached out to touch her hand, but stopped short and placed his hand in his pocket.

"My girl is gone," she sobbed. "Gone."

"I'm sad for Cassidy too," Beast said, sounding choked up.

"What did the police say?" Felon asked.

"They don't know shit. Stupid muthafuckas trying to tell me that Cas was out there on the stroll."

"That's bullshit," Felon said "Cassidy wasn't on it like that."

"Shit, I know that. That's why none of this shit adds up to me. Had she just been killed, it would've been sad, but not suspicious. Somebody arranged it to look that way. This wasn't no random murder, Felon."

"Eve, are you trying to say that someone singled Cassidy out?"

"Whoever did this not only wanted her dead, but they wanted to destroy her character in the process."

"Any ideas?" he asked.

"Nah." She shook her head. "This shit is so fucked up, I can't even think straight." Eve closed her eyes in an attempt to clear her head, but as soon as she did she saw Cassidy's battered face. "Damn, Felon. I don't know what I'm gonna do without her," she croaked. Eve's face was streaked with tears.

Felon went to touch her, but to his surprise she jerked away. He looked into her blue-green eyes and saw that the hurt was replaced by anger.

"It's cool, ma." He assured her.

"Nah, it ain't *cool*. You think my feelings are a fucking joke?" she snapped.

"Evelyn, what are you talking about?" This time when he reached for her, Beast sprang into action. He gripped Felon by the arm and yanked him from the stoop. The behemoth had a maddened look in his eyes that Felon had never seen before. Beast wrapped his free hand around Felon's neck, completely encircling it. Felon tried to fight him off, but Beast was far too strong. Just as Felon was about to draw his pistol, Eve laid a hand on Beast's thigh.

"Enough," she whispered.

Just as suddenly as the madness had come, it faded from Beast's eyes. He gave Felon a brief squeeze for good measure, then set him down. Felon glared at Beast with murder in his eyes, but the sorrowful look Eve gave him took away some of the anger. Keeping his eyes on the giant, he returned to his seat beside Eve.

"I saw you with her," she said, barely above a whisper. "You and that girl."

"Marcy?" he asked, surprised. "Baby, she was taking Eric some weed. He's on the Island."

"Felon, you don't have to lie. I'm not your *girl*."

"Evelyn Panelli. Let me put you up on something. I might be a lot of things, but I'm no liar. If I'm fucking a bitch, I'm gonna say I'm fucking her. I don't make excuses for anything I do. Eve, I know you got issues, but who doesn't? I wanna be there for you, but you gotta let me in, ma."

She looked at him but said nothing.

Felon reached out to touch Eve, and when Beast didn't object, he pulled her close to him. Eve broke down on Felon's chest while he held her as if she would fly away. He could feel the pain flow from her and into him, and he gladly accepted it. He would accept a thousand times worse if it would take away his Evelyn's suffering.

26.

Felon stood in the kitchen of his West Harlem apartment, sipping coffee and squinting into the morning sun. He had sat up with Eve until the birds started to chirp. He tried to get her to let him walk her home, but she didn't want to be alone. Being the gentleman he was, Felon invited her back to his place. Beast protested but went along with it when Felon told him he could come too. It was only a one-bedroom, so Beast had to sleep on the couch while Felon and Eve occupied the bedroom.

They had lain in each other's arms for a long while without saying a word. Felon cradled her like a newborn and planted soft kisses on her lips and forehead. He was hesitant when she urged him to make love to her. She was vulnerable and he didn't want to take advantage of her condition. She planted soft kisses on his neck and chest, making him a slave.

She pushed him down on his back and straddled him. Felon watched in amazement as the sunlight that invaded their privacy played tricks with her eyes. They flickered from blue to green and looked at him sorrowfully. She removed her shirt, then undid her pants. She ran her tongue from his navel and circled each nipple. She repeated this process while massaging his genitals. When Felon was fully erect, Eve wiggled out of her tight jeans.

This time she was the aggressor. She straddled him, then reaching back, rubbed his penis against her vagina until it was moist. Slowly she inserted him, first the head, then part of the shaft. It still hurt, but Eve needed the pain to take her mind elsewhere. When she built up the courage, she took it all. The lovemaking wasn't wild and impulsive like the first time. This was slow and calculated. When she came, she dismounted and curled into a ball on the far side of the bed.

It didn't take long before Eve finally dropped off to sleep. She was tired, physically and mentally. To be so young, she had gone through so much and was still here. You had to admire her strength. Even with her face swollen the way it was, she was still a vision. Felon watched her for a while before going into the kitchen.

Cassidy's murder had rocked everyone who knew her, but it nearly destroyed Eve. She and Cassidy had been tight since they were young. They argued most of the time, but they still loved each other like sisters. Wherever you saw one, you saw the other. Now her other half was gone.

Butter was another issue altogether. He proved to be damn near inconsolable after Felon had delivered the news. The only things that stopped his rampage were liquor and exhaustion. When Felon left him, he had passed out on his bed. He would have a terrible hangover when he woke up, but at least Felon didn't have to worry about him for a few hours.

Felon had already called Teddy and gave him the four-one-one. He also instructed him to have someone keep an eye on Eve's apartment building for suspicious activity. God forbid something happened to her, he would surely fall to pieces. Cassidy's murder had hit too close to home for him. You hear about this kind of thing every day, but it never really registers until it lands in your backyard.

Felon sat on one of his breakfast stools and lit a cigarette. In his mind he examined everything that had happened. Someone had singled Cassidy out; the question was why? Maybe a scorned lover? Cassidy was a good chick, but she had scandalous ways. She was one of those chicks who played on the emotions of men or their insecurities in order to get what she wanted. You couldn't live your life fucking people over and not expect it to come back, but not like that.

No one seemed to have any idea who killed Cassidy or why. The ripple effect cut Felon to the quick. Two people he cared a great deal for were hurting because of it. Butter would be the biggest issue. With Butter being in such an emotional state there was no telling how it would affect his decision making. He needed his partner to be on point. If his head wasn't in the game, it could get sour real fast. Felon liked the turn his life had taken and couldn't see it backsliding.

Eve waited until Felon had gone off to take his shower before sliding from his bed. She woke Beast and together they left the apartment. She would've told him she was leaving, but she didn't want him trying to convince her otherwise. The way she felt, it wouldn't have taken much convincing for her to climb back into Felon's bed and make love to him for the rest of the day. She appreciated his being there for her in her time of grief, but she needed to be alone with her thoughts.

Beast walked her to her building before going his own way. She climbed the broken-up stairs and let herself into the apartment. Uncle Bobby was sitting in front of the living room television watching something on CNN about the situation in Iraq. He gave Eve a nod but didn't turn from his television program. On his lap sat his trusty bayonet, which he was cleaning with an old rag. Eve looked like she wanted to say something to him, but instead she walked to her bedroom.

When he heard her door close, Bobby turned his attention from the television. He felt for his niece. He had lost many friends over the years, so he knew just how bad it could hurt. A few moments later, she came back out of the bedroom and headed for the front door. He thought about going to her, but was all but certain that she would reject the advance. She was bull-headed, like her mother and father. He decided to bide his time. When she needed him, he would be there.

Eve stood outside the apartment door, staring at her Air Maxes. Her hand lifted the iron knocker but hesitated. A lump formed in her throat as she took in the familiarity of the doormat. The brown and green mallard duck print had faded slightly, but it was still as Eve remembered it. The knocker connecting with the door boomed like a blacksmith's hammer in Eve's ears. The lady's speed stick began to melt from under her arms with the rapid beating of her heart. The locks clicked and Eve looked up, expecting to see Cassidy standing on the other side of the door and laughing at her for falling for the prank. Instead, Sheeka opened it and invited her in.

Eve stepped across the threshold and followed Sheeka into the living room. Sitting by the window was Cassidy's mother. Even sitting down you could tell where Cassidy got her height. Liz's hair partially covered her face, but her sad eyes were visible. She just stared out at the horizon.

"She's been like that ever since," Sheeka whispered.

Eve moved closer to Liz but made sure she didn't invade her space. Her eyes were swollen and tear-streaked, but she maintained her vigil over the city. She turned to Eve with a faint smile and went back to her gazing. Eve thought about trying to strike up a conversation, but decided it wasn't the time. Liz was clearly somewhere else, so Eve decided not to deny her that.

She walked up the hall, following Sheeka, who had moved to the bedroom. Pictures of Cassidy and a toothless Sheeka hung from the wall. It took all of five seconds before the warmth of tears began to tickle the rims of Eve's eyes. She faced the floor and took a seat on Cassidy's bed.

"How you holding up?" Eve asked, trying not to let her eyes go back to the picture.

"I'm good." Sheeka sighed. "Gotta stay strong for Mom, ya know?"

"Right." Eve nodded. "Anything new from the police?"

"That's a joke, right?" Sheeka asked with a sarcastic chuckle. "They don't give a shit about who killed my sister. Just another prostitute who got caught out there. This shit will probably go down as another unsolved murder." The tears Sheeka had been fighting back began to escape down her face.

"Don't cry, sis. It'll be all right," Eve assured her, leaning over and placing a hand on Sheeka's knee.

"Bullshit!" Sheeka hopped up. "You saw the pictures, Eve. This ain't never gonna be all right. The police ain't gonna do a god-damned thing outside of roust a few pimps, who they know ain't got nothing to do with it anyway. My sister is dead and we can't do shit about it! The muthafucka that killed Cassidy is a bastard. He didn't have to do it like that, Eve. Not like that. I want him dead! Just like my sister."

Eve sat there watching Sheeka as she ranted. The stress of losing her sibling had seemed to add years to her once-youthful face. She knew there was plenty of truth in Sheeka's words. The police were convinced that Cassidy was a streetwalker, so there wouldn't be much effort behind their investigation. As she replayed the vision of Cassidy's battered face, pure hate crept into every fiber of her being. They might've been victims in this, but they were far from helpless.

"Look at me, Sheeka," Eve said in low tone. Sheeka stopped her pacing and focused on Eve. Her eyes flashed rage, but her face was now completely blank. "Cassidy was my heart. I couldn't face myself every day if I let this ride."

"Whatever you got in mind, I'm with you, Eve," Sheeka said seriously.

Eve wanted to tell her no, but Cassidy was Sheeka's blood. Just like when they were kids, the two women huddled on the bed together and whispered of plots and vendettas to be loosed when the time came.

Andy leaned against his banged-up Nova and waited for the runner to come back with his product. He was dressed in brown slacks and a yellow jacket. Any smart cop wouldn't be caught dead buying his own drugs, but Andy was too cheap to pay someone to do it for him. While he waited, he made small talk with Mike, one of the lookouts.

"I can't see how you guys can sling this shit out in the open like that. Ain't you worried about the police running up on you?" Andy asked.

"Police ain't gonna do shit. You got Black women being killed in the streets and they ain't doing shit about it," Mike informed him.

"What, you mean that broad in the Bronx?" Andy showed his knowledge of current events. "She was a working girl."

"You better watch your mouth," Butter said, coming out of the building. A light beard covered his squared jaw, and his clothes were wrinkled. His bloodshot eyes shot daggers at the man bold enough to disrespect Cassidy's memory within earshot of him. "I don't think you know what you're talking about."

"What do ya mean? Buddy, it was all over the paper. Anybody with eyes knows what happened. She was working and somebody off 'd her," Andy said.

"Honkey, get the fuck off my block!" Butter shouted.

"Hey, be cool," Andy shouted back. "You don't know who you're talking to."

"I don't give a fuck who I'm talking to." Butter took a step forward. "I said get the fuck off my block, talking shit you don't know nothing about."

"You listen to me, you fucking street punk," Andy pointed, "I don't know who you think you're talking to, but I ain't some prick who came down to the hood to get a quick high. I'm connected, ass wipe. Now, why don't you call that little runner of yours to get my shit before I start kicking assess around here!" Andy poked his chest out, challenging the stocky youth.

Butter was a blur when he moved. He whipped the cubed pistol from his pocket and drew a bead on Andy's chest. Mike barely had time to move before the first bullet whipped past him. Andy took one to the chest and fell back. The Nova broke his fall, but a bullet to his shoulder shook him. Someone shouted something, but the fatal shot being fired drowned it out. Andy's face splattered on the passenger's side window of the car.

"What the fuck!" Teddy screamed, as he burst from the building with his gun drawn.

Butter remained silent for a moment. He hadn't intended to shoot the loudmouthed white guy, but his temper moved quicker than his reasoning. "Help Mike get this nigga in the car," Butter said over his shoulder.

Teddy stood there frozen, taking in the scene. A white man, with a chunk of his cheek missing, was stretched out next to an old car. Butter was tucking a pistol in his pants and looking up and down the block. Knowing that they had to get the body off the block, Teddy moved to help them clear the scene. After helping Mike get Andy into the backseat, Teddy searched the glove compartment for some sort of identification. When he saw the badge and gun, he almost shit his pants.

"Fuck!" he shouted.

"What's the matter?" Butter asked, moving to see what was wrong with Teddy. He cursed at the top of his lungs, but it still didn't change the fact that he had fucked up. "We gotta get rid of this nigga."

Teddy slid into the driver's seat and turned on the ignition. Before the engine could completely start, he had the car in gear. Mike almost got dragged, trying to climb in the backseat with Andy's body.

Butter's mind raced, trying to think what to do. He was panicking, but he had to maintain a calm façade in front of his crew. They had to get rid of a body, so that meant a trip out of town. Most likely, they'd hop on 80 West and bury him on the side of the road somewhere. Felon was gonna be pissed when he caught wind of it. But that was something Butter would just have to deal with when the time came.

27.

"You see this shit?" Carlo asked, pointing to the headline about the off-duty officer who had surfaced in a lake outside Westchester. "Somebody whacked out Lapelsky."

"Fucking-A," Tony said, leaning over Carlo's shoulder to get a better look at the article. "Says they found him in Westchester County. Fuck was he doing up there?"

"Trying to find a detox," Steve mumbled from his seat in the corner.

"What're you, a fucking comedian?" Carlo asked, facing Steve. "Your mouth has been pretty fucking smart lately."

"Hey, I'd be pissed too if I worked for a prick like you," Tony joked.

"This ain't no laughing matter." Carlo turned to Tony. "Lapelsky worked for my father. Whadda ya think he's gonna say bout this?" The room went silent. "Exactly. Gentleman, we've gotta get a handle on this thing."

"Why do you think he was killed?" Sal asked.

"Think it had something to do with that broad?" Tony asked. He started to elaborate further on the issue, but the look Carlo shot him stayed his tongue.

"The whole thing stinks to me," Carlo said. "Andy Lapelsky was a dirtbag and he could've got whacked for a number of reasons. That still doesn't change the fact that he was one of ours. Gentleman, this doesn't look good on us. We've got to get a handle on things. I want you guys to see what you can find out about it. Get on the streets and see what turns up. Tell everyone that there's a twenty-grand reward for the information."

"What're you gonna do?" Tony asked.

"Got a date," Carlo said, straightening his tie. "Steve, go get the car."

Cassidy's viewing and funeral were done on the same day. The family didn't want to drag the event out any longer than they had to. Dozens of floral arrangements crowded every free corner of the room. Because of the extensive damage to Cassidy's face and the time she had spent in a rodent-infested alley, the mahogany casket she rested in had to be closed.

Eve quietly occupied a seat in the back of the chapel. She could see the mourners in attendance as well as those coming and going. Quite a few people had turned out. Friends, relatives, even old boyfriends. Eve watched them all.

Felon sat across from Eve. He was dressed in a black suit and wore tinted glasses. Every now and again she would notice him looking at her, but he'd quickly turn away if their eyes threatened to meet. He tried to get her to sit with him, but she declined. Her pain was hers alone, and she didn't feel like sharing it. Teddy was at his side, but there was no sign of Butter. No one had seen him over the last few days.

From where Eve sat, she could see Cassidy's immediate family lining the benches in the front row. Liz sobbed uncontrollably, while Sheeka tried her best to console her. Eve wanted to go to her and try to offer words of encouragement, but what could you say to a mother who had just lost her daughter? Instead, she sat quietly and watched.

The funeral had almost come to an end when the real show started. Big Steve slipped through the door and scanned the sea of faces. Once he was sure that no one was going to jump up and attack, he held the door for his charge. Carlo came into the chapel dressed in a gray suit. His eyes swept the room, hidden by sunglasses, as he made his way down the aisle. Steve leaned against the wall near the door while his boss approached the casket.

Eve leaned forward and studied Carlo. His steps were slow and methodical, as if he were walking the green mile. When he got to the casket, he removed his glasses and dabbed his eyes with a silk handkerchief. He drew quite a few curious glances as he went through the motions of sobbing over his murdered lover.

"Oh, baby," he sobbed, running his fingers over the picture of Cassidy that sat atop the casket.

She looked over at Felon and saw his jaw muscles tightening. Teddy made to get up, but his mentor's hand on his forearm held him steady. She looked back to see Steve twisting his face up as if he had just smelled something rancid. When he had seen enough, he turned and left the chapel. When Carlo was done with his performance, he made his way back up the aisle. On the way out, he mouthed something to Felon before making his exit.

Felon paused at the chapel exit to compose himself. When the assembled guests lined up to pay their last respects, he hung back. He knew Cassidy was dead, but it didn't really set in until the funeral. Poor Eve had cried through most of it. More than once he thought about trying to console her, but he didn't want to break down in front of her. Cassidy was one of them. They hung together, drank together, and fought together. It was hard for him to accept the fact that he would never hear her big-ass mouth again. She was another testament of how mortal they all were, and how dirty the world could play.

He stepped out into the warm sunshine. The air outside stank, but it was a welcome change from the death-tainted chapel. Carlo was standing near his car with his back to Felon, talking to a young girl. He laughed and flirted with her while someone he was supposed to have cared about was being put to rest. Felon's skin began to crawl as he approached.

Carlo noticed Steve staring at something over his shoulder and turned to see Felon approaching. He knew how the scene must've appeared, so he tried to look as if he wasn't being a bastard. He greeted Felon with a smile, but the gesture wasn't returned.

"Shorty, beat it," Felon addressed the girl. Knowing how to take a hint, she did. "Why don't you show some fucking respect?" he hissed at Carlo.

"Felon, it wasn't what it looked like."

"Carlo, you know how that shit would've looked if that girl's family had seen you out here playing R. Kelly?"

"Take it easy," Carlo said, trying to sound authoratative. "I said it wasn't like that."

"You know what? I don't even care, man. You said you wanted to talk, so talk."

"Geez, what is it with all this antisocial behavior? Forget it. What do you know about that cop they found up in Westchester?"

"You called me out here to ask about some fuck-ass cop that got killed in Westchester?" Felon asked angrily.

"That fuck-ass cop worked for my father," Carlo told him.

"Then let your father conduct the investigation. I'm a drug dealer, not a detective."

"Don't get cute," Carlo warned. "The only reason I'm asking you is because Andy Lapelsky was a regular uptown. On and off-duty. I hear he had a drug problem and if I remember correctly, nobody gets high in Harlem unless they buy from one of your spots."

"Carlo, I ain't heard nothing about that cop other than what they ran on the news and in the paper. I cant keep track of every fuck-up trying to get a blast."

"What kind of king doesn't know what's going on in his kingdom?" Carlo asked, glaring at Felon.

Felon tensed up. "What you trying to say?"

"What I'm trying to say is, my father is gonna throw a fucking shit fit about this. Our guys down at the precinct say that he was killed somewhere else and the body was dumped up there. It's not gonna look good if this trail leads back to any of our doorsteps."

"I'll see what I can find out," Felon said, turning to walk back to the church.

"Say, Felon," Carlo called after him. "Where's your pal?"

"What?"

"Butter. Where is he? Knowing how he felt about Cas, it's just a little strange that he wouldn't be here."

"Guess it was too much for him to deal with." Felon's expression didn't change.

"I'll bet," Carlo smiled wickedly. "Why don't you see if he's heard anything?"

"I'll do that, if I see him."

"If? Don't you mean when?"

"You know what I mean, Carlo. If I find anything out, you'll be the first to know."

"You make sure, buddy."

Felon's wheels were spinning on the walk back to the church. When he got word of Butter's fuck-up, he knew it would be trouble. If Franko suspected they were involved in the death of his man, it would fall on Felon as their leader. In his mind, he had a vision of Big Steve running up on him and putting a bullet in the back of his head. He had to force himself not to look over his shoulder.

Butter's temper could've very possibly fucked them all. Carlo was enough of a pain in the ass, but the thought of Franko riding down on his crew didn't sit well with him. Killing a cop would carry a life sentence, if Butter even survived to see trial. Killing a cop who was connected to the mob was surely a death sentence.

* * *

One by one, Cassidy's closest friends and family approached the casket to pay their last respects. Eve stood between Cassidy's next-door neighbor, Mrs. Childs, who would fall out every fifth step, and an older man who kept trying to rub against her. The closer she got to the box, the weaker she felt. It was as if her legs had suddenly become rubber. She thought that she would fall out before she got her turn.

After two of Cassidy's uncles managed to hoist Mrs. Childs off the floor and out of the way, Eve had her turn to say good-bye. Her heart was beating out of her chest, but she tried not to appear shaken. The varnished casket seemed much longer than she re-membered Cassidy being. Running her finger along the top of it, she reflected on all the good times she and Cassidy had had over the years.

There was no way she could really be gone! She looked over her shoulder, expecting Cassidy to come in and expect everyone to laugh at her tasteless joke, but it never happened. Suddenly the room began to spin, and pain gripped her about the chest. The lump that welled in her throat threatened to suffocate her. Feeling the first tears trying to force their way to the surface, Eve took rushed steps to the church exit.

She burst through the doors and took greedy breaths. Had it not been for the wall, she would surely collapse. Tears flowed freely down her face as she mouthed Cassidy's name. Her best friend was truly gone. She needed to be away from that place so she could get her thoughts together.

As she was making her way up the block, she spotted Felon and Carlo. They seemed to be locked in some kind of heated debate. Felon appeared to be barking at Carlo about something. A young girl, who Eve knew only by face, strode past her, giving up a nod. Eve tried to piece the situation together, but her mind was in a mil-lion places at once. The two men were so engrossed in their conver-sation that they never even noticed her pass them.

28.

Carlo sat on the sofa in his father's study, flanked by Sal and Tony. Neither of his companions looked happy to be dragged into the meeting between father and son. Franko had summoned him to the house but hadn't disclosed the reason why. Carlo tried to keep a casual air about him, but he was really on edge. He had been a busy man over the last few weeks, and wondered if his father had gotten hold of something he wasn't supposed to.

Franko came into the study, wearing a red velvet smoking jacket. He chewed a cigar, but it wasn't lit. Cold eyes swept the men on the couch, causing them all to avert their eyes. The mob captain took his time as he crossed the room to his mammoth oak desk. He lowered himself into the antique chair and glared at the trio. After several uncomfortable moments, Franko spoke.

"So, how are my three little stooges?" he asked in his gravely tone.

"Everything is peaches, Dad," Carlo responded for the group.

"Peaches, eh? So tell me, little peach, how is our little experiment going?"

"The stuff is moving like hotcakes. Right now, we've secured about eighty-five percent of the trade in Harlem and a good cut of the Bronx. We don't really touch Brooklyn, on account of the other families might get wise to what we're doing. Things have slowed down a little, but we're still not in the red. Felon is making it happen, just like I told you he would."

"I see," Franko said, striking a match. "The new king of Harlem is maintaining his court. So, what do you think about this Lapelsky thing?"

"Crying fucking shame, Pop. He had a wife and kids for Christ's sake."

"Horseshit," Franko croaked. "Andy Lapelsky was a degenerate and an adulterer. Whoever whacked him out did his wife a favor. At least she's gonna get a check every month. That's more than that guy ever did for her in life. As much of a bastard as he was, Andy had his uses. More to the point, a murdered policeman causes quite a stink."

"Yeah, those guys in Westchester are gonna have some sleepless nights over this one."

Franko placed his knuckles on the desk and pushed himself up. He strode around it to stand in front of the three men. Sal and Tony stiffened in the presence of the looming killer, but Carlo only mirrored his father's blue-eyed gaze. In one swift motion, Franko snatched him to his feet.

"You sneaky sack of shit! Now you told me that you were clean on the Jimmy V job and I took your lying word for it, but don't insult my fucking intelligence. Lapelsky's body was found in Westchester, but our boys downtown got somebody fingering Harlem as the crime scene!" Franko rained spittle in Carlo's face.

Carlo could feel the color drain from his face. He knew what his father was capable of doing with his hands, and wondered if they'd be brought into play that evening. Luckily for him, Franko stopped shaking him long enough for Carlo's mind to put together a response.

"I didn't know," Carlo blurted out.

"Carlo, do you know how bad this is?" Franko slammed him back down to the couch. "These pigs are screaming bloody murder. They're up my ass to hang somebody for this shit. You and these fucking spades you hang around with are supposed to have a handle on this kinda shit, and they let one of ours get murdered like a dog! I provided you with a means to become a fucking millionaire, and you can't control a few square miles? Jesus, I didn't raise you to be a fucking shmuck!"

"Dad, on my eyes, I knew nothing about this." Carlo straightened his tie. "If he was hit in Harlem, it'll get handled. The cops will get their killer."

"You better fucking hope so. If the heat comes down for it, it's your ass that's gonna burn!" Franko warned. "Now get the fuck outta my office!"

The three men got up and quickly filed out of the door. Carlo brought up the rear, but he hesitated in the doorway. He looked back at his father and thought about trying to make some added reassurances, but figured it would be pointless. Harlem was his domain, and by association, it made Franko responsible for whatever went down. A cop being murdered was something not even money could fix. The police wanted a killer, and to save his own ass, Carlo would give them one.

Felon and Teddy rode in the back of the Harlem cab in silence. Each man was engrossed in his own thoughts. Felon had a very nasty situation on his hands. A cop being murdered did not go over well on the streets. The police were riding down on everyone, demanding the murderer be handed over. Spots all over the city were being raided. Felon himself had lost three spots to their fury.

There were speculations about someone from Felon's team being behind it, but no one had any solid proof. Needless to say, the remaining drug czars didn't take it very well. It was bad enough that Felon's product was making it hard to eat, but the extra police attention added to the lean on their pockets. There was already animosity toward his crew for being on the come-up, and this just gave the haters a reason to try something stupid. Butter's beef was hurting their profits.

The cab turned off at the Gun Hill Road exit, east. Once they were past the train station, the vehicle pulled over near the projects. Felon paid the driver and told him to wait. He and Teddy drew some stares from the locals as they entered the building, because they were new faces. No one did more than stare, though. Teddy let his jacket hang open, exposing the twin .45s he carried in the shoulder holsters.

They exited the elevator on the fifth floor, where Teddy led Felon down the hall to a corner apartment. Felon hadn't seen Butter since before the shooting, but this was where he was said to be laying low. Purple Haze could be smelled though the door. Definitely a sign that Butter was somewhere within.

They knocked on the door and waited for a few seconds. Teddy had the key, but neither of them wanted to risk startling the fugitive and getting shot by accident. After a few seconds, light came through the peephole. Several locks and chains were removed before the door actually came open. When Felon saw Butter standing there, he almost didn't recognize him.

Butter was sporting a nappy Afro and his face hadn't seen a razor in quite some time. His tank top was yellowing under the arms from the combination of sweat and the holster that held Butter's magnums. In addition to the two guns dangling from under his arms, his trusty shotgun sat by the front door.

"What's good?" Felon asked, stepping into the apartment and giving his friend dap. Butter smelled like he could use a shower, but Felon still embraced him tightly.

"Maintaining," Butter replied, hugging Felon back. Teddy locked the door behind them and the three men walked into the living room.

The living room was bare, except for a couch and a dining room table tucked in the corner. A wooden chair was facing the window, giving Butter a clear view of anyone coming in or out of the building. He retook his post, leaving Felon and Teddy to occupy the couch. As soon as they were seated, Butter began to speak.

"Sorry I missed the funeral," Butter said, turning his gaze to the children running through the playground. "How was it?"

"It was nice," Felon said. "As far as funerals go. Carlo came through to holla at me about this shit with Lapelsky."

"I know I fucked up," Butter said, never taking his eyes from the window. "Everything happened kinda fast, ya know? I know you're pissed off at me right now, but I didn't mean to get you caught up in this, Felon. Man, he was talking shit about Cassidy and I just lost it." Butter wiped the tear from his eye and tried to compose himself.

"This shit is real ugly," Felon said in a low tone. "Police is running all over the place shutting shit down, and the mob is in our asses for a killer."

"Fucking dagos," Butter chuckled, reaching for a cigarette. "I'll bet Carlo is loving this shit. He was just looking for a way to get me out of the picture, so he could get closer to you. Probably telling you to throw me to the wolves. You here to give me an ultimatum?" When Butter asked the question, he made sure to look Felon in the eye.

"Picture that," Felon said, looking at Butter as if he had lost his mind. "You did some real dumb shit that's probably gonna get both of us killed, but that don't change the fact that I love you. From the cradle to the grave, son. You know how we do."

"You always was my favorite nigga." Butter lit his cigarette, "You'd never turn your back on a friend."

"Butter, I'd give my life for you," Felon said sincerely, "but you've still fucked us. To say that I'm mad would be an understatement. If you were anyone else, I would've sent Teddy up here to put a bullet in your head. Because of your fucking temper, we could all be living on borrowed time. Carlo thinks you had something to do with it, but he isn't sure. The police want a killer, or they're gonna shut us down."

"They can't shut us down. We built this shit!" Butter said angrily.

"You're right," Felon said, lighting a blunt clip that was in the ashtray. "We built this shit, but your stupidity might play a part in its destruction. Not only is the mob tight, but the streets are looking at us funny. A dead cop in Harlem fucks up everyone's pockets."

"We can fix this shit," Butter rocked, "just like we always do. You got a plan in mind?"

"Shit, I wish. We gotta do something, but I need time to get it together. Just stay low and let me figure something out."

"Fo sho." Butter smiled. "Imma keep outta sight. When I come through the block, won't nobody know I'm there."

"Are you fucking crazy?" Felon asked. "If you show your face on the block, someone is liable to put a bullet in it. I don't know what the police know yet, but I do know that Carlo is looking for an excuse to whack your stupid ass. Just chill and let me try to think of something," Felon massaged his temples and tried to devise a plan to save his best friend's life.

Eve sat in the passenger's side of Bullet's Cutlass, chain-smoking cigarettes. The car was positioned so that they could see everything that went on in the block. The same block where Cassidy was murdered. It was hard for Eve to be there, but she had to. The police were looking into Cassidy's murder, but Eve was conducting her own investigation.

For the past two nights, she had been having Bullet drive her up to Hunts Point. There was more to Cassidy's murder than just some random act of violence. There was a definite motive behind it, but she wasn't sure what. The homeless man who found Cassidy's body had given the police his story, but it really didn't hold the clues she was looking for. She knew that the best people to ask were the prostitutes who worked the area.

They were sure to know something. The only problem was there were too many working girls to question them all. Eve decided that it would be best to stake the block out and see which girls worked the area regularly. One of them was sure to have seen something. Bullet tried to convince her that the plan wouldn't work, and Eve was beginning to get discouraged. Just as they were about to call it a night, Eve spotted a familiar face.

The girl was slim and appeared to be in her early twenties. She was one of the few girls whom Eve had noticed working the block on a consistent basis. There were one or two other girls, but Eve has pegged her because of the way she moved. She seemed to know all of the crackheads on the block, and made it a point to disappear a few seconds before the police would make their sweeps through the block. She was definitely someone who knew what was going down in the area.

Eve tapped Bullet. "Check shorty."

"The lil brown-skinned bitch?" he asked.

"Yeah, you disrespectful muthafucka. That's the chick I was telling you about."

"You wanna run up on her?"

"Yeah. I wanna holla at her, but I don't wanna scare her off. Check it, I'll hop out and walk around the block. You pull up on her like you want a date and I'll do the rest."

"I ain't down for no fucking kidnapping, Eve," Bullet warned.

"Be easy," she said, opening the car door, "I just wanna talk to her." Before he could protest further, she disappeared around the corner.

Bullet fired up the engine and coasted the car up the block. A few of the other streetwalkers tried to get his attention, but he ignored them and coasted to a stop in front of the girl Eve had pointed out. She kept her distance from the car, trying to decipher friend from foe. A working girl had to beware of predators on the track. If the police weren't trying to entrap you, the various pimps in the area were trying to make you choose.

"What's going on, baby girl?" Bullet shouted.

"The rent," she replied.

"I'm trying to have a good time. Get in."

"How do I know you ain't no cop, or a pimp?" she asked.

"Get in the car," a voice said from behind the prostitute. She wheeled around and found herself staring down the barrel of Eve's berretta. She thought about trying to run, but she doubted she could top the bullet's speed. Eve directed her into the backseat while she climbed in beside Bullet.

The trio rode in silence as Bullet bent the corner. The prostitute looked from the scar-faced driver to the female with the pistol and wondered if she was going to die. She had heard horror stories about prostitutes encountering demented tricks, but until then she hadn't had the misfortune. She could try and fight, but that would most likely lead to an ass-whipping or a bullet in the ass. Her abductors didn't seem to be crazy, so she tried to reason her way out of it.

"Listen, the jewelry is fake, but y'all can have everything I made for the night," she pleaded.

"Bitch, we ain't after no paper," Bullet snapped.

"Chill," Eve touched his arm. "Baby girl, ain't nobody gonna hurt you. All we need is some information," she assured her.

"I don't see how I can help you. I don't know nothing about nothing," the prostitute said.

"A girl was murdered up here a few nights ago," Eve said, looking out the window.

"I don't know nothing about no murder," the prostitute said nervously.

"Listen to me." Eve turned to face the prostitute. "The girl was a friend of mine. You ever lose a friend? Her name was Cassidy. She was eighteen years old, probably not much younger than you. She was beaten to death and thrown on the street. The police don't care about a Black girl getting murdered, but I do. I need to find out who was responsible," Eve tried to keep her game face, but she couldn't hide the emotion in her voice.

The prostitute examined Eve to see if she was trying to run game. She knew that there was something funny about the murder and it could be dangerous to speak of it, but there was something about the girl that touched her. She looked at Eve and could see the tears welling up in her eyes.

"I'm sorry about what happened to your friend," the prostitute whispered. "Nobody should be done that way. I don't know who killed her or why, but I did see the men who dumped her body." The prostitute went on to recount the events of that tragic night.

She and another girl were working the block when a black truck rolled in with its lights off. The girl ran, but she took cover behind a Dumpster, fearing that they were stickup kids. A big dude, as she described him, got out of the truck with a white guy and pulled a rolled-up carpet from the trunk. The prostitute knew they were up to something, so she watched from her hiding place.

She knew there was something wrapped in the carpet because it took two of them to carry it. They dumped whatever they were carrying and took off in the truck. Curiosity led the prostitute to investigate the scene, but when she came upon it she wished that she hadn't. The men had dumped a the body of a young girl.

"Why didn't you call the police?" Eve asked, sobbing.

"I don't know!" The prostitute cried. "I was scared. I just ran as fast as I could. When I came out the next night, I heard the body had been found."

"The men who dumped her, what did they look like?" Bullet asked.

"One was a big Black dude," she recalled. "Looked like he could've been a football player."

"One guess who that was," Eve said.

"Steve," Bullet grumbled.

"What about the other guy?" Eve asked.

"He was a thin white guy," the prostitute answered.

"Think it was Carlo?" Eve asked Bullet.

"Doubt it." He rubbed his chin. "He wouldn't be stupid enough to get that close to a murder scene. He has people like that fuck Steve to do his dirty work for him."

"Can I go now?" asked the prostitute.

"Yeah," Eve said, handing her a fifty-dollar bill. "Thanks for your help."

Bullet pulled the car over and popped the locks. The prostitute slid from the car and started up the block. She paused and came around to the passenger's side window. "Listen," she said to Eve, "for what it's worth, I'm sorry about what happened. I hope y'all catch the black-hearted bastards that did this before the police do." The prostitute gave Eve a weak smile and disappeared into the night.

"Muthafuckas!" Eve punched the dashboard.

"Easy, Eve." Bullet patted her arm. "They're gonna get what's coming to them."

"Damn right they will. I'm gonna make sure of it."

"Sounds like you're thinking about going against the mob?" Bullet joked. He looked over at Eve and saw that she wasn't smiling. "Eve, I know you're not thinking what I think you're thinking."

"She was like my sister," Eve said clutching the gun. "Steve and whoever else had a hand in it are gonna pay!"

29.

Felon eased down the hall clutching his Glock. With his back to the wall, he eased his way to the front door. He didn't allow people to pop up at his house unannounced, but someone was knocking at his door. Raising the gun to chest level against the door, Felon looked through the peephole. Seeing a friendly face, he uncocked his gun and opened the door.

"Hi," Eve said, standing in the doorway. "You gonna invite me in, or just stare at me?"

"Ah, come in." Felon stepped back and allowed Eve into the apartment. Eve was dressed in a pair of faded jeans and Air Max. Her hair was brushed back into a ponytail, showing off her pretty face. She looked better than she had in the last few days, but Felon could tell she was still grieving.

"You want something to drink?" he asked.

"I'm cool," she said, sitting on the couch. "I kinda need to talk to you."

"I kinda need to talk to you too. Listen, the other day—"

"What's done is done," she cut him off. "That's not what I came to talk to you about, though. I've got some new information about Cassidy's murder."

"Eve, you still on that? You're gonna worry yourself sick."

"I can't just let it go, Felon. She was my friend. Your fucking partners killed her and I can't let that ride," she said heatedly.

"Hold on, what are you talking about?"

"I spoke to a hooker up on the Point and she saw Big Steve dump Cassidy's body."

"Wait, wait. Eve, this is crazy. You come in here telling me that Steve killed Cassidy, on the word of some prostitute?"

"She saw him, Felon. Steve and a white guy dumped Cassidy's body. She couldn't identify that bastard Carlo, but I'm sure he's involved too. I'm going after them," she stated.

"Evelyn Panelli, have you lost your mind? You can't go at the mob because some hooker says she thinks she saw something. These people are killers, baby."

"I think they've proven that already." She folded her arms. "But they've fucked with the wrong person. I'm going after them."

"Eve, we're all upset about what happened to Cassidy, but you can't just go pointing fingers at people. Especially Carlo De Nardi."

"Why the hell not? She was one of us. Twenty-Gang since grade school! Instead of sitting here trying to talk me out of it, you should be helping me figure out a way to get at these niggaz."

"Eve," he said, sitting beside her, "what you're talking about is suicide. Baby, think about this."

"I don't believe this shit," she said, glaring icily at Felon. "How are you gonna side with them?"

"I'm not siding with anyone. I'm just not in a rush to throw my life away."

"Fuck this shit," she said, heading for the door. "Carlo might have your heart, but he don't put no fear in me."

"Eve, where are you going?" he called after her.

"I gotta go."

"Hold on, let me talk to you." Felon reached for her, but she pulled away.

"I'm sorry," she said softly, "I have to do this. Goodbye, Felon." Without giving him a second look, Evelyn Panelli walked out of Felon's apartment and his life.

Eve took hurried steps down the block, wrapped up in her own thoughts. The meeting with Felon hadn't gone quite as she had expected it to. Of all the people in the world she thought she could turn to about this, it was Felon. They all came up together, so it was only right that they ride on Cassidy's killer. When he shut her down, it hurt, but it didn't deter her.

After the prostitute told Eve what she had seen, she immediately started spinning a plan. Felon was to play an intricate part in her revenge scheme, but since he wasn't with it, she'd have to improvise. She pulled out her cell phone and dialed Sheeka. After the third ring she picked up. Eve made arrangements to meet up with Sheeka. She placed a call to Kiki.

"What's going on?" Eve asked.

"Ain't shit." She yawned. "Still on that thing."

"Good. Anything yet?"

"You know I got you, Eve. When he's not guarding his boss, he's an errand boy. Carlo keeps him pretty busy. Doesn't seem to enjoy his job much either."

"That helps, but I need something I can use."

"Well, here's something that I thought you might be interested in," Kiki began. "They must got some freaky shit going on up in that apartment. Just about every other night Carlo and Steve go out and pick up girls. I figured them to be prostitutes, cause neither one of them seem like they got much G."

"So, he's a freak. That still doesn't help me," Eve said, beginning to get irritated.

"Nah, Eve. That ain't the weird thing about it. All they fuck wit is young Black and Spanish pussy. Bout the same age as us. Sometimes Steve just leaves Carlo up there. I never get close enough to see em real good, but they all walk outta there like they got the devil on they heels."

"A'ight, Kiki. Stay on em for a minute. I'm trying to piece something together. Good looking, Twenty."

"All day, my sis." Kiki ended the call.

Eve paused and let the clues roll around in her mind. Could Steve and Carlo be into some kind of crazed sex act with the girls? She could picture them making them perform tricks while they pissed on them. Just thinking of what they might've done to Cassidy before they killed her almost made her buckle. This only added urgency to the plot.

Uncle Bobby was sitting at his post in front of the television when he heard Eve come into the apartment. She gave him a nod, but was silent as the grave. They hadn't done much talking since Cassidy was killed. His niece was going through a terrible time, and as was their way, she held it inside. Bobby decided to break the silence.

"Hey, Eve." He smiled.

"Sup, Uncle Bobby?"

"Ain't seen too much of you in a while, let alone held a conversation. What's going on?"

"Nothing, just trying to keep busy," she lied.

"Right. So, how you feeling, baby?"

"I'm good."

"You sure?"

"Very," she replied.

"You know." He wheeled over to where she was standing. "We ain't really spoke about what happened. Sometimes talking helps."

"Uncle Bobby, I'm straight," she said, heading toward her bedroom.

"Eve, if you need me I'm here. You know that, right?"

Eve looked over her shoulder and gave him a faint smile, then disappeared down the hall.

* * *

Felon leaned against the back of Carlo's Range Rover, steaming a
blunt of haze. Steve sat behind the wheel talking to Sal, who sat in
the passenger's seat. Carlo had left word that he was taking care of
something and he would be down in a few. A million scenarios
played in his mind as he waited for his partner.

Carlo came walking out of the building with a caramel thing on
his arm. She was cheesing as Carlo whispered something lame in
her ear. When he noticed the doorman watching, he palmed her ass
through the short-shorts. Felon waited patiently while Carlo
slipped her some bills and sent her on her way.

"What it is, my man?" Carlo smiled and extended his hand.

"Smooth as silk," Felon said, giving him a light shake. Felon
reached into his jacket pocket and pulled out three thick envelopes.
He held them up for Carlo to inspect, then tossed them in the car to
Steve.

Carlo rubbed his hands together greedily. "Always on time,
buddy."

"Streets are starting to open back up, so I got a little more
mobility."

"Good, good. Say, where's your pal these days?" Carlo asked.

"Had to go out of town to see some sick relatives," Felon said.
The lie was a weak one, so he was sure that Carlo had peeped it.

"Convenient."

"Say what?"

"I said, convenient. It's convenient that your right-hand man
ends up having to leave town in light of a cop getting murdered in
one of your hoods."

"Don't start this shit, Carlo," Felon said, his tone threatening.

"Hey." Carlo threw his hands up. "I gotta ask. You got a name
for me then?"

"I'm still working on it."

"You ain't working too hard, chief." Carlo put his hand on
Felon's shoulder. "Felon, you and me ain't never had a misunderstanding. It's your friend that's bringing the headaches. I got love for

him, because you're a friend of mine, but he ain't a friend of ours."

"Carlo, your people are gonna get their killer. Just hold your head and let me see what I can do."

"Clock is ticking," Carlo said, walking around him to get in the back of the truck. "Say, there's gonna be a little get-together down at this spot in the Village Saturday night. Why don't you come through? I can finally introduce you to the old man."

"A'ight." Felon nodded. "I'll stop through." Felon made his farewells and took two steps back. He waited until the truck had pulled off before walking up the block to his Windstar. He still didn't know what side of the fence Carlo had tossed him to amongst the old heads in the family.

The whole time he was talking to Carlo, he was thinking of Cassidy and wondering if he was really that foul. Felon pushed the thought from his head and focused on paper.

Eve leaned against a lamp post, waiting for Sheeka. She had traded her fitted jeans and sneakers for black army fatigues and Timberlands. A cool breeze rode in as the temperature began to drop. She shifted the weight of the knapsack she was carrying, tugging her collar up so she could light her cigarette.

Sheeka finally came stolling down the block, dressed in sweat pants and a leather jacket. A loose strand of hair fell from beneath her fitted hat and tickled her eyelashes. Much like Eve, she sported bags under her eyes from the many sleepless nights.

"Sup, sis," Eve said, hugging Sheeka.

"What up, Eve?" Sheeka said, hugging her back. "What you doing out here dressed like a damn combat soldier?"

"Come on, Sheeka. You know how I do it. But look, I didn't call you out here to discuss fashion. I got something."

"You heard something about Cassidy's murder?" Sheeka asked excitedly.

"Yeah, I spoke to a girl up there. I'll spare you the details, but I got a lead I'm running with," Eve told her.

"I'm wit you!" Sheeka slapped her fist against her palm.

Eve shushed her. "Chill. It ain't even going down like that. You're gonna get yours in, but I need *you* to make the plan go."

"You ain't even gotta ask me twice," Sheeka said.

"A'ight, it's kinda complicated, so pay attention."

Butter cruised up Madison Avenue in his rented Chrysler. He had a blunt hanging out of his mouth and a compact Uzi on the passenger's seat. When he got the word that the streets were beginning to cool off, he had decided to stretch his legs. Felon had warned him to stay low, but Butter couldn't stay away. Harlem was his home and he needed to be with his peoples. He felt like a caged rat sitting up in the Bronx. All he did was smoke weed and watch videos. He need to get out of his rut.

His first stop was to the barber shop. It had been a while so his hair was starting to look crazy. A few cats from the block recognized him and showed love when he entered. They all wanted to know where he had been, and Butter hit them with a story about a spot out of town. He didn't know who knew what about the murder, and he wasn't stupid enough to put himself out there.

After leaving the shop, Butter decided to take a slow ride through Harlem. It felt good to be back in his element. He almost couldn't believe that he had been so easily forced to leave. He knew the Italians wanted to question him and the police wanted to fry him. He took in the sights, but he wasn't stupid enough to linger.

Butter made a loop of the hood before he made headed back to the Bronx. He spotted Teddy holding the corner down and hit him with the horn. Teddy squinted to see who was in the car, but Butter was moving too fast. Butter headed for the highway and his project retreat. He was feeling so good about getting out that he never noticed the tan bucket that merged into the lane behind him.

After the ten o'clock news, Uncle Bobby decided to call it a night. There was no telling what time Eve was coming in, so he wasn't going to wait up. He wheeled into his bedroom and began the process of balancing himself into bed. His eyes happened to fall on his partially opened closet door. Uncle Bobby knew it was impossible for him to have done it, because he hardly went into it.

Sitting back down in the chair, he wheeled over to the closet and pulled it open. His old army suits and paraphernalia were as they should be, but his steamer chest had been moved. Uncle Bobby noticed the lock was sprung. No one had been in the house but him and Eve. Taking a quick inventory, he assessed what was missing and wondered what the hell his niece was up to.

Eve sat behind the wheel of Bullet's Cutlass, listening to the radio. After making sure Sheeka knew everything that was up, she set out on her mission. Kiki phoned her with the location and she was on the trail. She was parked under the shadow of a tree off Eighty-ninth and Broadway, looking through a pair of old binoculars. Carlo was in a restaurant seated with Steve and two other Italian men, eating dinner.

She imagined herself running into the restaurant and putting a bullet in each one of them, but she wasn't in a rush to see the inside of a jail again any time soon. They would get theirs in due time. She checked her watch and went back to her spying. She had been following them all night, trying to find a kink in their armor.

A few minutes passed and the men were joined by two young ladies. Eve watched the girls flirt and fawn all over Carlo and his gang. The brown-skinned one stepped to Steve, leaving the dark-skinned one for Carlo. He was smiling and flashing his jewels like he was king shit. The chickenhead girls cackled like he was Eddie Murphy every time he said something. Carlo was quite the showman and Eve took it all in.

Eve watched for another half hour or so, until the girls decided to take leave of their new friends. She saw Carlo hand one of the girls what looked like a flyer. After saying their good-byes, the girls went their way and Carlo's crew went theirs. Eve was about to tail them when the text-message alert went off on her phone. She looked at the screen and nodded her head in approval.

30.

The night of the party seemed like it took forever to get there. Felon normally shunned the whole club scene, but this was business to him. He was finally about to get next to the man. Neither he nor Carlo knew it yet, but Felon had big plans for the operation.

Butter being out of the picture was both a gift and a curse. He missed his crime partner dearly, but the hood was quiet. The crew was putting up numbers and there wasn't so much heat. Felon had warned Butter time and again about his rash temper; now he was under the gun because of it. Felon hoped that the situation could be mended over time, but for now, Butter had to leave town. Once he was sure it was safe, he was putting Butter on a plane.

Felon leaned against the bar, sipping a rum and coke. For the event, he was dressed in a black suit and rimmed glasses. He was going for taste, so the only jewelry he rocked was his platinum bracelet and the matching pinky ring. Carlo never specified a time for them to meet, so he popped in early to case the joint. Zero's was an up-and-coming club that Carlo had an interest in. The crowd boasted everything from upper-class whites to Hip Hop heads. It was definitely a happening place.

Felon tried to post up and look cool, but his nerves wouldn't let him. He couldn't help but think about Eve's assessment of the situation. If Carlo and Steve had something to do with Cassidy's murder, things were gonna get real hectic along the way. He had grown up with Cassidy, and her death couldn't go unpunished, but what could he do? He had a strong arm, and loyal soldiers at his disposal, but he wasn't about to fool himself into thinking that they were any match for the mob.

It didn't take long for Felon to spot De Nardi's crew. Big Steve cleared a path through the crowd, while Tony's eyes swept back and forth for signs of trouble. Sal brought up the rear, with Carlo in the center. Carlo spotted Felon leaning against the bar and directed the group in his direction.

"What's up, buddy?" Carlo asked, shaking Felon's hand and patting him on the back. "Glad you could make it."

"Thanks for inviting me."

"Come on. Got someone I want you to meet." Carlo led Felon and the rest of his entourage toward the back of the club. Making their way through the sea of bodies on the dance floor was like trying to swim in syrup. Club-goers danced, fucked, and rioted to the DJ's mixes.

In the rear of the club, just off the bathrooms, was a large iron door. A trunk of a man, wearing a black suit, inspected the group as they approached. Upon recognizing Carlo he stepped aside and held the door open for them. The inside of the office contained a desk, a couch, and a computer. There was a man stationed behind the door and one sitting at the desk. Franko occupied the couch.

He glanced from his son's face to the Black man at his side. Franko's sagging jaw folded up into a slight frown as his cold eyes examined Felon. Felon tried to fight off the natural intimidation he felt being in the presence of Franko De Nardi. He knew that the mob capo could have a man's life snubbed out on a whim. Franko wielded a power reserved only for the legendary in the underworld. A power that Felon craved.

"Dad." Carlo stepped forward. "This is Felon." He motioned toward him.

Franko sat up slightly. "I heard a lot about you." Clouds of cigar smoke wafted into his face and eyes, but he didn't seem to notice. "My son tells me that I have you to thank for the success of our little venture?"

"I'm just trying to do my part, sir," Felon said humbly.

"This guy," Franko chuckled. "It's a good thing you're doing, kid. The moves you're making show that you know how to sling poison, but can you hustle? I mean, what do you really know about crime?"

"Mr. De Nardi, I like to think of myself as a businessman. Whatever the hustle, I'm gonna do what's necessary for my family to eat."

"Sure ya do, kid. Let me tell you something. There's a lot of money in Harlem, and I don't just mean in drugs. In the old days, Harlem generated a mint for the family. Liquor, women, numbers. You name it. Most of the guys I came up with have given up on it, but not me. I believe there's still millions to be made in Harlem and I intend to cash in. How would you like to be a rich man, Felon?"

Felon smiled. "Who wouldn't?"

"I'm telling you, Dad, he's the one," Carlo said.

Franko silenced Carlo with a look and continued speaking to Felon. "As my son is always so quick to point out, I hear that you're a man who knows how to get things done. I need a man like you at the forefront of the new renaissance. You're large now, kid, but I'm talking about putting you in orbit. What I would like to know is, can I count on your continued support in the near future?"

Felon looked him in the eye. "It's like this, sir. I'm just trying to do my part and see some of this money. Carlo can tell you, I can smell a dollar. Anything you need, just call on me. All I want is an opportunity."

"Spoken like a true gentleman." Franko smiled. "Felon, I think you're going to see a lot of money. Each of us is. You'll be a welcomed addition to the family, but not just yet."

"Excuse me?" Felon did not like the look Carlo was giving him. He knew the man was thinking something sinister, but the kind of power he was offering was too tempting not to at least hear him out.

"Before you can be welcomed into the fold, you have to prove yourself. A problem has been brought to my attention and I think it only fitting that you handle it. Call it a show of good faith."

"I don't have a problem proving myself," Felon said, trying to sound cooler than he was. "What do you need me to do?"

"I'm sure you heard about the murdered police officer?" Franko studied his face. "By your expression, I'm sure you have. Anyhow, there were several fingers pointed at your partner, Butter."

Felon looked over at Carlo, who wouldn't meet his gaze. "I've heard about the murder. Carlo brought it to my attention, and I assured him I'd look into it. Butter being the shooter is unlikely, though."

"Well, my sources tell me otherwise." Franko leaned forward. "Andy Lapelsky was one of mine! Someone has to hang for this."

Felon matched Franko's stare. "With all due respect, Butter is a friend of mine. I've known him since we were jerking off for kicks. These accusations don't even have merit. I'm giving you my personal guarantee that the police will get their killer, but it won't be Butter."

Franko clamped down on his cigar. "You cocky little bastard. Do you know I could have the both of you whacked out and squash this whole beef?"

"Yes, sir," Felon said coolly. "I'm very aware of who you are and what you can do, but you have to understand my position in this. Butter is like a brother to me, and I am loyal to my family. I can't hand him over for a murder that he might not have even committed. Even if he did, I would be more inclined to clean it up, rather than hang my friend."

"Do you believe the balls on this kid?" Franko asked one of his bodyguards. "Felon, you've got balls of steel. You know I could kill you where you stand, yet you remain loyal to your friend. I like you, kid." Frank grinned.

The wave of relief that washed over Felon was so strong, he almost collapsed. The whole time Mr. De Nardi was speaking, he kept seeing his life flash before his eyes. He knew this would be his last night on earth, but he was still alive.

"Tell you what." Franko stood. "You get this mess cleaned up and Butter gets a pass. Something like this happens again and you both go." Franko reached out and patted Felon on the cheek. "You're gonna be a star, kid. You watch what I tell you."

There were smiles all around the room. Carlo leaned against the wall, smiling at Felon. His moving up in the ranks would be a boon for Carlo also. He had brought Felon in and had a stake in the operation. When they opened the books, Carlo could convince the old man to sponsor him for membership. He would have the best of both worlds.

As Felon was making his way through the club to the front door, his cell went off. With a finger on one ear and a phone on the other, he tried to make heads or tails of what the caller was saying. As the message became clearer, Felon's smile broadened. An interesting turn of events indeed.

Dre exited the bar, accompanied by a young lady in a miniskirt. From his uncoordinated steps anyone could tell he had been drinking. He staggered toward his car, with the young lady helping him keep his balance. No sooner had he taken the key from his pocket than an unmarked van skidded to a halt a few feet from them.

The back of the van slid open and Teddy hopped out, holding an AR15. Spoon and Vinny followed, holding two silenced .22s.

Vinny stood outside the bar door while Spoon and Teddy approached Dre from opposite sides. By the time the drunk and his girl realized what was going on Teddy had the AR trained on them.

"Bitch, if you scream, I'll blow your head the fuck off!" Teddy warned. The scream immediately died in the woman's throat.

"Fuck is going on!" Dre shouted.

"Shut the fuck up!" Spoon hit Dre in the head with the pistol. He tried to collapse, but Spoon held him upright.

The sounds of shouting brought one of Dre's people out to investigate. As soon as he stepped from the doorway, Vinny put a bullet in the back of his brain. Seeing that the men meant business, Dre calmed himself.

"Take my money, man. Just don't hurt me," Dre pleaded.

"We don't want yo money, nigga." Teddy grabbed him by the arm. "We gonna have a little chitchat." Teddy and Spoon half dragged, half walked Dre to the van. Vinny motioned for the woman to follow, and fear made her do as she was told. Vinny joined his peoples and the van sped off.

Felon stood outside Zero's, smoking a cigarette. His mind was spinning with the possible opportunities his new alliance with Franko De Nardi would bring. In addition to stepping it up, he had successfully bargained for his friend's life. He decided to ring Butter and tell him the good news.

Felon dialed Butter's cell and got his voice mail. He tried the number again with the same result. He wondered why his friend wasn't picking up. Even if Butter had been hardheaded enough to leave the safe house, he would've still had his cell on him. Felon was about to dial Teddy when a feminine voice caught his attention.

Sheeka, Rah, and another girl Felon didn't recognize were coming toward him. Sheeka and Rah were working their fits, but their friend could only be described as eye candy. Most of her round face was obscured by the cat-eye Gucci frames she wore, but her crimson lips were inviting. She had blood-red hair that hung down to her shoulders and feathered out at the ends. The red dress she wore hugged her hips but dipped low in the front, showing off her full breasts. Felon could feel himself harden just at the sight of her.

He smiled. "Sup, ladies? Y'all going in the club?"

"You know that," Sheeka said. "We heard this spot is jumping."

"It's a'ight." Felon was talking to Sheeka, but looking at the redhead. "Mixed crowd and the music is okay, but you know I don't do the club like that."

"For someone who doesn't do the club like that, I see you in enough of them," the redhead said.

"I'm afraid you've got me mistaken," Felon told her.

"I've seen you around a couple of times."

"Baby, I think I'd remember if we'd met." Felon stared at the girl's face and did see a resemblance to someone. He flipped through his mental rolodex of faces and tried to place hers. Just as she lowered her frames, it dawned on him. "Eve?" he asked, shocked.

She smiled. "It's Evelyn tonight." Her hair was dyed brighter than her natural red, and her makeup made her skin appear darker, but it was Eve.

"What have you done to yourself?" he asked, still stunned by her appearance.

"You like?" She spun around for him. "Sheeka did it."

"You know I had to hook my girl up," Sheeka said, fixing Eve's hair.

"Wow, you look good." Felon grinned. "I'm gonna have to keep an eye on you tonight, huh?"

"I guess we can have a drink or something," she said nonchalantly.

"Oh, it's like that, Eve?"

"Listen, boo. No disrespect, but I didn't come here to hang at the bar and reminisce. I came to take care of business."

"Business? Eve, I know you didn't come here to get into it with Carlo. Don't do this." He said in a pleading tone.

"Felon, I appreciate your concern, but I don't need it." She fixed her shades. "We spoke about this already and you told me how you felt. Cool. I'm gonna handle mine."

He grabbed her by the arm. "Eve, I'm not gonna let you do this."

"Really?" she said, looking at his hand like it was dirty. "Let me tell you something, boo. I'm gonna do what I gotta do. Anybody who tries to get in the way of that is food, straight cheese." Eve jerked loose and stepped into the club, followed by her friends.

"I don't know nothing, man," Dre pleaded through a busted lip. For the last half hour, he had been strapped to a chair inside an abandoned apartment while his inquisitors grilled him for information. Somehow they got it in their minds that Dre was involved with the attempt on Butter's life. They weren't wrong in this assumption, but he couldn't figure out how they had come about the information. Other than himself and Johnny, the only other person who knew of his involvement was the man who paid for it.

"Muthafucka, we know you was down," Spoon said, punching Dre in the face.

"You got the wrong dude!" Dre shouted.

"We might as well kill this muthafucka," Vinny said, chambering a bullet into his .22. "He ain't gonna talk."

"That's because we haven't been employing the right methods," Teddy said, standing near the stove. When he turned around, he was holding a hunting knife. The end was scorched from his holding it over the open flame. Teddy walked over to Dre and stood beside him.

"Hold on, man." Dre squirmed. "What you gonna do with that?"

"Easy, old-timer." Teddy smiled. "I just wanted you to answer some questions, but you wanted to give us a hard time. So, we'll try it this way."

Before Dre could plead further Teddy placed the hot knife to his throat. The skin on his neck smoldered and scorched under the heat. Dre screamed at the top of his lungs but couldn't move away. Pain shot throughout every fiber of his body. Teddy removed the knife before Dre could pass out.

Teddy grabbed him by the face. "Now, you listen to me. Somebody tried to have my friend killed, and I wanna know who it was. If you think this thing did a number on your neck, wait till you see what it does to some other body parts." Teddy moved toward Dre's eye with the knife, but it wasn't necessary.

Dre turned his face away. "Okay, okay!" he shouted. "Look, I knew about the hit, but I wasn't in on the contract. The guy's name is Black. Johnny Black. The first try was a test run. He's the real killer."

"Muthafucka!" Teddy cursed, pulling out his cell phone.

"What's the deal, son?" Spoon asked.

Vinny popped him in the head. "Johnny Black."

Teddy hit the send button and cradled the cell to his ear. If Johnny Black was involved, then the situation was far more dire than they thought. Johnny Black was a killer made from the stuff of legends. No one knew exactly where he came from, but death always followed in his wake.

PART THREE

WOMAN IN RED

31.

Carlo sat at a private table with his team, sipping drinks. As he had expected, the meeting between his father and Felon had gone over well. He took to the young man just as Carlo had upon meeting him. Until then, Franko had been reluctant to give Carlo the leeway he needed to build his own thing, but with someone like Felon at his side, he had no choice but to respect their hustle. The money in Harlem was rolling in and they were responsible.

Carlo was searching the crowd for the waitress when he saw Big Steve making his way through the crowd. The bodyguard was accompanied by two of the girls they had met the other night and another he didn't know. Carlo licked his lips hungrily as the quartet approached the table.

"Well, well." Carlo smiled. "What do we have here?"

"You remember Sheeka and Rah from the other night, don't ya?" Steve asked, pulling chairs out for the ladies.

"I remember the other two, but who is this vision?"

Eve met Carlo's hungry stare. If it weren't for the Gucci shades she might not have been able to hide the contempt in her eyes. Just feet away from her were the two men who had played a role in the death of her best friend. It would have been simple for her to try and take them out right there, but the chances of her dying in the process were just as high. This needed to be handled with tact.

"Say baby, I never got your name." Steve said to Eve. Something about her nagged at his memory, but he couldn't place her.

"Evelyn," she purred. Eve could feel all the men at the table watching her. This was just as she had planned it. Men would always slip for a piece of ass. All she had to do was play nice and the killer would expose his own throat.

"Lovely Evelyn," Carlo said, kissing her hand. "A pleasure."

Franko looked at his son fawning over the young Black girl and shook his head. "If you'll excuse me," he said standing, "I've got some business to handle. Tell Felon I'll see him around." Franko made his way around the table.

As he headed for the exit, he had to pass within mere inches of Eve. When he passed Eve his cold eyes landed on her. It was the first time she was getting an up-close and personal look at the notorious Franko De Nardi.

Something about his face nearly sent her into a panic. A scene played over in her head, but it moved too fast to make sense. As the mental reel began to slow, Eve finally understood. Franko De Nardi was the man who had executed her parents years before. The room seemed to start spinning at a hundred miles an hour and she knew she had to get out of there.

"Excuse me," Eve said, heading for the bathroom.

Carlo watched the young redhead leave and let his perverse thoughts wander. Evelyn was young and fine. He would be the envy of many men with her on his arm. His wicked little brain began to piece together a plot to get her into his bed.

Butter was parked outside Marcy Projects, smoking a blunt. He bobbed his head to the sounds of Nas *Illmatic* coming from the speakers. He had tried to force himself to stay in the safe house, but he hadn't gotten his dick wet in over a week and was about due for a romp. The projects he was hiding in didn't boast the most attractive women, and it was too hot for him to check any of his Harlem shorties, so he found himself calling Tahlia.

Tahlia was a chick that Butter called only once in a great while for two reasons. One, she lived all the way in Brooklyn, and two she lived with her baby daddy. He had called her about a half hour ago and told her to meet him downstairs. Now, forty-five minutes later, he found himself still waiting.

About ten minutes later, Tahlia came strolling out of the projects. She was wearing a tennis skirt and a tank top. Her large ass made the skirt ride up in the back, leaving little to the imagination. Butter tapped the horn twice, knowing she wouldn't recognize the rental. Tahlia slid into the passenger's seat and Butter pulled off.

"Damn, what took you so long?" Butter asked, irritated.

She sucked her teeth. "Nigga, my baby daddy is upstairs. I had to tell him that I was running to the corner store, so we gotta hurry up."

"Cool, baby." Butter drove for about two blocks and parked the car. No sooner did he kill the engine than Thalia went to work. She took his dick from his pants and put it in her mouth. She sucked him expertly while Butter rolled his head back and enjoyed it.

Johnny walked casually down the sidewalk, whistling a tune. He slipped on his black gloves and pulled a .380 from his coat pocket. He watched Butter through the rear window while he screwed on the silencer. Then Johnny drew his hand back and smashed the driver's side window. Thaila happened to be coming up for air and screamed as the window was shattered. Butter felt three things in succession: glass peppering his face, fire invading his chest and side, then oblivion. The night wind hissed twice more, then all was silent again.

Felon couldn't believe how Eve had come at him. He started to go after her and try to force her to listen to reason, but knowing Eve, that would probably lead to a fistfight. Only the sound of the plastic casing on his cell phone cracking under the pressure of his grip made him ease up. Eve couldn't seem to understand he was only trying to save her life. That fool girl really thought you could come at Carlo De Nardi's crew and win.

With the De Nardis, Felon could finally see the mountaintop. Eve's mission of vengeance would compromise that. The deal would put him on top, but he loved Eve. By her running in and trying to play cowboy, he would soon be forced to choose a side. Love or riches?

Eve leaned against the bathroom sink, trying to compose herself. Memories she had tried so long to suppress for so many years all rushed to the surface. She could still feel the weight from her mother's dead body trying to protect her from Franko's bullets. For years after the execution she had been plagued by nightmares. Sometimes she would wake up in the middle of the night and see those cold blue eyes hovering over her bed. She felt tears of pain welling up in her eyes but forced them back. She had to shake off the childhood demons and get it together. She needed to be strong. The order of business was Cassidy's murderer. As much as she would've liked to repay Franko for his crimes, she couldn't compromise the current mission. First, for Cassidy. But later . . . she stared in the bathroom mirror, eyes cold. Later, payback for her parents.

She returned to the table, where everyone was drinking and having a good time. Franko's entourage had cleared out, leaving Carlo and his stooges. Rah was whispering in his ear, while Sheeka made conversation with Tony and a reluctant Sal. Eve sat in the seat closest to Steve, which he didn't seem to mind at all, and crossed her legs seductively. Steve followed the movement with his eyes.

"So, what do you do?" she asked Steve.

"Oh, I'm in security," he said proudly.

"Really? Private or commercial?"

"Private," Carlo said, interrupting. "He works for me." He smirked and pretended he didn't notice the look Steve was giving him.

She turned her attention to Carlo. "You must be an important person to need security."

He grinned. "VIP. I deal in large sums of money, so it gets hectic from time to time."

She flashed him a bright smile. "Sounds interesting."

"I'd love to tell you about it some day."

"Sounds like a plan."

Steve watched the exchange and felt like stomping Carlo and the golddigging redhead. She had already chosen, and now Carlo was cock-blocking by bragging on his paper. Not trusting himself to control his anger, Steve excused himself from the table to go get more drinks. On his way to the bar he passed Felon, who was making his way to the table.

It enraged him to see his boo making time with another man, but he refused to give her the satisfaction of showing it. He was quite surprised to see how quickly she had worked herself into Carlo's good graces. Whatever she had planned, it would serve Carlo right for slipping so easily.

"Hey, Felon," Carlo called out. "Sit down and have a drink with us."

"Can't," Felon said, keeping his voice even. "Got something to handle. Just came to tell you I was getting outta here."

"That's too bad. I wanted you to meet the girls. This is Sheeka, Rah, and Evelyn." Carlo nodded down the line.

Felon nodded to each of the girls, but his gaze lingered on Eve. She returned his stare, remembering the intimate moments they shared and the years they avoided telling each other how they felt. Over the last few weeks it seemed as if they were on the brink of discovering something magical, only to have it torn apart by greed and revenge.

As she looked at Felon, she could see the hurt in his eyes. She longed to wake up in his arms tomorrow and realize this had all been a bad dream. They would laugh about it and discuss plans for some weekend getaway with Cassidy and Butter. But it was only a dream. Cassidy was dead and justice still needed to be issued.

"You guys know each other?" Carlo asked, noticing the extended eye contact.

Felon continued to stare at Eve. Her face was perfectly still, but her eyes pleaded for understanding. This was something she needed to do. "No," he answered. "Listen Carlo, I'll catch you later. Nice meeting you, ladies." Eve gave him a look of thanks, but Felon didn't even see it. He put his head down and left the club.

32.

The happy group partied well into the night. Everyone got lifted off the endless flow of champagne, courtesy of the De Nardis. As the first rays of the sun began to peek over the horizon, Carlo offered to give the girls a ride home. It was an obvious ploy to get some early-morning ass, but Eve wasn't as drunk as she pretended to be.

Carlo, on the other hand, was slithered. He almost fell twice getting into the truck. The entire ride uptown he made advances at Eve. She whispered softly in his ear and told him of the things she wanted to do to him. Carlo was near foaming at the mouth when the car stopped on Ninety-sixth Street.

"Say, baby. Your friends are calling it a night, but that doesn't mean we have to." He placed a hand on her thigh.

Eve wanted to rip his arm out of the socket, but she held her composure and smiled. "Not tonight, sweet daddy. I gotta take my mom to the doctor this morning. I'll call you, though."

Carlo finally unclamped his hand from Eve's thigh long enough for her get out of the truck. Sheeka followed her, but Rah stayed in the car. When they looked to her for an explanation, she rubbed Steve's thigh and gave them a wink. Eve nodded in understanding and waved good-bye to her friend.

Teddy tried Butter's cell one more time and still got no answer. He had been trying to raise the man all night, but was unable to get through. Had these been normal circumstances he wouldn't have been worried, but they weren't normal circumstances. One of the best hired killers in New York City had been set on Butter's trail.

"Still nothing?" Spoon asked from the passenger's seat.

"Muthafucka still ain't picking up!"

"You think Black got to him?"

"I doubt it." Teddy shook his head. "Only me and Felon knew where Butter was hiding at. Even if someone had an idea on where to look, the Bronx is big as hell. He's safe as long as he sticks to the house."

"So, what do we do now?" Spoon asked.

"It's late. Let's handle dickhead." He motioned toward the backseat. "Butter's probably fucking off somewhere and I really don't feel like dealing with his antics. I'll keep trying him. If it comes down to it, I'll send somebody to check on him. Other than that, we'll go check Butter in the morning."

Spoon hopped from the truck and opened the back door. With some assistance from Vinny, Dre came spilling out onto the ground. His face was bruised and he had burn marks all over his skin. He was beat to hell, but thankful to be alive.

"On your feet," Spoon said, yanking Dre upright. "It's time to raise the curtain."

Spoon dragged Dre across the street to the threshold of the precinct. Dre shook like a leaf as he was escorted to the front door. The thought of what the men might do to his girl if he didn't go along sent ice down his back. He looked for some means of escape or bargaining tool, but still came up blank. When Spoon noticed his hesitation, he shoved him through the doors. Inside, the night shift was bustling about, performing various task. Dre walked timidly to where the desk sergeant sat and waited to be addressed.

"Can I help you?" the beet-faced sergeant asked in a bored tone.

"Ah," Dre looked over his shoulder and could see Spoon, still standing outside the glass doors. "Yeah. I wanted to confess to a murder. A police officer was killed the other day and . . ."

Dre went on to tell the story as he had been coached. The sergeant called some officers from the back, who were all too eager to take Dre down to the holding cells. He knew that the police would likely beat him within an inch of his life for killing one of their own, but at least he had a chance with them. If he was lucky, he might survive to see trial.

Steve finally managed to get Carlo home. For the entire ride he had talked out of his ass and made advances at Rah. She didn't seem to mind, but it was pissing Steve off to no end. He was glad when Sal and Tony helped Carlo stagger his drunken ass into the building.

He was finally able to be alone with Rah. She wasn't as pretty as the redhead or her friend, but she seemed like a freak. While they were dropping their passengers off, Rah had been playing with his dick in the front seat. He offered to take her out to breakfast, but to his surprise, she refused. Rah wanted to get straight to it. "Ass for cash."

Rah suggested a short-stay hotel on 145th and Broadway. This suited Steve just fine. He figured if he was going to pay for the pussy, he refused to come out of his pocket for an expensive hotel room. When they got there, Steve gave the clerk an extra twenty to overlook the mandatory identification. After they got the key, Steve led Rah up to the room.

When they got to the room, Rah didn't waste any time. She stripped down, showing off her petite body. Rah might be slim, but she was nice to look at. She worked his dick into stiffness, then put him in her mouth. Rah sucked his shaft and licked his balls. When she spit on his rod and sucked it off, Steve felt like he was going to pop. She lay Steve down on the bed and mounted his huge penis. Rah worked her hips like a vet as the bodyguard grunted beneath her. To turn him on further, she flipped on her stomach and started fingering her ass. She handed Steve a small tube of K-Y Jelly and beckoned for him to enter.

Rah's face twisted in pain as Steve crammed himself into her ass. Every time she thought about asking him to stop, she thought of what they did to Cassidy. Her sheer hatred of her partner made her endure it. Steve plowed into her ass like it was the sweetest shot he ever had. He came in ten minutes and was sleeping in fifteen.

Rah slipped from the bed and began gathering her clothes. She dressed hurriedly in the dark, so as not to wake Steve. Their business had been conducted and she didn't want to spend any more time with him than she had to. Rah was almost to the door when he called out to her.

"Where're ya going?" he asked.

"I'm going downstairs to get a pack of cigarettes," she said. "You want something?"

"Yeah, bring me a bottle of water," he said, but never offered her any money. Rah agreed and slipped from the room.

Steve lay there with his eyes closed, thinking about the wild sex he had just had with Rah. She was a hood rat, but she knew how to work it. He had originally felt funny about her charging him after drinking it up all night, but after he got the pussy he decided it was well worth it. He even pondered the idea of making it a regular thing.

A few minutes later, Steve heard the door open. He never opened his eyes when Rah climbed back into bed with him. She ran her tongue from his nipples to his collar bone, causing Steve to moan. When he reached up to pull her down on top of him, something cold pressed against his neck. Steve opened his eyes and found a familiar face staring down at him.

"Surprise, big boy," Eve said, adding pressure to the knife.

"What the fuck is going on?" Steve asked, trying to peer at her face through the darkness.

"Shut up, you murdering sack of shit!" Eve slapped him.

"Listen, shorty. I don't know what all this shit is about, but you're making a big mistake," he said, nervously.

"Nah, you're the one who made the mistake." Eve gently ran the knife along his neck. "You killed my best friend and now you're gonna answer for it."

"I think there's been a misunderstanding. Let's talk about this," Steve pleaded.

"Did you give Cassidy a chance to bargain for her life?" she asked, cocking her head to the side.

Hearing Cassidy's name, Steve finally understood what it was all about. He had been singled out as the girl's murderer. Someone had implicated him in the murder and now some chick was holding a knife to his throat. The room was relatively dark, but Steve could see the familiar cat eyes of the redhead. She had traded in her dress and high heels for army fatigues and Timberlands. As his eyes adjusted to the darkness he realized that he knew the person holding a knife to his throat. His wheels spun and realization set in. The reason he thought she looked familiar at the club was because she did. The redhead and Bullet's young apprentice were one in the same.

He couldn't believe that he had been so easily duped. He wanted to laugh, but the look of madness in her eyes told him it was a bad idea. He knew if he didn't do something, his life was over. Using all of his strength, he bucked his midsection and tossed Eve from the bed. She crashed to the carpet, momentarily disoriented. This was all the time Steve needed to make a dash for the door. When he yanked it open, a large hand clamped around his throat. Beast carried him back into the room, smiling menacingly.

"Y'all are making a mistake!" Steve rasped.

"Quiet," Eve barked, turning on the light. "You've got some nerve. You murdered my friend in cold blood, and now you're pleading for your funky life. Why should I show you compassion when you couldn't do the same for her?"

"Because I didn't do it," he said, choking up. "Listen to me."

Eve thought about it for a minute, then motioned for Beast to let Steve go. Beast released his grip on his neck, but not before bending one of his arms behind his back. Steve figured he could take the big man in a straight-up fight, but they had the drop on him. His only hope to survive the ordeal was to be as honest as possible. Maybe when they heard what really happened he would be released so he could track down that dirty tramp Rah.

"Talk," Eve ordered.

"I didn't kill your friend," Steve blurted out.

"Bullshit!" She slapped him. "You were spotted dumping the body."

"I helped to get rid of the body, but I swear I didn't kill her. It was just so crazy."

"Tell me a story," Eve said, pulling out a pistol. "If I believe you, then you don't get a bullet in the head."

"It was all so crazy," Steve said again, lowering his head. "Carlo didn't like how Cassidy had played him, so he wanted to put her in her place. They argued on the phone, but he convinced her to meet with him and sort it all out. I picked Cassidy up from her block and took her to the hotel where Carlo was waiting. They talked for a while, but then they started arguing. Cassidy took a swing at Carlo, so he punched her. They tussled for a while, but then it turned ugly. Carlo pushed Cassidy off him and she fell. It was an accident."

"You're a fucking liar!" Eve raged. "I saw the pictures and read the autopsy. Cassidy was raped and beaten. She died from blunt head trauma."

"No, no!" Steve shook his head. "The bruises were from her and Carlo's fight. Cassidy tripped on the carpet and her head slammed into the glass coffee table. She was dead when she hit the ground. We all panicked. Having a dead girl in his hotel room was something even his father couldn't fix. We all agreed to dump the body, but the seman was Carlo's idea. She and Carlo had been fucking on the regular, so there were bound to be signs of penetration. He had a few of us jerk off and smeared the seman on her vagina and underwear. He figured if the police thought she was a prostitute, they wouldn't probe as deep into the murder."

Eve covered her ears. "You're lying."

"On everything I love, that's the truth," Steve said. "Lady, you don't know how much sleep I've lost over what happened to that girl. I might not have killed her, but I'm just as guilty for not doing something about it. For what it's worth, I'm sorry. I hope that sick muthafucka Carlo gets everything he deserves."

Eve sat on the edge of the bed and tried to process what she had just heard. The mystery of Cassidy's death had finally been solved. It might not bring her back, but it would allow the family some type of closure. Accident or not, it still didn't soften what Carlo had done. He would still pay for the crime, but Steve had to be dealt with first.

"Let him up, Beast," she said. He reluctantly complied.

"Listen," Steve said, massaging his arm. "You don't have to worry about me warning Carlo. I'm on the first thing smoking out of town. I'm through with the De Nardis and everyone like them."

Eve nodded. "Yeah, you're through." She gave Beast the signal and he wrapped his hands around the back of Steve's neck.

"Wait, you said you wouldn't kill me!"

"No." Eve gave him an icy glare. "I said I wouldn't shoot you. Beast, break his neck."

Steve tried to struggle, but Beast's grip was unbreakable. He struggled for about twenty seconds before the bones in his neck snapped. Beast wrapped Steve's body in a sheet and threw him over his shoulder. A well-placed hundred-dollar bill insured that the desk clerk was out on break while the body was carried out.

Carlo was awakened from his drunken stupor by the sound of his cell phone ringing. His head spun so bad from all the liquor he had consumed that he couldn't make out the numbers on the caller ID. When Carlo answered the phone, the caller said two words: "It's done." After that, the line went dead. Carlo allowed himself a triumphant smile before he drifted back to sleep.

33.

Felon sat in the driver's seat of his Lincoln Navigator, smoking a cigarette. He was both relieved and worried. The police had their killer, so Franko had opened the lane up for him, which was a good thing. But there was still no sign of Butter. He and Teddy had checked the safe house, but it didn't look like Butter had been there in a minute. His men had searched all of Butter's haunts, but they found no sign of him. This made him uneasy.

More and more Felon thought of the man called Johnny Black. Was it possible that he had gotten to Butter? Not likely; someone would have heard something by now. As he glanced out of the window, he saw Teddy walking in his direction holding a newspaper. The expression on the youngster's face was a grim one.

"Got some bad news," Teddy said, hopping into the passenger's seat.

"What's going on?" asked Felon.

"Take a look at this." He unfolded the newspaper and pointed to an article on page five. A young Brooklyn girl named Tahlia

Deeds was reported missing two nights ago from the Marcy Projects in Brooklyn. The girl's baby father said that she was supposed to be going to the store, but witnesses reported her getting into a car with a light-skinned man. No one had seen Tahlia since.

"Ain't that the shorty that Butter used to fuck with?" Felon asked, trying to hide the fear in his voice.

"Sure is." Teddy nodded. "They've been on and off for a minute. She disappeared around the same time Butter did."

"I don't like this shit." Felon pulled on his cigarette. "My gut tells me something is wrong."

"Don't jump to conclusions just yet," Teddy said, trying to calm him. "For all we know, Butter could've gotten paranoid and left town. Let's go out and look for him before we panic."

Felon gave Teddy a half smile. Butter hated being away from Harlem, let alone New York. Even if he were do decide to go OT he would've contacted Felon or Teddy. He would've liked to believe that he was just overreacting, but in his heart he already knew that his friend was gone. He might not have been able to save Butter, but he would see to it that Johnny Black was hunted down.

Eve sat at her kitchen table picking at a plate of bacon and eggs. She appreciated her uncle going though the trouble of preparing breakfast, but she didn't have much of an appetite. There was too much going on. All through the meal Uncle Bobby tried to make small talk, but she only half listened. Seeing the disturbed look on his niece's face, he decided to cut to the chase.

"Eve, what's been wrong with you lately?" he asked.

"Nothing," she said, chopping her eggs with the fork.

"Don't feed me that. I know something is bothering you. Talk to me."

"There's nothing to tell, Uncle Bobby. I'm just trying to live my life. Why does something have to be going on?"

"Anytime my niece is stealing old military equipment from me, something is definitely going on. Now, you gonna tell me what's up?"

"There's just a lot going on right now." She sighed. "I'm trying to stay focused, but it isn't easy. A lot of people are depending on me right now."

"Depending on you for what? Eve, what are you into?"

"Tell me something. Back in your army days, if someone messed with one of your squad, what would you do?"

"Well, I'd do what I could to protect him. In the trenches, all we had was each other."

"So that same rule applies to the streets, then?"

"That's different. We were at war."

"And we're not?" she asked. "Uncle Bobby, I know you don't spend a lot of time on the streets, so you really don't understand what's going on. There are people out there preying on young girls and nobody seems to give a fuck. Every time you look in the paper, somebody's daughter or sister is falling victim. When is somebody gonna stand up and say enough?"

"Eve, they got the police to handle that kind of stuff."

"But what happens when the police can't or won't do anything about it?"

"Baby girl, sounds like you might be getting into something that's way over your head. I know you're hurting about what happened, but in time the pain will fade," he tried to console her.

She chuckled. "Uncle Bobby, this ain't just about Cassidy. This is about a little girl's nightmares and finally being able to put them to rest." Eve kissed him on the forehead and left the apartment.

Uncle Bobby sat there pondering the conversation with Eve and wondered what he should do next. No matter what the girl said, he knew something was up. She was hardly ever home, but when she was, she was walking around whispering on her cell phone. A definite sign that something was going on. Not only was her attitude different, she was different. Eve had dyed her hair and brought a whole bunch of clothes that did not fit who she was. Bobby might've been old, but he wasn't a fool.

He thought about their exchange over breakfast and his wheels began to spin. "A little girl's nightmares finally being put to rest" is what she had said. Ever since she was a little girl, Evelyn Panelli was never one to fear anything. There was only one thing he could think of that had ever caused his niece to lose sleep.

Bobby wheeled down the hall and removed the picture of Eve and her parents from the wall. He ran his fingers across the photo and smiled. "Looks like the game ain't over just yet," he whispered.

"Where the fuck is this guy?" Carlo flipped his cell phone closed.

"Trouble, cousin?" Sal asked.

"Fucking Steve isn't picking up his phone. I've been trying to get him on the line since this morning."

"Maybe he's still laid up with the Black broad?"

"Probably." Carlo scratched his chin. "Speaking of broads, what do you think of that redhead number from last night?"

Sal smiled. "You know I don't do dark meat, but I'd like to do her."

"Did you check that sweet ass?" Carlo clutched his heart. "I'm getting a hard-on just thinking about her."

"So, when are you gonna try to pop her?" Sal asked.

"As soon as possible. Sally, I gotta have that broad!"

"I don't understand you, Carlo." Sal shook his head. "All of the white women in this city and you chase Black tail. What the hell is wrong with you?"

"It's an acquired taste," Carlo said, resembling an addict thinking of a fix. "I mean, I've screwed my fair share of white broads, but they don't match up to Black pussy. There's nothing like crawling between a pair of warm brown thighs."

"If you say so." Sal frowned. "I'll stick to my own."

"Suit yourself." Carlo shrugged. "But don't knock it till you try it."

Carlo flipped his phone back open and dialed the redhead's number. After the third ring, Eve answered. "Guess who?" Carlo sang.

"What's going on, big time?" she said, as if she was overjoyed to hear from him. "I thought you had forgotten about me."

"Never," he told her. "I've just been busy. Got a lot on my plate."

"So I hear."

"What's that supposed to mean?" he asked curiously.

"I do my homework, Carlo De Nardi. I hear you're the man to see," she said in a sultry tone.

"That's what I've been trying to tell you." He grinned. "Enough about me, let's talk about us. I wanna see you."

"I don't know, baby. I'm a pretty busy girl myself," she teased.

"Well, make yourself unbusy."

"Carlo, as bad as I wanna see you, I have a very hectic schedule. A girl's gotta eat, ya know?"

"If money's all that you're worried about, I got enough of that to keep you occupied for a while," he boasted.

"Carlo, I don't know what kind of girls you're used to dealing with, but money don't make me moist. Only hard dick motivates me."

"Well, I got that for you too," Carlo said excitedly. "Come on, Evelyn. Don't make me beg."

"Of course not, boo. The begging comes later. Tell you what, let me handle what I need to handle and I promise to see you sometime this week."

"Sometime this week?" he asked, disappointed. "Baby, Carlo De Nardi doesn't wait for anything."

"Not even for this sweet pussy?" she asked, her voice low and soft.

"Hmmm, that's a hard one."

"Tell you what. For you being such a good boy and waiting, I promise to make it worth your while."

"I'm gonna hold you to that, and it better be worth it," he told her.

"Oh, it will be. I'll give you a call later." Then Eve ended the call.

Carlo sat back on the sofa, touching himself. Evelyn was a prime piece of ass. Of all the Black girls he had laid, she was the most prized catch. Cassidy was good, but she had mileage and a reputation. Evelyn was a fresh face. Suddenly he forgot all about Steve's abrupt disappearance and focused on what he wanted to do to young Evelyn.

After hanging up with Carlo, Eve pulled out her regular cell phone and dialed Kiki to put the next phase of their plan into action. Eve knew that there was no way to make Steve disappear without raising suspicion, so she planned for it. Not only had she had Steve murdered, but she was going to destroy his credibility. Just as they had done to Cassidy.

"Sup, Twenty?" Kiki said when she answered the phone.

"Chilling, sis," Eve replied. "How'd everything go?"

"As smooth as you said it would, ma. I passed by two barber shops and three hair salons with Rah. We made sure the story got out. The rest is on the rumor mill."

"Good looking, sis," Eve said.

"You know Twenties look out for their own. I wish I could be there to see the look on Carlo's face when he catches wind that his bodyguard was sharing information with the Feds."

Al & Son's car lot in Jamaica, Queens, was usually pretty quiet. They did enough business to keep their doors open, but there was never an overabundance of activity. That morning was quite different. Police tape blocked the entrance to the lot while plainclothes officers swarmed the place, looking for clues.

A customer had come in that morning wanting to purchase a car that was on the lot. When the salesman looked at the tag, he realized that it wasn't one of theirs. After a brief search of the car, they realized it was a rental. Upon further inspection of the car, they found two bodies in the trunk. One belonged to the missing girl and the other was an unidentified man. They both had bullet holes in their heads.

34.

Carlo sat and listened as Tony recounted what he had heard. Tony was one of his most trusted friends, so he knew that he wouldn't bring him that kind of information unless there was some truth to it. Even though he was hearing it, he found it very hard to believe. Steve had worked for the De Nardis for quite some time. Carlo trusted him with his life. The man had always been loyal and diligent in his work. Steve's usefulness had never come into question until then.

"I can't believe it!" Carlo slammed his fist into the wall. "How could Big Steve turn on us?"

"Hey, I'm just as shocked as you are," Tony said, "but that's the word. They said the police picked him up in connection with that hooker who got clipped. This is bad."

"You think I don't fucking know that!" Carlo snapped. "Jesus, he could hang us all. We gotta get to him."

"Not likely. I called some of our people downtown and no one knows anything. My guess is that the Feds got him and they're keeping things real hushed."

"Fuck, fuck, fuck!" Carlo screamed. "We gotta call a meeting. Tony, we gotta get this thing cleaned up before my father finds out."

"Don't worry, Carlo." Tony patted him on his back. "Franko will understand. We're gonna straighten this whole thing out."

Carlo wished he shared his friend's confidence, but he didn't. Steve knew some of his darkest secrets. Carlo had said and done things in front of Steve that not even his father was aware of. Because of him, the whole De Nardi empire could take a hit. Son or not, if Steve implicated Franko because of something Carlo let slip, he was a dead man.

Eve watched Beast as he frolicked with a stray puppy he had found the night before. He had such a childlike innocence about him. Eve had involved him with Steve's murder when she knew she shouldn't have. She had already caused him so much grief that it was selfish of her to have him risking his life for her vendetta. A tear almost escaped her eye as she thought of never seeing him again.

"What's the matter, Eve?" he asked, noticing the sad look on her face.

"Nothing, just thinking." She smiled. "I got a lot to do."

"Are we going out again? Like the other night?"

"No. I've got to do this alone."

"Eve, you're my friend. I wanna help," he said, protesting.

"You've already helped me more than you know." She patted his hand. "This will all be over soon, and I'm going to have to leave."

"But why? If you make all the bad men go away, then you don't have to leave, right?"

"I wish it was that simple. Even after I take care of these bad men, more will come. They'll keep coming until I'm dead."

"Then we'll fight them," he said with conviction.

"No, Beast. I've already lost one friend. I don't want to loose another."

"I won't let you go," he cried, hugging her leg.

"You have to." She fought back the tears. "I've come too far to turn back, but its not too late for you. I'm sorry, Beast, that's just the way it has to be."

Unexpectedly he jerked away from her and stormed across the room. He hefted his twenty-seven-inch TV off the stand and hurled it against the wall. Glass and sparks flew all over the furniture and carpet. Next he moved to the wall and proceeded to punch holes in it. Eve felt for the big man. He just didn't seem to understand.

"Beast, you have to calm down!" She placed a hand on his shoulder.

"Eve, if you leave, who'll take care of me?" He looked up at her through tear-filled eyes.

"You're going to be okay, Beast. I promise. I just gotta work this thing out. After everything is taken care of, we'll hook back up," Eve lied. She knew that the chances of her finishing the job and living to reflect on it were minimal. But telling Beast that wouldn't help to soothe him. "Everything is gonna be fine." She cradled him.

Beast cried like a newborn while Eve stroked his head. Besides Cassidy, he was the only friend she ever had. She couldn't risk losing him because of her need for revenge. She held him for a while longer before he finally cried himself to sleep. Eve kissed her friend's forehead and slipped from the apartment.

When Felon received the news of the police finding Butter's body, he was beyond distraught. For as many years as he could remember, he and Butter had put in work together. They came from small-timers on the block to the niggaz running things. Everything they had accomplished was done together. They were a team.

Felon always knew that something awful would come from Butter's ill temper, but he thought he could fix it like he always did. Butter turned it up and Felon smoothed it out. That's how it had always worked. Apparently there was no fixing this one.

He downed another glass of liquor and thought on his problem. There was no doubt in his mind that Carlo had something to do with the hit. Even after he had bargained with Franko for his friend's life, he was still executed. Butter had tried to show him the writing on the wall, but he was too blinded by the promise of riches to see it.

The blinders were off now. When they took his friend, all bets were off. Felon's closest road dawg had been taken from him and that was unforgivable. Carlo would finally be put in his place and Felon would just accept whatever consequences that came with it.

For the last couple of days Eve had been playing a dangerous game of cat-and-mouse with Carlo. He had asked her time and again, but she still hadn't officially gone out with him. They had gotten together a couple of times, but it was never more than for a few minutes at a location of her choosing. Whenever he came thorough to see her, she would make sure she was wearing something trashy. If it wasn't shorts riding up in her ass, it was outfits that showed off way too much of her body. She would allow him to kiss her and fondle her, but whenever he tried to go the extra mile, she would stop him. It made her physically ill to have Cassidy's murderer touching her, but Eve kept her game face. Soon it would all be over.

Eve looked up from her Amtrak schedule when she heard footsteps to her rear. She looked over her shoulder and saw Sheeka approaching. She now wore her hair in a short cut, showing off her cute face. She came around the bench and sat down beside Eve.

"Going somewhere?" Sheeka asked, pointing at the schedule.

Eve shrugged. "Thinking about taking a trip. Things are gonna get pretty uncomfortable around here soon."

"Eve," Sheeka said, hesitating, "I don't know if you've heard or not, but they've found Butter."

"The police picked him up?"

"No. He was murdered."

"God, no." Eve covered her mouth. "When? How?"

"The police found him and another girl inside the trunk of a rental," Sheeka told her. "They were executed."

"Carlo," Eve hissed.

"You don't know that. Butter had a lot of enemies," Sheeka said.

"Yeah, he had a lot of enemies, but he was connected to the mob. How many street niggaz you think would've been stupid enough to challenge that? Just one more reason Carlo needs to die. I'm gonna take him out before he takes any more of mine!"

"Eve, you know you don't have to go through with this. Steve is dead, and Carlo is gonna end up getting himself killed sooner or later. If you decided to give up, no one could be mad at you."

"God, if it were that simple." Eve sighed. "Sheeka, this thing has gotten so much bigger than Cassidy. I have to do this. Not just for her, but for my parents."

"What do your folks have to do with this?" asked Sheeka.

"It's a long story. The point is, the De Nardis die."

"I wish you would rethink this," Sheeka said, pleading with her.

"Either I'm gonna kill them, or they're gonna kill me. Either way, this all ends."

Sheeka saw the conviction in Eve's face and decided that it was pointless to try and sway her. Once Evelyn Panelli set her mind to doing something, only an act of God could sway her. All Sheeka could do was to keep Eve in her prayers and never forget what she had done for her and her sister.

After leaving Sheeka, Eve bumped into Felon. He was the last person she wanted to see the way she was feeling. Things hadn't been the same between them since he declined to help her with her plan. She tried to stay mad at him, but she couldn't. Not everyone was in a rush to die. She thought about avoiding him by going the other way, but they had danced around what had happened for too long. It was time to bring closure to their situation.

"Hey," he said as she walked up.

"Hey yourself." She smiled. "How you doing?"

"I've been better," he said, swigging from the pint that he was holding.

"Listen, I'm sorry to hear about Butter," she said sincerely.

"Yeah. I'm gonna miss him. That was my nigga, and somebody touched him. He's gone from here, but at least he ain't gotta worry no more."

"I hear you. Felon, I need to talk to you about something."

"That's funny, cause I need to talk to you about something too. It takes a big man to say when he's wrong, but I was. I should've listened to you when you warned me about Carlo. I don't know why I was too fucking stupid to see it. Now my partner is gone," he said.

"Felon, I don't blame you for not wanting to go out in a blaze of glory with me. I guess it was even a little selfish for me to ask you to. This is my fight."

"But it should've been ours," he said. "I shouldn't have let you run off like that. I could've tried harder to stop you."

"Felon, you know damn well you couldn't have stopped me. I would've probably kicked your ass," she said with a smile. "But that's neither here nor there. Let the past be the past."

"So you forgive me?"

"How could I stay mad at such a beautiful face?" She touched his cheek.

"Evelyn," he cupped her face, "I've loved you from the first time I saw you. I don't know why I've never found the courage to say it. Guess the only reason I'm saying it now is because you can never tell if you're gonna wake up in the morning."

Eve was so caught off guard by Felon's statement that she didn't know how to respond. Here she was, possibly on the threshold of her own demise, and someone she cared a great deal about was confessing something that she had carried in her heart for years. For as much as Felon thought he loved her, she loved him even more.

"Felon, I . . . ," she began.

"Don't say anything." He placed a finger over her lips. "Baby, I don't know what's gonna happen because of all this, but I don't wanna ruin the moment with words." Felon leaned in and kissed her. He kissed her as deeply and as passionately as he could and she returned it. For those few moments, they were the only two people on earth.

"I love you, Evelyn." He pulled away. "And when this is all over, I'm gonna show you how much. Right now I got some things that I need to take care of, but I'm gonna come see you in a few days. Until then, I want you to hold onto this for me." Felon handed her a small orange key.

"What's this?" she asked.

"I've got some paperwork in a locker at Penn Station. I'll come get it from you in a few days so I can show you what I've been up to. Until then, keep it and yourself safe."

Eve took the key and held it in her palm. She wanted to tell Felon about what she had planned and confess that she was scared to death, but she didn't want to ruin the moment. She tried to fight back the tears but they came anyway. Eve reached up and hugged Felon as tightly as she could. She didn't have the heart to tell him that it would probably be the last time they ever saw each other.

Carlo paced back and forth in his living room, smoking a cigarette. His nostrils were beet red from snorting cocaine all morning. He had tapped into all his resources and still couldn't get a line on Steve. It would've been far simpler for him to go to his father and enlist the aid of his people, but that would be a last resort. He was trying to show Franko that he could handle things on his own.

He stopped his pacing long enough to answer his cell. "Hello," he barked in an irritated voice.

"Sorry, did I catch you at a bad time?" Evelyn asked.

"Oh, hey, Evelyn." Carlo softened his voice. "What's up?"

"Thinking about you."

"Oh, yeah. What were you thinking?"

"How much better your hand would feel than mine, touching my pussy." Evelyn always knew what to say to get Carlo going, but this time he didn't bite.

"You know what, I'm starting to think you're full of shit," he told her. "We play this game . . . what, three or four times a week? You get me all hot and excited and then leave me hanging. I'm not used to taking this kinda shit from a broad."

"I'm sorry, baby," she said softly. "I know I've been hard to catch up with, and I wanna make it up to you."

"Yeah, and how do you plan on doing that?"

"I'll show you when we see each other tonight. Why don't you come pick me up about seven?" she asked.

"Seven is no good." He looked at his watch, "I gotta stop by my dad's restaurant. I won't be long, though."

"I wouldn't mind riding along," she said, seeing an opportunity to kill two birds with one stone. "We could get a bite to eat, then we could move the party back to your place. I just bought a new garter set and I'm dying to model it for you."

Carlo's first thought was to tell her no. Even though he wasn't going to the restaurant on official business, he still didn't think Franko would like the idea of him parading around in his joint with the young Black girl. Then again, if he told her no, she might call the whole thing off. Just like with most men, he allowed the little head to lead the big one.

"Okay, I'll come pick you up," he said, "but you gotta be ready by seven. I don't want to be late."

"Okay, daddy," she sang. "I'll be waiting." Evelyn ended the call.

Carlo wanted to pump his fist in the air. Evelyn's high-yellow ass had been playing games with him since he met her. He had just about given up on her until he got the phone call. With the thought of fresh pussy in his mind, he had almost forgotten he was even considering it. He was finally going to get his chance to crack for some of what she had tucked between her legs. Carlo had decided that when they made the date, she was going to give it up whether she wanted to or not.

35.

When Carlo pulled up the corner of Ninety-sixth and Amsterdam, Evelyn was already waiting for him. She was tastefully dressed in a black, one-piece pantsuit and black three-quarter-inch mules. The Glock .40 she carried gave her purse an extra sway. Evelyn swept her crimson mane behind her left ear and gave him her warmest smile.

"Damn, you look good," he said, stepping out to give her a hug. He cupped her ass with both hands. "Ready to go?"

Evelyn smiled. "Sure am." She looked in the driver's seat and saw Tony behind the wheel. "Where's Steve?"

"He had to go outta town," Carlo said, holding the back door for her.

She wasn't too worried about killing an extra man. When she had originally put her plan together, she calculated having to take out two targets. Carlo was a coward and Tony was too fat to match her reflexes. When she climbed in and saw Sal sitting in the passenger's seat, she started making adjustments.

As Evelyn sat beside her soon-to-be victim, she could feel the deodorant begin to liquify. She was teetering on the line between vengeance and certain death. Both fear and anticipation made her lightheaded. From that point on, she had to choose her steps wisely or it would all be in vain.

Not only was she faced with killing three men, she had to decide which De Nardi she wanted to kill. She could kill Carlo before they got to the restaurant and make her escape. This was clearly the smarter plan, but Evelyn wanted it to be done with. She would ride into the devil's mouth and exterminate them both. She just hoped that the cards could be on her side for once.

When they got out into traffic, Carlo fired up a blunt of hydro. The pungent odor quickly filled the truck and stung her eyes. When it came around to Evelyn, she took several deep pulls. Her PO violating her was the least of her concerns. If she was gonna go out, she would go out blasted.

The traffic was light, so the ride to the restaurant was a short one. They exited the West Side Highway at Fifty-sixth Street and crossed over to Ninth Avenue. Evelyn expected some five-star restaurant, but Poppa Frank's was anything but that. It was a quaint little eatery that housed several wooden dining tables and a bar. Carlo held the front door for her as she stepped into the place that would serve as the stage for the final battle.

Before the car could come to a complete stop, Teddy was hopping out. He instructed Spoon and Vinny to wait while he ran upstairs. He had been trying to reach Felon all day, but got no answer. Normally, it wouldn't have been unusual for Felon to withdraw for a few days, but recent events had made the circumstances anything but normal.

Not bothering with the elevator, Teddy jogged up the four flights of stairs to Felon's apartment. He rang the doorbell but all was silent. He banged on the door but still got no response. His instincts were wailing that something was wrong. Fearing the worst, Teddy used his emergency key.

Felon's apartment was dark and quiet. Teddy searched every room of the house for signs of what might've happened to Felon. Except for some dirty laundry strewn on the bathroom floor, everything seemed to be in order. Teddy had decided to leave the apartment and search elsewhere for his boss. As he passed the kitchen he noticed a sheet of paper taped to the refrigerator. Teddy took the note and began to read.

> *My nigga, Ted,*
>
> *I knew it would only be a matter of time before you came to investigate my disappearance. You never were a dumb nigga, and that's why I took a liking to you from the beginning. If you're reading this note, then the shit has probably hit the fan already. These last few weeks have been good and bad to us. We've made more money than we know what to do with, but at what price? I've had many sleepless nights knowing I've sold my soul for riches. We got into this game to try and better ourselves and our situations, but somewhere along the line, larceny changed the plan. I was a fool to trust Carlo. I know that now. Because of him, I've lost the best friend I've ever had and turned away the only woman I've ever loved. Just as Butter always said he would, Carlo has destroyed the foundation of our thing. There's no turning back for me now. I've already spoken with our old connect and told him that you'll be running things from now on. With my last words, I urge you to leave this life behind, and do something righteous with yours. You're still young and the possibilities are endless. Right now, you probably wanna ride out and bring it to somebody for what has happened to me, but you can't this time. I have no one to blame for the tragedy of my life but myself. Tell the crew that I went out so they wouldn't have to.*
>
> *Felon*

His eyes watered up as he read the letter again and again. Shit had been crazy, but he never expected this. In the blink of an eye, he had lost both his mentors. He raged and rained punches on the refrigerator until his fists bled. When he had exhausted himself, Teddy slid down to the floor and cried.

Carlo led Evelyn into the restaurant where Franko was seated at a table in the back, flanked by his two bodyguards. She drew some stares from the other patrons, but she kept her eyes focused on her prey. Even years later, the girlish fears crept into her mind. She shook off the bloody images of her parents and reined in her composure as they approached the table.

Carlo smiled. "Hey, Pop."

"I didn't realize we were having guests," Franko said, casting his icy glare on Evelyn.

"This is a friend of mine," Carlo said, placing his hand around her waist. "Evelyn, this is my father, Franko De Nardi."

"Pleased to meet you," she said, extending her hand. Franko looked at it as if she had just removed it from the toilet.

"You have something for me?" Franko asked, turning his attention back to his son.

"Yeah." Carlo motioned for Sal to come over. Sal placed a leather briefcase on the table in front of his uncle. "It's all there."

"I don't doubt that," Franko said, never bothering to touch the case. He and Carlo were making small talk, but his eyes kept going back to Evelyn. She was beautiful, even for a black girl, but that wasn't it. Something about her seemed familiar. "Evelyn, don't I know you from somewhere?"

"Nah, you don't know her, Dad," Carlo said.

"Actually we have met." She smiled. "I was a little girl at the time, but you probably remember my father, Joe-Joe Panelli."

Franko stopped chewing his food and searched his mind. The name did ring a bell in his head, but he couldn't place it. Suddenly he recalled the man and his family he had been sent to kill all those years ago. By the time it dawned on him, she had already snatched one of the steak knives from the table.

Tony stood outside Poppa Frank's, smoking a cigarette. He could think of a million other things he'd rather be doing than watching Carlo's back. It was a beautiful night and he was anxious to hit the club and do some drinking. A figure stepped from the darkness to his left. Tony went for his gun, but eased up when he recognized who it was.

"What's up, Felon?" he asked with a smile.

Felon returned his smile, then hit him with both barrels of Butter's shotgun.

Carlo shrieked as Evelyn caught him with an elbow to the nose. He tried to swing, but she countered and dazed him with a left hook. When the first bodyguard tried to get up, she plunged the knife into his cheek. The man clutched at the utensil, but the blood squirting from the wound made it hard to grip. He fell backward, knocking Franko to the floor.

Evelyn had managed to retrieve her pistol from her purse when Sal put her in a choke hold. She tried to knock him off but lost her footing in a puddle of blood. The momentum caused Sal to release her or risk falling himself, but it also put her on her back and her gun under a table. As she looked up at the faces of her enemies, all hope fled.

She knew there was a possibility of the hit going wrong, but in the wake of her impending death it became very real. She had come so close to avenging her loved ones only to fail. Just as Sal was reaching for her, the front doors to the restaurant exploded.

Felon stepped through the shattered glass doors, holding the smoking shotgun. Blood coated his face, and murder lurked in his eyes. Sal turned from Eve to the new threat, but he was too late. A hail of buckshot hit him in the back and sent him skidding across the floor.

Carlo tried to make a run for it, but Eve tripped him up. He tried to scramble away, but the floor was slick with blood and food. Eve managed to grab hold of his hair and yanked him back, then gave him a sharp knee to the ribs and flipped him over on his back. She channeled all of her rage and hurt into her fist as she bashed his face bloody.

By now, the second bodyguard had managed to draw his gun and opened fire on the man wielding the shotgun. Innocent diners took stray bullets and buckshots trying to get clear of the gunfight. Felon dove for cover behind the table that was closest to the kitchen entrance where he crouched and reloaded the gun for another attack.

He cursed silently for underestimating Eve. He not expected her to be in the restaurant when he made his hit. He thought that if he moved quickly, he could have it out with Carlo before she put the last phase of her plan into motion. Now she was smack dead in the middle of the bullshit he was trying to protect her from. What had begun as a suicide mission had turned into a rescue.

Felon prepared for his next assault. Eve had Carlo tied up, so all he had to worry about was Franko and the remaining bodyguard. Just as he stood to let off a blast, pain shot through his back. Felon's left arm instantly went numb, causing him to loose his grip on the shotgun. He turned around and found himself confronted with the waiter holding a bloody kitchen knife.

Carlo lay on the floor almost unconscious from Eve's beating. She spared a glance over her shoulder to see how Felon was faring. Of all the scenarios Eve had played out in her mind, Felon bursting through the doors like some wild cowboy wasn't one of them. She didn't know whether to kiss him for saving her or kick his ass for crashing her party.

Felon found himself in a bad way. On one side of him was the bodyguard trying to get a bead with his pistol, and on the other the waiter slashed at him with the kitchen knife. He fended the blows off as best he could, but his useless left arm made it difficult. He had to gain the advantage so he could help Eve.

The waiter lunged at Felon, giving him the advantage he needed. He stepped to the side and flipped his shotgun around. Using the rifle like a club, he brought it around and bashed in the back of the waiter's skull. The man crumbled at his feet and blood pooled out around his body. Felon dropped the shotgun and pulled his nine from his waistband. He turned around just in time to see the muzzle flash of the bodyguard's gun.

"Noooooo!" Eve shrieked. The bullet struck Felon in the chest and sent him crashing into a table. He tried to get up but didn't have the strength. He lay on the floor gasping, but he was still alive. The bodyguard advanced on him with the intention of finishing the job.

Eve couldn't allow it. She had lost everyone else she cared about to the mob and she refused to let them add Felon to that number. Completely forgetting about Carlo, she got to her feet and rushed to help Felon. She had only made it a few feet when a mammoth hand grabbed her by the hair.

"You fucking bitch!" Franko snarled. "I thought I had killed you with your nigger-loving father, but I guess you survived. It doesn't matter though. I'm gonna finish the job today." Franko slammed his fist into Eve's face, breaking her nose. She almost blacked out, but the pain of his holding her up by the hair wouldn't let her. Franko rained blows onto her face, sending blood and spit flying everywhere.

As much pain as she was in, all she could think about was the bodyguard who was now leaning down to slit Felon's throat. Franko tossed her around like a rag doll, kicking her viciously every time she tried to go down. Eve's vision lost and regained focus at least a dozen times during the beating. She saw Franko pull a small handgun from his pocket, but didn't have the strength to do anything about it. At least if she had to die, it would be with Felon.

* * *

Felon lay on the floor, fighting to stay conscious. He had lost all feeling in his arm, but his chest burned terribly. He managed to move his head enough to see Franko beating the hell out of Eve. He tried to call out to her, but he had no voice. He knew she was going to die, but there was nothing he could do about it. As his eyes closed on the bodyguard approaching him, all he could do was hope that he died first so he wouldn't have to watch her suffer.

The bodyguard approached Felon with a hard look on his face. Slowly he unsheathed a butterfly knife and flicked the blade out. He smiled triumphantly as he leaned in to finish Felon off. Suddenly he paused to investigate a humming sound coming from the doorway.

Uncle Bobby's wheelchair came rumbling over the broken glass that was once the entrance of Poppa Frank's. The bodyguard tried to raise his pistol in defense, but he was a little too slow. He managed to get a shot off, but not before Bobby speared him with the bayonet that was attached to the end of his army-issue machine gun. A wicked grin crossed his face as the man shook once, then died.

"What the fuck is this?" a shocked Franko asked.

"Payback, muthafucka!" Bobby shouted as he squeezed the trigger.

Eve rolled out of the way just as the first shots hit Franko. The mob captain whipped back and forth as lead entered and exited his body. It seemed like an eternity before the shooting finally stopped. When the smoke cleared, Franko lay on his side, with blood leaking out of at least a dozen holes. His cold eyes stared into space as the life drained from his body.

Eve crawled from her hiding place under the table to assess the damage. Carlo had managed to slip out at some point, but with his father not being around to protect him, it was only a matter of time before he managed to piss off someone else. Cassidy's killer had escaped, but Eve had finally managed to lay her family's demons to rest. Franko lay on the ground with holes decorating his face, chest, and legs. Eve spat on his body before rushing to Felon's side.

"Oh, baby," she sobbed, "hold on, we're gonna get you some help."

"No," Felon croaked. "Too late for me."

"That's bullshit and you know it!" She screamed. "You better not die on me."

"Eve." He took her hand, "I love you, ma. . . . If I had it to do over again . . . I'd have told you sooner."

"I love you too!" she cried. "Now don't try to talk. We're gonna get you to a hospital."

"You gotta go," he said, his voice raspy. "You gotta go."

"Felon, I won't leave you here. You hear me!"

"Too late." He coughed out a mouth full of blood. "Please . . . go."

Eve continued to kneel by Felon's side, shaking him. His loving eyes took in her measure one last time before they glazed over. Felon was gone.

"How did you know?" she asked her uncle, without looking up at him.

"You're my blood," he said, his expression sober. "I knew you couldn't let this debt rest no more than I could. I wish you had come to me."

She broke down crying. "I'm sorry, Uncle Bobby."

"You quit that crying." He helped her to her feet. "The police will be here soon. Somebody is gonna fry behind this shit here. You gotta get outta here, Eve."

"What about you?"

"Don't worry about your uncle." He tossed the machine gun aside. "I should've been dead years ago. The only reason I hung around this long was to try and raise you right and settle up with Franko. It's done now, baby. Your parents can rest."

Eve hugged her uncle tightly as they both cried freely. All those years she thought he was just a bitter old man, but Bobby had his demons too. Eve wiped her eyes and kissed her uncle's forehead. She wanted to say something, but he pushed her away. Eve took one last look at the last what remained of her life and fled into the night.

* * *

The police stormed Poppa Frank's and were in total shock at what they saw. There were several bodies lying about, but the most astonishing was that of Franko De Nardi. Uncle Bobby confessed to the murders, but the police had a hard time buying it. They couldn't see how an old man in a wheelchair had managed to murder a mob capo and his bodyguards. Like it or not, that was the story he gave them. Bobby would spend the rest of his days behind bars, but it was a small price to pay for his niece's freedom.

BITTERSWEET

It had been three months since the murder of Franko De Nardi and his bodyguards. The mob had been trying to locate Carlo to find out what really happened, but he decided he wasn't ready to talk yet. Maybe they would buy his story, maybe they wouldn't. He figured, why risk it? He began traveling from city to city to stay one step ahead of his pursuers. His port this month was Philly.

The weather had begun to change, so he decided to pick up a few fall items from the mall. He strode down Market Street, carrying his bags, smoking a cigarette. Carlo had made it all the way to his car when he felt someone behind him. He tried to turn around, but the wire had already been looped over his head. The more he struggled, the tighter the noose became. After a few minutes his body dropped limp to the sidewalk.

"Eve sends her regards," Bullet whispered. He spat on Carlo's body and disappeared into the night.

* * *

Somewhere in Monaco:

Beast drew quite a few odd stares as he stepped off the small boat. Fisherman as well as merchants stared curiously at the giant as he made his way through the port. He pulled a stack of postcards from his backpack and read the top one again. "You've always got a friend," is what it read. He had been receiving the cards and small sums of money regularly for the last month or so. The only return address he could find was that of a small post office in Monaco. When his curiosity couldn't take it any longer, he decided to investigate.

As he lumbered down the boardwalk, he noticed a woman staring at him. She had a short black Afro and her eyes were hidden behind a pair of dimestore sunglasses. When Beast returned her stare, she only smiled. When he was within feet of her, she removed the glasses.

"Eve!" he squealed. Beast charged down the gangway, scaring quite a few people. When he reached Eve, he lifted her over his head. "How'd you get here?"

"It's a long story." She chuckled. Before Eve had left the city, she decided to see what was behind the door that the little key opened. Inside the locker was Felon's driver's license and birth certificate. In addition to his identification, there was a large duffel bag. It was wedged in so tight that Eve ripped the bag trying to pull it from the small locker. Sticking out of the bag was a large stack of money. She peeped into the bag and saw that the stack had a lot of company. There was almost two hundred and fifty thousand dollars in the bag. Eve sent a hundred thousand to Felon's mother and vanished with the rest.

"Eve, I thought you had left me forever!" he shouted.

"I told you, we'd always be there for you." She smiled. Their touching reunion was broken up by a small pug nipping at Beast's ankles.

"What's that?" Beast put Eve down to examine the creature.

"It's a dog, silly." She scooped up the pug.

"Looks like a pig or something." He scratched his head. The dog let out a high-pitched bark in response.

"Her name is Cassidy. She lives with me."

"You live here?" Beast asked.

"Yes. And you can too, if you want."

"I don't know, Eve. This place is pretty, but I don't know nothing about it. What happens if you have to leave me again?"

"You don't have to worry about that." She patted his cheek. "I think I'll be staying for a while. Evelyn Panelli is tired of running."

K'wan Foye

K'WAN is a multiple literary award winner and bestselling author of more than twenty titles, which include *Gangsta, Road Dawgz, Street Dreams, Hoodlum, Eve, Hood Rat, Blow, Still Hood, Gutter, Section 8, From Harlem with Love, The Leak, Welfare Wifeys, Eviction Notice, Love & Gunplay, Animal, The Life & Times of Slim Goodie, Purple Reign, Little Nikki Grind, Animal II, The Fix, Black Lotus, First & Fifteenth, Ghetto Bastard, Animal 3, The Fix 2, The Fix 3* and *Animal 4.*